Between Us Girls

Sally John

HARVEST HOUSE PUBLISHERS
EUGENE, OREGON

Scripture verses are taken from the Jerusalem Bible © 1966 by Darton, Longman & Todd, Ltd. and Doubleday & Company, Inc.

Cover by Garborg Design Works, Savage, Minnesota

Cover photos © omgimages, hoangkhainhan, warrengoldswain / Bigstock

Back cover author photo © Tim John

The author is represented by the literary agency of Alive Communications, Inc., 7680 Goddard Street, Ste. 200, Colorado Springs, CO 80920.

This is a work of fiction. Names, characters, places, and incidents are products of the author's imagination or are used fictitiously. Any resemblance to actual persons, living or dead, is entirely coincidental.

BETWEEN US GIRLS
Copyright © 2014 by Sally John
Published by Harvest House Publishers
Eugene, Oregon 97402
www.harvesthousepublishers.com

Library of Congress Cataloging-in-Publication Data
John, Sally
Between us girls / Sally John.
    pages cm.—(Family of the Heart Series ; Book 1)
ISBN 978-0-7369-5465-5 (pbk.)
ISBN 978-0-7369-5467-9 (eBook)
1. Christian fiction. I. Title.
PS3560.O323B48 2014
813'.54—dc23

2013048187

Printed in the United States of America

14 15 16 17 18 19 20 21 22 / LB-JH / 10 9 8 7 6 5 4 3 2 1

For
Jonah Timothy Johnson

Welcome, little guy.

Acknowledgments

As always, I want to thank my family for their continued, unflagging support. Husband Tim sustains me on so many levels. Granddaughter Aliah reminds me to giggle. Granddaughter Kaiya provides adjectives and details on a host of topics. Daughter-in-law Tracy is a brainstormer extraordinaire. Son Christopher is my nature and farming go-to guy. Son-in-law Troy is my go-to sports guy. Daughter Elizabeth gives me writing music and fiction insight. And grandson Jonah—well, at nine months, he just is.

For bringing this book full circle, I couldn't ask for a better team. Thank you to my editor, Kim Moore, and to everyone at Harvest House. Thank you to my agent, Andrea Heinecke, and everyone at Alive Communications. You all make it so easy.

Thank you to everyone who kindly shared their expertise about cats, tornadoes, desert geology, stents, the Spanish language, and Navajo information: Cindi Cox, Tom Carlson, Peggy Hadacek, Karlie Garcia, and Kelly Glisson.

Thank you to my SDCWG writing friends who time and again brought me back to the passion of writing fiction: Elizabeth Van Tassel, Ann Larson, Sandi Esch, John Welch, Bobbe Van Hise, Tomi Leslie, Susan McFarland, and Tiffany Hayden.

A special thank-you to my long-lost cousin, Elizabeth Carlson Hurst, who found me during the writing of this story.

And always, always a big thank-you, dear Readers, for your encouragement.

In loving memory, I thank two people who blessed my writing journey for many years: website designer Kristen Balsis and agent Lee Hough. You are greatly missed.

My God, how great you are!
…You advance on the wings of the wind;
you use the winds as messengers.

PSALM 104:1,3-4

Residents of the Casa de Vida Cottages

Olivia "Liv" McAlister, owner

Riley and Tasha Baker

Noah and Déja Grey

Sean Keagan

Piper Keyes

Charles Chadwick Rutherford IV

Inez and Louis Templeton

Coco Vizzini

Samantha Whitley

Beau Jenner, maintenance man

One

March 15
Valley Oaks, Illinois

Jasmyn Albright watched the sun wink its first beam on the horizon. The light shimmered, a runner on a starting block, and then—*whoosh*. It raced lickety-split across field after field of rich, black earth. It hurdled the fence and streaked over the backyard, bumped into the porch steps, bounced up to her stocking feet, and then—*wham*. It splashed her entire body with light so unbearable she had to shut her eyes.

"Mornin', Jasmyn."

At the sound of the familiar rasp, the *whoosh* and the *wham* went *poof*. She opened her eyes. Where Zeb Swanson should have been standing were only yellowy flickers. "Good morning, Zeb. Coffee?"

"Don't mind if I do."

Blinking away the light, she went into the house. It was the fifteenth of the month, the date Zeb always hand-delivered, at the crack of dawn, his rent check to her. He trusted neither the U.S. Postal Service nor electronic banking.

The man was as old as the dirt he tilled and a creature of habit. His routine on the fifteenth of the month was to gulp coffee, gripe about corn and soybean prices, and mention that he wasn't sure how long he could keep leasing land from her at the rate she charged. He'd take another gulp of coffee and toss the remainder into the spirea bushes or down her kitchen sink, depending on the season. Then, at long last, he would pull the neatly folded check from the front bib pocket of his overalls.

With her best customer-is-king waitress smile, she'd take the check and the cup from him. They would tell each other to have a good day. While he walked off to the barn, she would unfold the check and breathe a sigh of relief.

Every single month she did that. Her best friend said Jasmyn was stuck in a rut with both ends walled shut.

Jasmyn disagreed. The rut kept her safe. It offered *whooshing* and *whamming* and a grumpy man who helped her pay off the six hundred fifty acres that would not sell for more than she owed on it.

She filled two mugs with coffee that had brewed during the spectacular sunrise, retied her plaid flannel robe snugly, and headed back through the mudroom.

The rut also came with a cocoon, a two-story farmhouse with walk-up attic, built by her great-great-grandparents. It was too large for one person and in need of updating, but Jasmyn didn't mind that she could not afford new appliances or window treatments or a couch that did not sag. The place was home and she kept it pristine, just like Gramma June had taught her. The mere thought of leaving it gave her the willies.

Jasmyn smiled to herself. She was only thirty-five and as much a creature of habit as old Zeb Swanson.

He waited on the wraparound porch, leaning against the post at the top of the stairs. "Thank you." He took the mug from her and gulped his first gulp, right on cue.

Zeb reminded her of her late grandfather. Grizzled. Ornery. Dour. Hardworking. She was glad their paths did not cross often.

"Gonna get in the field tomorrow," he said.

"Really?" Her grandfather had never, ever planted in March.

He gazed off in the distance and lowered the brim of his green *Nothing Runs Like a Deere* cap. "It's been hot as blazes for three weeks straight. Spring never did show up. Don't expect it will now."

That was true. The lion that usually ushered in the month of March had failed to roar. Instead, the lamb arrived way ahead of schedule. Crocuses were already in full bloom, grass had greened, and daffodil shoots promised April blooms. But still.

"It's only March."

He scowled.

Jasmyn bit her lip before saying something else stupid. Of course he knew the date. Of course he knew frost was a real possibility until April fifteenth. Of course he knew corn and frost were not friends.

"It's a gamble, I admit," he said. "But an early harvest means the best prices we've seen in years. If the weather cooperates."

Of course he knew what would happen if the weather did not cooperate.

He shrugged. "Farming always was and will be a gamble." Zeb owned a large farm himself and added to it by leasing smaller tracts from others. Twenty years ago he had begun leasing from her Gramma June after her grandpa's death.

Whenever Jasmyn thought about avoiding Zeb Swanson, she reminded herself what a godsend he had been.

He reached into his back hip pocket, pulled out his neatly folded check, and handed it to her. "I've been meaning to say I appreciate you not raising the rent all these years."

First a discussion about planting, and now words of gratitude? And the check was in his *back* pocket? Whoa. He was way off the grid today.

"Uh, sure. I'm, uh, I'm glad it's worked out all these years."

"It's a prime piece of land. I'm happy to keep it in use. Your grandparents were good people."

Jasmyn could have clued him in on the realities of life with Jerome and June Albright. Probably best that she did not. He might get testy and stop leasing from her before he planted his early crop. She smiled instead.

He drained his mug and gave it to her. "You take care now."

Huh? Take care?

He was halfway across the yard before she found her voice. "Have a good day, Zeb."

He paused and turned. "It's a weird one. Can you feel it?"

She shook her head.

"Barometer's dropping."

Maybe that explained his weirdness.

"Storm's coming." He walked away.

Jasmyn unfolded the check and sighed a sigh so different from her typical fifteenth-of-the-month sigh that she had to sit down on the porch step.

Zeb had doubled his check amount.

The barometer must have dropped clear through the floor.

⁄⁄e

Two days later

Jasmyn slid onto the padded stool in front of the bedroom vanity and grimaced at her friend reflected behind her in the mirror. "Okay, the guinea pig is ready to roll."

Quinn Olafsson laughed. Her latest goal was to become a hairdresser in her spare time. "It'll only take ten minutes, I promise." She gently brushed Jasmyn's long dark hair back from her face. "We'll do a French braid this time. Nothing fancy. So, finish your story. What did Zeb say about his check?"

"He drove off before I had a chance to talk to him."

Quinn stopped brushing and met Jasmyn's stare in the mirror. Since kindergarten they had been as close as twins, though no one would mistake them for blood relatives. Quinn had an athletic build, super short hair—naturally blond and naturally curly—big pale blue eyes, a cute turned-up nose, and confidence as big as the outdoors.

Jasmyn, on the other hand, resembled the photograph in the eight-by-ten frame on the dresser: a helpless, not-in-this-lifetime-cute preemie. The only difference was that she now had hair.

"Zeb drove off? Jasmyn, he should have been in the barn. What's going on with him?"

"Air pressure. Have you noticed a big change?"

"Do I look like a farmer?" She combed Jasmyn's hair and began parting it into sections. "What are you going to do with the extra money?"

"Hire Zeb's grandsons to haul this vanity over to your house so you can play beauty shop whenever you want."

Quinn smirked. "Oh, I wouldn't want to mess up the feng shui you got going here in your little cocoon."

Jasmyn glanced around the frilly yellow room that had been her mother's from birth until she passed away three years ago. "Mom's hand-me-down furniture is not the secret to my blissful cocoon."

Quinn laughed so hard she let go of the hair strands. "Oops." She ruffled Jasmyn's hair, undoing the braid. "Starting over." She brushed again. "'Blissful cocoon?' That's a good one, Sunshine."

Sunshine. The nickname was compliments of their third-grade teacher. According to Miss Fowles, Jasmyn smiled a lot and her last name was Albright. How perfect was that?

It turned out to be not in the least bit perfect. Classmates put their own spin on her name. They wondered why a student who was *all bright* would be in the Panda reading group, the pokey Pandas. That was probably the year Jasmyn first felt the enormous safety of home, of the cocoon. Even with a gruff granddad, a super strict gram, and a wacky mother, the place was always far better than the war zone, aka her school and peers.

"Earth to Jasmyn. I said, please hand me—never mind." Quinn reached over Jasmyn's shoulder and took a ribbon from the vanity top. "Got it. I probably shouldn't ask the client to hand me things. Where were you?"

"Third grade."

"David Webb!" Quinn named the boy she'd had a crush on. Typical. It was how she kept track of her school years.

Jasmyn groaned.

"What? He was nice." Quinn handed her a mirror and nudged her around the stool. "Ta-da! Check it out. Not a strand out of place and note the green ribbon for St. Patty's Day. Pretty cool, huh?"

Jasmyn tilted the mirror to see the back of her head. "It is definitely cool. You should be a beautician."

"Thanks. Now why on earth did you zone out to third grade? That year was nasty. Except for David Webb." She took the mirror and bent to face Jasmyn nose to nose. "Hon, are you okay?"

"I'm fine, Quinn." She smiled. "I'm just fine."

She was always just fine. Was there another choice?

Two

March 17
San Diego, California

Samantha Whitley tried to smile. She gave it her best shot, stretching her lips to unaccustomed distances. She showed her teeth, hid her teeth, made the corners of her mouth defy gravity.

The camera went *click, click, click* and Sam gave up. It would be better to express her solemn, professional self than look like a flibbertigibbet. Besides, supermodels never smiled.

Click, click.

Not that she was supermodel material.

Click, click.

Good grief. What was up with the photographer? If he hoped to catch the tall, black-eyed, black-haired, black-suited woman smiling genuinely in the back row of a group of twenty-some people, he would be snapping for a long, long time.

Sam considered texting insults to her boss about his idiotic decision to send her to the event. Randy had insisted the assignment was necessary. It was a boost up the ladder for her. And besides, no one else was available. The guy was a hoot a minute.

At last the photographer lowered his camera and the group dispersed, laughing and chattering. Sam wondered if it was too soon to leave.

She retrieved her oversized handbag at her feet, unclipped the name-tag from her lapel, and dropped it in the bag. Enough with the PR already.

Samantha Whitley of Collins and Creighton Engineering Firm was going back to the office to do some real work.

"Excuse me."

Sam turned toward the voice. It belonged to a teenager with long blond hair, horn-rimmed glasses, and a long deep crease between her brows. Sam said, "Hi."

The girl gave a quick nod. "Would you mind telling me what you did?"

"What I did?"

"Here." She swept her arm in a wide arc.

The gesture encompassed the building behind Sam, a playground, a parking lot, shrubbery, fences, housetops peeking over them, and the cloudless Southern California blue sky.

What had she done there? Well, she had shaken hands politely, per Randy's instructions. She had pronounced the name of her firm clearly into the microphone as she said thanks for the certificate of appreciation. She let others cut the ribbon. She had her picture taken countless times with a couple dozen strangers. She had even tried to smile.

"I mean..." The girl pushed at the bridge of her glasses and did not hold direct eye contact. "I mean, your work."

Sam watched the girl's face turn hot pink and saw herself fifteen years ago, blushing and stammering in front of a stranger.

The woman had been a guest at her high school's Career Day. Typically a collection of locals spoke, people the kids saw at work every single day of their lives. The Arizona town was too remote for outsiders to bother with. Except that one time. Irene Hibbs blew in like a puffy white cloud, a thing of amazement that hovered long enough for Sam to dare to approach.

She was the only one who had cared to approach the woman. Classmates were bored silly and acting like it. No surprise. The video player was on the fritz. No surprise. It was monsoon season and water plopped loudly into buckets around the room. Even the woman's laptop seemed jinxed. She had resorted to passing around a coffee-table book.

The girl standing before Sam now said, "Did you...did you build it?"

It was the same question Sam had asked Irene Hibbs. *Did you...did you build it?* She had referred to a Chicago skyscraper photographed in the book. The girl referred to the structure behind Sam. The answer, though, would be the same as the one she had heard.

"What do you think?"

The girl blinked and nudged her glasses upward again. "They said you're an engineer with Collins and Creighton."

"Yes."

She exhaled. "Really?" The word rode on her breath, as if Sam were a thing of amazement.

Inwardly Sam squirmed. That was no skyscraper behind her, only a simple community center, its most remarkable feature a gym. She wanted to slink off. But the girl's reddened cheeks and avoidance of eye contact was doing a number on her.

"It just takes a lot of math and science."

"But you built it."

"If we don't count architects and construction people."

"Their work wouldn't happen without yours."

Sam's mouth twitched. "How do you know?"

"My little sister draws pretty pictures and my little brother plays with Legos. Sometimes I put them together."

"And you get an aesthetically pleasing structure that doesn't fall apart."

"Not always." She shrugged and met Sam's gaze at last, her expression an unabashed desire for knowledge she had not yet been able to acquire.

Sam understood. "Do you want to take a tour behind the scenes? I'll tell you about base isolation and what we did with the beams and columns that allows energy to dissipate during an earthquake."

The girl's eyes did not glaze over.

Sam went on. "I can explain why we put the gym on the north side and the kitchen on the east, how the passive and active fire protection systems were designed."

The girl nodded. She was hooked.

It was Sam's turn to blink. If she still wore glasses instead of contact lenses, she would be adjusting them on her nose. She'd met a soul mate. "Sound fun?"

A more vigorous nod.

"Okay. Keep in mind that there's a whole team of us. I'm still doing entry-level stuff. I only worked on the beams and columns."

Another nod and a tentative smile.

Sam put out her hand and shook the girl's. "I'm Sam Whitley."

"Nice to meet you. I'm Lisa Kingman."

Kingman? As in… "Are you related to Mayor Kingman?"

"He's my dad."

Sam nearly burst out laughing, but she only smiled, a genuine expression this time. She was schmoozing the mayor's daughter.

That might be worth two boosts up the ladder.

Three

March 17
Valley Oaks, Illinois

Between the lunch and dinner shifts at the Flying Pig Rib House, Jasmyn sat in a corner booth in the empty dining room and wrapped silverware place settings in thick paper napkins. Muggy, summerlike air floated through the open door. The late winter day was so warm she wore black capris with a short-sleeved white blouse and had even bicycled to work.

She sang along with the Dixie Chicks, using her own country-girlish twang that she thought was pretty good. Not that she could hear it very well above the music blasting from the speakers. Quinn liked the volume on extra loud.

The kitchen door swung open now and Quinn backed out through it, singing in her clear, full soprano. She bopped around, a large tray of salt and pepper shakers in her hands. None of them rattled. With the graceful ease of a gymnast who taught dance exercise classes, she made her way to the middle of the room and set the tray down. "Sing it like you mean it, Albright."

Jasmyn continued her quiet sing-along. Although she liked the tune, the message had never made much sense to her, so singing like she meant it was out of the question. The words were all about wide open spaces and leaving home to find a dream. She already lived smack-dab in the middle of wide open spaces, and why would she leave her comfy home?

According to the ladies, the answer was to find a dream. Well, she had that too. She wanted to pay off medical bills left by her grandparents and mother. Strokes and cancer were expensive affairs. After that, maybe she would visit Chicago again. She had liked the Shedd Aquarium that one time she'd gone with Quinn.

When she wanted to get really wild and crazy, she dreamed of being the owner's right-hand helper. Assistant Manager would be going too far because Danno Johnson had no need of one.

The Flying Pig was an old establishment, built in the early 1900s of brick, like many of the buildings in town. The dining room walls were paneled in dark fake pine. Windows lined one side, a booth beside each one. At the far end French doors led to a screened-in porch. The decor consisted of Valley Oaks school team photos: sports, academics, and band members from throughout the years. The kitchen had been updated in the '80s.

Still, it was Jasmyn's home away from home and she adored it.

Danno, longtime owner and creator of the amazing barbecue sauce that had put Valley Oaks on the map, welcomed her twenty years ago. She was still in high school, in need of a part-time job and—she understood now—a place to hide. Surprisingly, she was a natural at waitressing. She effortlessly memorized orders and anticipated diners' needs before they voiced them.

The job became her great escape from the rest of life. That third-grade year as a pokey Panda had been only the beginning of school issues. Sunshine aside, she was forever Awkward Jasmyn on the sidelines when it came to friends and decent grades. But at the Pig…she smiled now. Well, at the Pig, everyone agreed Jasmyn ruled.

The Chicks faded into Johnny Cash, and Quinn plunked salt and pepper shakers on her table. "Andrew has a friend." She shimmied in her black Bermuda shorts to the next booth.

Jasmyn shook her head. Andrew was Quinn's current heartthrob. He might even be the One. Quinn believed that Jasmyn needed a guy too, a heartthrob and potential the One. Jasmyn did not agree. She'd been there, done that, and got the T-shirt. Or crushed heart.

"Oh, man." Quinn paused in her work and put her hands on her hips. "Look at him out there."

Jasmyn followed her gaze to the French doors and saw Danno dragging plastic chairs and large round tables across the concrete floor. She shrugged. "Everybody at lunch wanted to sit out there and griped because the tables weren't set up."

Quinn scrunched her nose, lips, and eyes together until she resembled a dried apple with short, curly blond hair. "Honestly, it's just way too early in the season for this."

"That's what I told Zeb, but it really is warm enough to sit outdoors. Danno is going to be ready for the dinner crowd. You know how he loves to keep his customers happy."

"To a fault. It'll probably snow next week and then he'll have to redo it all again. The guy is sixty-five years old. He should slow down. Or he should hire the part-timers now instead of waiting for summer—"

Woo-ooo...the air-raid siren shattered the calm. It drowned Quinn's voice and Johnny's. *Woo-ooo*...

The sound crescendoed and faded out. There was a brief pause, like a screamer stopping to take another breath. Then the wail came again. *Woo-ooo*...

Quinn said loudly, "Rats. I wanted to run over to the pharmacy before dinner—"

Woo-ooo...

Jasmyn said, "You'll have time. This will blow over."

"Ladies!" Danno barreled down between the tables like a bull. "Let's go!"

In Valley Oaks, the threat of tornados was a way of life. Springtime and summertime meant bone-rattling thunderstorms and wild clouds. Every Midwesterner had stories to tell about green skies and moments of eerie quiet.

Hours were spent in dank basements with flashlights and battery-operated portable radios, listening to weather updates, waiting for a tornado watch to turn into a tornado warning. A watch meant conditions were ripe. A warning meant one had touched down. Air-raid sirens wailed so everyone knew that it was seriously time to take cover.

Although winds had wreaked their damage throughout the years, no one could recall that a tornado had actually hit the area. Still, old-timers like Danno took the possibility for real every single time. He ushered them into the kitchen, pausing to close windows. Quinn headed down the basement stairs. Jasmyn went to shut the back door and stopped.

Set a few steps above the gravel parking lot, the doorway offered a view from the edge of town. The angle flattened acre after acre of rolling hills. Open farmland stretched forever before a true horizon showed up.

Jasmyn's farmhouse sat about two miles out, as the crow flew. She could see it from where she stood, a tall white-framed structure with a few outbuildings, all little more than specks behind a stand of oaks in front of a patch of pines.

No breeze stirred. The air felt empty, as if it had been drawn out somehow, encasing the world in a vacuum. A translucent curtain of algae green hung over everything.

The siren kept up its incessant cry.

Barometer's dropping. Was that what Zeb had said?

"Jasmyn!" Quinn screamed.

She didn't budge. She could not leave the sight before her.

In the distance, a funnel touched the earth like a finger of God. It twirled silently, spinning along a path from her left to her right.

In the middle, between the left and the right, sat her farmhouse.

Suddenly the roar of a freight train drowned out the siren. It engulfed her. It slammed against her ears.

"Jasmyn!" Danno shouted. "Get your keister down here!"

If not for her boss's big arms lifting her away from the door and setting her on the top basement step, she would not have moved.

"Go!" he yelled in her ear, clutching her elbow and pressing her down the old wooden steps before yanking shut the door behind him.

They sat, the three of them, on old stools in the northeast corner. Cases of canned food were stacked against the concrete block walls. Bare lightbulbs shone from the ceiling's crisscross of two-by-fours.

The freight train noise was dulled underground.

No one spoke. Quinn bit her nails, Danno wheezed, and Jasmyn shook, her heart pounding.

She was glad for her boss's presence. She had often wished he was her father. He was a bit older than her mother, Jerri, would have been, but like her he was born and raised in Valley Oaks. When she asked her mother if she and Danno had ever dated, Jerri had laughed and laughed and said the name of his restaurant fit him every which way and then some. He was a total pig.

Jasmyn begged to differ. There was something solid about him. Sober and nicotine-free for decades, he wore plaid shirts in size triple-X. Compliments, he said, of his own good cooking. He kept his hair buzzed, the style he'd worn since his army cooking days in Vietnam.

The lights winked off.

Danno flipped on two camping lanterns. "No worries, ladies."

Then everything shuddered.

And Jasmyn knew deep in her bones that there were indeed going to be worries.

Four

Sam sat at her kitchen table after a long day that felt longer than long because of the public relations stint followed by a surprise chat with her boss.

She wore flannel pajamas, ate homemade meatballs and spaghetti, and watched an evening newscast on the small television that sat next to the toaster oven on the countertop.

Yes, pj's, a made-from-scratch dinner, and a portable television in a kitchen that featured an avacado green stove. It all seemed old fashioned for a young professional, which, according to age and income brackets, she was.

She worked with people who got the news on their smartphones and ate takeout and trolled clubs on a nightly basis. They lived in high-rise condos with ocean views and direct-deposited rent checks to a faceless management agency. They did not live in a compound of stucco cottages built in the 1920s, in the old San Diego community of Seaside Village, three blocks from the beach. Their landlady did not live on the premises and hand out her homemade dishes like a jolly Santa with toys and a dozen good boys and girls.

But it suited Sam. She sometimes wondered why the Casa de Vida complex, aka House of Life, remained her sanctuary after four years and a monthly salary that surpassed what her mother had ever seen in a year. It could be that deep down she was still simply Samantha the Weirdo, bucking the system without really trying.

She hoped the girl she'd met earlier in the day, Lisa Kingman, would not be saddled with that same moniker for the next twenty years. Maybe having a dad as mayor would make a difference.

At least her boss, Randy, accepted her for whatever she was. That afternoon, when she had told him about the PR session ending with the Lisa Kingman personal tour, he stood and reached across his desk to give her a high five.

"Way to go, Sam!" His grin had been unbelievable.

"Yeah, well, thanks, but don't send me again anytime soon, okay?"

"Okay." He had paused, keeping eye contact in his way that both unnerved her and made her feel safe.

She liked Randy Hall a lot. Forty plus years, marriage, and fatherhood were attractive on him. His three towheaded boys looked like mini versions of their dad, minus the expanding waistline. He understood engineering inside out and always had her back.

She had seen his eye lockdown thing before. He was concocting some wild plan. He wanted to color outside the lines. Somehow, she was involved.

"Sammi."

Oh, no. He used the nickname. It was a dead giveaway.

He blinked away the lockdown and his hazel eyes shone. "I have an idea."

No kidding.

"Here, take a look at this." He spun his laptop around.

The screen showed a page from UC Berkeley.

She bit her lip and reminded herself that once in a while his schemes did not see the light of day.

"Trust me," he said. "See this?" He clicked and scrolled, clicked and scrolled. "Six weeks and you'll have these two courses under your belt. You haven't taken these, right?" Not bothering to wait for an answer because he already knew it, he went on. "It's perfect for Collins and Creighton. You're already our go-to person for environmental remediation, but the firm is still lagging. Just six weeks out of your summer—and wow. You're on your way to another master's, maybe a PhD, and you make us look good, really good."

He wasn't talking about a boost up the ladder. This was serious business impacting the firm. She had earned her master's in civil engineering at UCLA. The environmental side of things intrigued her. She'd dabbled in it enough to pad her credentials.

But…summer school? Out of town?

It was way worse than the PR gig at the community center.

"Randy, I can do it online."

"And lose your sanity." He glanced at her. "Sam, you already give us twenty-four/seven. Besides, there's no hoity-toity factor in that."

In spite of herself, she smiled. Prestige was C and C's middle name. Randy liked poking fun at it.

"And it would take too long."

"Too long for what?"

He gave a one-shoulder shrug.

The gesture indicated something was up, something big, but he couldn't discuss it with her. "Think of it this way. It's not PR."

She muffled a groan. "Berkeley?"

"You'll love it there. But don't pack your bags yet. I have to run this by Collins. Ever been to San Francisco?"

Now, in her cottage, she groaned out loud and opened another plastic container from her landlady. No, she'd never been to San Francisco. Not interested. Not interested in a PhD, either.

She took out a brownie. Cream cheese filled. Ooey-gooey milk chocolate frosting.

Who was going to feed her at Berkeley? More importantly, where would she sleep? She did not want to move, even temporarily. She was home. Casa de Vida was the best home she'd ever had in her life.

Sugar melted on her tongue as she watched the news. A video was running from the Midwest. Frame after frame after frame of rubble.

She swallowed and placed the brownie back in its container.

What would it take to construct a completely tornado-resistant school or house? Maybe she'd learn that at Berkeley.

She snapped shut the lid, moved aside her plate, and slid her laptop into its place. No reason to delay apartment-hunting. At least the relocation would be for only a short while.

And, at least, unlike those people on the news she would have a home to come back to.

Five

September 3
Seaside Village, California

Standing in the arched gateway of her courtyard, Olivia McAlister watched a stranger pace back and forth just a few yards away on the grassy tract near the street's curb.

The woman—a wisp of a thing in a sleeveless yellow dress—babbled on and on. Was she talking to herself or into some wireless device? It was tricky nowadays to tell the difference.

Her dark brown hair was pulled back into a disheveled ponytail. A striped beach bag, oversized and overstuffed, hung from her shoulder, weighing it down, making it droop. She was clearly agitated and—

And what did it matter?

Liv sighed. She was not, she absolutely was not going to get distracted by a needy person today. She had promised herself to devote the day to friends. No matter that it was a holiday and that holidays—even a minor one like Labor Day—tended to upset the street people already burdened by so many—

Oh, no.

The woman had stopped pacing and was now hunched, bent nearly double, leaning against a parked white SUV. Her arms crossed her stomach, as if she were in great pain.

Liv stepped from the gateway, her promise to ignore the needy a fading memory as she strode quickly down her walk and across the public side-walk to the woman.

"Excuse me, dear. May I help you?"

The woman looked at her with the loveliest eyes she'd ever seen, a shade deeper than blue, almost a violet. They glistened with unshed tears. "I parked it here! I'm sure I did!"

"Your car?"

"Yes! Oh, this can't be happening. This cannot be happening." She sank onto the grass. "Not again!"

Again? Liv didn't ask. A more urgent question was if she knelt on the ground beside the stranger, would she be able to get back up? She considered the distance between her knees and the ground. Although she was fairly nimble for being within sight of seventy years, the hours spent gardening yesterday had left certain reminders in her joints.

The young woman burst into tears.

Liv went down on her knees. "Oh, honey, don't you worry your pretty little head. We'll figure this out. I'm Olivia, call me Liv, McAlister." It was always how she introduced herself, offbeat enough to help people remember her name. As a businesswoman, that was a plus. "What's your name?"

"Jasmyn," she blubbered, and then she took a ragged breath. "Albright." Faint crow's-feet at her eyes suggested over thirty but south of forty.

"Nice to meet you, Jasmyn Albright." Liv touched the woman's arm. It was an olive tone, lightly tanned. There were traces of dried salt water. Swimsuit straps were visible above the neckline of her dress. Typically street people were tanned much more darkly. They did not wear suits and swim in the ocean. Perhaps Jasmyn was not, after all, homeless.

"Are you absolutely sure this is the right place?" Liv asked. "Seaside Village looks a lot like the other beach communities."

"I'm absolutely, positively, completely sure!" Her voice matched her slight stature. Even in a high pitch of distress, it was soft. "Seaside Village is my favorite."

"Well then, you know that the streets all look alike here. It's quite easy to confuse them."

The younger woman shook her head, adamant. "This is Westwind Avenue." She gestured toward a distant corner. "And that's Surfrider Street. I've parked here in this exact same spot every single day for the past week."

Liv eyed the endless row of vehicles smushed together, bumper to bumper, up and down the long block. It was true that her street was ideal for parking because it was only three blocks from the beach and, unlike spaces closer to it, had no meters to feed. From Memorial Day until Labor Day, it looked like this. To find the exact same spot every day would have been impossible.

"The exact same spot?"

Jasmyn nodded. "I come early."

"How early?"

"Six thirty."

"My, you must really like the beach."

Jasmyn pulled a large towel from her bag and wiped her face with it, leaving dots of sand on her freckled, sunburned nose. "I love the beach." Her voice dropped to a hushed, reverent whisper. "I could live here."

"Where do you live now?"

Her chin trembled. "Out of my suitcase."

"Oh." So much for Liv's conclusion that Jasmyn was not homeless. "And that suitcase was in your car?"

Tears gushed again. Her mouth formed an *O*, and out came a heart-rending wail.

Liv leaned over and wrapped her in a hug. She smelled of fruity shampoo and coconut suntan lotion.

The scents were curiously clean for a person living out of her suitcase. Like the swimsuit and new tan, other things did not add up. Her toenails and fingernails were neatly painted a pretty shade of coral. Then there was the matching beach towel and bag, their stripes bold and the fabrics unworn.

Perhaps Jasmyn Albright was new to the homeless business.

Movement on the sidewalk caught Liv's attention. She looked up to see a neighbor, Sean Keagan. There was a question in the tilt of his head and humor in the slight curve of his lips.

Liv almost burst out laughing. His sudden appearance was no surprise. Keagan—as he preferred to be called—had a knack for showing up whenever she was about to get involved with a total stranger.

The girl whimpered into the beach towel.

"No worries." Liv gave her one more squeeze and raised an elbow for Keagan to hold as she stood. "The cavalry has arrived."

Her one-man cavalry would never be mistaken for—what was the slang term?—a hottie. He was most definitely neither muscle-bound nor handsome. His hair was a nonshade between brown and blond that he kept short as stubble. A whisper shorter than her own five foot ten, he had a compact physique.

Nevertheless, his strength rivaled a pair of oxen's. One time she had watched him haul half a dozen bags of cement mix on his shoulders down the block.

"What's up?" he said.

"Well, this is Jasmyn, and this morning she parked her car right here. That SUV is not it."

"Hmm." He pulled out his cell from a pocket of his jeans, decisive as always about what to do in any given situation.

That was the other cavalry-type thing about Keagan. He hummed with an energy that radiated competency and security.

He punched in a number and put the phone to his ear. "Now what are the odds of having a car stolen right in front of Liv McAlister's gate?"

She chuckled. He knew the odds were good. Lost lambs had been showing up on her doorstep for years by various means. A car theft, however, was a first. Rather dramatic as well.

So much for her silly notion to avoid needy people that day.

Six

Jasmyn pressed the damp, sandy towel against her face and cried as hard as she had ever cried in her whole entire life. She must look like an idiot, sitting there in the grass, bawling. But what else could she do? Everything was gone. Her friends were halfway across the country. She had no money, no clothes, no phone. She had sand in her eyes and—

"Jasmyn, dear." The stranger spoke. Something about her low voice comforted. Maybe it was the way she said *Jasmyn dear* as though it were one word. As though *Jasmyn* and *dear* meant the same thing and one couldn't be said without the other.

Her tears slowed. She craned her neck to look up at the woman, now standing. What was her name? *Olivia, call me Liv.*

Liv smiled and her whole face twinkled, not just the blue eyes behind silver rimmed glasses. "My friend here is calling the police. Are you—"

"The police!"

"Well, yes. We have to tell them your car was stolen."

"Stolen! Stolen?"

"Oh, my. You hadn't realized that?"

Jasmyn shook her head. "No. I was just…I just…" Just what? She was just stuck in a black hole with a whole lot of confusion and panic. Were all of her belongings really gone? How did this happen twice in one lifetime? Why—

"Honey? Can you talk to them?"

"Them?"

"The police."

Jasmyn took a shaky breath. "Okay."

"Thatta girl. This is Keagan, my neighbor."

A man stepped around Liv. He nodded at her, talking into a cell phone. "I'll put her on." He handed the phone to her.

It felt hot and too large in her hand. It was a newer model than hers, one of the smart kinds that always made her feel dumb. She put it to her ear, hoping it was right side up. "Hello?"

A kind female voice replied, and Jasmyn wondered if everyone in California was nice. She had yet to meet a grump.

The woman's straightforward questions put her at ease, helping her to rattle off all the car information. Her knack for details was why she never wrote down customer orders and why her friends called her the queen of trivia. Names, numbers, and directions were always at her fingertips. She never lost her keys.

No way on earth could she have forgotten where she parked her car. No way could she have forgotten the time she had parked it; its make, model, or license plate number; or the name and location of the rental agency.

She ended with, "Why on earth would anyone want to steal a plain little white two-door rental?"

The policewoman chuckled. "You'd be surprised."

When the conversation ended, Jasmyn stared at the phone. "I don't know how to turn it off."

The man called Keagan took it from her. "Your car is a rental?"

She nodded and thought about standing up. But seriously. Was there any reason to stand up? She had nowhere to go and no way of getting there.

"Jasmyn, dear, where are you from?"

"Illinois. Valley Oaks, Illinois."

"Oh! Then you're here on vacation?" Liv sounded surprised.

"Yeah."

"Is someone traveling with you?"

As Quinn would say, *Uh-oh, red flag.* She'd say that California had earned its nickname, the Land of Fruits and Nuts, for good reason, and it wasn't because of agriculture. Friendly did not mean trustworthy, and Jasmyn should always be on her guard against weirdos.

If Quinn could see this guy Keagan, she'd tell Jasmyn to hightail it out of there ASAP. *He was friendly enough to make the phone call, but come on,*

Albright, give me a break. Scary. No expression whatsoever. Have you seen him smile? No. I am not even going to mention those two mirrors hiding his eyes. Check out the hair. Hair? What'd he use? A brown marker? That's one bona fide kook for sure.

Liv said, "Can we call someone for you?"

Jasmyn shrugged, not wanting to give personal information, and she wondered why such a nice woman would hang out with the likes of Keagan. It was probably all an act. The two of them were in cahoots.

Liv went on. "You said you were living out of your suitcase. Are you staying in a motel?"

Jasmyn's neck ached from looking up at the strangers. She bent her head and focused on shoving the towel back into the beach bag, trying not to cry again. If she didn't shove Quinn's imaginary voice in the bag with the towel, she'd be sitting there all night in the grass because really, she was beyond frazzled.

She had no choice but to trust these kooks.

"I'm here by myself. I checked out of a motel this morning." She got to her feet and smoothed out her cover-up dress. "That's why all my luggage was in the car. I was leaving from the beach to go to…to go to…" Her breath caught. "To Disneyland. I had a reservation at the resort."

"Oh, honey." Liv reached out and squeezed Jasmyn's arm. "You'll get a chance to go there and you will love it. For now, though, we'd better get you settled in. You'll want to cancel credit cards and reservations. You need food and a place to sleep."

She blinked away fresh tears. It was too much to think about. "Any motel is fine. Whatever is close. I'll pay you back, I promise."

"Now, now, no worries about money. And no motel room for you. I live right through that gate over there, and we have a room with your name on it. As a matter of fact, we have an entire cottage. Come on. Let's go home." She turned on her heel and walked away.

A cottage with her name on it? *Uh-oh.* Should Jasmyn follow? Was she being kidnapped?

Quinn's voice again.

But Quinn had not met this woman.

Liv was tall and large-boned. Probably in her sixties. She wore sandals, khaki capris, and a brightly colored floral print blouse. Her twinkling eyes and quick smile were the stuff of fairy godmother tales. In a deep voice on the verge of a giggle, she had made the car issue disappear like a puff of smoke and offered to take Jasmyn home.

Home.

Could Liv McAlister be Hansel and Gretel's hag in disguise?

Keagan moved beside her. "Olivia's the real deal, Jasmyn Albright." Without another glance or word, he trailed after the woman.

Jasmyn watched their retreating backs. What should she do? Spend the night on a park bench or follow the bighearted woman and her mind-reading friend?

Her heart thumping in her throat, she picked up her beach bag.

Quinn would have a cow.

◦∞℮

Jasmyn walked toward the wall she had noticed every day she had parked in her spot. It was impossible not to notice it. At least half a block long and probably twelve feet high, it was covered with green vines and gorgeous hot pink papery blossoms.

In the center of the wall was a wide archway with a gate—more like a solid door—that, unlike now, had always been shut. To its right was a small sign made of tiles painted with flowers and lettering that read *Casa de Vida, 157 Westwind.*

Jasmyn approached the doorway, now open, where Liv waited alone. Keagan was nowhere to be seen.

The woman spread her arms wide and grinned. "Welcome to the Casa de Vida." She pronounced it *casa day veeda.* "The House of Life."

Uh-oh. House of Life? Jasmyn was walking into some wacky cult place.

"Come into the courtyard and meet my other neighbors."

Cringing at the image of herself as Gretel, Jasmyn followed Liv through the gateway, stopped in her tracks, and gasped.

Liv chuckled. "Everyone does that the first time they come inside. Isn't it lovely?"

Lovely did not begin to describe the festive paradise before her. It looked like a movie set. Actors would have Italian accents.

Plants grew everywhere, absolutely everywhere she looked. There were green leaves, from tiny to huge jungle-like. There were palms, tall and squat, strung with patio lights. There were pots of every size and color.

There were blossoms of every size and color, up high and down low, giving off scents so sweet and thick she tasted honey.

Several people sat or stood near a trickling fountain or at patio tables shaded by red umbrellas. Everyone talked and laughed.

Almost hidden behind the garden and the people were the cutest little cottages she had ever seen. They were connected side by side, each one white and flat roofed with colorful window boxes. They sat in a crooked circle around the courtyard.

Oh, she hoped it wasn't a cult. "What is this place?"

Liv laughed. "An apartment complex."

"An apartment complex? In Valley Oaks that's a three-story brick schoolhouse built in 1926."

"Is that where you live?"

"Sort of." Yes, she did live in that building where everyone in town over the age of seventy had gone to middle school when it was a middle school. The building still smelled of chalk dust and glue and musty books. But it wasn't where she was supposed to live. It was not her house. Not her home.

"Sort of?" Liv asked.

Jasmyn shrugged, her throat too tight to speak.

"Well, dear, it sounds full of history, like this place. The Casa was built in the 1920s too by a one-armed World War I veteran. All sorts of people have lived here. War heroes, television stars, movie stars, world champion surfers, a senator's mistress, a gangster on the lam, an admiral with amnesia—well, the list goes on and on. Are you hungry? You arrived just in time for our Labor Day potluck picnic. Let's put your bag on this bench here for now." She lifted the bag from Jasmyn's shoulder. "We'll get you settled into number Eleven in a bit, okay?"

Jasmyn glanced over her shoulder. The gate was still open. It could be her last chance to hightail it out of there.

Suddenly it didn't matter. She had no idea what she was walking into, but she sensed that with Liv McAlister, everything was going to be all right.

And she hadn't felt that since the morning of St. Patrick's Day.

Seven

Sam groaned under her breath, a trick she had learned within the first week of moving into Casa de Vida.

Much as she liked her home—okay, after her summer stint at Berkeley in a two-window studio apartment above a Vietnamese restaurant, she could admit that she probably loved her home. And, yes, Liv's cooking was an added perk. But despite her homemade meals, the matriarch of the Casa was…

Well, she was impossible to describe. Something about her bugged the living daylights out of Sam. If they had to speak on a daily basis, Sam doubted she would have lasted for the past four years. She might have smothered to death by all the groaning under her breath.

There Liv was now, dragging in yet another stray off the street, introducing her to everyone at the picnic, handing her a bottle of water, and ignoring the poor woman's deer-in-headlights expression.

Sam set a box of cupcakes on the serving table and uncovered it. Purchased bakery items were her typical contribution to the Casa's occasional potlucks. Who had time to cook? Well, not counting the other residents who were either retired, unemployed, or worked part-time, nowhere near the sixty-plus hours she usually put in during a week.

She watched Liv make her way through the courtyard, the stranger in tow. Sam guessed her to be a little older than herself, maybe around thirty-five and, judging from the deer eyes, in dire straits.

Of course she was in dire straits. Liv did not pull in well-adjusted, happy people.

Sam sighed again. In all honesty, she included herself on that one.

Four years ago, desperate for an apartment or condo that was located no more than three freeway exits from her new job, she had wandered the streets of Seaside Village, the last possible choice and nowhere near her first. Its laidback, beachy culture felt shallow. Hemmed in by the freeway and ocean, it felt confining.

She'd sat in a coffee shop, drawing thick lines with a black marker through listings that had sounded hopeful on paper but turned out to be positively putrid, nearly sick to her stomach at the thought of returning to the dingy motel room she had lived in for three months. Why hadn't she taken that job in Los Angeles rather than the one in San Diego? Was it too late to change her mind?

Someone nearby had kept clearing her throat until finally Sam turned and saw a stranger, tall and large-boned, with glasses and fluffy silvery-brown hair and a smile.

"Excuse me, dear. You need a place to live."

Right off the bat, Sam sensed comfort and safety. But, Sam being Sam—socially inept—she bristled at the tender vibes.

Liv had rattled off the pertinent details. Two bedrooms, hardwood floors, charming but updated, crazy unheard-of low rent, and one block from Jitters, the coffee shop where they sat. An hour later, Sam had signed a lease.

True, she had not been happy or overly well adjusted at the time, but she had presented herself as if she were sane. This newcomer appeared fragile, a waif in imminent danger of a major meltdown. What was Liv thinking?

Sam continued to watch as Liv introduced the woman to the residents and their families and, good grief, even to Beau, the handyman, who looked like a linebacker but had a Gentle Ben personality.

Sam referred to herself and these neighbors of hers as the Detainees. Why such a mismatched band of people had come together baffled her, but they were now smiling at the newcomer. Typical.

Inez and Louis Templeton, Cottage Eight, were great-grandparents and had that role down pat, dousing everyone under the age of seventy with parental adoration. Naturally, Inez greeted the total stranger with a hug.

There was Piper from Four. Model beautiful, she worked part-time in a department store.

Chad from Two was model handsome. He and Piper made a good-looking couple, but they were not involved, probably because he was an aimless, perpetual college student whose rich parents paid for his lifestyle.

Cottage Six neighbors Riley and her daughter, nine-year-old Tasha, were introduced next. The little girl, who had Down syndrome, surpassed Inez when it came to being lovable. She hugged the woman fiercely and told her about the cupcakes she already knew Sam had delivered.

Noah, aka the Stork from Five, smiled and introduced his teenage daughter, Déja, who did not live full-time with him. He was, as far as Sam could tell, a part-time dad, part-time musician, part-time choir director, and part-time chef.

Coco Vizzini, from Twelve, grinned and waved from her wheelchair next to a patio table. Her lipstick was smeared. Her mascara was thick on her lashes as well as her cheeks. Not a strand of her blond hair, however, escaped the perfect bob, which was a wig. She wore a rhinestone-studded jacket. She was the epitome of old-fashioned glamour. No one knew her age, but she told story after story of her Hollywood career in the 1940s and 1950s.

Keagan from Cottage One was missing. He mingled even less than Sam did. She had yet to figure out Mr. Kung Fu Dude. According to Liv, he ran a gym and held some sort of martial arts honor. According to his constant facial expression, he ate a lot of lemons.

Liv owned the property, all twelve cottages. She had inherited the place from her father. When her husband died about ten years ago, she had moved into Cottage Ten to manage as the resident busybody.

Busybody probably went too far. Liv did not interfere with Sam in the least. She gave her warm greetings and food. At times Sam still bristled. In fair moments, she admired the woman's independence and hard work. In unfair moments, she groaned.

Liv approached her now. "Samantha, this is Jasmyn Albright from Valley Oaks, Illinois."

"Hi." Sam shook her small, cold hand. "I'm Sam from Seven. Have you memorized all our names and numbers yet? Liv's going to test you."

Jasmyn's smile slipped. She tried another with the same result.

"Oh, Samantha." Liv's smile never slipped. "Don't make her feel worse. Her car was stolen right out in front of the Casa."

"No way."

"Yes way, with all her belongings. Isn't that odd? These things don't happen here."

Indeed, they did not happen around there. Seaside Village had its share of malcontents and crime. The Casa property, though, along with its street and the alley out back, was never involved. Even litter was a rare thing. Sam had always felt physically safe.

Liv touched her arm and grinned. "No worries, dear. I'm sure it was a one-time incident. And now we've met Jasmyn."

Sam knew from experience that she should simply accept the leap between two unrelated events. If she tried to decipher what car theft had to do with happily meeting someone new, she would be there all night.

Liv's expression turned somber. "She's lost her clothes, phone, and purse. Isn't that awful? We notified the police, but that's not going to take care of tonight or the foreseeable future, is it?"

"N-no, it's not." Sam hesitated. Jumping onboard with Liv carried with it the possibility of being pushed out of her comfort zone.

Sam had numerous examples. One time when a mouse had been spotted inside Riley's cottage, Liv talked Sam into letting Riley and Tasha spend the night with her. It turned into three nights before the creature and its friends were dealt with. Because her spare bedroom served as an office without a bed, she let them stay in her bedroom while she slept on the couch.

Liv said, "Eleven is vacant, you know, so Jasmyn can stay there."

Sam felt relief and then guilt. "But it's empty."

"Which is why I'm lining up a few necessities. Jasmyn insists a television is not a necessity, but I was wondering about that little one you have in your kitchen that you said you don't use all that much."

Only for news programs. Mornings and evenings. Every day. "I'll get it for you. What about a chair? I have a fold-up rocker."

"Perfect."

"Towels?"

"Yes, we'll need those. And pillows, sheets, and blankets. Inez has a roll-away but is short on linens because two of her grandkids are coming this week. Do you have a TV tray or two? Chad has a card table, but you know Chad. It's buried treasure and he doesn't have a map."

Sam nodded, noticing Jasmyn shift her weight from one foot to the other and crumple the water bottle. Her face reddened and her eyebrows were all but lost up into her hairline.

Sam sensed the meltdown was approaching while Liv went on and on about linens and TV trays. "Okay, so you've talked to the police. What about credit card companies and your phone service provider?"

Jasmyn shook her head.

Liv said, "We'll get to that. I thought some friendly faces and food might be comforting before all that other business."

At last the woman spoke. "Really, I'm not very hungry." The voice fulfilled Sam's expectation. It was tenuous and soft, like a little girl's.

Fully aware that it was not the woman's fault that she spoke in syrupy sweet tones, Sam found it off-putting anyway. But it called for help, and Liv was dropping the ball.

Sam tilted her chin and crossed her arms. "Liv."

"Oh." Liv caught on to her disapproval. "You think business first?"

"Yes. She'll be hungry later."

"You're right. Right as rain, like always. Why don't you take her into my office and show her around?" Liv looked at Jasmyn. "I told you Sam was the bright one."

Sam nearly laughed out loud. *Bright one.* Yeah, right. Liv had just finagled her into donating several items to the cause and helping Jasmyn wade through headache-producing details.

At least she would not be sleeping on her couch tonight.

Eight

Alone in the Casa's office, Jasmyn sat at a desk, on the phone with Quinn. As she had imagined, her friend assumed Jasmyn had stumbled upon the sort of group that made national freaky headlines.

"You should come home right now. Tomorrow."

"When I said everything was stolen, that meant my purse and my wallet and my driver's license. You can't get on a plane without ID. I'll call in the morning about getting it replaced."

"Oh, no. What are we going to do?"

"Quinn, I'm fine. Really and truly."

"Would you know if you weren't? Nope. Cult wackos are always super nice at first. That's how they get you to trust them. Tell me again about the scary guy."

"I said he was kind of intimidating, not scary."

"Mm-hmm."

Jasmyn wondered how to describe the energy she'd felt when Keagan said with such certainty that Liv was the real deal. "He's like Sheriff Cal. You wouldn't want to cross him, but he makes you feel safe."

"This guy sounds bizarre. Who names their kid *Keagan*? It's probably his special cult name."

Jasmyn stifled a sigh and looked through the office window. Everyone milled about the pretty courtyard and seemed to be having a good time. Liv was easy to spot, tall and laughing.

"Liv is one big heart walking around on two legs."

"Every cult needs a mother figure and an enforcer. You've met them both. What are the others like?"

"Quinn, honestly, they're just regular people. Sam is a little uptight. She's the one who got me online. She has short, coal-black hair. You'd call her chic. I thought she was the manager, but she told me Liv manages and owns the place."

"You should check out the office. See if you can find any incriminating evidence."

"What in the world would that look like?"

"I have no idea, but you'd recognize it."

"Right." Jasmyn swiveled in the chair and took in again the pretty room that, according to uptight Sam, was originally one of the cottages. It had been divided in half to create an office and a laundry room. "I don't see any. The room looks like a big heart must have decorated it."

Quinn moaned. "Okay, fine. I'm just concerned."

"No need. I'm looking at pretty pink floral curtains and wallpaper. Comfy chairs. A rose in a crystal vase. Old photos on the walls. A kitchenette with a super cute teapot on the counter. Only a lovely person has an office like this. I will be fine, Quinn. How's the picnic going?"

"It's going."

Jasmyn pictured her friend right now at the Valley Oaks Labor Day picnic, out at the park by the baseball fields with half the town. Her natural curls would be wound extra tight because of the humidity and sticking to her head like a blond swim cap, but she wouldn't give a hoot.

"Jasmyn, don't change the subject. You can't go through loss like this again, especially not with a bunch of strangers, no matter how regular they seem. We have to get you home."

Home. *Home*...

Funny thing. San Diego felt like home. Two weeks ago, she landed, drove straight from the airport to the beach, and dipped her toes into the ocean—the Pacific Ocean!—and an indescribable sense of coming home, of *homecoming*, washed over her. It was as real as the wave that immediately knocked her flat.

Amazing, awesome, and really, really weird.

Then things got even weirder.

The feeling didn't go away. For days on end she swam in salt water that drenched her over and over again with a deep, bone-melting, laugh-out-loud happiness. She had come home.

Liv slipped naturally into the home scene. She was the fairy godmother, the heart on two legs, the mother figure. A version of *mom* that Jasmyn wished she had experienced.

How on earth was she going to explain such things to Quinn?

In the end, Jasmyn did not try to explain such things to Quinn. She gave her friend Casa de Vida's address and phone number and made a bunch of silly promises, such as she would lock the door, lock the windows, and not give out any PIN numbers or passwords.

Beyond exhausted now, Jasmyn followed Liv through the rooms of Cottage Eleven, blinked, and tried not to cry at the gift being handed to her. Was she awake or asleep? She wasn't sure.

The tour ended back in the living room.

Liv turned to her. "Jasmyn, dear, what's wrong?"

She shook her head and shrugged. "It's so…so…" She shrugged again.

Liv leaned in until she was eye-level with her. "Good or bad?"

Jasmyn whispered, "It's so good it's almost bad."

Liv clapped her hands once and laughed. "I know just what you mean."

Jasmyn wasn't sure she did, but how else could she say it? Not two hours ago she had the clothes on her back, a pair of sweats, and a stack of magazines inside a beach bag, and nothing else. Now she had a roof over her head and a home that was filled with necessities and then some. Was it too good to be true?

Of course it was too good to be true. Everything was borrowed. The home was temporary.

"Just remember that you are welcome to stay for as long as you need. Or want." Liv smiled. "I'm right next door in Ten if you need me. Coco is on your other side in Twelve, but she couldn't hear fireworks set off in her kitchen. Now get some rest. We'll tackle the details tomorrow."

She was out the door before Jasmyn could thank her properly. But what was *properly* for such an enormous gift?

She roamed back through the cottage. It was small, quaint, and almost as pretty as Liv's office. The walls were a soft yellow. The hardwood floors gleamed. The bathroom and galley kitchen were spotless.

While she had been on the phone, Liv and the others had created a haven. The living room invited her to sit and relax with a padded rocker, floor lamp, and small television. A fragrant bouquet of flowers graced the wide, built-in seat in front of the bay window.

The kitchen was empty except for a few dishes and cups in the glass-front cupboards, a coffeemaker on the counter, and food from the picnic inside the fridge.

Even sparsely furnished, the bedroom surpassed her motel room when it came to cozy. A multicolored quilt covered the rollaway. On top of it sat a stack of fluffy sea-green towels. Soft light shone from a single reading lamp on a TV tray.

Clothes hung in the closet and toiletries were spread across the vanity in the bathroom. Piper, the beautiful young woman from Four who worked at a department store, had provided all of those things. Apparently clothes and cosmetics were her life, so she had plenty to spare and loved equipping others with them, but still…

It was so good it was almost bad.

Jasmyn giggled. Then she cried. Then she took a shower, slipped into a lavender cotton nightshirt that still had the tags on it, and crawled into bed.

Nine

Before any of her tenants had opened the blinds on their bay windows, Liv was out and about, making her morning rounds in the courtyard.

She smiled. Syd, her late husband, had coined the term *making her rounds*. He said she was doctor and security guard rolled into one. Through the years, other people had called her Mama Liv, angel, prayer warrior, crazy coot, and odd duck. And those were only the ones she knew about.

But, as young people said nowadays, whatever. She was fine with the labels because they suited her. Believing that those who lived at the Casa had been placed there for her to watch over was the axiom she lived by. She began each day with a stroll around the courtyard, a pause before each cottage, and a prayer for the occupant.

Facing the courtyard that still lay in shadows, Liv sat now near her front door on an Adirondack chair, a teapot and cup beside her on a table. All the cottages had similar chairs, their colors chosen to match each front door. Hers was holly red, Syd's favorite color on her.

Tobi, her RagaMuffin cat, purred on her lap. She was a beauty with her mouth and nose centered inside a triangle of white fur. Her right eye and ear were surrounded by dark fur, the left ones by orange.

Birds chirped their predawn song while Liv jotted notes on a pad. She needed to get to the market and the library and tend to those sad mums under the sycamore. The burned-out lightbulbs in the laundry room and the Templetons' drippy faucet were chores for Beau, her maintenance man.

She heard Eleven's door open and close, a swishing sound nearly lost in the swelling birdsong. That would be the new girl now, trying not to disturb anyone. She seemed a bit on the mousy side with her soft, small voice. It was a wonder Liv had convinced her to spend the night at the Casa.

Liv leaned forward, eager for Jasmyn to appear. The cottages were not lined up in a straight row, but in a staggered circle around the courtyard. Each front door was set back in an alcove. The lovely design created corners and privacy, an excellent feature for such a compact area. But for an odd duck who moonlighted as a mama, it fostered impatience.

Liv waited her limit of three seconds and called out, "Jasmyn, dear?"

The girl peered around the corner of her cottage. "Liv?"

"Good morning!"

Jasmyn emerged, a mug in her hand and wearing a pale yellow robe that fit her to a tee. "Good morning."

Liv patted the arm of the chair next to hers. "You look bright eyed and bushy tailed."

"Do I?" Jasmyn sat and smiled. Even in the grayish light of dawn her almost-violet-colored eyes shone. Dimples appeared in her rounded cheeks. "I do, don't I?"

"You must have slept well."

"Oh, I can't begin to tell you how well I slept. Did you know with the window open you can hear the surf from here?" She paused as she heard her own question. "Of course you know that."

"It is lovely when the wind blows just right."

"And the scent! Oh my gosh. Sweet flowers are right outside the window."

Liv nearly clapped her hands. She hadn't thought of the large plant growing near the back corner of Cottage Eleven, the one she had pampered and coaxed into blooming again. "That's jasmine."

"Really?"

She nodded.

"Isn't that funny? Well, between the smell and the sound, the room was so soothing. But still I can't believe I slept. I mean, on a rollaway in a strange house wearing someone else's clothes. How goofy is that?" She drew a deep breath, her smile and twinkle fading. "Especially since I haven't really slept in almost six months."

"Six months?"

"There was a tornado." She inhaled again deeply and blew out loudly. "My house is gone and everything I owned. Well, except for my bicycle because I rode it to work that day, and that's where I was when the tornado struck. It didn't hit the restaurant or the town, for that matter. I live— I lived on a farm."

A tornado? The poor child. "I'm so sorry. You and your family weren't harmed?"

"No. I mean, I wasn't. I don't have any family. No siblings or cousins. My grandparents are gone. My mother died three years ago. There were only the four of us."

"No dad?"

"Uh, my mom, uh, wasn't sure who he was. He was just passing through town. She was only eighteen."

Oh my! "I'm so sorry. But you had friends to help you after the tornado? A special young man? Oh, dear. I'm snooping. Bad habit."

"That's okay. I think I need to talk. Friends, yes. Special guy, no." She grimaced, as if to say there had been one at some point and that it had not ended well.

"These past months must have been about the worst in your life."

"Yeah." She breathed out the word, as if grateful for Liv's two cents' worth of sympathy. "I'd say *the* worst. So, you see? It doesn't make any sense why I could sleep here right after I lost everything again. But then, nothing has made sense since the instant I stuck my foot in the ocean and felt like I'd come home. Everything about San Diego is familiar. Even the freeways. Back home, Valley Oaks doesn't have one stoplight and the highways are two-lanes through farmland. The very first day I got here, I zipped along six lanes of traffic as though it were old hat and I drove straight to the Seaside Village beach without taking one wrong turn."

Liv held the teacup to her mouth to hide a smile. On second thought, Jasmyn Albright was not in the least bit mousy.

"Then my things were stolen, but I was rescued and treated like a princess. I didn't even have to ask for cream for my coffee. It was right there in the fridge. *Poof!* Like magic. And I slept for the first time since my house was crushed into a pile of matchsticks. To tell you the truth, it's getting a little scary. And I can't believe I'm telling you all this."

"My goodness, that is a curious chain of events, isn't it?" Liv set down her cup on the small table between the chairs and cleared her throat. "Why did you choose the Seaside Village beach over the others?"

"I read about it online." She shrugged. "It sounded like the prettiest one."

"I think it is. Well. Would you like my take on things?" She had learned to ask permission. In her crazy coot days she'd had a tendency to jump in with both feet and splash others who did not want to get wet. They seldom came back for more.

"Okay?" Jasmyn's voice went up as if she asked a question.

Liv heard it as assent, though, and measured her words. If she said that the Holy Spirit prompted her to stand at the gate yesterday so that she would see Jasmyn in distress and be able to help, the girl might run off. If Liv explained that she had walked through Cottage Eleven, sprinkled holy water around, and prayed for Jasmyn to feel like a princess in it, the girl would hightail it out of there for sure.

Liv chose neutral territory. "Life is a mystery, and it hardly ever makes sense. All I know for sure is that you ended up here when you needed help. And it was Labor Day when no one was working, and we could easily pool our resources. Coco, by the way, donated the cream. She insisted that you have it because she uses it in her coffee."

Jasmyn gave a little smile. "Why could I sleep?"

"You felt safe here."

"I felt safe enough in my Valley Oaks studio apartment. I even felt safe at the Marriott. But I didn't sleep well in either place."

Lord, have mercy. The girl couldn't sleep well in those other places because deep down she did not feel truly safe, not yet. How could she? Six months was nothing. Last night happened only because…

Well, Liv knew why.

She jumped in with both feet and tried not to splash too much. "Then maybe you slept here because I prayed a special blessing on your sleep. It had been such a dreadful day for you."

Jasmyn inched forward in her chair, no doubt preparing to skedaddle.

Liv smiled gently. "That sounds zany, I know. But I pray about everything."

"Is this…" Jasmyn whispered haltingly. "Is this place a, um, a cult?"

"A cult?" Liv pressed her lips together before a burst of laughter escaped.

She cleared her throat. "My goodness. I've never been asked that before. No, Jasmyn, dear. We're not a cult. You just happened to catch us at one of our infrequent all-Casa parties. I suppose each of us is a little kooky in some way. No one, though, is what I would call off-the-chart strange."

Jasmyn bit her lip and looked down at her mug.

Liv said, "Maybe you think I'm off-the-chart strange?"

She looked up, her eyes wide. "I don't know anyone who prays about everything and gets answers."

"Well, now you do." *Oops.* She hadn't meant to say that out loud.

To Liv's surprise Jasmyn scooched back in the chair and smiled. "Yes, now I do. So is it all right if I spend another night here?"

Liv grinned her reply, not wanting to give voice to the thought that was forming in her mind like a video on fast-forward.

Cottage Eleven was going to be Jasmyn Albright's new home.

Ten

Sam parked her black Jeep Cherokee and cut the engine. Despite the ibuprofen she'd taken while inching along the freeway in rush hour traffic, her head throbbed. She removed her sunglasses and covered her face with her hands.

Typically her days did not end like this. Typically work energized her. She arrived at the office early, left late, stopped off at the gym three days a week, and ran at the beach the other two. She went in on weekends. Her friends were those other people in the office early, late, and on weekends.

Work was her hobby, her passion, her social life, her *raison d'être*. She was content and satisfied.

Until today.

A sudden rap on her window startled her. She jumped and turned to see Charles Chadwick Rutherford IV grinning like a goofy little kid. Her heart pounded along with her head.

He mouthed a *Sorry* and made a rolling motion with his hand.

She turned the key and hit the automatic button to open the window. "Honestly, Chad!" He went by his middle name. Apparently after three variations on Charles, the family had run out. "What is wrong with you?"

His grin went sideways and he put a hand to his chest. "Rakish" should have been his middle name. "You know I can't pass up an opportunity to set you off, Miss Whitley. You are completely irresistible when you're exasperated. Your eyes are wild and you're blush—"

"Put a lid on it."

The guy was too cute for his own good. Clear hazel eyes that always made dead-on, disarming contact. Perfectly straight white teeth. Six feet tall. Broad shoulders that made white T-shirts look like haute couture. Slender face. Thatch of unruly dark brown waves. He was textbook material for a men's cologne ad.

He leaned on the car, his arms folded on the window opening. "What are you doing?"

She gave him her best *duh* stare. "Climbing Mt. Everest."

"Seriously, Sammi, it's five thirty. You're not due home for hours."

She glanced away. Chad was only twenty-five, a spoiled brat, and a pesky nuisance. He was also her best friend at the Casa. *Go figure.* "A huge project was just dumped in my lap."

"What's the problem? You love huge projects, and they're always dumped in your lap, right?"

Right. But…

Sam gazed down the alley, trying not to see the excitement on the faces of Randy and her coworkers. Trying not to feel the hypocrisy in how she had matched them grin for grin.

The alley was bordered by fences, garages, an apartment building, and the Casa's high wall. Most of it was a no parking zone. She paid extra for her spot, only one of four next to the Casa's back gate. Liv used one, the Templetons and Riley leased the others. Except for Chad, who rented a garage for his little Audi, Casa tenants parked on the streets wherever they happened to find space.

Every once in a while, like now, the whole scene felt constricting. The thoughts of freeways enveloping Seaside Village like octopus arms and of three million people driving on them threatened to cut off her breath altogether.

Chad poked her shoulder. "I said, what's the problem?"

"Oh, nothing." She lied through her teeth. "It's just kind of a big nerveracking deal. I'll have to go out of town periodically. Out to Lotanzai."

His brow furrowed and he stared at her for a moment. Then his jaw dropped. "Whoa, Nellie! The Lotanzai Indian Reservation?" He grinned, nodding knowingly. "You're building that new hotel, casino, and golf course."

She lifted her hands in surrender.

He gave a low whistle of approval. "Well, well. You are moving up in that hoity-toity firm of yours."

Maybe. For four years she had worked for them on schools and parks and community centers. She did well with schools and parks and community centers. Probably because she liked schools and parks and community centers.

She did not like hotels, casinos, and golf courses. She did not like leaving town. If the Lotanzai project was moving up, she'd prefer a demotion.

"It's only because of those eco-engineering courses I took this summer, and they needed—"

"Get over it, Samantha." Chad held up his palm. "You did good. Give me five."

She met his slap and tried to smile. "Move. I'm closing the window."

He stood back. "Did you hear about the powwow tonight?"

She let go of the window button. "No."

"Seven o'clock, Liv's place. Mark my words. She's handing out assignments for her latest project: Make Jasmyn Feel Welcome."

Sam groaned.

"Tsk, tsk. No frowning allowed. Better bring your peace pipe. *Ciao.*" He strode off.

Sam caught her frowning reflection in the rearview mirror. Crow-black hair. High cheekbones. Broad face. Olive complexion.

Powwows. Peace pipes. The rez.

Would she never get away?

Maybe she'd just sit in the car for a while and scream.

✿

Liv McAlister did not email. She did not text. She did not put up notes in the laundry room. She called meetings by word of mouth. They were not mandatory, but if Sam wanted to stay in the loop, she needed to attend.

Besides that, Liv served home-cooked food.

"Thank you all for coming." Liv addressed her guests from the bend of the "L" where the living room and kitchen met at the counter that separated them.

Chad, seated on a braided rug next to Sam, a dinner plate in his lap, winked and forked a piece of lasagna. He came for the food too.

Except for Piper and the newcomer Jasmyn, everyone was in attendance, occupying the couch and chairs and most of the floor space. Keagan, who seldom joined such gatherings, stood in the kitchen area behind the counter to Liv's side. Tasha was behind him, eating at the table with her mother, Riley.

Liv's long, flowery skirt billowed around the stool as she sat down. She was an earthy dresser, sort of Hippie Meets L.L. Bean, Senior Style. "I won't keep you long. As cheeky Chadwick has already asked me, is this meeting about saving Jasmyn?"

Laughter rippled through the group. Everyone knew only Chad would ask the question. They also knew the answer.

By "saving," Liv meant making the stranger feel welcome. When Sam had first moved into the Casa, there had been a similar meeting. She didn't know about it until after Piper had moved in and Sam was part of a meeting to save Piper. It was then she realized why each resident had managed to do special favors for her in those early weeks.

"Jasmyn will tell you her story when and if she wants to, but she gave me permission to share a few things. About six months ago she lost her house in Illinois and everything she owned when a tornado hit. She came here for a little vacation. Then, as you know, her rental car was stolen along with all of her things. Talk about a double whammy."

A murmur of sympathy rolled through the room.

"New credit cards and a temporary driver's license are in the mail, but she has no clothes or food aside from what we provided last night. Piper has taken her shopping tonight. I'm sure Jasmyn will pay her back." Liv glanced over at Keagan.

Deadpan Keagan did not respond.

He and Liv had an odd relationship, somewhat like that of a president and her secret service agent. No question about it, the guy watched over her. Liv would have given Piper money for the shopping trip simply because she trusted Jasmyn's character. Keagan, on the other hand, would have run a background check on her last night and taught her—if she did not already understand—how to electronically pay Liv back.

"So." Liv brought her hands together in a single clap. "What do you all think? What can we do for Jasmyn?"

Casa people were a brainstorming bunch. Suggestions flowed from everyone but Keagan and Sam. Keagan was being Keagan, and Sam was thinking about work. On second thought, she too was just being herself.

Tasha walked over to Liv and laid a hand on her arm. It was the little girl's polite way of letting Liv know she wanted a turn to speak.

Sam's heart came as close to melting as possible, although she never let on that Tasha affected her like that. It wasn't pity over the fact that Down syndrome heaped special challenges on the youngster. It was, rather, an almost reverence because there was absolutely no guile in her.

Liv patted Tasha's hand. "What's your idea, honey?"

The little girl flashed her thousand-watt smile. "Let's give Jasmyn lots and lots and *lots* of hugs."

Laughter ended the meeting and Sam slipped away.

Liv caught up with her at the front door. "Samantha, dear, might I put a bug in your ear?" She went on, not waiting for a reply. "Jasmyn is a runner." She smiled, squeezed Sam's arm, and turned back inside.

Sam went out into the cool evening air and considered that Jasmyn factoid for about two seconds. Liv's bug was nothing compared to the lions growling in Sam's path.

Maybe she could talk Randy into giving her a different assignment. Maybe—

"How does she do that?"

She jumped at Chad's voice over her shoulder. "Chad!"

"Whoops, sorry. Seriously, how does she do it?"

There was no need to ask whom he was talking about. "Do what?"

"Make me want to take part in her crazy scheme."

"She put something in the lasagna."

"Aha! It worked on you too, didn't it?"

Sam stopped and faced him, her hands on her hips, determined to deny his assumption. Instead, the tiny white patio lights glittered in the jacaranda tree and the palms. The fountain sang gently like an ancient lullaby. She saw herself last night gathering linens, lifting the portable television from her kitchen counter, and hauling everything over to Eleven.

Chad laughed. "It's nothing to be ashamed of, Sammi. Mama Liv is not exactly a bad influence on us. So what's your assignment?"

"I don't have an a—" She pressed her lips together.

"Mine is to do something fun with her, like go to the zoo. It can't look like a date, though. She's probably old enough to be my older sister. I think I'll ask Piper to join us."

"No wonder you're on board with the crazy scheme."

He raised his hands and shrugged. "Maybe the love of my life will say yes this time."

"Right. Fantasies come true all the time. See you." She walked toward her cottage.

"You didn't answer my question." Chad was beside her again.

"Jasmyn runs."

"Perfect!"

"I don't have the time."

No time. No time and definitely no emotional space for another new project.

Eleven

Late Tuesday night, Jasmyn sat in her borrowed rocker in her borrowed cottage and, using a borrowed cell phone, she phoned Quinn.

No way was she going to tell her about how Liv prayed and thought she got answers or how Jasmyn felt definite mom vibes coming from the woman. But she did describe the sense of homecoming to end all homecomings.

"Quinn, it feels like I've been away for such a long time and now I'm back. I'm back home."

"You're back home. In California. Jasmyn, that's the loopiest thing you have ever said. But then again, you are loopy. I mean that in the most affectionate way."

It was a running joke. Jasmyn was loopy, Quinn was sassy.

Quinn sighed. "It sounds more like heaven. No work, no humidity, no bugs. Movie stars around every corner. Not to mention you're on vacation, loafing on the beach, and doing those number puzzles to your heart's content."

"I haven't seen a movie star."

"You wouldn't recognize one in the flesh. On the street they look just like us."

"Oh, Quinn, it's more than that kind of stuff." How could she describe the impact of Southern California?

She was a country girl who had never been anywhere before. She loved the Midwest and its beautiful, changing seasons. By now the cornstalks would be elephant-eye high, the soybeans beginning to yellow, the air wobbling with late summer heat. Potted mums of every color would be on everyone's front stoop. Tree-covered hillsides would soon be masses of brilliant reds, yellows, and oranges.

Which was why the effect of the crowded city and its ocean surprised her so much.

"It could be that California feels good simply because it's not Valley Oaks where a tornado turned your life on its ear."

"Maybe. But still…" Still, it felt as if she had landed in a never-never land of unbelievably exquisite sights and smells. Sights they had seen on television and smells they paid for. "Quinn, you know how we buy dried eucalyptus stems at the craft store?"

"Yeah. So?"

"So guess what. Eucalyptus trees actually grow here. Whole entire blocks smell like our little bouquets. And the flowers. Oh my goodness. Jasmine blooms outside my cottage. Jasmine! Walking down the street is like walking past the perfume counter at Dillards. And the sky! It's every shade of blue rolled into one and coated with a pearly glaze. And the ocean! Surfers ride on the waves, on *top* of the waves with seagulls and pelicans and *dolphins*. And people are so happy. They're always smiling."

Quinn laughed. "Well, yeah they're smiling. They're all either on vacation or they get to live there full-time at the perfume counter with the seagulls and the pelicans and the *dolphins*."

"That was mean."

"Sorry. Hey, I get it. I do. After what happened here, I don't blame you for feeling at home somewhere else. A vacation was definitely in order, but I really think you should cut it short."

"Why? I planned to stay four weeks. It's only been ten days, and I haven't been to Disneyland yet, and some people here said they'd go with me and even loan me the money if the debit card doesn't get here soon."

"But all your new stuff was stolen! It's like you're jinxed. At least back here you know people. Not to mention I miss you like crazy. We all do. Customers ask about you every day. Danno's having fits over the new girl, who is absolutely clueless. No kidding. I'm talking true-blue space cadet."

Jasmyn could imagine Danno scowling at the new girl the exact same way he had scowled at her when she started, pretending he didn't have a heart of gold.

"Work is a total drag with Miss Airhead. Sorry. That was mean. Again. I'm nicer when you're here. You know, we don't call you Sunshine for nothing."

Suddenly Jasmyn felt tired, way down, bone-deep tired. She wished with all her heart she had a safe place to go to. Living in a borrowed cottage with borrowed things and surrounded by borrowed friends did not exactly fill the bill.

But then neither did Valley Oaks anymore, not since the tornado.

Twelve

In a grassy area at the base of a bluff, across the street from the beach, Jasmyn pressed her hands against the back of a park bench. With one leg extended and her head down, she smelled the just-off-the-rack scent in the lime green T-shirt. Her socks were unworn brilliant white, and her running shoes a very cool neon yellow. Piper the fashionista had voted for them.

Unbelievable. For the second time in less than six months she had bought a brand-new basic wardrobe. Jeans, shirts, underwear, socks, shoes, pajamas, and running clothes. Piper had pressed her to buy a skirt, sweater, and some nice slacks, but Jasmyn resisted. She didn't need everything all at once. The basics were enough.

Jasmyn switched legs and glanced over at Sam, who was in the middle of a flamingo stretch. Limber as the bird itself, she effortlessly pulled up one leg until her foot seemed to touch above the waistband of her black shorts.

At least five years younger and several inches taller, Sam would run circles around her.

"Did you run cross-country or track in school?"

"No." Sam released the leg and lifted the other one. "I just ran. How about you?"

"Just ran." Jasmyn let go of the bench and laughed. "Not even the cross-country team wanted me. I'm slow, really slow."

"This isn't a competition." Sam's smile came and went like the flicker of a lightning bug. She tugged a black ball cap lower on her forehead, stuck tiny earbuds in place, and fiddled with the iPod in the holster on her upper arm. "Ready?"

They jogged down the narrow lane called the Strand. To the left were endless stretches of beach, ocean, and sky. To the right were homes stacked on top of each other, a crazy mix of dumpy cottages, trendy all-glass structures as tall as the bluff behind them, and every style in between.

Jasmyn loped crookedly, stumbling along like a newborn colt.

Sam slowed and pulled out one earbud. "You okay?"

No, not really. "Guess I haven't found my California legs yet."

"Shorten your stride a little."

Jasmyn wanted to sit down and cry. But a run was what she needed, so she followed the advice and finally fell into a rhythm. "Back home it's all rolling hills. Nothing like this."

"Hmm." Sam had replaced the earpiece and was fiddling with the iPod.

"Did you grow up here?"

"No." She increased the pace.

So much for small talk.

Her first impression of Samantha Whitley as an uptight, aloof career woman still held. Which was why she had been surprised to be invited to run that evening. Although Sam was polite—offering to take her on a three-mile route—she apparently considered a run was a run, not to be confused with a social outing.

Jasmyn would have agreed if it weren't for her loneliness. For as long as she could remember, she had run for the quiet, for the escape from life's uglies. Now, though, she felt a friendship void. Despite everyone's kindness at the Casa and Liv's comforting mom demeanor, Jasmyn wasn't exactly at home. Nor was she exactly on vacation. She was an outsider in a no-man's land.

She should go home. But…she didn't want to go home. Not yet.

Jasmyn's leg muscles ached already. No wonder. For days on end she'd been sitting or playing in the waves, not exercising.

The beach was nearly deserted, nothing like the jam-packed place she had enjoyed. It was the end of summer, and people had gone back to school or work. Back to their regular lives.

Tears stung her eyes and the scene blurred. Even if her things hadn't been stolen, she wouldn't be going back to a regular life. She didn't have a regular life back home, either. She really didn't have a home.

But she knew how to throw a pity party. That had to count for something.

Jasmyn concentrated on the slap of her feet against the pavement, one after another. She breathed deeply through her mouth, in and out, in and out.

Eventually she noticed a huge, multistory condo structure. It blocked the beach route, but they followed the Strand as it curved up a gradual incline and intersected with a street. They hopped onto a sidewalk, eventually passed the condos, and came face-to-face with a harbor.

Jasmyn breathed out a *whoa* at the picturesque scene. A red, white, and blue lighthouse replica rose above a sea of sailboat masts.

"Arizona."

Jasmyn glanced at Sam. "What?"

"Arizona. That's where I grew up." She spoke between huffs, the earbuds on her shoulders. "In the north. I ran through wilderness. Think Grand Canyon–type topography."

"Wow. That would be different from this."

Sam's smile flashed. "A little."

"Do you miss it?"

"No." A few strides later she said, "Yes."

"Me too." Lungs afire, Jasmyn panted. "No and yes. I miss— Can we stop?"

"Sure."

They slowed to a walk and drank from their water bottles. Across a parking lot they reached a sidewalk that led them along the harbor. Docked yachts and smaller boats bobbed. Rigging clinked softly. In the distance, the sun ducked behind low-lying clouds.

Jasmyn wiped her sleeve over her sweaty face. "I miss the wide open spaces. The cornfields and the woods."

"I miss the wide open spaces too. Canyons and mesas."

Jasmyn smiled. "This city is sort of confining, isn't it?"

"Like a straitjacket."

"Exactly. Well, except for the ocean. It's so incredibly beautiful. I had no idea."

"You'd never seen it before?"

"Nope. Never seen a mountain or a desert either. I really couldn't afford to travel before the tornado hit. You heard about that?"

"Liv mentioned it. I'm really sorry."

"Thanks. The upside of it all is that I made a lot of money from the house insurance. Then I sold the land and my grandparents' farmland to a development company. For the first time in my life I could afford a brand-new car and a vacation. A long vacation, like a whole entire month in Southern California."

Sam winced.

It was too much information, but Jasmyn's pent-up thoughts tumbled out. "I never really fit in as a kid. I was from the wrong side of the tracks…or the cornfield. The only place I felt safe was by myself. Valley Oaks is a wonderful place. Everyone rallied around me after the tornado. Unbelievable charity. But then I sold the land and whoa. People were not happy. I mean, I still have friends— Well, it's not like we get together a lot. Except for Quinn. Her parents invite me for holidays. And my regular customers are always sweet, but…"

Jasmyn frowned. The next part was awfully difficult to admit. She went on. "The thing is, the company I sold to is putting in a strip mall between the town and the interstate. Yikes. It'll be such an easy stop for travelers. Too easy. They won't have to come into town to shop or eat." She paused for a breath and a peek at Sam, who kept right on walking, her profile a stoic mask, her businesswoman brain probably thinking how Jasmyn had robbed her town.

Which she had.

Jasmyn sighed. "I know, it sounds awful and I admit that part bothers me too. It was a hasty decision and I can be so gullible. I could have lived on the insurance alone for a while, but this company came to me. They'd been scouting the area for months. What was I supposed to do? I didn't want to rebuild. I listed with a Realtor, but nobody was interested in buying. The farmer who leased land from me is old and he didn't want to— Well, you get the picture. I guess. Look, I'm sorry for running off the mouth like that. My grandma called me a vocal fire hydrant for good reason."

That tidbit usually got a smile out of people, but not Sam.

Jasmyn felt like a total idiot for gushing on and on. "So. You said you don't miss some things about home either, huh?"

Still no reaction.

Way too personal.

They walked past several docked boats and headed out to what appeared to be the arm of land that separated the harbor from the ocean. She spotted a restaurant and a motel.

Even after her land sold and the village cold shoulder aimed itself at her, Jasmyn had not considered changing anything about her life. After all, she had dealt with plenty of hardships. Her grandparents died. Her mother died at fifty-one. Growing up, she'd worn used clothing and was teased for it as well as for her not-so-bright grades. She dated a few guys. Two were losers; one upset her. Okay, he snapped her heart in two as though it were a twig, and by the time she got over him, she'd sworn off men.

Seriously, what was one little tornado?

After a few weeks she had moved from Quinn's couch into a furnished studio apartment, no big deal. When she dropped a platter of barbecue ribs and the sauce splattered the ceiling tiles and three diners, including the school board president, Danno said yes, it was a big deal. No, he said the tornado was a *huge* deal.

He told her she was a basket case and to take a vacation. He told her to go find her smile. And that San Diego was his all-time favorite place for finding smiles.

His words struck a chord. She realized she was living not only under a black cloud, but inside of it as well. How had she not seen that before? When she hugged Quinn goodbye at the airport, the darkness lessened. When she set foot on the beach, it went away. *Poof.*

Then came the car theft, and now there she was again, on the verge of tears, running off the mouth to a virtual stranger, putting on her dark basket-case self again as though it were a sweatshirt, wishing—

"What I don't miss..." Sam glanced at her. "I don't miss breathing the same air I breathed when I was a kid living in the middle of a nightmare. I don't miss living near those memories of not feeling safe with others. Like you."

The words resounded in her head, as loud as the cracking of an old oak in a storm. Trunk, limbs, and words all hit the ground with an echoing boom.

Memories of not feeling safe... like you.

That described her to a tee.

Thirteen

Two weeks after moving into the Casa, Jasmyn poured a cup of coffee, her first of the morning. Quinn's voice filled the cell phone at her ear, but warm fuzzies muffled her friend's words. What had brought on the happy attack? A dream? What could make her so deliriously giggly?

Her temporary ID and replacement credit and debit cards had arrived. She had her own new cell phone too, a smarter one than her lost one. Its built-in camera was better, and it meant she didn't have to replace her camera yet. But those things made life easier, not exactly a cloud nine experience.

Two weeks at the Casa could easily explain it. Nestled under Mama Liv's wing, she couldn't help but feel good. *Mama Liv.* That was what others called her at times. She clearly affected everyone with her nurturing vibes.

The woman would not let her pay rent. Instead, she gave her chores, little ones. Jasmyn cleaned the laundry room and the office, weeded flower beds, swept the courtyard, and ran errands. Almost daily she and Liv either ate together or went to the coffee shop down the street.

And the neighbors. They kept inviting her to do things. Well, all except for Keagan. Jasmyn was okay with that because he wasn't exactly friendly. Liv said he was an angel, but the woman tended to be over-the-top with positive thinking.

Everyone else, though, treated her royally. She'd gone running three times with Sam, went to the ice-cream shop with Riley and Tasha, played Monopoly with Noah and his daughter in the courtyard, eaten meals at

Inez and Louis's, gone with Piper and Chad to a Japanese restaurant where they cooked everything right at the table on a huge surface, and watched an old video with Coco, the generous cream sharer.

Smiling, Jasmyn added cream to her coffee now, tilted the phone from her mouth, and said to the soundproof wall that divided her cottage from the neighbor's, "Thank you, Coco."

"Coco?" Quinn interrupted herself. "You're having hot cocoa in the land of perpetual summer?"

"No. I was talking to Coco Vizzini. I told you about her."

"I can't keep them all straight."

"She's the sweet, doddery ex-movie star in Cottage Twelve. I should say, *film* star. That's what she says. She's so cute."

"Is she there?"

"Where?"

"With you, Miss Sun-Soaked Brain. In your little *cottage* number whatever."

Jasmyn rolled her eyes. "Nope. I was just using the second carton of cream she's given me, and so I thanked her through the walls. Did I mention she danced in a 1950s movie that was nominated for a Best Picture Oscar?"

"You're talking to some nonexistent woman."

"She exists."

"Somewhere else. She's not there with you."

"Sheesh, you sound grumpy." Teasing sometimes took the edge off Quinn's demeanor. "Have you had your coffee yet? Mine is so good with this cream. Mmm." She slurped from her mug.

"It's September seventeenth."

"The seventeenth. Okay. I'll take your word for it. I just got up and haven't looked at a calendar, not that I have a calendar to look—"

"September *seventeenth*, Jasmyn."

September seventeenth.

She leaned against the kitchen counter and looked around the room. The walls were bare. If she lived there, truly lived there, she would hang up a calendar, a pretty one with garden scenes. No, ocean scenes. Or wild animals from the zoo that Liv said she wished they had time to visit—

"Jasmyn Albright, I called to commiserate with you," Quinn scolded.

"Or celebrate. Or something a friend would do like she's done once a month for the past six months. I guess you didn't need it."

On second thought, maybe she'd skip the calendar part and hang up paintings of flowers or ocean. That way she wouldn't have to look at months and dates.

Quinn said, "Six months is a milestone. A whole half a year."

Six months. When had she stopped counting?

In the beginning she had counted, first in hours, then in days and weeks, finally in months. She counted the passing of time since the tornado ripped a dividing line into her life. Before the tornado. After the tornado. Everything fell on one side or the other. The two did not meet.

How long was long enough before the After enveloped the Before and she could get on with life? Was it happening now? Did that explain the warm fuzzy attack? The fact that she had stopped counting? Or simply could stop counting.

"Honestly, I didn't realize today's date."

"Sorry for bringing it up." Quinn's tone didn't match the apology. She was seriously grumpy. "At least you heard it from me instead of being smacked by some reminder while you're standing in line at the grocery store or something. Remember how you got blindsided that day in Farm 'n Fleet by a pair of rain boots? I practically had to carry you out to the car."

It was true. Odd things triggered memories. She would be reminded of a possession that was gone, completely gone. Then she would totally lose it.

"But for me *not* to get all anxious about the date is a good thing, right?"

"Sure, if it's for real. I mean, you're still on vacation in La-La Land where apparently the wonders never cease. Even months and days go bye-bye."

"Why are you being so snarky?"

Quinn didn't reply for a moment. "I guess I just miss you. You've been gone a long time."

"Four weeks on Saturday. You knew that was my plan from the start. And you know that's when I'm coming home."

"Yeah. Okay. I'll talk to you later."

"I needed a break, Quinn. I just needed a break."

"Yeah."

Their goodbye felt awkward.

Jasmyn set her mug on the counter, walked into the adjoining living room, and sat in the rocker.

Six months of loss. It might have felt a breath less devastating as five months. Except...

Except it now seemed that Quinn's friendship might be added to the loss.

They had had their moments since kindergarten. Annoyances, disagreements, awkwardness, moodiness. But never the outright and senseless jealousy she'd just heard in Quinn's voice.

Maybe it was understandable. Jasmyn had been able to stop counting the months of loss because a group of strangers in a strange land loved on her.

And her best friend was not part of that equation.

A deep exhaustion hit her. It was familiar, all too familiar. It came out of nowhere, like those memories. It sapped her of all strength, all energy, all emotion.

She made her way to the bedroom, laid down on the little rollaway, and went back to sleep.

Fourteen

Liv's teapot was empty. A choir of morning birds sang at the top of their tiny lungs, and the first shaft of sunlight lit the upper fronds of the tallest palm. Tobi sprang from Liv's lap and wandered back indoors, her little love tank all filled up for the day.

And still Jasmyn was nowhere in sight.

"Hmm."

Jasmyn had lived at the Casa for only two weeks, but they had a morning ritual going. Usually by now the two of them would have chatted and planned some event, if only an afternoon walk to Jitters coffee shop for a latte. Liv would have prodded a bit and been given another peek or two inside the young woman's heart.

It seemed somewhat of a lonely place despite Jasmyn's cheery description of life in her small hometown. Her family was gone. She loved her job at the restaurant and had a good friend, but since the tornado, things in Valley Oaks seemed to have lost their glow.

"Good morning, Liv."

She turned toward the voice and saw Samantha approach, a highly unusual Monday morning sight. She wore blue jeans and a long-sleeved white shirt, also an odd thing.

"Well, good morning to you, Samantha, dear."

She stopped near Liv's chair. "I just wanted to let you know I'll be out of town for a few days. Probably until Friday."

"Work related?" The woman never went away for fun.

"Yes." She didn't offer details. "Do you think Beau could put in a new showerhead for me? It's on the kitchen counter. I couldn't get the old one off."

"You know you don't have to do things like that. That's why we have Beau."

"I'll pay for it. The old head works fine, but I would prefer a different one."

Liv smiled. "I've been meaning to put in those low-water-usage ones ever since you explained droughts to me." She did not begin to comprehend Samantha's work. All she knew was that the genius in Seven built things and tried to protect the environment at the same time.

"Whose land are you saving this week?"

Samantha shifted her weight and rolled her shoulders, a familiar mannerism of hers when she seemed uncomfortable. "I'm working at the Lotanzai Reservation. We don't know yet if there's anything to save."

"I read about that. The newspaper interviewed people who say there's plenty to save. You go, girl."

Samantha turned her head as if to deflect the comment. A ray of sunlight glimmered on her coal-black hair. Against the backdrop of shadowy foliage, it looked like a halo.

Liv kept that observation to herself.

"Controversy sells newspapers. Anyway, I didn't want you to worry about my absence."

"Thank you. Have a good week and remember to just be yourself."

Samantha squinted as if she did not understand. "Thanks?"

Liv smiled. "I imagine you're going to get pressured."

"That's a given."

"Exactly. People are going to fuss at you. They're going to think they know more than you do. But you are wise beyond your years, Samantha Whitley." It wasn't the first time Liv had declared such a thing to her. Affirmation, though, bore repeating, especially when there was no evidence that it had sunk in. "Don't let them walk all over you, okay?"

"O-okay."

"That didn't sound very convincing."

"I gotta go." Samantha turned and waved over her shoulder as she walked away.

Liv raised her voice. "Say it like you mean it, hon. *Okay!*"

There was no response, but Liv glimpsed in her profile a rare smile.

"Oh, child," she whispered. "What are we going to do with you?"

Samantha disappeared behind a patch of six-foot-tall bird-of-paradise near her cottage. A moment later she pulled a suitcase around the corner of her place and down the walkway toward the alley gate, its wheels thumping rhythmically.

"Lord, have mercy," Liv mumbled. "A sheep off to a den of wolves. You're sending an angel with her, right?"

ɔℚℓ

Pondering whether or not to knock on Jasmyn's door, Liv went inside and refilled her teapot.

Whether or not to knock was probably not the question. It was more like *when* should she go knock on the girl's door.

Stepping back outside, she found Keagan in the chair next to hers. She almost told him he couldn't sit there because it was Jasmyn's seat. "Good morning."

"Morning. I saw Sam leaving with a suitcase."

"Yes, she's off to the Lotanzai Reservation for work. It was thoughtful of her to tell me so I wouldn't worry. You know, I can't figure out why she doesn't move. She's well established in her job and familiar with the city. You'd think she'd want a more hip place with a manager who doesn't give two hoots about her comings and goings."

"You're slipping, Mama Liv." His mouth didn't move, but tiny crow's-feet appeared around his eyes as if he were indeed smiling.

He had amazing eyes, a luminous blue-green color. There was seldom a hint of a smile around them.

He and Sam were very much alike. Aloof. Smart as whips. Private. Extremely private. Inscrutable, even.

Liv knew little about either one of them. Keagan had been born and raised in New York City. She had no clue what he had done for a living before he moved to the Casa and became part-owner in a gym. He simply said he had been in software. Right. Her suspicions revolved around careers that involved secrecy and physical prowess, such as a special military outfit or the CIA.

Samantha had gone to UCLA and then taken a job in San Diego. She had grown up in Arizona. She only referred to it as *in the northern part of the state, Flagstaff was the nearest big city.* That left a lot of wiggle room. Sometimes Liv saw Native American features. Other times Samantha's cheekbones seemed not in the least bit high and her eyes lost their slightly almond shape.

"What do you mean I'm slipping?"

"Typically you would have this figured out by now."

She opened her mouth to protest and then closed it. She was in her mid-sixties. Okay, maybe the later side of the mid area, but goodness, that was nothing like being in her *eighties.* She was not slipping. Deep down she knew why Samantha stayed at the Casa. It was because she was supposed to stay. God wanted her there at the Casa for His own reasons.

She pursed her lips. *Whew!* That sounded a bit high and mighty even to herself, and she was all about lofty, mystical explanations.

She sighed. "It's clear Samantha simply puts up with the rest of us. It's not like she has a close friend here. So why does she stay?"

"Because there's no one else in her life like you who gives two hoots about her comings and goings."

"Ah." She thought about that for a moment. "But at her age, in her position, why would she want that?"

"Liv, who doesn't want that?"

"Well, for one, an independent, successful career woman who should be hanging out with friends and meeting a significant other."

"Don't let her veneer fool you."

Liv met his gaze. Samantha wasn't the only one who kept a veneer in place. "Is that why you stay? Because I'm a mother figure?"

He winked.

An unusual gesture.

"Nah. I stay because you'd be lost without me."

She grinned. "You're almost as cheeky as Chadwick."

"Now that's a contest I don't care to win." He stood. "Where's your little helper?"

"You mean Jasmyn?"

"She's late for your morning routine."

Liv didn't bother to ask how he knew that. Keagan seemed to know most things.

"Anything I can do?" His question wasn't all that odd, but something was. The timing? His tone? His eyes? That wink for sure.

"Do you mean anything you can do in general or about Jasmyn?"

"Either." He slipped on his sunglasses, hiding the laser beams.

"Nothing I can think of at the moment."

"Okay. Have a good day, Liv."

She watched him walk away, grateful as always that he did indeed stay on at the Casa for whatever reason. She would be lost without him.

He wasn't movie star handsome like her Syd had been, but frankly, if she were forty years younger, he'd be starring in her daydreams.

When her husband Syd died ten years ago, she had been completely lost. Slowly she found her way into a life without him. She sold their condo and moved into the Casa, which her smart cookie of a father had bought in the 1960s. He had held on to it because his daughter loved the place so much and begged for the opportunity to inherit it.

Life worked for her at the Casa. Still, there was a void. When Keagan had shown up a few years later, she knew what was missing. He brought with him a good dose of masculinity, an attribute a single businesswoman needed to lean on now and then.

And there were the subtle things. Like this morning, how he stopped and chatted for a spell exactly when she needed it. Puzzled by Samantha and concerned about Jasmyn, she had indeed been feeling a little bit lost.

Fifteen

Jasmyn awoke from a deep sleep, not quite sure where she was.

Sunlight filtered through partially open venetian blinds. She saw a giant bouquet of fernlike stems sprouting in a patch of blue sky. It was not an oak tree.

She thought about turning her back to the view, but her body refused to respond. The familiar inertia had been triggered, she remembered now, when she talked with Quinn about the date. The anniversary. Was it still the seventeenth? Maybe she had slept all the way through it.

Probably not. The heaviness would have lightened if it were the next day.

Its sensation always reminded her of walking at the creek's edge as a kid with Quinn. Their feet would sink deep into squishy mud, sometimes halfway up their shins. The mud became a monster with strong hands that yanked off shoes and socks. They squealed in delicious fear and played tug-of-war with it, freeing their legs at last.

Now her whole body was being sucked down and trapped in the monster's clutches. Squealing in delicious fear never entered the picture. Eventually, though, the heaviness would pass, strength would return to her muscles or to her willpower—she wasn't sure which—and she'd get up. Eventually. By the end of the day.

At least that's what had always happened so far.

The bouts were lessening. In the beginning they had come daily. Lately not so often. They hadn't knocked her out for a whole entire day since… Well, not since her arrival in California. Had Quinn really needed to tell her the date?

Jasmyn lost herself in the memory she so badly wanted to forget.

The siren's *woo-ooo*. The translucent curtain of algae green. The funnel, like a finger of God, twirling. The roar of a freight train slamming against her ears. The waiting in the basement.

Then… the seeing. The seeing of a reality so dreadful they should have draped it with a cloth. They should have averted their eyes.

Her home, her cocoon, was a pile of unrecognizable trash. The spaces between the walls, where she cooked, cleaned, bathed, slept, breathed… gone. Gone. Absolutely gone.

And so the day of the sixth month anniversary passed in Cottage Eleven.

 ℘

"Jasmyn, dear, are you all right?" Liv smiled in the doorway, a plate of brownies in her hand, the patio lights behind her already lit in the dusky courtyard.

Jasmyn had lost the whole entire day. "I'm fine." It wasn't a lie. Compared to not being able to get out of bed, she was really pretty much okay.

"Well, I became concerned when I didn't see you all day. Not that I keep track of everyone's comings and goings." Her shoulders rose and fell. "Okay, sometimes I do. Especially you single gals because, well, just because who else will make sure you're home safe and sound? Anyway." She handed her the plate. "Chocolate. It's good for whatever ails you."

Jasmyn caught a whiff of warm chocolate. "Thank you." She placed a hand on the door, ready to shut it at the first opportunity.

"I bet you thought chicken soup was the cure-all."

"I'm fine. Really."

The creases in Liv's forehead said she clearly did not believe Jasmyn was fine. "I'm just a little tired."

Liv nodded. "You've had quite a couple of weeks."

A couple of weeks. Try six months. Whatever. "I need to go home."

"Home! To Illinois? Oh goodness, not before Saturday, surely! I mean, Chadwick has planned a trip to Disneyland for you on Wednesday. He's talked Riley into taking Tasha out of school. Inez wants to bring the twins, her great-grandsons."

"I don't know—"

"You just go now and rest up. We'll talk tomorrow." Liv turned and hurried away.

Jasmyn shut the door and leaned against it. She did not want to talk tomorrow! She did not want to go to Disneyland!

Oh, what was happening to her new safe place with its batch of warm fuzzies?

A great sob erupted. She slid to the floor and muffled it with her arms, not wanting to disturb the neighbors who had welcomed her.

Sixteen

The office door was open. Liv liked to smell the damp night air and hear the trickling fountain while she worked at her desk. Work tonight meant snooping into a probable tenant's background.

She removed her glasses, propped her elbows on either side of the computer keyboard, and pressed her forehead into her hands. "Lord, what is wrong with me?"

Liv did not doubt her presumption that Jasmyn Albright was a probable tenant. It was a knowledge given to her, visceral, deep, and inexplicable. Such things happened now and then, often enough for her to sense when they were true.

She imagined they came from God. Why? It didn't matter. Why weren't a timetable and a to-do list included for her? It didn't matter.

Except this time it mattered. A fear gnawed at her. What if the someday were eons from now? She wanted Jasmyn there right now on a permanent basis. She'd never felt such a crazy notion.

The sound of a discreet throat clearing told her Keagan stood in the doorway. She looked up and saw him.

"Knock, knock?"

"Come on in."

"What's up?" He sat in the armchair across the desk.

"What makes you think something's up?"

"It's after eleven and the front gate was open."

"Open!" Liv moaned. She never forgot to close and lock the gate before dark at the absolute latest. Never.

"Are you feeling okay?"

She replaced her glasses. "How do you mean?"

"Olivia." He fixed his laser beam gaze on her. "You forget the gate about once a year. Either somebody died or the doctor gave you bad news."

She waved a hand and almost said *nonsense*, but Keagan didn't speak nonsense. He most likely was not capable of doing so.

"Well?" He leaned forward. "Which is it?"

"Neither." She shook her head. "All right. I'm tied up in knots about Jasmyn."

"The visitor who's leaving Saturday. Why?"

"Well, because…" She glanced around the office. From a wall a photograph her late husband, Syd, smiled down. It was an eight-by-ten black and white glossy head shot. He'd had it taken as a joke because she always called him movie star handsome. He'd even scrawled *Best Wishes* and signed his name, *Sydney Engstrom*, like Robert Redford would do.

The man had kept her going. They married late in life; she was forty-six, he fifty. She hadn't taken his last name because by then she was well known in the business world as the owner of McAlister Realty, which had been around since her father founded it in the 1950s. Syd didn't mind. He wasn't the sort to be threatened. They had enjoyed only a dozen years together before he passed away too soon. Way too soon.

She suddenly felt very old and very alone.

"You don't get tied up in knots about strangers. Overly concerned and involved maybe, but not upset."

"I know." She swiveled the monitor so he could see it. "Look at these." She clicked through several online photos.

"Let me guess. It's not a pile of toothpicks."

"No, it's Jasmyn's farmhouse after the tornado."

The scenes could have been taken in a war zone. Rubble was scattered across fields of tilled soil. The only partially recognizable things were a toppled, leafless oak and a chunk of green metal identified in the caption as a combine fender.

"Tornadoes were in other parts of the Midwest that day that caused a lot of destruction, but nothing in her area except her home. The local newspaper devoted pages to her story. The article says the funnel's path went straight through the Albright property. Jasmyn's house and two barns and all their contents were totally demolished. Nothing was salvageable. Isn't that heartbreaking?"

"That's a tough one."

"Check out the date. It happened six months ago *today*. What an awful anniversary and, as far as I can tell, she spent it all alone inside her cottage. Probably crying her eyes out. I knocked a few times throughout the day, but she didn't answer until tonight."

"Hmm."

"Poor thing comes out to California for a little R and R and what happens? The few things she has replaced are stolen. She was actually almost rude to me. Jasmyn Albright, rude! She said she needs to go home." Liv pointed at the monitor. "Home. Do you believe it? She doesn't have a home! She doesn't even have any family!"

"You know better than anyone that sometimes friends are home and family."

"Except for her best friend, she doesn't have enough friends back there to hang her heart on."

"Is that what she said?"

"Well, not exactly." Exactly, Jasmyn had said her hometown was a wonderful place. "But it's easy to deduce from her tone that she'd rather be here."

Keagan leaned back in his chair. "It's not her cottage."

"What?"

"You said she spent the day inside her cottage. It's not hers."

"Yes, it most surely is her—" She cut off the babbling. Her voice had risen an octave and her words were running together.

"Liv, Jasmyn hasn't paid rent or moved in. The place is not technically hers. Correct?"

She shrugged.

"You probably had one of your hunches, but you're jumping the gun here. You've known her all of two weeks."

She swallowed and lowered her tone. "I don't want her to leave."

He didn't reply for a moment. "People have come and gone from the Casa for years. You always give them a healthy shove out of the nest when you know their wings are ready to fly. This morning you were ready to give Sam a nudge. When they leave, you get a little sad, but not afraid. A season is over. Such is life. And besides, everyone always comes back to visit you."

She nodded.

"What's different about Jasmyn Albright?"

Liv replayed the two weeks since Jasmyn's arrival. On that first morning, there had been a deep heart connection. Since then they had spoken freely on whatever subject came up as if they'd known each other for years.

Liv had taken her around Seaside Village and introduced her to people at the market, the coffee shop, and the library. She had even explained the work involved with running the complex and the girl was quick to catch on. They had simply enjoyed each other's companionship the way a mother and a daughter would.

Oh.

Where had that come from?

Keagan reached over and, with a few strokes on the keyboard, logged out and powered down the computer. "Have some tea. Go to bed. If you're still this needy in the morning, I'm moving you into that assisted living care facility over on El Camino." He smiled his almost smile and walked out the door.

Well. She released a pent-up breath. "Well."

A hug would have been nice. Jasmyn would have hugged her.

Seventeen

Sam had never visited the particular area of the desert where she now ran, but her body recognized it. The uneven terrain hummed in a familiar way beneath her feet. The dry scents of mesquite and sage enveloped her, a security blanket that never failed to deliver.

She ran and ran, not following a marked trail but keeping the sunrise to her right. Intuitively she found sure footing in the sandy dirt, leaped over stones, and skirted boulders and low-lying vegetation.

She ran and ran. The first rays of the dawn streaked across the landscape. The black mountains to her left burst into golden hues. The color flowed from their peaks downward as if a giant swept a paintbrush across them.

She ran and ran, trusting that the lone coyote in the distance up ahead would not mistake her for a rabbit.

She ran and ran until the love-hate relationship with the desert no longer burned in her chest like hot coals.

At last she slowed to a jog, removed her visor, and wiped the hem of her T-shirt across her face. Whoever had decided to start the engineering project in one-hundred-degree September weather should be locked up.

She turned until the rising sun was on her left and then retraced her steps.

Less than sixteen hours had gone by since she had arrived at the Lotan-zai Reservation, and already she'd mentally resigned from the company three times. At least she hadn't said it out loud. Although she figured that Randy knew.

She recalled last night's conversation with him as they had sat knee-to-knee in two wicker chairs, aka the motel lobby. If she had reached over her shoulder, she could have touched the check-in counter.

"Sammi." His big brown eyes and puppy dog expression masked his Attila the Hun work ethic. "Are you nervous about joining the big league?"

"N-no."

He grinned. "That was convincing. Hey, no worries. It's understandable, your first time out on a project like this. We wouldn't have chosen you if we didn't think you could handle it."

"Thanks. I'm fine. Really."

"You seem more ticked off than usual."

She gave him a small smile. His comment was a private joke between them, one she used on him now and then. Her work ethic matched his, and their demeanors were sometimes mistaken for irascibility.

"Seriously, Sam. What's going on?"

"Nothing."

"'Nothing.' My wife's famous last word right before she falls apart." He rested his elbows on his knees, leaning forward until they were almost nose to nose. The scent of peppermint gum filled the space between them. "Listen." He spoke in a low voice. "I know you couldn't wait to grow up and get off the rez in Arizona. I understand if being on one now unsettles you. The thing is, I'm counting on more than your technical expertise here. You have a deep insight that none of the rest of us can begin to fathom."

She shook her head. "Just because three-fourths of my ancestors were Navajo doesn't mean I understand diddly."

"Yes, it does. You have a connection to this land and this people whether you're conscious of it or not."

"It's not my land. They're not my people."

"Yeah, yeah. I get that." He waved a hand, batting away her words. "Trust me, Sammi. There's something different about you."

Tears of frustration gathered, and she gazed at her hands in her lap, blinking. She had spent a lifetime trying to escape the *something different* label, and now Randy wanted to glorify it.

"Listen, all I'm asking is that you put aside the childhood junk, but don't dismiss your respect for all the rest. Use it to enhance your work. Okay?"

Not trusting her voice, she had nodded just to get him to stop talking.

"Thanks." He stood. "And no meltdowns allowed until we get back to the city."

She didn't do meltdowns. She ran.

Now she quickened her pace. The morning sun had risen well over the peaks.

Shadows atop a flat, low-lying boulder caught her attention. They outlined three or four bowl-shaped indentations. A common sight, they should not have affected her. But she slowed and walked over to the boulder, blaming Randy for whatever subliminal message he'd planted.

She stroked the smooth interiors of the shallow depressions. They were *morteros*, a pre-Crate and Barrel version of a mortar and pestle. Ages ago women had ground acorns, hollowing out the bowls over time.

Sam sat on the boulder and let the landscape envelop her. The desert floor. Its scrubby plant life. The mountains, purple to the east, golden in the west. The cloudless blue canopy over it all. The quiet. The ineffable quiet.

Randy respected the land. The Collins and Creighton Engineering Firm was committed to using it wisely. They would figure out how to work with its contours and its layers of decomposed granite, volcanic remnants, siltstones, and even marine fossils. They would mold and shape and remove and not disturb the past or harm the future. Their sole purpose was to bring the land into the twenty-first century so that it might provide the necessities for work and play, for life itself.

Like the ancients had done except with a bit more flair.

Sam doubted she would find ancient burial grounds or proof of environmental issues. Her early research indicated the area was clear. These *morteros*, several miles from the site in question, were no matter. They merely proved that the Lotanzai had lived here, a fact not in dispute.

She, her boss, the company, and the Lotanzai were all in agreement about disturbing as little as possible. Yet Randy wanted more from her, some deeper insight into the impact of the project.

She didn't have it.

Her father had had it and had tried to teach her, but he died when she was a child, long before she could comprehend his words and his stories as they walked in the desert.

Sam propped her feet up on the boulder, wrapped her arms around her legs, and pressed her face against them. Randy's rule against meltdowns was about to be broken.

Eighteen

"Jasmyn." Inez Templeton's smile rivaled Liv's when it came to expressing sheer joy. "I am so glad you join us."

"Me too." Jasmyn grinned. She was at Disneyland. For real. Seated on the bench with her was the Casa's resident grandmother.

"Disneyland is such a happy place." Although seventy-five years old, Inez could have passed for sixty. She had thick dark brown hair, clear topaz eyes, a healthy glow, and a confident air. Her heavily accented English rolled *r*'s and mixed verb tenses. She called her husband *Loo-ees*, making it, like most of her words, a soft, tender sound.

"Yes, it is *such* a happy place," Jasmyn agreed, although for the life of her she could not explain why she had come. The last thing she remembered was sitting in Liv's office, making sure that her return flight reservation was in order. It would be four weeks since she had landed in California, plenty long enough for any vacation. Right now she should be packing her few things and putting the little cottage in order, not having her picture taken with Mickey Mouse.

Jasmyn imagined Quinn's response to Disneyland. She'd say of course it was a happy place. Once people paid an arm and a leg for admission and another arm for a cup of coffee, they were in a state of shock. They had already slid on into a fantasy world. Disneyland was the La-La Land to beat all La-La Lands.

But Jasmyn loved it. She loved the music and bright colors at every turn, the life-size Mickey and Minnie, the scary pirates, the Jedi training show, the futuristic museum, the carousel and Dumbo rides with Tasha…the hours of escape.

She really had to get Quinn's voice out of her head.

"I am especially glad you are here because I do not want to take care of Chad alone by myself."

Jasmyn stared in surprise at her. "You were worried about Chad? Not your great-grandsons?"

"No. My great-grandsons are smart nine-year-olds. They look after each other since babies in the cradle. They know I am on this bench in Fantasyland. I know they are on Space Mountain. We have cell phones, but they will not stray from our plan to meet here."

"But Chad might?"

"Might? Ah, he will for certain. He is—how does Louis say it?—'the boy is unpredictable.' I love him to pieces, but I do not want to be responsible for him. His latest indiscretion? True, it was some months ago, but still, not good. He arrive home in the middle of the night, intoxicated." She whispered the last word. "He cannot open the front gate. He shout and shout until Keagan hear him. Then Olivia wake up, and he fall into the fountain. This time she say he is on probation. She will evict him if it happens again. I do not understand how he think he can win Piper's heart— Oh, dear, now I am a gossip."

"I won't tell anyone."

Inez laughed and patted her arm. "Everybody know, *querida*. Just like everybody know I enter the United States illegally."

"I didn't know that."

"No?"

"No." She winked. "But I did hear that your ancestors were royalty in Spain."

Inez laughed again, a sound like tiny wind chimes. "That is a much better story. Piper tell you this."

"Yes, she did." Jasmyn thought how Piper had been her source for juicy tidbits. Liv never divulged personal details. Coco was too absent. Riley was too wrapped up in caring for Tasha to gossip. Sam made smart-aleck observations but probably did not know many juicy tidbits. "Tell me about your background."

"Oh, the royalty was many, many centuries ago. It matters nothing. Are you going to ride these things?" Inez gestured toward the wide sidewalk.

Through a wall of passersby, Jasmyn caught a glimpse of Tasha and her mother in line to ride Alice in Wonderland's giant twirling teacups. Her stomach knotted. "Uh, I'll sit this one out."

"Too much hot dog and flying Dumbo?"

Jasmyn laughed. "Maybe."

"You are like a little girl having fun. This is good for you. You are in a very difficult time of life."

She shrugged. "It's not too bad." Well, two days ago had been completely, totally bad, but she had survived, hadn't she? "I lost my things in the storm, but I didn't get hurt. No one did."

"Do not underestimate the devastation of this loss. Your home is gone. You have been wounded." She touched her chest. "Deep inside."

Jasmyn shrugged again, her throat tight.

"Good news, Jasmyn! You are not alone. Many of us at the Casa arrive in much pain. Riley's husband divorce her. He not deal well with his little Tasha's needs." She made a *tsking* noise. "Noah, his wife leave him. Piper's fiancé is killed in Afghanistan. Samantha, she runs from something. Olivia is a widow too soon." She shook her head. "Sad stories everywhere. But that makes us good together, like family."

"What about you?"

"Not so sad after I meet Louis. But before…" Inez leaned forward and whispered. "My father was a *bracero*, a guest farmworker in the United States. World War II time. After, he does not get green card and he go home, to Mexico. There, much poverty for us, and he is ill. I am seventeen and—oh, *mi Dios*." She crossed herself. "I pay a coyote to bring me here to work."

"A coyote?"

"A man. He sneak people into the country. Everyone at home and my auntie in San Diego give me money to pay him. I live with Auntie and I get a job and I pay them all back." She straightened and spoke in a normal tone. "My job is at the Casa de Vida."

"The Casa!"

"Yes! I am cleaning lady for Olivia's father. She is young girl. Funny and smart. Tall. So tall."

"How did you get a job?"

"Mr. McAlister, he not check identification, but I think he know." She shrugged. "He is desperate for a cleaning lady. And then…" She paused, a smile lighting up her face. "One day I take a walk on the pier and I meet Louis Templeton. Oh! Such a handsome navy man."

"Love at first sight?"

"*Si*. Love at first sight. I speak no *inglés*. His *español—ay!*" She laughed. "But it is enough. The problem, how can a navy man marry an immigrant with no papers? I go home so we can love each other in Mexico too. We marry in church with the padre. Then I am legal. I come back Mrs. Louis Templeton."

It was like a fairy tale. "And you lived happily ever after."

Inez shook her head and smiled. "We live life. A wonderful life all over the world with United States Navy and *mis cuatro ninos*. But happy, sad, easy, hard, fun, scary. Like you."

Jasmyn nodded. "I seem to be stuck in the sad, hard, scary part. That's never happened before. I could always see the silver lining."

"A tornado never happen before. This bump in the road is most worst for you."

Inez's words rang true. Yet why hadn't her mother's death been the worst bump for Jasmyn? Or even the years spent nursing her through cancer?

Or what about the lifelong shame heaped on her because she'd been born out of wedlock to a teenager and never knew her father's name?

"*Querida*." Inez looped her arm through Jasmyn's and leaned against her. "Louis and I grow old. The house, the yard, too much work. It is our most worst bump, but we move to *la Casa* and we are happy. You move into *la Casa* and you be happy too. Everyone take care of you. *Si?*"

An attack of warm fuzzies burst through her. Jasmyn melted inside. For one brief amazing moment the shadowy corners of sad, hard, and scary were ablaze in light.

But…

"I'm on vacation."

Inez shrugged. "So? Go get your things. Vacation over."

Go get your things. Those would be her new car and a jacket. But seriously. Move to California? Away from her hometown, the only place she'd ever known, and her job, and—

"Look at this." Inez pointed at the crowd and sighed. "My boys come. Chad, I see nowhere. Am I surprised?" She looked at Jasmyn. "This is why

I put van keys in my pocketbook. If he no show, you drive but first you call Keagan because we don't know the way home."

They didn't? *Uh-oh.*

"When we women need rescue, he always there for us. He is our knight."

A knight. That was a new one. Her first impression of Keagan had been all about sheriff vibes. Sam's nickname for him was Mr. Kung Fu Dude because he had some sort of belt and apparently could break a stack of two-by-fours with his bare hands. Now Inez added shining armor and a white horse to the guy's intimidating reputation.

Between a knight, a mama, a grandmother, kind people, and unbelievable peace and beauty, the place had everything.

Still, though, no matter how attractive it was, no matter how much it had given her, Casa de Vida was not her home. The thought of permanently leaving Valley Oaks was off-the-chart ridiculous and certainly not the solution to getting herself over the worst bump in the road.

No, she would return home as planned on Saturday, where she belonged, and just live her life, bumps and all.

Nineteen

If Liv had married what's-his-name decades ago, before he shipped out to Vietnam, she might have a daughter now around Jasmyn's age.

"Foolish thoughts, Olivia." She spoke aloud to herself. "Foolish thoughts that do you no good whatsoever."

She and the cute Marine had been wild about each other. If she were the impetuous sort or even a romantic, she would have accepted his proposal. But she was not and she did not. He never contacted her again.

And she never loved anyone as wildly again until Syd.

She sighed and petted Tobi on her lap. They sat in the recliner, both just awake from catnaps. Dusk had fallen and the living room lay in shadows. Outside the bay window the jacaranda tree shone with vertical strands of twinkle lights. An automatic timer lit them and brightened a corner of the courtyard where the source of her foolish thoughts stood with Samantha.

Liv tried not to feel like a beady-eyed private investigator. Snooping simply came with the managerial territory. It was a necessity, right? She managed better if she remained abreast of what was going on.

A small wheeled suitcase was propped beside Samantha. She was probably arriving home after her work week in the desert. Jasmyn, thankfully, had no suitcase in sight.

Not yet anyway.

Liv's eyes burned and she blinked rapidly so the tears would not fall.

Jasmyn was scheduled to fly back to the Midwest tomorrow. Liv had suggested she stay longer, that the theft experience had interfered with her vacation, that it had subtracted days from her emotional time of R and R, that she owed herself at least another week. Jasmyn only said she needed to get on with her life.

"Lord, she wants to stay. When we ate at Betsy's Café, she said she could see herself working there. She was dreaming about life here. I know she was. She should give it more time."

Outside now, Jasmyn and Samantha appeared to be laughing.

Odd. Liv had thought Riley would be the one to tug Jasmyn's heartstrings. They were closer in age, more alike than different. Jasmyn was small-town sweet and—Liv imagined—a crackerjack of a waitress because she easily put regular people at ease.

Samantha was anything but regular. Mum about her background, overeducated—why the summer postgrad studies?—and consumed with work, she walked around in a Plexiglas bubble.

Hmm.

"Lord, Jasmyn could be a good influence on Samantha. And Samantha could be, well, she might very well be the friend Jasmyn needs. What do You think?"

Liv did not have to sit long with the question. She immediately recognized her dishonesty.

The truth was, ever since Jasmyn's arrival, a deep loneliness had taken hold of her unlike any she'd known since Syd's death.

The truth was, she had begun to hope that the something wondrous she assumed was in store for Jasmyn might actually be in store for herself. Was that too foolish? Too selfish?

Yes, but…

"All right. The truth is, Lord, I want a daughter. Jasmyn's the best candidate. It's my last season of life and the biological clock seems to be ticking. Better late than never? I don't know. You're the one who dropped Jasmyn Albright on my doorstep. So now what?"

There, she'd quit hemming and hawing.

Tears stung again, and this time she let them fall.

Twenty

Sam stood in the dusky courtyard with Jasmyn. With her suitcase beside her and a casserole from her boss's wife heavy in her arms, she laughed and laughed.

Laughed. For real. Out loud. It felt like when an antibiotic kicked in and her body sensed the absence of illness and an energy zinged every nerve ending with new life.

Jasmyn was describing her trip to Disneyland. Mostly she talked about goofy Chad at Disneyland. Her sweet voice still bugged Sam, but it also pulled her in, the call of honey to a bear.

Which made Sam the bear?

"Chad finally showed up, in the dark, on Main Street after the parade as if that had been our original plan all along. Inez had Keagan on the phone because Chad wasn't answering his. He told me he'd made a new friend."

"I bet he got her phone number."

"Yes, he did. You know, he's so adorable. None of us could stay mad at him. Tasha was exhausted, and he carried her to the car. But first we stopped at a store because she wanted Minnie Mouse ears and Riley was out of money, so he bought them. Then the whole way home he and the twins chattered on and on about rides they hadn't taken together."

"What did Inez say?"

"She shook her finger at him and said, 'You must grow up someday.' He hugged her and said, 'But not today. Peter Pan cannot grow up at Disneyland, *a-a*—' What does he call her?"

"*Abuela*. Grandmother."

"That's it. How does he get away with being Peter Pan?"

Sam heard concern in Jasmyn's tone. Despite the differences of age, body type, and voice pitch, she and Liv could pass for clones. Which was downright spooky.

"Big safety net. He'll inherit millions and just keep on keeping on."

"Seriously?" Jasmyn looked appalled.

"Yeah. His family is filthy rich."

"No, I mean you think he'll just keep on being completely aimless?"

"Who knows? We can't fix him."

"Inez said Liv gave him an ultimatum. If he messes up again, he has to move out. I think Liv's on to something. He needs boundaries. He needs a job. I need a job."

"Oh?" A woman after her own heart.

"Definitely. You can't go to Disneyland every day. Or be on vacation forever. This aimlessness is getting old."

"What would you like to do?"

"What I've always done. It's not exactly rocket science, but then I'm not a rocket scientist. I love working at the Flying Pig. I'll go back to it, easy-peasy."

"Did you ever dream of doing other things?"

"Not really. In Valley Oaks, it's not like I had a lot of options. That must sound really boring to you."

"No. It sounds insanely difficult because I'm not a people person like you."

"For a while I wanted to be a nurse."

"Ew. Now you've gone too far. You really have to be a people person for that one."

Jasmyn smiled. "I loved taking care of my grandparents and my mother. Of course, I had to waitress the whole time they were sick and that went on for so many years..." She shrugged. "It's a little late in life to start over."

"Liv says thirtysomethings are baby chicks. You know, there's always a news story about some woman getting her college degree when she's like eighty-zillion years old. It's never too late to reinvent yourself."

"Reinvent?"

"Imagine yourself in a different role and then take the first step toward living it."

"I hadn't thought of it like that."

Sam had always thought of it like that. If she hadn't created a life for herself beyond the role some labeled half-breed— No reason to go there.

Jasmyn said, "You really think I could reinvent myself?"

"Sure. You're in a sweet space, Jasmyn. Single. No family or house to tie you down. A job you could probably do anywhere."

"Put that way, it sounds just plain sad."

"Just plain sad can be a catalyst. Off the top of your head, what's the wildest thing you can think of? If nothing could hold you back, what would you do?"

Jasmyn frowned.

Spontaneity and the waitress from Illinois probably did not meet on a regular basis.

"Um." Jasmyn smiled shyly. "Seriously?"

No. Impulsively! "Go for it."

"I'd like to manage an apartment complex."

Spoken like a true Liv clone. "Okay." She couldn't let it go. "Um, you're sure? You don't want to join the Peace Corps? Climb Machu Picchu?"

"No."

"Write the Great American Novel?"

"No."

"Be a movie star?"

"Nope."

"You want to be Olivia McAlister.'"

"No. I want to be Jasmyn Albright." She smiled. "Anyway, I'm going home tomorrow."

Sam let the words sink in, and then she said with conviction, "I'm sorry."

"Me too. But vacation is over."

"I suppose it has to end."

Jasmyn wrinkled her nose. "There's a little corner of me that would rather do the Peter Pan–Chad thing."

Sam chuckled and shifted the weight of the heavy dish in her arms. "Hey, I have this mystery casserole from my boss's wife. It's probably full of chicken and a creamy soup and could feed an army. Do you want to come over and eat?"

Jasmyn's jaw dropped. "Really?"

Sam understood the surprised response and, if it weren't so pathetically true, she would have laughed again. The detached businesswoman who disliked everyone was inviting a guest for dinner?

She was. The thought of having an uninterrupted conversation with a like-minded woman felt...nice.

Sam said, "No, not really. I'd rather have pizza."

Jasmyn laughed with her.

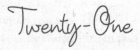

Twenty-One

At airport security, Jasmyn gathered her things from the gray bins on the conveyor belt. Shoes, sweater, handbag, belt, bracelet, bag of liquids, and the beach bag she was using as a catchall.

Sheesh. What a lot of fuss. Practically undress while standing next to a bunch of strangers who were also undressing. Wait. Get scanned. Wait. Carry everything to a bench. Put it back on or back into a bag or a pocket. Search for the boarding pass shoved into her purse. And what had she done with her ID?

At least she hadn't been detained and wanded or had to stand by while a guard dug through her bag the way she saw happening to others.

At least everyone was nice about it all.

Nice. Something she was not feeling or exhibiting. She should be ashamed of herself.

She slipped on the outrageously priced sandals Piper had talked her into because they were, in all honesty, the most comfy things she'd ever had on her feet. She hugged the purse and beach bag to herself, and stared at the escalator. It moved people upward, but it somehow appeared insurmountable.

She really, truly did not want to go home.

There. She'd admitted it at last. After a night of tossing and turning—her first since that first night at the Casa—she was too exhausted to fight it any longer. She wanted to stay in California.

The questions of why, how long, and when would have to wait for answers. For now she would get on the plane, return to her studio apartment, go to work tomorrow, and then…Well, and then she would plan another vacation.

Danno would tell her to take it ASAP. He had sent her away in the first place to go find her smile. Well, she had found it in California. The trouble was, she'd lost it that morning somewhere between the Casa and the airport. It was not getting on board with her. It would not be going with her to the Flying Pig tomorrow. Leaving a strange place should not be this difficult, should it?

Sam had driven Jasmyn to the airport and basically repeated Inez's *Go get your things.* "Maybe it's time for a new start. What better place for a reinvention than in California?"

Sam had meant well, and Liv had meant well as they hugged goodbye in the alley behind the Casa. Choking back tears, she repeated three times that Cottage Eleven was Jasmyn's home whenever she returned, which she hoped was two shakes of a lamb's tail away.

Their words haunted Jasmyn now. What happened to Valley Oaks being home, the place she had always belonged?

She sighed. That one was easy. Stupid tornado. Stupid hurt feelings because she did what she had to do by selling the property. Stupid dead-end job. Stupid, ugly apartment.

Stupid memories that still defined her. *She doesn't have a dad. She's Jerri's daughter. You know Jerri, the slutty one. That grandpa of hers is a real piece of work. The grandma's not much better. Do you believe she sold that land? It'll put her boss out of business. That was really smart.*

Jasmyn got on the escalator.

Upstairs, hordes of people milled around a gift shop and a Peet's Coffee counter. They strode past her from every direction. They lined up at gates and filled row after row of seats as far as she could see.

She found her gate and an empty seat near it that faced a window. Pouting had always been at the bottom of her list of favorite pastimes, but she freely engaged in it now as she gazed at the runway and distant hills dotted with houses.

Quinn had been happy to hear she was coming home. Happy? More like ecstatic. She promised to pick Jasmyn up at the airport that evening, which meant she had to get off work early on a Saturday night, the busiest shift of the week. It meant a sacrifice of major tips. It meant—

"Jasmyn."

She blinked and saw Keagan looking down at her. "Keagan?"

Mr. Kung Fu Dude slid onto the seat beside her. "You can't leave." His black leather jacket rustled as he smoothed the jeans against his thighs. He turned to her, a deep crease between his blue-green eyes. His usual intimidation factor was missing.

"What do you mean I can't leave?"

"Liv had a heart attack."

Jasmyn scurried after Keagan, who never slowed his pace, not even on escalators. They trotted down one now, an outdoor one that descended steeply into a parking lot.

Quinn would totally have a cow over this latest decision. Jasmyn was staying in San Diego because someone she barely knew had a heart attack? Because that all-but-total stranger told the weird kung fu guy, while they had waited for the paramedics, that she needed Jasmyn? Baloney.

No, not baloney. She owed Liv McAlister for all she had done for her. If the woman said she needed Jasmyn, then Jasmyn was there for her. Flight or no flight.

They reached the sidewalk at the bottom of the escalator and she jogged to catch up to him. "What did she mean, she needs me?"

"Beats me." His sunglasses hid his eyes. Her beach bag was slung over his shoulder.

She stepped off a curb and walked smack-dab into Keagan's outstretched arm. A car cruised past them, too fast for a parking lot. Without a word, they continued on their way.

The guy was just plain odd. Who was he anyway? He could have made up the whole entire story about Liv and was kidnapping Jasmyn because he was a serial killer. And how had he gotten through security?

"How did you get through security?"

"Don't worry about it."

"I am worrying about it."

His sunglasses flashed in her direction. "It was an emergency. I talked to the right people. They let me through."

The right people? Sure. From what she heard about TSA, the only right people would be in Washington, DC. Why would they believe his emergency story? And what about her checked baggage?

"What about my checked baggage?"

"It's been X-rayed for bombs. It's on a domestic flight. It'll reach its destination. Maybe a friend can pick it up for you."

Her friend would be too busy having a hissy fit.

Of course it wasn't as if Jasmyn had had many things to pack. She could let it go to wherever unclaimed suitcases went. What was one more lost batch of clothing? She should be getting used to not owning anything by now. There were those neon yellow shoes, though. She really liked them.

Keagan stopped next to a motorcycle. Jasmyn remembered Liv telling her that he did not own a car.

It was a shiny, dark blue monster. He unlocked a storage compartment, pulled out two helmets, and stuck a white one in her hand.

She held it back out to him, her own hissy fit gathering steam. He'd totally invaded her space, all but yanked her off a plane by her ponytail, and now she was supposed to get on a Harley? "I can't ride this thing."

"Why not?"

"I don't ride motorcycles."

"Your dad's rule?"

"My grandpa's."

He cocked his head, his lips a thin line. "What happened?"

Her throat closed up and her heart pounded. She whispered, "A friend died."

"An accident?"

She nodded.

"Years ago? When you were a teenager?"

Again she nodded. They had been sixteen. He was Quinn's boyfriend.

"It's time to get over it."

She shook her head. "I'll find a cab." Her voice squeaked.

"Jasmyn, take a deep breath."

She took a deep breath.

"Another." He slid his sunglasses onto his head and watched her with kind eyes as she breathed. "One more. Okay. Now give me your hand."

His hand was calloused and gentle around hers. "Listen. My driving record is perfect. My bike is top of the line with all the safety features."

"Right. It has airbags? I don't think so. I've seen you guys out there on the freeway, cutting in and out between cars, riding the lane markers, racing faster than the craziest drivers."

"Riding the markers is legal and safer than being in the way of traffic—Okay, okay. I hear you. I won't do any of those things. I promise."

A fizzy sensation went up her arm. It spread through her chest and down her other arm like a feathery tickle along the inside of her skin. A sense of calm enveloped her.

"Jasmyn, we'll go to the hospital. It's only twenty minutes away. Trust me. Your presence will make all the difference for Liv."

"Why do you say that? We hardly know each other."

"Call it a woman thing." He shrugged off his jacket. "Here. Put this on. Your sweater won't be warm enough. And the helmet too. Please."

A few minutes later, swimming in his coat, her bag and purse stowed away, she sat astride the bike. A wave of sheer terror flowed through her. She wasn't going home. She'd lost all her belongings once again. Dear, sweet Olivia might be dying or dead even. And she was going to ride a motorcycle.

Keagan turned the key and the blue monster roared to life. "Hold on!" he yelled.

Jasmyn hesitated. There wasn't anything to hold on to except Mr. Kung Fu Dude, who reached back with both hands and pulled her arms around his waist.

It felt like a stone wall covered in a cotton T-shirt.

Inhibition fled. She clung for dear life and pressed her helmet-covered forehead between his shoulder blades.

God, I promise if we make it, I'll be nicer to everyone and not complain about Quinn and I'll go home as soon as I can...

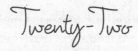

Twenty-Two

Liv hadn't planned on having a heart attack that day. True, she wasn't feeling well when she'd gotten out of bed, but what was a little nausea and sweating? They were evidence of fatigue. They were inconveniences caused by a restless night and anxiety over Jasmyn's departure.

And so she had worked, planting sweet alyssum—they did so well in the coastal winters and filled the courtyard with their intoxicating fragrance—and then boom. She could scarcely breathe.

Now, lying in a hospital bed, she felt suspended, a marionette with feet—or in this case, backside—not quite touching the earth. She was awake, but not fully. She was asleep, but not fully. She was drugged, but not to the point of pain-free. She spoke coherently, but because no one responded, she assumed the conversation was an internal monologue.

"Apparently, I am alive. Otherwise Syd would have shown up to greet me. Instead, I got Keagan and paramedics."

They said it was a mild heart attack. Mild.

"*Mild.* I suppose that means it was a pickup and not a semi that parked itself on my chest."

The thing had immobilized her right in front of the fountain. Naturally, Keagan was the one to find her there, gazing at the blue sky as though she were sunbathing. She heard his typical, unruffled voice long before she saw his face bent over hers.

"Olivia, what are you doing? Taking a break?" When he knelt, he was already talking into his cell to a 911 operator.

Everyone else at the Casa had left for the day. It was Saturday, their day to play, run errands, or, like Sam and Piper, to work extra hours. It was Jasmyn's day to go back to Illinois.

Back to Illinois. Less than twenty-four hours after Liv had dared to ask the Creator of the Universe what He was going to do about her undeniable, aching desire for a daughter that had begun to grow all out of proportion the day He plopped Jasmyn Albright on her doorstep...

"You know, Abba, You could have just taken me home. Have it over and done with. I've had a good run, a solid six decades and then some. I would have been fine with leaving. But no. My biological clock starts ticking. Whoever heard of such a thing? I'm pushing seventy and I end up flat on my back, whining and gasping, making a fool of myself. 'Keagan, oh Keagan. Please, *please*, bring Jasmyn back. I need her. I just need her here.'"

Not that she thought for one minute that God had zapped her with a heart attack. *Applesauce*. That was her own fault. She ate an appalling diet, forgot on a regular basis to take her prescribed blood pressure and cholesterol medications, and she walked briskly the third Tuesday of every other month.

But the timing. Ah, the timing was curious.

Jasmyn had no reason to stay in Seaside Village, and Liv had had no right to keep telling her she could. Or to think a heart attack gave her an excuse to ask her to.

Sending Keagan after the girl had been wrong. Liv felt like a conniving old biddy. Syd wouldn't recognize her. Or would he? Maybe it was her true self coming out. She hoped Keagan failed.

Liv heard approaching voices now and knew he hadn't. No surprise, really. He never failed at anything.

"Oh!" Jasmyn's whispered breath overflowed with compassion. "She looks so...so..." Her voice trailed away as if she did not want to express how perfectly ghastly Liv must look.

A throat cleared. Keagan. "Well, she did have a heart attack." His neutral tone slipped a tiny bit.

Liv smiled and opened her eyes. Nothing appeared before them, not even ceiling tiles. She sighed. Like the smile, it was probably real only inside her head. Okay, she could go with that, if only Jasmyn and Keagan were not imaginary.

She heard the bedrail go down and sensed a weight on the mattress. A soft hand touched her arm.

Well, that seemed real enough.

"Liv." It was Jasmyn, her voice firmer. "You look a little peaked, that's all. But my goodness, who wouldn't after what you've been through?" She spoke as if Liv were fully engaged. "Other than that, you look wonderful."

Wonderful? Right. Liv hooted in the silent way she had going.

"Can she hear you?" Keagan said.

"You never know. My grandpa was out of it for weeks after his stroke. Then one day he sat up and griped about specific things we had been saying and doing."

Keagan made a noise that almost resembled a chuckle. "We don't have to worry about Liv griping."

"No, we don't." Jasmyn stroked Liv's arm, gently and rhythmically. "She's not like that."

Silence filled the room.

It was a deep, comfortable silence, and Liv felt embraced by it. One by one the anxious thoughts slipped off into the blurry edges of her mind. The marionette fell gently against the pillow and mattress.

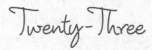

Twenty-Three

In the hospital cafeteria, Keagan leaned across the table until he was almost between Jasmyn and her spoon. She stopped stirring the coffee and looked at him.

He sat back. "Thank you for coming."

As though she'd had a choice. He had slipped through airport security as if it did not exist, shocked her with *Liv had a heart attack*, and marched off with her beach bag. Now she had missed her flight, had no clothes except the ones on her back, and had no plan in mind. What was she doing?

Jasmyn ripped open two more nondairy creamer pods—she'd already added two others—and poured them into her mug.

"That stuff will kill you."

Coffee sloshed from the cup. She set the spoon on the white Formica tabletop and clenched her fists on her lap. "I'd do anything for Liv, but I'm a little…"

"Discombobulated?"

"What does that mean?"

"Like it sounds."

"Hmm. Like I'm a water balloon and I just went *splat*?"

"You got it." He squeezed a tea bag over his cup. "At the moment, you're mentally halfway to Illinois with an image of a healthy Olivia. You'll catch up to reality shortly."

"She seemed perfectly fine this morning. Maybe tired, but her usual self."

"That's how these things happen."

"But the doctor said she'll be okay, right?" Jasmyn had asked the question at least half a dozen times already, ever since the doctor had spoken to Keagan when they first arrived at the hospital.

"Yes, that's what she said." Keagan repeated his answer in a tone of infinite patience. "The angioplasty went without a hitch. Liv can go home in a day or two."

She nodded. Okay. It was serious, but not as bad as it could have been. "I still don't understand why she wants me here. I mean, she has dozens of friends who are closer to her. Inez is closer. You're closer."

"Inez has her dotty moments, and I'm a guy. Nowhere near the same impact. Her dozens of other friends don't live at the Casa."

"I don't live at the Casa."

"She thinks you do." A corner of his mouth made a tiny indentation. It might have been a smile.

He was actually a nice-looking guy.

"But I *don't* live there. I am on vacation. I have no clothes. Again. No household stuff. No home to put it in if I did."

Keagan lifted his jacket from the back of his chair and unzipped an inside pocket. "Nothing has been moved out of Cottage Eleven." He pulled out Liv's stretchy coil key ring and a cell phone and slid them across the table. He fingered a key with a brown dot painted on it. "This is the office key. Inside the top desk drawer you'll find your cottage key. Chad's bringing her van over for you to use. All of our numbers are programmed into her phone. You'll want to let the others know what happened. Organize visits. Probably meals too."

Jasmyn stared at him.

"A few deep breaths always help."

"Keagan, I can't."

"Breathe?"

"No. I can't live here and take care of Liv."

"Because you were doing something else?"

Not exactly. "She trusts me this much?"

"Is there a reason she shouldn't?"

"Will you stop answering questions with a question?"

"Jasmyn." He leaned forward again, forcing eye contact. "She trusts you completely. You need to trust yourself."

She frowned.

"Just now, when we first saw Liv, she was agitated. The moment you started talking, she relaxed. You light up a room, Ms. All Bright. You make a difference. Just be yourself." He touched her hand, light as the brush of a butterfly wing, and then he stood. "Why did you come back?"

"Because you made me."

His left eyebrow rose. Clearly he didn't buy that answer.

And clearly, she could have simply said no. Except she hadn't wanted to go home.

"By the way, I already called Piper," he said. "She'll pick up some clothes for you."

Jasmyn tried taking a deep breath. It caught in her throat. More clothes. At least Piper was a smart shopper and understood Jasmyn's simple tastes. Except for those neon yellow shoes and the comfy sandals.

Keagan put on his jacket. "And I called Sam."

"Sam?"

"She'll be the most affected."

"Sam?" Jasmyn wondered why he thought that about the Casa's most together tenant. What else was she missing about her new friends?

"Drink the tea," he said. "Skip the coffee. You'll feel better. Later." He walked away.

Jasmyn wanted to run after him, the only familiar person in this whole weird scene. But fear rooted her to the chair. What had she just agreed to? Or at least not disagreed to?

You light up a room, Ms. Albright.

But he had said it in two distinct words. All Bright.

Just be yourself.

Discombobulated could not begin to describe the turmoil inside of her.

Deep breaths. Drink the tea.

Maybe she should try things Keagan's way.

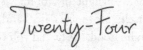

Twenty-Four

Sam stared at the panel of buttons inside the hospital elevator. The numbers blurred. Which didn't matter a whole lot because she didn't have a clue what floor she wanted.

"Ma'am, are you all right?"

Ma'am. What was up with *ma'am*? Liv was a *ma'am*. Inez was a *ma'am*. Since turning thirty, Sam had become a *ma'am* to salesclerks and waiters. It was as if there was some rule about age thirty.

She glanced at the person beside her, a woman in greenish scrubs. A short, young woman who probably had not yet been called *ma'am*. "I…" Her heart hammered in her throat, cutting off her voice.

"Where are you going?"

She gulped. "ICU. I can't find it. I keep asking people. I've been on sixteen elevators and down a dozen corridors."

The woman smiled and punched a button. "This place is a maze. I'll take you to ICU."

"You don't have to do that."

"I'd better before you collapse."

"I've been running." Which she did several times a week. Therefore she was in good shape. Why couldn't she breathe?

The stranger deposited her at the ICU waiting area. "Good luck."

Sam found Jasmyn seated on a couch behind a plastic potted palm. "Jasmyn."

Her friend turned.

Her friend? She'd never had one, not really. She wasn't sure what it entailed.

Jasmyn Albright, the woman she had dropped off at the airport. The one from Illinois who should not be at the hospital and involved with Casa business. The one with the overly sweet voice who liked Canadian bacon and sauerkraut pizza and wanted a job. The one who seemed to enjoy Sam's company.

The one who cared for Liv as much as Sam did.

Jasmyn rose from the couch and wrapped Sam in a tight hug. "They let me see her. She's going to be all right."

Sam squeezed shut her eyes and held her breath. Big girls didn't cry. Ma'ams certainly did not cry.

But they hugged. It was okay to hug because that's what friends did.

The rest of them arrived, every Casa de Vida resident. Chad, Piper, Riley, little Tasha, Inez, Louis, Coco, Noah. Even Keagan. For that matter, even Sam herself. And, good grief, even Beau, the self-employed handyman who should have been working on a Saturday.

They filled the waiting room with chatter and made it standing room only. An ICU nurse shooed them off. Jasmyn suggested the cafeteria, and the noisy bunch straggled down the hallway.

Sam positioned herself behind Keagan, the only one she trusted to lead them directly there and back.

"Hey," she said to his shoulder.

He turned halfway, slowing until she was beside him.

"How did you and Jasmyn get in to see her? I thought it was family only."

"I explained we were the closest thing to family Liv has." He shrugged. "One nurse bent the rules."

No stretch of the imagination was needed to believe him. She said, "Can you tell her I'm family too?"

"Are you?"

Sam did not like Sean Keagan. He was aloof and enigmatic and talked like a robot and asked more questions than he answered and he was special to Liv.

He touched her elbow and halted. The others kept on going. "Sam, you are family."

The lump in her throat returned.

"You and Liv care about each other."

Sam blinked and blinked. Family…Another concept so cobbled up in her past it meant nothing. "I pay rent. I respect her. She's a good businesswoman. She…she…"

"She makes your home feel like a safe place. She watches over you. She cooks and bakes for you. She prays for your well-being."

Sam kept blinking, but the heat in her eyes remained.

"Samantha, did no one ever do those things for you?"

Made her feel safe? Cared for her? "My dad," she whispered. "A long, long…" She took a deep breath. "Time ago."

Sam didn't know who moved first, but the tears spilled and then his shirt was soaking them up, Keagan's arms around her.

⁂

Liv appeared to be sleeping peacefully, but she wasn't exactly herself. Her gray skin matched the matted hair. Her chin was jowly. The ugly blue floral garb hung crookedly at her neck, the furthest thing from L.L. Bean imaginable. Liv would have used it to scrub down the courtyard fountain before wearing it.

Sam exhaled. "Ohhh."

Behind her, Keagan said, "She'll be fine."

"Yeah, right." Her ears felt on fire, a sure sign she should be quiet. "She won't be fine, not without some major lifestyle changes. She needs to walk *every* day, down to the beach instead of the coffee shop for glazed donuts and lattes. She needs to eat more vegetables. And she needs to hire Beau full-time so she doesn't do it all. He gardens too. He doesn't do just handyman stuff. She knows that."

"It's understandable why you're angry. We get like that when we're afraid."

Sam clenched her jaw.

"Jasmyn thinks she can hear us."

"Good. I hope she can. Liv, look, I know you're tired and hurting and you probably want to quit. But you are not, I repeat, you are *not* checking out on us. We need you here. Do you understand? I need you here."

I need you here?

Sam brushed past Keagan and sprinted from the room as if a wildcat were in pursuit.

Sam's father died when she was seven. A heart attack.

Like his mother of Swedish descent, Jimmy Whitehorse was blue-eyed and a much-loved high school math teacher. Like his Diné father, he wore his black hair in a thick braid halfway down his back and served on the tribal council. Like both of them, he was gone at a young age.

When Sam was old enough to understand the strange workings of marriage, she realized that her mother—much younger than her dad and still in her late twenties—had been cheating on her father for a long time. As a seven-year-old fatherless child, with no extended family, she only knew that the day after they buried her dad, a stranger moved into the house, a man she had never met.

He was a rough construction worker who took care of her mother and the three sons they proceeded to create in quick succession. He basically treated Sam as if she were invisible except when she was in his way. Then he snarled and called her names. Her mother? She was emotionally absent to her firstborn, unaware of her presence except when a cook or babysitter was wanted.

Much later, Sam realized she was bright, brighter than the adults in her house. She also realized that that fact intimidated them. They verbally struck at her most vulnerable point, her heritage, which was an oddball grandmother of Swedish descent who happened to visit the rez in the 1940s and marry a Navajo man.

School was no different. Kids went for the jugular. It was hardwired into their little brains to call others derogatory names. *Teacher's pet* cut as deeply as did *half-breed, outsider, bilagáana*. She wasn't the only smart one or the only one of mixed heritage, but she seemed to be the only one who carried both identities.

Sam no longer blamed her classmates. The way she flew off the handle, she had been a fun target for them. Through it all she had learned how to take care of herself, how to fight as a little kid and how to be mouthy as a teenager. Some teachers understood and nurtured her better side. She focused on studies rather than cliques and boys.

But at home? That wasn't fair. That wasn't right.

And the only one who understood it all was dead.

I need you here.

She couldn't lose the only one who had ever shown her the same kindness that her father had.

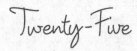

Twenty-Five

By the time Jasmyn made her way from the hospital to the Casa, darkness had fallen at the end of an unbelievably long day. She was frazzled to within an inch of sitting down on the alley's dirty asphalt and bawling her eyes out.

Driving Liv's bulky minivan on the freeway and parallel parking it in the alley had been no picnic. Now she stood in front of the tall back gate, as solid as any steel door between the twelve-foot walls that surrounded the complex. Under a burned-out streetlamp, she fumbled with Liv's bright orange coil with umpteen keys on it, none of which fit the back gate's deadbolt.

"Oh!" She threw down the keys and they clanked against the concrete. "I quit! I quit!"

"Really, Jasmyn?"

Her heart skipped a beat, but she saw it was only Keagan coming down the alley.

"You quit?" He bent and picked up the keys. "Have you even started?"

"Yeah. I started this day and I am totally, completely done with it."

"Understandable." He held the keys up in the dim light and sorted through them. He chose one and tried it on the lock. Then he tried a different one. "I was hoping you weren't quitting the other thing."

"The other thing?"

"The woman thing I told you about earlier."

She took a deep breath. The woman thing. All right, there was something to that. She connected with Liv in a way Keagan probably could not.

It was obvious while she sat with Liv at the hospital that afternoon and evening. Despite the environment, time passed peacefully. When Liv was awake, she said things like *Bless you, Jasmyn, dear. Thank you for coming. Do you mind staying a few days? I'll be fit as a fiddle in no time.*

When Jasmyn asked her what she could do for her, she replied, *Just be you.*

It was the most loving thing Jasmyn had ever been told. *Just be you.* No need to perform, no need to change her looks, words, or behavior. Just be herself.

She watched Keagan try yet another key. "No, I won't quit on Liv."

"Thank you." His voice was soft, his head down as he fiddled with the lock.

Jasmyn marveled at the hint of emotion. Once again, his intimidating manner disappeared. "You really care about her, don't you?"

He stopped moving but didn't look at her. "I lost my parents when I was twelve." He straightened. "This isn't working and I don't have my keys. I thought hers for the gate was the one with the pink dot."

"The green one matches the gate." Liv had coded her keys with dots of various colors of nail polish. "You tried it?"

"I tried the whole rainbow. Let's go around to the front. And next time, don't stand out here by yourself in the dark. Call me first."

She walked beside him down the alley and almost giggled. What had Inez said? *You call Keagan. When we women need rescue, he always there for us. He is our knight.* Apparently, he didn't always need a phone call.

The distance around to the front gate was nearly a block, plenty of time to ask Keagan all about his childhood, but Jasmyn sensed that the tidbit he'd just shared was his limit of self-revelation. No wonder he sometimes called Liv *Mama Liv.*

At the front gate, he punched in the code on the automatic lock and it clicked open. They walked into the courtyard. Even at nighttime its peaceful aura swept over her. The fountain trickled and tiny lights hung from various plants.

She held out her hand for Liv's keys. "Thanks for getting me inside."

"I'll walk you to the office."

She was too tired to tell the knight he was off duty.

As they reached the cottage-turned-office, an exterior light automatically blinked on, brightening the entrance area.

Keagan easily chose a key and unlocked the door. Then he reached inside and flipped a switch. The table lamp came on. "I'm sure there's food in Liv's fridge and pantry." He handed her the key ring. "Red dot for her cottage. You should eat something."

And then he was gone, as quickly as he had appeared.

He truly was an odd guy.

⁂

Inside the office, Jasmyn tried to make herself feel at home. It wasn't happening.

Although she had spent time on Liv's computer, taking care of her own banking business and whatnot, sitting at the desk with Liv nowhere on the premises did not seem right. She opened one desk drawer after another, searching for her cottage key. Where exactly had Keagan said it was? She should have asked him to find it.

"Hey."

She looked up and saw Sam come through the open doorway. "Hey, yourself. Do you know where Liv keeps the cottage keys?"

"Top right." She closed the door.

"I already searched every—oh. Here it is. I feel like I'm snooping."

"No reason to. Liv doesn't mind." Sam sat on one of the overstuffed armchairs. "So, welcome back. I guess?"

"I guess."

"Liv's okay?"

"Yes. Groggy, but she was alert enough to talk for a few minutes. Are you okay? You look…" Jasmyn didn't want to say that Sam looked worse than Liv, although she did look decidedly worse. "You look a little peaked."

"I'm…" Sam's lips flattened into a straight line. Her eyes seemed focused on the Oriental rug at her feet.

Jasmyn stepped around the desk and gave Sam a quick hug. "Yeah, I know. I'll make us some tea."

The kitchenette area at the rear of the one-room office felt less personal than the desk. Jasmyn had made tea and coffee for Liv and herself on several occasions. Now she easily went about turning on the electric kettle and taking cups, saucers, tea bags, and napkins from the cupboard. Instead of putting cookies on a plate, she added the owl-shaped cookie jar to the pewter serving tray. When the water was ready, she poured it into her favorite teapot, the one with the lemon-yellow daisy design.

She carried the tray to the table between the armchairs and sat down. "Care to share a cookie jar?"

Sam flashed her half smile. "Mmm, comfort food. Chocolate chip?"

Jasmyn lifted the owl's head and sniffed. "Yup."

"When they're gone, I bet we could find some of her special mac and cheese in the freezer. Her homemade stuff."

Jasmyn laughed and held out the cookie jar.

Sam took three and started munching. "You have this whole thing down pat, you know."

"What's that?"

"WWLD."

"WWLD?"

"What Would Liv Do. She would do exactly what you did. Give me a hug, tea, and cookies. You're a natural."

"Really?"

"Really. You don't think I make things up just to be nice, do you?"

"Well." Jasmyn poured the tea.

"Be honest."

"No."

"Right. If I say something nice, I mean it, but I'm not a nice person who just naturally says nice things all the time. I told you I'm not a people person. I'm not Liv. I'm not Jasmyn Albright. I'm Samantha 'don't come any closer than arm's length' Whitley who says something once in a while that happens to be nice."

Jasmyn handed her a cup. "Chamomile. It's supposed to be calming."

"You think I need calming?" She shut her eyes and sipped.

"Liv is going to be all right, Sam. The doctor said so, and you know Liv. She'll bounce back in no time."

Sam inhaled deeply and opened her eyes. "I suppose you're going to start praying next."

"Why would I—oh. Because Liv would. WWLD."

"You're catching on."

"It's not exactly a habit." She smiled. "But I think I actually prayed this morning on the back of Keagan's motorcycle."

Sam's eyes widened. "You were on Keagan's bike?"

"That's how I got from the airport to the hospital."

"He doesn't let anyone touch his bike. Oh, we're all falling apart here. Chad went to his parents' house to spend the night, which he never does. Noah's been pounding on his piano all evening. Riley and Tasha have been at Inez and Louis's with Coco for hours. I ran ten miles. Ten. You didn't go back to Illinois."

"Mama Liv means a lot to all of us."

"You have some big shoes to fill."

"I can't—"

"You can't say you can't." Sam's phone beeped and she took it from her sweatshirt pocket.

"Well, I can't."

Sam chuckled and slipped the phone back into her pocket. "All right, maybe you can't because I think you forgot something huge. Chad just texted one word: Tobi."

"Tobi! The cat! Oh my gosh! Where is she?"

"Probably inside Liv's cottage."

Jasmyn went to the desk and picked up the key ring. "Red dot, right?"

"Holly red. Shall we look for the mac and cheese?"

Jasmyn smiled. "Definitely."

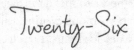

Twenty-Six

Much later that night, after Jasmyn and Sam had stuffed themselves with macaroni and cheese—Liv's comfort-of-all-comfort food—and Sam had gone home, Jasmyn sat on the floor in Liv's cottage, deciding what to do with the cat.

Tobi snuggled on her lap, purring like a little engine. Jasmyn had tried to carry the cat to her own cottage, but Tobi had complained loudly, jumped from her arms, and raced back to Liv's door.

Jasmyn understood. Who wanted to leave a home that felt cozy and safe? It was probably the real reason she had not gotten on the plane that morning. Cottage Eleven, even with its temporary furnishings and all-but-empty closet, provided more cocoon-ness than anything waiting for her in Valley Oaks.

It wasn't just inside Cottage Eleven. The whole entire Casa exuded comfort and security. Maybe it had something to do with the high surrounding wall and the nearly circular layout of the cottages. It was straight out of a storybook. If she hadn't already met everyone, she would not have been surprised to see hobbits living there.

The cottages all had bay windows that faced the courtyard. Their front doors were a different color, bright against the white walls. The interiors were simple with hardwood floors, old-fashioned rounded walls, and French doors that opened onto tiny back patios.

Each one felt homey, though Liv's most of all. Entering her cottage was like stepping into a teddy bear's hug. Jasmyn thought about crawling up on the floral print couch and spending the night inside that hug.

"But that seems presumptuous, don't you think?" She held Tobi up to her face. "I'm going home. Are you coming?"

The cat tilted her head and gazed at her. She was a pretty one, long-haired and multicolored. Her green eyes said she was staying put.

Jasmyn set her on the floor, and she scurried off toward the bedroom.

"Okay," she called after her. "Be that way. I'll check on you in the morning."

Outside, Jasmyn paused to soak in the nighttime courtyard. The air was cool and yet humid, a mixture of briny and sweet alyssum scents. A few stars were visible through the trees. It was near midnight, and the fountain had automatically turned off at eleven. The tiny lights that hung in trees and bushes would stay on until dawn.

What would Liv do?

The question poked its way into her thoughts without warning.

"I don't—"

But she did know. She had spent enough time, up close, with Olivia McAlister to replay a dozen similar scenes.

Liv, in the courtyard late at night, her shoulders thrown back, her face upward, inhaling deeply and breathing out a whispered, *Thank You, Lord.*

Liv, gently shaking a mum from its pot and placing it in the hole she had dug. *Bless you.*

Liv, smiling at a foamy latte. *Thank You.*

Liv, on the sidewalk, bending over, her hand atop a toddler's head. *Bless you, child.*

The woman prayed all the time, over and under and about everything, always thanking God for whatever was right there in front of her, always blessing others.

Jasmyn sighed. She figured there was something unseen at work. The cornfields and the woods had told her that since she was a kid. The ocean only made a concept of God more obvious. But making a personal connection the way Liv did? The thought had never entered her mind.

Except that day when she saw His finger.

She had asked Liv about it as they sat in the coffee shop one time. "I don't literally think it was God's finger. The idea popped into my head right then while it was happening."

"Maybe in that incomprehensible moment you came face-to-face with the Ultimate Incomprehensible."

Jasmyn heard the capital letters in Liv's tone. "You mean it's absolutely impossible for us to understand God?"

"Exactly. His ways and His nature are beyond us. We give Him human attributes, like fingers, to make it easier to relate to Him. And easier to blame."

"You think I blame God for what happened?"

"I would."

"Seriously?"

"I'd be deeply hurt and angry, like I was when Syd died. Couldn't God have stopped that? Was He punishing me for something?" She paused, her forehead creased.

Jasmyn could only stare at the woman who seemed to have it all together.

A few moments passed before she went on. "Eventually I ran out of steam. It took too much energy to be bitter. To be self-righteous. I realized that for the most part I'd been responding to God either as though He were a genie in a bottle who gave me things if I performed correctly, or like an ancient Greek god who zapped me if I did not perform correctly." She had smiled. "But those were starting points. Necessary baby steps."

Jasmyn's attention had gotten stuck on the zapping image. When Jasmyn was seven, her Grandma June abruptly quit going to church and taking Jasmyn with her. Her only explanation had been something about catty women blaming her for her daughter's pregnancy and if that was what God was like, she wanted no part of Him. Since then, Jasmyn assumed God was all about blaming, about zapping. She had, for the most part, kept her distance.

"The tornado felt like a personal zap."

"Of course it did." Liv nodded. "That's a baby step toward recognizing Him."

Jasmyn had frowned.

Liv had smiled. "I can't explain why this world is full of such pain and heartache and evil and beauty and goodness and wonder. All I know for certain is that God is God and I am not. He's not a genie or a zapper. That takes a huge weight off my shoulders. It frees me up to simply share the journey with others."

"And pray about everything."

A funny expression crossed Liv's face, almost a wince. "I can't explain that either. It's a mystery why I think He's listening. But I believe He is listening because I inexplicably believe that He loves me."

"It doesn't make sense."

"Exactly, Jasmyn, dear." She patted her hand and changed the subject.

Now, in the courtyard, Jasmyn asked Sam's question. What would Liv do alone in the dark after a crazy day like Jasmyn had been through?

Easy one. Liv would thank God.

She sighed. Why not? "Um, thank You." *Thank You.* For what? "For this beautiful, peaceful courtyard."

That was easy enough. Real enough.

What else?

"Thank You for Liv, who works so hard to keep it beautiful and peaceful."

Liv.

"Thank You that Liv is okay."

And?

Friends.

"Thank You for Quinn." Jasmyn had phoned Quinn from the hospital early in the day, her nerves totally frayed from the news of Liv's heart attack and missing her flight, not to mention that motorcycle ride. Although she wouldn't have blamed Quinn at all for being super upset, Jasmyn had felt desperate for her friend to be sympathetic.

"And she came through. She wasn't overly dramatic, and she didn't make me feel worse than I already did. She even offered to pick up my luggage and ship a few things, like the neon yellow shoes. Now that was downright unbelievable."

Was there anything else?

Jasmyn looked up at the stars. She glanced around the ring of quiet cottages. She listened carefully and heard a faint whoosh.

"Ohhh! The ocean! Thank You for the ocean. How could I forget? And for the stars and the palm trees. For this whole entire place. The Casa. Everybody who lives here. Liv, Sam, Piper, Chad, Riley, Tasha, Noah, Inez and Louis, Keagan. Did I get them all? And Beau. And Cottage Eleven, the one with my name on it. Thank You that I met everyone and stay here…"

She met them all because her car was stolen.

That sounded as though she could be grateful for a stolen car.

Seriously?

Then why not for Liv's heart attack, which fulfilled Jasmyn's wish not to leave Seaside Village today? Why not for the tornado, which got her there in the first place and put her in the position of having her car stolen?

"Okay, this is getting a little weird. No, it's a lot weird. Too weird."

She shook her head, certain that she would hear a loose screw rattling around. Her cheeks felt flushed. It was embarrassing to act like a flake.

Besides, why would God bother listening after she'd ignored Him for so long? And why did she even consider that He existed in the first place? Who did she think she was, acting like Liv by praying about everything, acting as though God was interested?

Her eyes stung. She felt as if she'd swallowed a wad of bubble gum and it was stuck. "Honestly, God, we really do need her here. Please, please make her better. Really, really soon."

She didn't move.

There was more to say to the God she was unsure cared. But the words burned so hotly in her chest that she could not speak them aloud. *It would be so wonderful to live here.*

She exhaled and inhaled and exhaled, each breath going deeper. After a bit, her tears dried and the wad of gum melted away. And her doubts did not seem to matter anymore.

"Okay," she whispered. "Amen."

Ten minutes later she was sound asleep in her little rollaway, wearing a pumpkin orange nightshirt with the tag still on it.

Twenty-Seven

Sean Keagan sat in a chair the ICU nurses had reluctantly allowed him to put in Liv's room, near the foot of her bed. There was much eye-rolling when he said he would be occupying it throughout the night.

It wasn't that he didn't trust the staff to adequately watch over Liv. It was, as he pointed out to them, the fact that his one-to-one ratio beat their one-to-two, which often slipped to one-to-four due to break times, emergencies, and other situations he had witnessed earlier in the day. Simple arithmetic.

That and what Liv called his Clint Eastwood glare. She had said often that she expected him to say *Make my day*.

He wouldn't say that. His intention was not to mimic any tough guy. His persona simply came with the territory. He was orphaned at age twelve and rebellious as a teen despite kind grandparents, who wisely hauled him to counseling until he was eighteen and then backed his desire to enlist. After the military came a stint with the DEA. The rigorous lifestyles of both suited him, giving him discipline and direction.

When at last he had spun out his anger, he began what he referred to as the second half of his life. No bad guys to hunt and take down, no drug cartel business, no surveillance, no informants, no courtrooms, no guns.

Instead, he ran a gym where people exercised for health reasons and kids played basketball. He lived in an innocuous apartment and had a surrogate mother for a landlady. He surfed. He rode with a motorcycle club through deserts and mountains. Life was good.

Still, the persona remained, the air about him rife with some energy that compelled others to see things his way. He knew blood ran through his veins because he had seen it. Sometimes, though, he wondered about its temperature. Liv might say it tended to run on the cool side.

Unless she could see him now, alert at two a.m., watching over her because truthfully, he really did care.

His mouth twitched. He was getting downright sentimental.

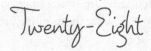

Twenty-Eight

One week and one day after returning home from the hospital, Liv sat in a lounge chair and watched Jasmyn carry two cups of tea across the courtyard. The girl wore her favorite yellow shoes. Thanks to her friend Quinn, she had enough clothes to get her through a few weeks without shopping again.

"What a gorgeous day!" Jasmyn handed a cup to Liv and slid onto a nearby bench. "I had to double-check the calendar to make sure what month it is."

Liv lowered her head and blinked rapidly until the tears stopped pooling. Jasmyn had a calendar. It had garden scenes and hung on her kitchen wall. It made things seem almost established, although of course they weren't. Jasmyn needed the calendar to keep Liv's appointments straight. The girl only stayed because, first of all, Keagan probably scared her into it. Secondly, she loved the beach. And last, she didn't have anything better to do.

For the moment.

For which Liv was grateful because, if not for Jasmyn's companionship, she feared that—well, she wasn't sure what she feared. The doctor said she was fine. She knew better. Something was off. Her emotions ran amok. She couldn't get a handle on herself.

She blamed the medical procedures. They had put that *thing* inside her body, that *stent*. Blood flowed freely now, going full speed. What else could her heart do but push out one extreme emotion after another, good and bad?

Jasmyn said, "It's October, but the weather is the same as when I first got here in August."

Liv shifted in the lounge chair, trying to get an internal grip. "Well, there are subtle differences. Look at the morning sunlight hitting the fountain."

"Okay."

"Squint. What do you see?"

"Morning sunlight hitting the fountain."

"Notice, though, it's at an angle. It comes in low between those palms, from the south-southeast. It was completely different just a couple of weeks ago."

"That's how you can tell it's October and not August?"

"Nor September. There's a nip in the air too."

"Nip? Liv, it'll be seventy-two degrees by noon. I swim in the ocean most days. Chad says I need a wetsuit, but I'm not cold."

"You still have a Midwestern thermostat. It'll change."

"How do the pumpkins know it's time to ripen? Tasha went on a field trip to the pumpkin patch and she brought home a nice plump one."

"You should ask Beau. He's the brainiac."

"Brainiac, electrician, plumber, mechanic, gardener. Whew! Aren't you glad you convinced him to put in more hours?" Jasmyn's dimples creased deeply.

Liv smiled, but it was a small, tight effort.

That was another thing. After all her years of independent decision making, she noted others' opinions. Suddenly Keagan's Clint-like gaze and Samantha's arguments about living smarter nagged at her. Jasmyn researched every medical question and talked to the doctors as much as Liv did. Piper, Chadwick, and Inez implored her to give up what they called her one-woman show. Noah voiced adamant opinions about everything under the sun. Even little Tasha clapped when she saw Beau in the court-yard two days in a row.

They all swayed Liv's decisions about business and about everyday things. Everyday things like tea.

She sipped from the cup Jasmyn had brought her, some sugar-free, dairy-free, caffeine-free concoction. She held back a grimace. "Hmm. Something new added?"

"Stevia. Piper brought it over. It's a sweet herb. And we put in some almond milk too. What do you think?"

"It's not half bad."

"How bad is it?"

"Seven-eighths."

Jasmyn laughed. "We'll play with it."

"I bet I could walk to Jitters today."

"That's about two blocks." Jasmyn paused, her lower lip puckered.

Liv had seen the expression often in recent weeks. Jasmyn was weighing the consequences of the idea.

Liv sighed inwardly. They all meant well. Still…

At last Jasmyn said, "Okay. Two blocks is a reasonable goal."

"One small latte sounds reasonable too."

"As long as it's decaf, fat-free milk, no sugar."

"How about half a glazed donut?"

"Liv!"

"A fourth. Two bites of a plain one."

"Don't you want to get better?"

She opened her mouth, but closed it before something stupid came out like *I have my moments.*

Jasmyn patted her hand and stood. "Of course you want to get better. It just takes time and a lot of hard work. I have to call Quinn. Inez said she'll be out to visit in a bit. And remember, the ladies from church are bringing lunch." She smiled and walked off to the office.

That was another thing. They all took turns babysitting her.

Lord…

Liv shut her eyes. She really didn't have anything to say to anybody.

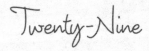

Twenty-Nine

Seated behind Liv's desk, Jasmyn surveyed her domain. Behind the computer monitor was a round crystal vase filled with flowers she had picked that morning: alyssum, daisies, a white rose, and a fern. The sunshine, with its peculiar October slant, came through the back window in the kitchenette area and touched her shoulder.

She wasn't sure how she had gotten to this place in life, but it seemed strangely natural. Liv and Keagan acted as if they just assumed she would step into the manager's role. Once, while still in the hospital, Liv had said, *Jasmyn, dear, would you mind organizing the mail and checking on Coco? And Tobi probably needs an extra cuddle or two.*

One thing led to another. No one else indicated they wanted to do it or that Jasmyn was a poor choice. Of course, they all had lives to continue, whereas Jasmyn didn't exactly have another life.

And so there she sat, Temporary Manager of the Casa de Vida.

She might not be perfectly tuned in to Liv's way of seeing and doing life, but she couldn't be happier trying. It gave her a purpose for staying in California, at least for three more weeks. She had just rebooked her flight home.

Not caring to dwell on that schedule, she turned her attention to the computer. Managing the complex was easy-peasy. Automatic online rent deposits and bill paying required little beyond getting Liv into the office and at the computer now and then. Beau Jenner—a delightful guy about Jasmyn's age—came daily now and made his own maintenance lists.

The Casa was a well-oiled machine. Technically speaking, it could go on without Liv for a while. But heart speaking? Well, that was a different matter. And that was her biggest challenge, filling in the other.

The *other*…Such a small word, but it encompassed everything else which was, really, the essence of Olivia McAlister.

Not that Liv had asked Jasmyn to consider such things, but that acronym Sam created had grabbed hold of her imagination and would not let go. WWLD. Keagan had called it a woman thing. Jasmyn called it complicated.

There was Liv's mothering influence on most of the residents. How could Jasmyn, a childless thirtysomething, mimic that? Little Tasha was not a problem, of course, but wild Chad? Confident Piper? Cool Sam? And *Keagan*? Yeah, right.

Then there were Liv's relationships with countless others, from the mail carrier to the trash collectors to the baristas down at Jitters to vendors at the farmers market to street people. Some of them recognized Jasmyn and asked about Liv. Already she was giving medical updates to virtual strangers.

But the toughest of all was following in the footsteps of Liv's prayer life. Jasmyn tried. She still felt like a flake and a fake, although she was getting pretty good with the gratitude. Who wouldn't, considering her situation: a wonderful home in a hobbit-like garden with an instant community of likable folks?

She thought of blessing people late at night, not in the moment. She didn't know if that still counted. And the bit about asking for things from the One who created the ocean? That remained far, far fetched.

But, as Sam would say, she was not Liv. She was Jasmyn Albright. She might mimic Liv, but it would be in her own way, which had always been a little backward.

She hoped it was enough.

 ℒ

"Hey."

Jasmyn looked up from the desk where she was sorting the mail and saw Keagan in the open office doorway. "Hey, yourself," she said.

"I have a surprise for you."

Jasmyn blinked a couple of times, unsure what to reply. In recent weeks, he would appear as he had at the airport and in the alley, out of nowhere, quiet as a mouse. He would ask about Liv, Casa matters, how Jasmyn was doing. Sometimes she imagined she heard a wink or a smile in his voice, though his face never outwardly expressed such things.

The guy was a little bit disturbing and a little bit comforting with no space in between the two.

"I don't like surprises."

He stared at her for a moment. The slanted sunlight caught in his eyes, making the unique blue-green color sparkle. "I imagine you don't. I apologize."

She shrugged. The tornado had been the biggie of surprises. Before that it had been her grandfather's volatile anger, her grandmother's sharp and embarrassing tongue, her mother's illness at such a young age. The car theft.

"I could go an entire lifetime without another surprise."

"This is a good one, though." He ducked outside and immediately returned, a suitcase in his hand.

A large, grape-purple suitcase.

Keagan set it down, pulled up its handle, and wheeled it around the desk to where she sat. "Good surprise?"

She gasped. "How— What—? Oh my gosh!"

"The police found your rental in a parking garage. Your luggage was still in the trunk, apparently not touched."

She leaned over, unzipped a front pocket, reached inside, and pulled out her purse. "They didn't take my purse?" She unzipped the big yellow-and-orange handbag she had splurged on for the trip. Her wallet and cell phone were nestled in their special pockets. She gasped again.

She laid the suitcase down and knelt. It felt heavy, as if everything she had packed so many weeks ago must still be in it. She unzipped the top and lifted it. Beneath were neat piles of clothing strapped in. Her clothing. Her jeans. Her tops. Her pajamas. Her sweater. Her cosmetic bag. Her shoes.

"Oh, Keagan. It's all here." She looked up. "How did you get this?"

"A friend."

"A friend?"

He tilted his head, obviously done explaining.

"How can I thank him? Or her?"

"Already taken care of."

Jasmyn looked again at the luggage before her. Never in a million years would she have thought she would see her things again. Not that there was anything special in the suitcase or her purse. Just everyday necessities that had been replaced easily enough. Still, it felt like a treasure.

"Keagan, thank you." She stood.

He wasn't there.

She hurried out the office door and scanned the courtyard.

He was nowhere to be seen.

Typical Keagan. He wouldn't hang around for a thank-you.

She wondered what sort of thank-you would mean something to him. Cookies? Cake? Liv would know.

Jasmyn turned to go back into the office and spotted her door. Like all twelve cottages, it was painted its own unique color. Hers was purple. Of course she knew that. Purple being a particular favorite of hers, she had seen that right away. What she hadn't noted until that very moment was its shade of purple. It was not lavender. Not violet. Not orchid.

Nope. It was grape. Deep, luscious dark grape, a Concord variety ready to be plucked off the vine. It was an exact match to her luggage.

What a curious coincidence.

Even more curious was the rush of sweet contentment flowing through her now, as if matching door and luggage mattered.

Jasmyn shook her head. This was like having a conversation with Liv.

Honestly, filling in for the woman was affecting her in really, really strange ways.

Thirty

Sam did not mean to eavesdrop, but given the proximity of Jasmyn and Liv, it could not be helped. She stood at the counter; they sat at Jasmyn's kitchen table within arm's reach. Their voices carried above others who filled the living room, balancing dinner plates on their laps and having their own conversations.

"Jasmyn, dear." Liv put down her fork. "I think true coincidences occur rarely. Very rarely. I won't say never, but I sometimes wonder."

Across the small kitchen table, Jasmyn gazed with wide eyes at Liv as if she were some ancient oracle. "Really?"

"Yes. I don't believe in flukes. Things happen for a reason, which by definition means that those things can't be coincidences."

"Even silly little things?"

"Those can be the best because they're easy to notice. They convey the simple fact that God's attention is on us."

Sam spooned a glob of casserole onto her plate and clunked the spoon back into the serving dish. *Good grief.* They were talking about God and Jasmyn's newly found luggage that happened to be the same shade of purple as her cottage door. A silly little thing. Was there a point to the conversation?

Sam wound her way through wall-to-wall people seated on the living room floor and made her way to Chad on the window seat in front of the bay window.

He smiled, his mouth full, and pointed at his plate, nodding vigorously in approval.

She sat. "Is it Noah's?"

"Mmm."

She took a bite. "Mmm. Mm-hmm." It was Noah's special mix of chicken, black beans, cheese, and his own version of fairy dust that made it scrumptious.

Chad swallowed. "Two thumbs-up for our little Liv clone. She has the hang of this impromptu potluck thing."

"Jasmyn is a natural." Sam glanced around at the crowd and saw evidence at how perfectly suited Jasmyn was to her role as assistant manager.

"We really should talk her into staying longer," Chad said. "As in permanently longer."

"Good luck with that. I don't see her changing her mind about leaving."

"Always the positive one."

Sam ignored his comment.

The group was a noisy bunch, talking, laughing, and eating. It was the first time they had gathered as a group since that awful day at the hospital.

Everyone had come, even Keagan. Even three of Inez and Louis's great-grandkids. Even Beau the handyman.

Jasmyn's cottage still had *temporary* written all over it, but the mishmash of furniture had grown in the past week. Inez had bought a new couch and so her old, good-as-new plaid one had been moved into the living room. Chad never found his card table, but he raided his parents' garage, where they stored unwanted items. Jasmyn now had a kitchen table with four chairs, an end table, and two floor lamps.

Chad said, "I hope this event will boost Liv's spirits. She seems a bit down in the dumps, don't you think?"

Actually, Liv had been a *lot* down in the dumps. "It's the effects of the detox. She hasn't had a latte or glazed donut in weeks."

"Nah. That would just make her cranky. This is something more. She's not herself. I've never seen her not herself. She hasn't had one cheery word for me since the heart attack."

They ate in silence for a few moments. Then Sam mentioned the weather. Chad mentioned the surf. Obviously neither of one them wanted to mention how they themselves might be devastated by an Olivia McAlister who did not regularly spout cheery words to them.

Sam and Chad were undoubtedly the two most self-absorbed Casa Detainees.

"Ooh," Chad whispered. "Empty seat alert." Without an *excuse me*, he shot across the crowded room and slid onto the floor next to Piper.

Sam rolled her eyes. He was such a puppy dog and so clueless. Piper had once been engaged to a Marine. She was not into clueless puppy dogs.

"Miss Samantha, mind if I sit here?"

Sam looked up to see Beau beside her. "Help yourself." She scooted sideways. The big guy would need a little more space than what Chad had vacated.

He sat, carefully balancing a plate that held an alpine ridge of food.

Gentle giant fit Beau Jenner to a tee. His extreme size suggested the opposite of his affable demeanor and soft voice.

Liv had hired him a few months ago when her handyman retired and recommended him. Sam guessed Beau was a little older than herself. She heard that he had played college football, turned down a pro offer, and ran his own business, which—she noted—consisted of him, his truck, his tools, his cell phone, and his hours.

He scooped a peak from his casserole mountain into his mouth and chewed slowly. "Mmm. This is amazing."

"Noah made it."

"That makes sense. He's a chef, right?"

"Oh, now and then." She winced. Beau's civility always made her snarkiness fall flat on her own ears. "I mean, he is a chef, but he's not actually working as a chef. You know, officially. As in a restaurant."

"Lucky for us." He winked and forked up some salad foothills. "Else we might not have this tasty dish here."

She ate, making careful, deliberate movements, yet squirming on the inside. She'd never met anyone like this guy.

First of all, he was the largest man she knew, at least six foot five and two-hundred-and-then-some pounds without an ounce of flab on him. His shoulders were so broad that the first time she saw him standing in a doorway she wondered why he was wearing shoulder pads.

He was smart, no doubt about that. He could fix anything and even teach her about apps on her tablet.

That little iPad session had been a fluke. She'd been in the laundry room, waiting for the dryer to stop, working with her new device, fussing quietly at it. Evidently not quietly enough. He overheard her from the courtyard, popped inside, and explained the problem like nobody's business.

Definitely a fluke.

Then there was his limited wardrobe. Not that she was into fashion, but he wore one outfit: blue jeans and a distressed-green denim work shirt. Above its left pocket was a small embroidered logo: a hammer in a deeper green shade, and, in red letters, *Fix-It Jenner*. Typically, he wore a matching cap that he would tuck inside his back pocket when, like now, he was indoors. The logo green matched his eyes, the red hinted at the reddish-blond shade of his short wavy hair.

It was, however, his Southern genteel mannerisms that got to her. It was like being tickled by a feather under her nose. Whenever he was near, she itched and twitched and behaved like an absolute oaf.

Naturally, she avoided him whenever possible.

"So." She took a stab at conversation, speaking to her plate. "I hear you'll be spending more time at the Casa."

He swallowed. "That's partially true. Between you and me and the fly on the wall, those chores Miss Olivia used to do by herself won't take me near the amount of time they took her."

Sam bristled. How dare he make light of Liv's needs. "She's very thorough. Details matter to her. It's why the Casa is always in tip-top shape. Everything works and the courtyard looks impeccable. All the time." She felt his eyes on her and turned to meet his gaze. "I'm just saying…"

"That if I cheat Miss Olivia, you'll nail my hide to a tree." He smiled and his eyes twinkled.

They actually *twinkled*. Like when sunlight hit a raindrop shimmying on a wide leaf of the tropical tree outside her front door.

"Well, yes. Generally speaking, that's what I'd do."

He chuckled. "Don't you worry your pretty little head, Miss Samantha. Doing business with Miss Olivia is exactly the same thing as sitting with my Granny Mibs on her front porch, drinking lemonade. It's sheer delight. Even if it weren't, I would never disrespect either one of those ladies."

"Please don't call me that."

"Whoops." He grimaced in an exaggerated way. "I apologize. Sometimes I forget it's the twenty-first century and women don't care for that sort of old-fashioned talk. I don't mean anything by it. Not that I'm saying your head isn't pretty. Because it is. And it's just the right size, not too small."

Good grief. Pretty little head? That line had sailed right past her. "I was talking about the 'Miss' part."

"The 'Miss' part?" He smiled crookedly. "Well, I can't promise anything about that. Granny Mibs practically yanked my ear off every time I addressed a lady incorrectly. She made one of those—what do you call it?—indelible impressions. I'll do my best, though, to not give offense. Would 'ma'am' suit you better?"

Sam blinked a few times and focused on twirling her fork in the casserole. "'Sam' suits me better."

"All right, then! 'Miss Sam' it is. You know, Miss Olivia always refers to you as Samantha. That's where I picked it up. I appreciate your clarifying things. Now, if you'll excuse me, I need to talk to Miss Jasmyn." He looked at her, as if waiting for her permission to leave.

"Uh, sure."

"Enjoy the rest of your evening." He made his way slowly across the room, slapping high fives with one of the Templeton grandkids, raising a thumb toward Noah, and complimenting Piper on her latest hairdo, which resembled spikes on a light brown porcupine.

Was Beau Jenner for real?

Who knew? Who cared?

Sam sat alone. Again. Or still. Whatever. She doubted anyone else would pick up on any empty seat alert.

Of course not. It was next to Sam, the snob.

She watched Beau sit down in the empty seat beside Jasmyn. She watched their easy exchange, words flowing freely back and forth, punctuated by grins and laughter.

Oh, well. She had work to do.

Thirty-One

"Keagan, I am not getting out of this vehicle." Liv, seated in the passenger seat of her minivan, crossed her arms. The movement made her chest hurt. The doctor had said it was her imagination. Still, it was there. She felt it. She uncrossed her arms. "I'm not budging."

Keagan chuckled from the driver's seat. "You know I can outwait you." He turned off the engine and with that went the heater.

She wanted to protest, but she couldn't summon the energy to do so. Besides, he was right. He could outwait her. Although she wore socks with her slip-on Birkenstock sandals and a jacket, the van was already chilly.

They were parked down at the beach, in a lot nearly empty at this late hour, and faced the night ocean. The inky water mirrored the sky, both full of shimmering pinpricks as if stars had been tossed high and low on two canvases. Far to the right, gentle waves swelled beneath the pier, their whitecaps briefly aglow in light cast from the vapor lamps high above them.

"Liv, you're not old and you're not dying."

"I am old and, for your information, we're all dying."

"You get my drift. You always say age is a state of mind. And yours has been focused on that one foot you've stuck inside the grave."

"What do you expect? I had a heart attack."

Keagan chuckled again. "*I had a heart attack.* You might want to reconsider that mantra. It's getting redundant."

The man went for days speaking no more than a dozen words. What was up with the Mr. Magpie routine? "If I get out of the car, will you stop talking?"

"Only one way to find out." He hopped from the car, hurried around to her door, and opened it.

She let him help her down. The sand-covered pavement crunched under her sandals. She inhaled damp, cool autumn air that carried smoky scents from campfires burning in a handful of rings on the beach.

She sighed. "Look at those stars."

"Hmm. Let's walk." He drew her arm through his and led her to the lane marked for pedestrians on the Strand. Its curb paralleled the beach. They turned south, away from the pier.

She suspected he chose the direction on purpose. He knew her first choice was always to walk the pier. Tonight, though, the thought of going up and down its ramp felt beyond her ability. Evidently he did not plan to push her physical limitations.

Just her mental ones.

They walked in silence—blessed silence—at a snail's pace. It wasn't their first nighttime stroll. Years before, soon after his arrival at the Casa, Keagan had spotted her around ten p.m., halfway out on the nineteen-hundred-foot-long pier.

She never again walked the pier late at night by herself. With that peculiar sense of his, he intuited whenever she was ready to go and he showed up, quiet and watchful, either keeping his distance or joining her.

She thought it totally unnecessary. Seaside Village was a safe community, and she could take pretty good care of herself. Her height and listen-up voice commanded attention when she wanted them to.

One time years ago she was in the alley performing her macho routine for three teenage boys who were up to no good. She did not have proof they were up to no good, but one carried a can of spray paint in his back pocket. When she asked them about it, they sassed her. Never one to be afraid to stand her ground or call the police, she was prepared to do both, but the need evaporated.

Out of nowhere Keagan appeared beside her. He spoke in a dead calm voice. "You'll be moving along now, boys. You won't be returning."

Without a word or backward glance, they scurried off.

Those boys never returned. Not a trace of graffiti ever appeared on her wall or the gate or the light pole or the dumpster. The neighbors' properties remained clean.

Those events cemented Keagan's role at the Casa. Liv hadn't asked for it, but she didn't mind. He wasn't obnoxious about it, and honestly, who wouldn't want an angel nearby? Or, as Inez called him, a knight? A little Clint Eastwood never hurt either.

On second thought, maybe she *had* asked for it. She'd complained enough about the Syd-shaped hole in her life, that male presence that complemented her role as a single female apartment manager. Voilà. Sean Keagan showed up on her doorstep one spring day.

Angel or not, he had earned the right to speak things she did not want to hear.

The stars flickered, above and below. Waves kissed the beach. Quiet beauty danced around her and eventually, slowly, it seeped inside.

She let go of his arm. She'd show him who had one foot in the grave. "Okay. Do you want to hear my side of the story?"

"Only if it might help."

"I'm scared, Sean." She seldom called him by his first name. He tolerated it from her, although she had the impression it carried sad memories for him. Still, at times like now, she desperately needed a son-type intimate more than an angel or a knight.

They walked several steps in silence.

Finally he said, "Of course you're scared. You experienced a lot of pain and a brush with death."

Silence built between them.

"Is there more?"

"No." She fidgeted. "Yes. What it's really about is losing control. About depending on others for the simple basics of preparing food and cleaning my home and walking across the courtyard and pulling my weeds. It's about feeling like God is so far away. So very, very far away."

He touched her elbow, steered her around, and they headed back toward the parking lot.

"Well," he said, "what can I say? Life is difficult."

"Yeah, and it stinks too."

He laughed. "At times."

Liv did not. "That's all you have for me?"

"Yes, Mama Liv, that's all either one of us has. Life is difficult and at times it stinks."

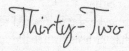

Thirty-Two

Jasmyn sat on a retaining wall. Below her feet lay mounds of boulders that protected a section of shoreline beneath the pier. The tide was low, leaving a stretch of beach and exposing barnacle-covered pilings. A steady stream of joggers and walkers paraded past her. Out in the water, surfers paddled toward the horizon, rode waves, were tossed off their board, and then started the process all over.

Filling in for Liv as a manager was coming easy for her. Even organizing last night's potluck—nowhere near her forte—had been a breeze. Of course, she knew how to serve people in a restaurant, but she had never ever entertained at home in her entire life. Having Quinn over for tuna-and-noodle casserole did not count.

But she wanted to express family support for Liv. She posed the WWLD question to herself. What she had seen Liv do was gather the residents together. The day Jasmyn first arrived, the annual Labor Day picnic was in progress, and Liv had been absolutely radiant. It was easy to see how much she adored her Casa family, how much it meant to have them all together.

And so Jasmyn decided to go way outside her comfort zone. Everyone had jumped on board at her suggestion, offering food and drink, promising to help set up and clean up. They obviously thought the world of Liv.

Reflecting on the evening, Jasmyn saw that the only downside was that the guest of honor had not exactly rallied for the occasion. There was no radiance or adoration coming from her. In fact, she'd even gone home early. Apparently, Jasmyn's efforts fell short of what Liv expected or wanted.

Maybe she wasn't cut out for managing an apartment complex. Not that it mattered. She would be leaving before too long.

"Don't worry about it."

Jasmyn jumped at the low voice in her ear and turned, coming almost nose to nose with Keagan.

He sat down, swung his legs over the wall, and faced the ocean. His profile revealed its usual deadpan expression.

She suspected he felt at least smidgens of emotion. After all, he had reached out for help from her, a stranger, because of his concern for Liv. He had even come to the potluck, a rare thing, according to Piper, for Liv's sake. And he had gone to the trouble of tracking down her luggage and retrieving it from his police friend, a kind gesture toward her.

But that set jaw of his and the dark sunglasses still threw her for a loop. She wasn't sure how to respond to him. Angel and knight talk were out of her realm.

If he were a customer at her table in the Flying Pig, she'd figure him for a drifter and a loner. He'd order the daily special—hold the sauce—and leave at least twenty percent. They would not make small talk because he would have his sunglasses off and he'd be looking at her with those intense peacock-blue eyes—more unnerving than the sunglasses—and her natural flow of small talk would dry up on the spot.

Then he would rev up his motorcycle, and within sixty seconds Valley Oaks would be a speck in his rearview mirror.

"What in the world are you talking about?"

"The potluck." He glanced at her and shrugged. "About Liv. It was a good party."

She stared at him, speechless.

"She didn't respond well. That's not your fault."

"Did I look like I was worried?"

"A little."

"I guess my timing was off. She wasn't ready to be cheered up."

"Liv is…how shall I put it? Independent to a fault sometimes. It's hard for fiercely independent people to have heart attacks and depend on others to cheer them up."

Jasmyn sighed. "Should I not even try?"

"Only if you resent her for it."

She looked at him. "Oh! I would never do that."

Beneath his sunglasses, his nose twitched and then his lips moved, quick as a flutter.

"Don't laugh. Really, I wouldn't."

He turned toward her. "I know you wouldn't, not on purpose. I wasn't laughing at you." He paused, as if he had something else to say, but the moment passed and he faced the ocean again.

Jasmyn studied his profile. He had a nice nose, slender and not overly long. He could have done with a shave. His hair hadn't seemed to grow one iota since they'd met almost two months ago. Maybe he shaved his head more often than his jaw. As usual, he wore athletic shoes, blue jeans, and a dark T-shirt—navy today—with faded lettering across the front, *Seaside Village Gym*, the name of the place he co-owned.

Why was she so silly about him? He wasn't scary. A little different maybe, a little odd, but thoughtful nonetheless.

His nose twitched again.

"So what are you laughing at?"

He didn't answer for a moment. At last he replied, "Your naïveté. Sorry. It's refreshing. Bottom line, Jasmyn Albright, you're doing a good job. Believe in yourself."

Naïveté? Refreshing? Good job? Believe in herself? Well…she had nothing to say.

They sat in silence. And after a while, the silence became comfortable.

Thirty-Three

From the passenger seat in Sam's car, Jasmyn watched the scenery zip by along the two-lane highway. Except for distant mountains, it was curiously similar to Illinois country: wide open, full of trees, rolling hills, cows and horses, little traffic.

She was so excited about her first visit to the desert that she could hardly sit still or stop jabbering about every tree they passed. "Sorry. I'm a little bouncy."

Sam glanced over, the scenery reflected in her sunglasses. "A little? That 'what would Liv do' business is nowhere in sight."

Jasmyn thought she heard teasing in her friend's tone, but she should probably give up trying to read Samantha Whitley. The only thing she understood for sure was that Sam most often resembled the big Jeep they rode in: dark, moody, and full of attitude, her interior concealed by tinted windows.

"You mean Liv wouldn't be excited about going to the desert with you?"

"She wouldn't be going in the first place." Sam scrunched her lips together and muttered under her breath, "Probably because I wouldn't invite her."

Jasmyn didn't bother to ask why. Sam was the most private person she had ever met. Jasmyn doubted she would invite anyone except maybe Chad. She hadn't exactly asked Jasmyn. "See, there's the difference between Liv and me. I didn't wait for an invitation. I barged my way in." She raised her voice to a falsetto. "'Sam! For real? You're going to the desert? I've never, *ever* been to a desert!' Hint, hint."

Sam smiled at her, a full-on, un-Sam-like smile. "No problem, as long as you don't need me to play tour guide. Besides, you needed a day off. You've been playing Liv for two weeks straight. Which, by the way, you do really well."

"I'm not so sure. I could keep the courtyard and laundry room clean in my sleep. The 'mama' part totally escapes me."

"You throw a pretty mean potluck, though. Very Mama Liv style."

Jasmyn felt her face blush. "I was so far outside my comfort zone."

"Really? You seemed like a natural, being all social butterflyish."

She laughed. "I guess it's similar to waitressing. But at the restaurant I'm only responsible for putting food on the table, not asking people to come to my place and then making sure they're comfortable. That's what Liv does so well. That's her 'mama' persona."

"Okay, no 'Mama Jasmyn' nickname. But honestly, the Casa would have fallen apart by now without you."

Two compliments from Sam? Quinn would tell Jasmyn to shut up and accept them. "Thanks."

"It's true. You're not Liv, but you are you and that's what we needed. Like a ray of sunshine. Hey, that fits your name, doesn't it? All bright."

Jasmyn groaned.

"You've been told that before."

"Once or twice."

Sam chuckled as she slowed the car and turned off the pavement onto a narrow dirt path.

They drove for several moments, up a hill, winding around boulders and low-lying bushes. The Jeep easily rumbled over rocks and crevices.

She braked and turned off the car. "Follow me."

The instant Jasmyn stepped outside, a sudden quiet hit her. It was physical enough to feel like hands clapping over her ears, deafening her.

She scrambled behind Sam on blond-colored dirt strewn with rock up a steep incline. Ahead she could only see its rim and above it the bluest of blue skies. She caught up to Sam at the top, saw beyond the rim, and gasped.

"Welcome to the desert, Jasmyn Albright."

The vista before them seemed larger than even the ocean. It stretched on and on and on. It was bigger than enormous. There were mountains in the distance painted in reds and browns and purples…boulders of all shapes and sizes scattered about like confetti…plants in gray-greens and browns, small and low to the ground. The highway looped like a thread in and out, behind and through it all.

Jasmyn exhaled. "Oh my gosh. I thought it would be…I don't know. Dull. I never imagined…" How could she have imagined? The desert was too vast and too beautiful for words.

"Next March this will be a carpet of flowers. The scents, unbelievable."

"Can we come?"

Sam chuckled. "Jasmyn, you can drive yourself here anytime you want. You saw how short and easy the route is."

"I could, couldn't I? I'll bring Liv. The ride would do her good. Maybe Tasha and her mom. Inez would enjoy it. Oh, Sam, thank you for showing this to me."

"You're welcome."

They stood for a while longer. Sam seemed to soak it in as much as Jasmyn did.

Jasmyn remembered how Sam had agreed the city felt confining, like a straitjacket. She wondered then why Sam didn't leave it more often. And if her home in Arizona was anything like this, why wouldn't she go back there, at least for visits.

Which begged the question, if Jasmyn also thought the city felt like a straitjacket, why would she dread going back to Valley Oaks and her beloved green fields?

She was dreading it.

But who needed to wonder about that right now? She was in the *desert*.

"Hey," Jasmyn said. "I thought you weren't going to play tour guide."

"I'm not. It begins and ends here. I just wanted you to see this." She pressed her lips together. She appeared to be having an emotional moment.

Sam? Emotional? Maybe she'd left dark and moody back in the car.

At last she spoke. "In all honesty, you know how it is to see something through someone else's eyes? It changes your perspective somehow. Things look brand new. Uncluttered." She paused. "I used to love the wilderness, but I'd lost sight of that. Today it's back. Thanks."

"Anytime." Jasmyn smiled. "You could return the favor. I used to love the cornfields and my hometown. Maybe if you came with me to Valley Oaks…"

"In your dreams."

"You could have ribs slathered in Danno's sauce."

"No, thanks. I hear it's cold there. Come on, I have to get to my meeting."

Jasmyn took one last gaze at the bigness and whispered, "Thank You."

It was what Liv would have done. And it felt good.

Thirty-Four

Sam stole a glance at Jasmyn as they drove past the highway sign that announced they had entered the Lotanzai Reservation. Jasmyn's face seldom disguised her feelings. Right now her eyebrows inched above her sunglasses, clearly suggesting some hesitation. It was an old reaction that Sam knew well.

She said in a solemn tone, "No need to worry, Jasmyn. They are a peaceful people these days."

"Oh, dear. How did you know? I didn't mean to— I'm sorry. The thing is, I watched one too many old Westerns with my grandpa."

"Indians were the bad guys."

"Exactly. We even found arrowheads on the farm to prove it." She groaned. "He was a difficult man."

Sam figured Jasmyn sugarcoated the truth about her grandfather the way she did most things. From the few hints Jasmyn had dropped, Sam imagined the old man was a misogynistic bigot who blamed his granddaughter for being born to his unwed daughter.

"Hey, Sam, can I ask you something personal?"

Sam decided to just go ahead and answer the question she assumed was on Jasmyn's mind. "Yes, I am an Indian."

"Now how did you know what I wanted to ask?"

"Because people have always asked me that. I legally changed my name from Whitehorse to Whitley after college and now they ask less. Apparently, I don't look Indian with a different name. I'm three-fourths Navajo."

"Really?"

Sam focused on the highway and the odometer, anticipating the unmarked road. She stuffed down familiar, ugly reactions. Things like, *Yeah I really am three-fourths Navajo. What of it?*

As a kid on the rez, she was defined by that one-fourth slice of non-Navajo heritage. As a college student off the rez, she was defined by the three-fourths. As an adult, she realized how much unwarranted shame had colored her world because of other people's reactions.

"You are the first one I've met."

"Something to write home about."

"I'm sorry." Jasmyn apologized often. "Am I being offensive?"

Sam sighed. In spite of her saccharine voice, Jasmyn was the most genuinely nice, wholesome person she had ever known. The woman would have to work at being offensive. "No, you're not. I'm just being my usual touchy self on the subject. So what do you think? Do I meet your expectations?"

"Well, you definitely dress better than the characters in the Westerns." She smiled.

"Seriously, Sam, in Valley Oaks we don't have much experience with other cultures. Ninety-nine point nine percent of us are descendants of Swedish farmers who came to America in the mid-1800s, married each other, and farmed."

Sam's mind's eye flashed to the faded photo she had of her grandmother, the grandmother with long blond hair and blue eyes. Her father's mother.

From the corner of her eye she saw the turnoff as they sailed past it.

"Nuts." She slowed, pulled off the side of the empty highway, and made a U-turn. "I missed the turn."

"The turn? We're in the middle of nowhere. How will people ever find this new hotel?"

"They'll go the front way, where a freeway and big signs for the turn-off into the town of Overland are located. I took this back route because it has the best wow effect for desert first-timers."

Jasmyn grinned. "Thanks."

"Yup." She slowed at the narrow, cracked asphalt road and turned. "The reservation covers about fifteen thousand acres. My grandmother was Swedish."

"Huh?"

Sam bit her lip. Those last words had slipped themselves into the conversation. She had nothing to do with it. Not even Randy had ever heard them, and she shared more with him than anybody.

"Swedish!"

Sam cleared her throat. "My father's mother. She died when I was a baby. I don't remember her at all."

"How…"

"Heart attack."

"I mean, how did she become your grandmother?"

Sam couldn't help but smile. "Jasmyn, let's save that talk for another time."

She laughed. "Not *that* talk."

"Oh! You mean how did she become my grandmother?"

"That's what I said."

Good grief. Sam was teasing and discussing her family. Jasmyn Albright was an atrocious influence.

"Hannah Susanne Carlson came to teach on the reservation in the 1940s and met my grandfather. Blah, blah, blah. They both died young, as did my father."

"Then you don't know much about them?"

Sam remembered the handful of stories she had heard as a child. "An elderly woman once told me that everyone adored Hannah. That she was a wonderful teacher and a kind person. I have no idea why she went to live with the Navajo."

"She needed to meet your grandfather so you could be born."

So she could be born? Sam tilted her head. What an odd comment.

"Trust me, Sam, I've thought a lot about these things. My mother never even knew my father's name. My heart has this spare room—oh, never mind. That's a long story. Where did Hannah come from?"

"Um, up north. Seems like it started with an 'I.' My dad told me when I was little. My mom refused to talk about his family."

"Illinois?"

"I don't know."

"Seriously? You don't?"

"I don't. Iowa, Idaho, Indiana. It doesn't matter."

"It's interesting, though. Why wouldn't your mom talk about it?"

Sam had asked her once. If she thought long enough about it, she could feel the sting on her sixteen-year-old cheek and hear the shrill voice. *You stupid girl, shut up!* "I figure Hannah and my mom did not get along for some reason. My mom is a difficult woman. She never said a nice thing about my dad. I don't know why she hooked up with him in the first place."

"There's only one explanation. Same one as why your grandmother stayed on the reservation. Your mom got together with your dad so you could be born."

"Come on, Jasmyn. That's ridiculous."

Jasmyn gave her a small smile. Enigmatic. A Liv-cloneish smile and attitude. "You never googled Hannah Susanne Carlson?"

"I did. Do you have any idea how many Carlsons there are in this country?"

"Yes. It's a good Swedish name. Half the people in Valley Oaks have a Carlson in their family tree." Then she giggled. "Who knows? We might be related."

ﾟ

The tribal council president's name was Deborah Brown. She was a stylish fiftysomething woman in a black business suit, a red silk blouse, and pearls. Her well-coiffed hair was short, thick, and black. She was intelligent and friendly.

She looked nothing like Sam's mother. She acted nothing like Sam's mother. There was no reason for Sam to react to her as if she were her mother. But she did.

Sam felt incompetent, ugly, stupid, and worthless. She hoped it wasn't showing.

"Randy." Deborah looked up from the sketches spread about the table where the three of them sat. "You didn't tell me your young associate was brilliant."

Randy shrugged. "What can I say? We keep Sammi out of sight. Can't have another firm hiring her away."

Deborah smiled and her whole face lit up. "The question is, what firm would it be? Evidently she's an engineer and an architect and probably has a host of other top-notch talents in her back pocket."

Sam squirmed in her seat. "I don't have a degree in architecture."

"I doubt that would matter." The woman gazed again at the drawings.

"Besides being more beautiful, your renditions flow better than the architect's. You've made a casino look like an extension of the landscape. It blends in like bighorn sheep camouflaged against the rocks and hills."

Randy caught Sam's attention and winked. He mouthed, *Told you.*

Deborah smiled at her again. "You said you drew these for fun?"

"Sort of." She made herself meet the woman's eyes. They were warm and caring. Her edginess dwindled and she softened her voice. "Yes. It's a hobby. They're not to scale; I don't have the skill. But…well, I couldn't help but take another look at the plans."

"Why is that?"

Sam still had a hard time explaining why, but she tried. "Because I wanted to take into account your history. I didn't find burial grounds or any environmental reasons to halt the project, but I highly suspect that this corner where you want to build is where your ancestors summered. Now you're going to welcome other people to come and play here. It seems a shame to obliterate the landscape any more than necessary."

"That's the most impractical thing I've ever heard."

"I know, right? And I'm one of the most practical people on the face of the earth."

Deborah's eyes were moist. "Me too. But this speaks to my heart."

Sam felt her own eyes burn, and she blinked quickly.

Randy hummed off tune. "Please don't tell anyone I was in on this conversation."

Deborah laughed. "I want to show these around. I'm sure the others will agree that we could ask the architects how much they can incorporate into what we already have on the table."

Sam resisted the urge to do a handspring.

They hashed out details. Although the new designs were Sam's creation, she wanted to give them to the professionals who could actually make plans that contractors could use to build. Randy insisted on some official paperwork that would give her credit. There was the question of fees.

They left Deborah in her office in the community center and made their way outdoors. Across the road they stopped beside Randy's car.

"Congratulations, Sam. I'm really proud of you."

She had no words, only a grin that wouldn't stop stretching across her face.

"You should celebrate."

She eyed the small town center, little more than a speed bump on a side road. There were some nondescript houses, a mobile home park, a school, a Laundromat, a gas station, a café. She assumed Jasmyn was nearby, probably with half a dozen new friends in tow. "I'll find my friend and we'll get some ice cream at the café."

Randy chuckled. "Be careful you don't overindulge."

"Actually, this whole thing doesn't feel real yet. I'm not sure what I'm supposed to do."

"Get used to it. You're gonna be a rock star. You should dress up and go to a fancy restaurant on the coast with a guy wearing a tie. Do you have one yet?"

"A guy in a tie?"

"Yeah."

"Nah. I don't have time for that."

He shook his head. "Give yourself a break, Sammi."

"But I love work. I'm fine."

Randy slipped on his sunglasses. "I'm going home to my wife, and we're going to make a list of all the eligible nice guys we know."

"Don't you dare."

He laughed and got in his car.

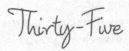

Thirty-Five

"But…" Jasmyn paused, unsure how to phrase her question.

The little woman seated in the pew beside her nodded as if she understood. From what Jasmyn had sampled of her wisdom in the past hour or so, she probably did understand.

They had met soon after Sam went into her business meeting, after Jasmyn finished wandering through the small town, which didn't resemble her small town in the least. There was no library, no pharmacy, and no post office, which were Valley Oaks staples. Few people were about in the middle of a hot weekday.

She had spotted a bell tower through a patch of trees, a white adobe Spanish-looking structure with arches and a tile roof. Next to it was a matching tiny church. A small sign read Mission San Pedro de Lotanzai, 1782. She peeked inside and saw an old woman sweeping the floor. The woman happily greeted her.

"Come, come." She gestured and propped her broom against the doorjamb. "The church is open."

As Jasmyn stepped out of the sun, between walls at least two feet thick and into the coolness, she felt transported. The place could have been a movie set for one of her grandfather's Westerns. It was dusky and had low wooden ceiling beams, simple pews on either side of the aisle, and little else. Several votive candles flickered from a table in a back corner near the door.

The best part, though, was the woman who introduced herself as Nova. She looked a little bit like a dried apricot trimmed with two silver gray braids, an embroidered white peasant blouse, a brown skirt, and a kind smile. Her voice was low, whispery, fitting for someone who obviously had been talking for many, many years.

Nova gave Jasmyn a tour of the church. It was, she explained, an *Assistencia*, or extension, part of the church's thrust inland from the main missions along the coast. For more than two hundred years, itinerant priests had conducted Sunday services, sometimes only once every other month. The one who came nowadays drove a Chevy truck and showed up every other week.

The tour over, they sat now on a hard pew, Nova's feet dangling above the uneven stone floor. The rough adobe walls were white, stenciled with colorful designs. Sunlight filtered through four stained glass windows, two in each of the side walls. Up front, beyond a rail, was a table, and behind that, high up on the wall, hung a large wooden crucifix.

Jasmyn admired Nova's ability to relay without bias a history that sounded basically like a long, hostile struggle between cultures and religions. The story upset Jasmyn. Which was why she was confused and could not frame a question tactfully. She gave up and said instead, "I wish I had your wisdom, Nova."

She chuckled. "I'm only ninety-two." She raised her arms high above her head and wiggled her fingers. "I've scarcely brushed the tips of the wise eagle's feathers."

Jasmyn smiled.

"There is time yet for you." She lowered her arms. "But to gain wisdom, you must ask the difficult questions."

Okay. Jasmyn nodded. *Ask it.* "The thing is, the history here is so awful, so tragic. I don't understand why this place hasn't been razed. Why would you revere where your ancestors were enslaved and forced to work for foreigners? Forced to claim a faith that had brought so much misery to them?"

Nova's dark eyes were depthless pools reflecting the candlelight behind Jasmyn. She laid a gnarled hand on Jasmyn's wrist. "Not everything can be explained. Through the years, many people experienced the reality of the Holy One. The ways of the church spoke to them despite their tragic history."

Jasmyn frowned.

"Forgiveness is a powerful tool." Nova spoke softly. "Life is a paradox,

Jasmyn. Have you walked the land where your ancestors walked out their story?"

Instantly she saw the farm. Her stomach flip-flopped. The farm's very first crop had been planted by her great-great-great-grandfather.

"Yes," she whispered.

"And have you sat in a room where they sat?"

Her heart raced. The farmhouse had been built by her great-great-grandparents. Her attic bedroom had at different times been a sewing room, a great-aunt's bedroom, and a distant cousin's temporary home when he came to help with the harvest.

"Mm-hmm."

"Heartbreak and joy, right? Both together. Never one without the other."

Jasmyn shut her eyes.

Hers had not been a storybook childhood in the least. And yet what had she known if not pure joy in that tiny room with its dolls and its view of stars and cornfields, where no one disturbed her? Or in the rambling woods? And even on the tractor she learned to drive at age nine?

Nova patted her arm and straightened. "I am an old woman. Someday this place will no longer speak to anyone except the ones who love olden days. And that is all right. These days the church needs air-conditioning and microphones."

Jasmyn opened her eyes. "It wasn't my choice to raze it. A tornado destroyed it."

Nova stared at her.

"My home. Mine and my family's, all the way back to my great-great-grandparents."

"Jasmyn, I am sorry."

"But then I sold the land."

Nova nodded. "Because it no longer spoke to you."

Jasmyn shrugged.

"Do you have siblings? Or children?"

"No."

"And it was a tornado?"

"Yes."

Nova did not respond for a long moment. "Then you can trust it was time to let it go." She pulled a handkerchief from a skirt pocket and dabbed Jasmyn's cheeks. "I haven't used it." She smiled.

"I'm sorry. I don't know why I'm crying."

"You cry because you have a sad story. Don't worry. Joy will weave its way through it in time. Would you like to pray?"

Jasmyn stifled a sob. Hot tears fell. Her body shook.

Nova knelt on the stone floor. "No air-conditioning, no microphones, no padded kneelers. How in the world do we keep going?" She giggled to herself, made the sign of the cross, and, with arms propped on the pew in front of her, buried her face in her hands.

The quiet enveloped Jasmyn as it had outdoors, at the entrance to the desert, a hush so loud it nearly hurt her ears.

Her tears subsided. Her breathing returned to normal.

She was still working on her Liv-style prayer, walking and talking to God in the courtyard, eyes open. Kneeling on a stone floor with her face buried in her hands seemed an odd way to pray. Maybe a little over-the-top.

The hush pressed in on her again. It pressed away the sad stories, Nova's and her own. It pressed her to her knees.

And she knelt there in a wordless, nameless embrace.

The scenery whizzed past them as they flew along the freeway. Sam jabbered, excited about her meeting. Jasmyn nodded and smiled.

"Good grief! We've switched roles. I'm talking and you're not," Sam said. "Tell me what you've been doing."

"Um. Well. I'm not sure exactly." And then, just like heat lightning that flashed across the sky back home, it came to her.

She had been meeting the Holy One.

And oh, how He loved her!

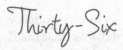

Thirty-Six

On the drive home from the desert, when Jasmyn had echoed Randy's suggestion that a special dinner was in order, Sam surprised herself and agreed. After all, it was happy news and friends celebrated happy news, right? They let someone else cook and even serve them at a table in a restaurant near the coast.

Now they sat at a table in a restaurant near the coast. It wasn't exactly what Sam had imagined.

Not because the table was long and covered with a linen cloth. Not because it was on a veranda, under a trellis, warmed by propane heaters, and lit by fake candles and patio lights. Not because a mariachi band strolled by, singing and playing festive music. Not even because others had joined them. Of course Jasmyn had invited others, phoning them from the car on their way to the city. And of course some came…Liv, Inez and Louis, Riley and Tasha, and Chad.

Nope. It wasn't any of those things that tied her brain into a pretzel.

It was because of the guy in a tie.

What was going on? First Jasmyn channeled Randy. Then Beau Jenner showed up, wearing a tie and looking nothing like the guy in a *Fix-It Jenner* work shirt, cap, and blue jeans.

"Miss Sam." He handed her a single red rose wrapped in white tissue paper. "Congratulations for the spectacular accomplishment you made today. I do apologize for my tardiness." He pulled out the chair across from her. There were two vacant chairs at the other end.

"It wasn't spectacular." She laid the rose next to her plate. "I sketched some buildings. The right people liked them. Not a big deal."

"You're an artist too?"

Her eyelids fluttered. She had no control over them.

From the other end of the table, Chad called out to Beau. "Hey, dude!" He touched the neck of his T-shirt where a tie would have gone. "Nice."

Beau gave him a thumbs-up and opened his menu. "What do y'all like here?"

Sam used to like the taco salad with chicken. She tuned out the chatter. What had she been thinking to agree to this? She wasn't good at chit-chat, at celebrating, at camaraderie. She wasn't all that good at being civil.

She most certainly was not good at keeping her cool while sitting across the table from an overly well-mannered, rose-giving, eye-twinkling guy wearing brown slacks, a robin's egg-blue shirt, a tie in spring green with blue dots, and some very pleasant cologne.

Thirty-Seven

Swell. Jasmyn tore her gaze from Sam at the other end of the table and picked up a fish taco from her plate.

That makes two for two. Apparently, she was not all that good at planning parties to honor someone. Liv's potluck last week had prompted only polite smiles from the woman. And right now, Sam was obviously not enjoying her celebration at all.

Earlier, Jasmyn had spotted a genuine smile or two. But then, in two whisks of a squirrel's tail, her friend had shrunk back into her turtle shell. What happened?

Sam had agreed to the dinner out. She'd agreed to the casual restaurant. She had even agreed—after a slight hesitation—to inviting Casa folks. She'd agreed to sharing the fact that she'd received extraordinarily good feedback on her work, but the details were not to be discussed. Jasmyn's lips were sealed. Sam did not want to invite her boss and his wife. Fine with Jasmyn.

So what was with the furrowed brow aimed now at Beau?

Jasmyn wished Keagan were there. The angel could decipher the problem, or at least remind her it was not her fault.

Okay, it was not her fault. Nor was it her responsibility to fix it. Maybe Mr. Fix-It Jenner could do that. He looked as if he could fix just about anything in that dress shirt and tie. Pipes, wires, lonely hearts.

Liv touched her arm. "Jasmyn, dear, what a delightful celebration!"

She swallowed her bite. "Really?"

"Yes. It's wonderful to make people feel special like this." She leaned closer and whispered, "Especially us single people. Who else is going to do it?"

Hmm. Unsure how to respond, Jasmyn watched Liv scoop a forkful of salad, the dinner Jasmyn had convinced her to order rather than the one she wanted: a deep-fried chimichanga with cheese, sour cream, and guacamole.

Since that morning at the reservation, a phrase from the old woman Nova had been on repeat play. Now it replayed once again. *To gain wisdom, you must ask the difficult questions.* Okay. She needed to ask Liv why the potluck had been a bad idea. But that seemed too in-your-face. Maybe she could ask it and skirt it at the same time.

"Liv," she whispered, "Sam doesn't appear to be feeling special."

"I noticed. Some people don't like attention."

"I shouldn't have invited others."

"Maybe not. But it may be that she's resisting the warm-fuzzies rush. It can be hard to handle. Stubborn old ladies who resent heart attacks behave in a similar manner." She winked, a slow, obvious lowering of one eyelid over the blue eye behind the large silver-rimmed glasses. "I truly appreciated the potluck, dear." She turned to Chad across the table from them. "May I have one tiny little bite of your chimichanga?"

Jasmyn chided. "Liv."

"Just a little." She sliced an end off of Chad's stuffed tortilla and put it on her plate. "Just one teensy, itsy-bitsy bite."

Chad took back his plate. "It's half gone." Holding out the plate, he spoke to the others. "Anybody else want what's left of my dinner?"

Louis accepted his offer.

The bantering began and Jasmyn turned to Liv. "You sound like your old self again."

"Oh, dear. Is that a good thing?"

"You know it is."

"I hope so. But I don't want to completely be my old self again. I may have learned a thing or two through the ordeal."

"Are you up for managing again?"

"I believe so." She sighed and folded her hands on her lap. "I wish you didn't have to leave in two weeks."

Ten days, Jasmyn silently corrected. Who wanted to count out loud?

After dinner, Jasmyn and Sam strolled along a crowded sidewalk toward the Jeep parked several blocks away, past boutique and souvenir shops still open in the late evening to cater to ever-present tourists.

If Sam were Quinn, Jasmyn imagined they would pop in and out of stores, giggle over the silly things, drool over the chic clothing, and buy chocolate and refrigerator magnets. It was the sort of thing they did in the mall at Rockville, Illinois, population fifty-two thousand.

Not so with cool Sam. From the looks of her tailored clothes, she probably shopped in that one store at the mall geared toward businesswomen. She wouldn't give these places a second glance.

"Jasmyn." Sam cleared her throat. "I, um, thank you for dinner. You didn't have to buy mine."

"Yeah, I did. Consider it thanks for the desert trip and congratulations on your work."

"Okay."

"You're welcome. I'm sorry if I pushed you into having all those people there."

"Don't apologize for doing something nice."

"But you didn't have a good time."

"I had a fine time."

"Come on." Jasmyn pointed at the plastic container in Sam's hand. "You didn't eat a fourth of your dinner."

"Why would you notice what I ate?"

"Didn't eat."

"Whatever. You're acting like Liv more and more."

"I'll take that as a compliment." Jasmyn nudged her. "Really, tell me what was wrong about tonight. I don't want it to happen again."

"Nothing was wrong. I have social issues, that's all."

"Yeah. You should get over that."

Sam snickered.

Progress. Jasmyn smiled. The whole day and evening had been progress until Sam went quiet at the table. It was as if she crawled back behind that wall she kept up, that fortress. Things were fine until after the food had been served— "Oh my gosh!" Jasmyn said. "You have a problem with Beau."

"No, I don't."

Jasmyn burst out laughing. Sam's answer had been way too quick. "You got all quiet after he came."

"I did not."

"Did too."

"Jasmyn! Good grief!"

She whispered, "Did too."

"If I got quiet after he came, it was because he monopolizes every conversation. I didn't know you invited him."

"Chad did."

Sam exhaled what sounded like a big lump of frustration.

"Hey," Jasmyn said. "Beau brought you a rose. Where's the rose?"

"I guess I left it at the table."

"Aw, Sam."

"It was over-the-top. He's over-the-top. Miss this and Miss that. Please and thank you and my Granny Mibs and all that homespun Kentucky jibber jabber."

"Jibber jabber?"

"Yeah."

Jasmyn giggled. "He knows how to push your buttons."

"He's obnoxious."

"He looked good in a tie."

"Nobody wears a tie for casual dining in San Diego."

"He's flirting."

Sam whipped around to face her, so abruptly Jasmyn thought she'd lose her balance. "He is not."

"He might be."

Sam faced forward again and they crossed a street, the parking lot within sight.

Jasmyn wondered what Sam had against flirting. Hadn't she ever dated anyone? Or fallen in love? Or had a crush on someone?

Jasmyn sighed. She refused to end the evening on such a note. She grasped Sam's elbow and steered them both back toward the shops. "Let's get some chocolate. I saw chocolate truffles in a window back there."

"I don't eat chocolate truffles."

"Mm-hmm. Maybe we'll get some refrigerator magnets too."

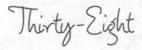

Thirty-Eight

Standing beside the trickling fountain, in shadows cast by the patio lights, Liv clasped her hands together and raved about the dinner to Keagan. "It was lovely."

"That explains why you feel well enough to make your nightly rounds." He turned toward his cottage. "Don't overdo it."

Liv watched him walk away and called out, "Jasmyn fits in perfectly, don't you think?"

He didn't even look back. A moment later he opened his door and disappeared inside.

Liv smiled. He knew what she was talking about.

Jasmyn added a lovely spark to the Casa. Liv noticed that Keagan noticed because although he had skipped the restaurant gathering earlier that evening, he had attended the potluck last week, a rare occurrence.

Samantha was touched too. To think that Jasmyn had spent the entire day with her, that Samantha had told her about some work accomplishment, that Jasmyn had thrown together a festive dinner and Samantha came, that they weren't home yet because they must be out enjoying life— Well, that all said a lot.

If Liv polled the Casa family, she was certain they would all agree that Jasmyn was a perfect fit.

Of course she was. "Because You brought her to us, didn't You, Abba? And my old lady biological clock seems to have stopped its incessant ticking. Unless that was just my heart acting up."

Smiling, she slid a cushioned chair out from a patio table and sat to enjoy the night's beauty. The damp coastal air enhanced every fragrance the courtyard offered, a heady mix of floral, pine, eucalyptus, cedar mulch, and plain old dirt. The patio lights cast a soft glow over it all. Solar lamps in the ground lit pathways to the cottages.

She heard Jasmyn and Samantha before she saw them. Jasmyn's infectious giggle was at full volume—which was never very loud—and then, wonder of wonders, Samantha's low chuckle escalated into a burst of laughter.

They emerged from the back gate area, spotted her, and walked over.

"Liv!" Jasmyn sat on a chair beside her. "You're up awfully late."

"For an invalid. I'm not an invalid anymore."

Samantha stood before them and thrust a fist in the air. "Yesss! Mama Liv is back."

Liv stared at her.

Jasmyn laughed. "Way to be excited, Sam."

"It's the sugar. Liv, she made me eat truffles." Samantha slapped a hand to her mouth and her eyes grew wide.

Jasmyn said, "Oops."

Samantha lowered her hand. "We would have bought some for you, but, you know, it's not on your diet. We did get a magnet for you, though."

Jasmyn dug into a shopping bag, pulled out a small sack, and handed it to her. "For your fridge. It says 'I *heart* Seaside Village.' The heart's supposed to remind you to take care of yours."

Liv took out a square magnet and chuckled. "Aren't you ladies thoughtful?"

"No," Samantha said. "We just felt guilty about the truffles. Speaking of which, the sugar crash is coming." She yawned. "Good night all." She turned and walked toward her cottage.

Jasmyn called out, "See you tomorrow, BFF."

Samantha waved over her shoulder.

Jasmyn whispered to Liv, "Do you think that was too much, the BFF part?"

"Best Friend Forever?" Liv smiled. "Yesterday, I would have said yes, but she's different tonight. The way she teased just now was simply amazing. I haven't heard her say a silly word in four years."

"We had such a great time today. She really loosened up."

"She's always so tense. I worry she's going to pop."

"Exactly. I think she has a lot of hurt inside. Are we gossiping?"

"Not quite. We're both concerned for her well-being." She squeezed Jasmyn's arm. "I must say that organizing the dinner for her was a stroke of genius."

"I'm so glad you think so. Is it what you would've done?"

"No. She's always been a puzzle to me. I love on her the best I can, make her soup or whatnot, and encourage her with words, but I never have had a clue how to honor her and include our family in on it. Only a BFF could've done what you did."

"It just came to me out of the blue, this wild idea to treat her to dinner. She was a little reluctant about inviting others, but I told her you and Chad especially would want to celebrate her accomplishment. Whatever it is." She grinned and leaned closer. "I think Beau has a crush on her."

"Really?"

"Really. And she was not happy about him being there. Not one bit."

"Hmm. Maybe the crush goes both ways?"

"Maybe. They're total opposites."

"Now we are gossiping."

"Yes, we are. But it's a fun thought. Love makes the world go round, right?"

"Right." Liv smiled. What was going on? Jasmyn's sweet voice sounded sweeter, more melodious than usual. The air positively shimmered with her bubbly energy.

There was more behind such happiness than chocolate truffles alone. Had something happened in the desert?

"Tell me about your day. All I've heard is that you loved the desert."

"Oh, Liv, I was in absolute awe of it. It's simply magnificent. It's so huge. Huger than cornfields. And Overland, the town on the reservation, is just a speck in the middle of all that hugeness, but it was…" She grew pensive. "Well." She turned to Liv. "It was magnificent too."

Ah. Now they were getting to it.

Jasmyn described her visit in great detail. By the time she finished telling her about the mission church and an old woman named Nova and the feel of a stone floor beneath her knees, Liv's cheeks were damp with tears.

Jasmyn wiped her own eyes. "I've been thanking God for things lately. I wasn't sure He was listening until now."

Liv nodded. "Jasmyn, dear, you experienced a thin place."

"What's a thin place?"

"Where the walls of this world go blurry and we get a glimpse of something Other. 'Other' with a capital *O*."

Jasmyn stared at her. "That was it."

"You never know where or when you'll stumble into one. Maybe in a church, maybe in Walmart. And what's thin for someone might be thick for someone else." She grasped Jasmyn's hand and gave it a gentle squeeze. "This was a gift especially for you."

They sat in silence for several moments. Except for the sound of the trickling fountain, the air was hushed.

Jasmyn breathed out a long sigh. "Love does make the world go round." She leaned over and kissed Liv's cheek. "Thank you."

Liv watched her walk under the jacaranda tree strung with tiny lights, past the bird-of-paradise, between the potted geraniums and mums, and to the grape-purple door of Eleven. Her heart, that thing she needed to take care of, felt ready to burst with gratitude.

Jasmyn knew she was loved. What more could Liv have asked for her? Nothing surpassed the mysterious heart knowledge that the Creator was within her and without, making the world go round.

Thirty-Nine

Midnight. Wide awake. Staring at the bedroom ceiling.

Sam groaned.

Beau Jenner was flirting?

"No way."

Would she even recognize flirting?

"Nope."

And what if she did? What was she supposed to do about it? Flirt back?

"Yeah, right."

She wasn't sure what that looked like either.

If she was brutally honest with herself—and it seemed a night for brutal honesty—she'd had a few crushes through the years. A few. Three to be exact.

There was the boy in high school, smarter than she was, a loner like she was. A perfect match. Except he was, unbelievably, more socially awkward than she was. They never attempted to have a conversation. Not a hello passed between them before they parted ways, he to Harvard, she to UCLA. She imagined that he had become a researcher. He would probably find a cure for cancer someday.

She met similar guys in college, brilliant and backward. Two relationships had progressed beyond *hello* and she enjoyed conversing with them about engineering. She even had coffee with one a few times and studied with the other before finals. They both dated bubbly chatterboxes who didn't know the first thing about the application of the mechanics of equilibrium to force systems, let alone the fundamentals of chemical reactions, kinetics of biochemical systems, or ion exchange.

Sort of like Jasmyn. Her BFF.

Sam grimaced.

She'd never had a best friend, girl or boy. She had acquaintances who generally did not giggle or do meaningless activities like buy refrigerator magnets. She gave those acquaintances the time of day probably because she did not do those things either.

And why was that? Besides the fact that those activities were silly. Was it because no one had included her in those things? Not that she'd ever been exactly approachable. Who purposely approached a porcupine?

Besides Jasmyn. She was different, enough of a fruitcake to ignore Sam's exterior.

Sam smiled. Okay. To some small degree, she had enjoyed herself that evening, not counting the time between Beau's arrival and departure. Liv, Inez, and Louis came to the dinner because they were nice people. Chad came for the food. Riley was a standoffish mystery who had her hands full raising Tasha by herself. She must have been desperate for company. And Tasha…

Tasha had hugged Sam, long and hard, and said *Congratulations.* That was a first. Everybody got Tasha hugs except Sam. Sam wouldn't dare hug Sam. Why would a little girl approach a porcupine?

That hug had felt indescribably good. So good, in fact, Sam had hugged her back.

Okay, when all was said and done, maybe she was on the verge of accepting friendly overtures, of joining the human race. Liv and Inez were not going away. Jasmyn would be there for a short while longer. Maybe she'd come back to visit. If her BFF wanted to go for a run or occasionally do something silly, Sam might be amenable to it.

Beau, on the other hand, was a no-go. That fish out of water feeling she experienced around him was…well, it was unsettling. Disorienting. She would simply ignore him. He would lose interest. Life would continue.

Sam flipped onto her side. Then she flopped onto her other side.

It was going to be a long night.

Forty

Jasmyn's boss called her Friday morning. It was their first chance to have a good long talk, and she filled him in on much more than he probably cared to hear about.

But Danno laughed his gruff bark at her stories. "It sounds like you're having the time of your life, Jasmyn."

She smiled. For the hundred millioneth time she wished the man was her dad. He had been a part of her life since she was a teenager, if only from the edges.

"Danno, I'm so grateful for you."

"Ditto, girl." He paused. "You know, I'd tell you if there was any chance at all we're related." He referenced her old wish, which she had said aloud to him once in an ooey-gooey gush after he'd attended her high school graduation ceremony. "I could have handled you being my daughter. You're a wonderful young woman."

Tears filled her eyes. "Thanks."

"As a matter of fact, you encouraged the wife and me so much with your extended stay out there that we're gonna follow in your footsteps. Except to Florida, not California."

"You're taking a vacation?"

"Nah, we're going whole hog. We're retiring and moving to warmer climes. Florida's warmer than where you are."

"Wow. That's...that's, uh, great."

"You think the Flying Pig is going under and we have to pull out and it's all your fault."

"Um, yeah. Basically." If she hadn't sold her land to those developers who were building businesses to take business away from Valley Oaks businesses—

"Jasmyn, it's not your fault. Technically, I'm old enough to retire. I'm overdue. And the restaurant will go on without me if someone buys it."

"But who would sign up for, you know…" She was on the verge of tears.

"Like I said, not your fault. People who want a McRib, they're taking care of a snack attack. They stop in at the new place, get a fix. That's not going to make or break the Pig. Now, this is between you and me. I have people interested in buying it."

"You do?"

"Yeah. But selling to two local guys wasn't my original plan." He cleared his throat. "I mean, they'll do all right. One has a business degree. They're young and gung ho. But I hoped you'd take it over someday."

"Me?"

"Yeah. You've worked here the longest. You have a head for the restaurant business and a heart for the customers. You'd be perfect."

Blinking no longer kept the tears at bay.

"It's easy to understand why that woman Liv thinks you're the cat's pajamas as her temporary manager."

Danno was paraphrasing what Jasmyn had told him. She swallowed. "When did you come up with this idea?"

"You were about eighteen." He chuckled. "Been a while."

"You never said anything."

"It wasn't the right time."

"Because I didn't have money and now I do?"

"Nope. Money has nothing to do with it. I would've worked something out so you could afford it and I'd still do it that way." He paused again. "The truth is, I didn't want to hold you back. You needed to get out of Valley Oaks, spread your wings and fly a little, build up some confidence."

She wiped at her cheeks. "I never fit in back there."

"You did so. You just never thought you did because your life was hard here. I understand." He exhaled. "Anyway, you should hear the customers. They're griping more than usual. Quinn has a fit when they tell her, 'Jasmyn would have done it this way. Jasmyn would have done it that way. Jasmyn never wrote down an order and always got it exactly right.' Blah, blah, blah. I swear, you've kept more people coming back here than the sauce."

He had said such things in the past, but he was famous for embellishing the truth.

"So anyhoo, those other guys aren't ready to commit just yet, and I told them I wasn't either, not before Christmas. I wouldn't expect you to buy it outright. We'd do a long-term deal. No pressure, Jasmyn. Just maybe something to consider."

Something to consider? Was he off his rocker? She was a waitress!

"Hey, don't let this mess with your head. It might not be what's best for you. You'll want to think long and hard about it. Hear me?"

"I hear you."

"And, well, I just wanted you to know how much I think of you."

They didn't exactly blubber through their goodbyes, but almost.

Jasmyn couldn't focus on anything except Danno's news.

She walked the four blocks down to the beach and trudged across it to the hard-packed sand at the water's edge, her thoughts far removed from eucalyptus trees and wind-whipped whitecaps.

Since the tornado, her life had been a series of hasty actions. From the moment her home disappeared, she had been caught up in a whirlwind herself, making snap decisions. Live with Quinn—sleep on her couch. Buy the first jacket and jeans she touched in the store—wrong sizes, ugly colors. Take the first available apartment—cramped, smelly. Sell the land—tell Zeb Swanson, who didn't want to buy it, that this year's corn was his last in her fields. Take a vacation—to someone else's favorite place.

There had been a short restful lull in San Diego, but then came the stolen rental car, and she fell right back into the whirlwind. Sleep here, wear this, do whatever a virtual stranger invited her to do. Don't get on the plane.

But...she smiled. Hadn't that last decision led to two weeks of bliss? Filling in for Liv. Feeling more like a Casa resident than a visitor. Seeing the desert. Getting to know everyone better, especially Sam. Getting to know God.

In the long run, not getting on the plane hadn't been a bad choice.

Now, with Danno's plans, the wind began to swirl around her again. She felt as if she were being turned inside out. Her heart thumped, a big bass drum keeping time with a Sousa march.

Very soon she would be going back to yet another upheaval. Danno already had one foot out the door. What was that called? A lame duck. He wouldn't matter all that much anymore.

New owners would matter. They might not keep her on. She might not want to stay on. If she bought the place— Well, that was totally beyond reason. What did she know about managing anything?

Jasmyn walked long and hard. The weather had turned chilly. The sky was a low-hanging, pewter gray canopy. She wished she had put on a heavier jacket. The denim one—yet another silly purchase—was too light. Oh, wait. She didn't *have* a heavier jacket. Did she have one back home?

Home. And where exactly was that?

No home. No job. What a mess! She needed to bounce her thoughts off someone. Not Liv, she was too emotional, too close. Same with Sam.

You call Keagan. Those were Inez's words. *When we women need rescue, he always come. He is our knight.*

Keagan? But she didn't need rescuing, just a friendly ear, maybe a word or two that would help her see things more clearly. He seemed to have a knack.

Jasmyn frowned. Maybe that added up to rescuing. The term didn't necessarily mean she was a damsel in distress. She would really truly dislike wearing that name tag. *Sunshine* was bad enough.

Zigzagging through a maze of short blocks, she made her way from the beach to the business area, a hodgepodge of beach culture and small-town flavor. The district was so homey that if it were plopped down in Valley Oaks, no one would notice.

Except for a few things, such as the large bubbly fountain on one corner, the movie theater on another, the touristy shops in between. And except for the fact that Seaside Village covered several blocks instead of two. And that there were palm trees and flowerbeds full of blossoms even now in mid-October.

But, like her hometown, there were restaurants, hair salons, barbershops, a post office, bank, market, and pharmacy. Everything anyone needed sat right there.

Also like her town, there was a gym. Keagan owned this one, or co-owned it. It was located on one of the side streets. Liv had pointed it out once.

Jasmyn had no idea what his work schedule was. From what she had observed of his comings and goings, he didn't have one. Because she hadn't seen him around the Casa earlier, she might as well give the gym a try.

The sign painted on the glass door read simply *Seaside Village Gym* with the hours printed underneath. She pulled the door open, a small bell jingled, and she stepped into an unpleasant memory: PE class and the locker room. Her nose twitched involuntarily.

A buff young woman in black spandex smiled from behind a counter. "May I help you?"

"Hi. I'm looking for Keagan."

"Who isn't?" She laughed. "That man has perfected the disappearing act. May I help you?"

As the woman eyed her, Jasmyn sank into another memory, one of feeling intensely uncoordinated, not good enough, and embarrassed at being the last in her class to need to wear a bra.

Her heart started up its Sousa rhythm again and it wasn't from the brisk walk. "No thanks. We're, uh, neighbors, and I just wanted, uh, to, uh— He's not here then?"

"Nope."

"Okay, thanks." She pushed open the door and its bell jingled again as it swished shut behind her.

What in the world was she doing? Keagan was totally out of her league.

She stopped in her tracks. *Seriously?*

Well, in all honesty, yes, *seriously*.

She was really and truly concerned about her and Keagan's leagues. *Uh-oh.*

Jasmyn looked up at the gray sky and shook her head. She was foolish. A nobody from Valley Oaks and a Southern California hotshot? *No way.*

She hurried along, weaving in and out of other people on the sidewalk. She neared the library, a large white stucco building with a spacious courtyard dotted with benches. Not exactly Midwest architecture. Another thing that would stand out.

Okay, Seaside Village could not be dropped into Valley Oaks unnoticed.

She had been silly about a lot of things. At least some good news came out of it. If she were attracted to Keagan, it meant that what's-his-name was history. Actually, she could probably even say the name of what's-his-name out loud and not feel nauseous.

"Nick Bloome."

She pressed her stomach. So far, so good.

Nick had been everything she could have wanted in a husband, but after eighteen months of lovey-dovey he declared she was not what he wanted in a wife. And oh, by the way, he had found someone who was. And, oh yeah, she was pregnant with his baby.

History.

Which she was not about to repeat in any way, shape, or form by paying attention to that annoying feather that fluttered in her chest whenever she saw Keagan. *Sean* Keagan. She had seen his first name in Liv's files.

Not paying the feather any attention was easier said than done because there he sat on one of those benches outside the library, his nose in a book, sunglasses atop his head.

And the feather tickled away. She swallowed and kept walking. There were several people between them, standing, talking, and walking. She would pass by and he wouldn't even notice—

He looked up.

Maybe he simply unnerved her. That sixth sense or whatever it was that told him to look up or show up at fluky moments was just plain weird. Not to mention the gaze that made her wonder if food was stuck in her teeth. Then there was the kung fu aspect. She swore the air shimmered with energy that said *You don't want to mess with me.*

Or…it shimmered with the unfolding of the safety net he pulled out of the blue for damsels in distress. Like now.

And she stood twenty feet away.

It was a huge net.

He gestured at the empty seat beside him. An invitation.

She accepted.

He moved to one side of the bench. "Have a seat."

She sat. "Hi." On a typical day, she would have asked about the book he was reading. Typical got lost two blocks back.

"What's up?"

"Um, nothing really." She hesitated. Liv would say their meeting was not a coincidence. Hadn't Jasmyn decided to talk to him? "But I was wondering...um, I mean, do you mind..."

"I don't mind." He shut the book. "What do you need?"

"A listener?"

"Is that a question?"

"No." She squared her shoulders. "I need someone to listen, and not like Liv or Quinn or Sam would. They're too, I don't know, emotionally involved."

"You think I fit the bill." A statement, a half smile. Or more like a quarter of a smile.

She gave him her own quarter of a smile. He totally fit the bill of not emotionally involved. "The thing is, I just found out my boss is retiring. He'll either sell the restaurant or close it down." The words began to flow more easily. "Which means I'm going home to major work changes, maybe even to no job within a couple months. I'm going home to no place to live. I mean, the ugly studio apartment doesn't count. Not really. Not that I can't find a better place. But life feels so chaotic, so up in the air."

"Probably because it is."

She blew out a breath. "I'm getting tired of up in the air."

"It makes walking with two feet on the ground difficult."

"What do I do about it?"

"What can you do?"

"I don't have a clue."

"Let me ask this. What is there to do besides go back and do whatever it is you have to do to get on with life there?"

"Not go back?" She met his eyes and something passed between them. She couldn't say what it was, but it seemed real. And a little bit awkward.

"Is that a question?"

"No. Sorry. I'm a little iffy today."

"You're vulnerable."

"That too. Anyway, *not* going back to Valley Oaks isn't really an option. I don't have a job here. My home is there. I mean, my roots are there. People don't uproot themselves to turn a vacation spot into their permanent place of residence."

"Is that a statistic you read somewhere?"

"No. It's just not done."

"Think outside the box. What else don't people do?"

She thought of Danno's ridiculous proposal. "People like me don't buy restaurants, even though my boss offered to sell it to me and make it work somehow financially."

Keagan's eyebrows went up and right back down. "That is outside the box. Why did he offer to do that?"

"He thinks I know the business and could do it. I think he's an old softy who hopes his dream doesn't die when he retires to Florida, and I've been there the longest."

"Can you imagine yourself doing it? What would it be like?"

"A huge responsibility. Danno taught me everything he knows. He's like Liv that way. But I couldn't do it alone. Quinn's the best waitress and my best friend since kindergarten. I'd want her for a partner. We would need a chef because neither one of us can cook. The place needs redecorating. I'd fire at least two of the wait staff and hire teenagers and teach them to do it right."

"You've thought about this."

"Only this very minute."

"What's the downside?"

"Quinn is a flake—lovable but a flake nonetheless—and folks might boycott the place because they're still mad that I sold my farm to a developer and then I'd lose the money I made from that deal."

"The upside?"

She shrugged. "I'd have a job?"

Keagan did not agree or disagree. And as usual, there were no clues in his body language as to what went on inside of him.

Kind of like a wall, which made him a perfect sounding board.

"You want to factor in the rest of your life," he said. "Whether or not Valley Oaks offers the real stuff you need, like family, friends, community, significant other."

Jasmyn felt a flush of embarrassment. Why did it cut so deeply all of a sudden? She had easily shared hurtful things with Sam and Liv, admitting that she'd never felt part of the Valley Oaks community, that there was no special guy, that her dad had never been in her life.

"There's no family. None. Not much in the way of community outside of the restaurant, and there is definitely no significant other since—oh, never mind. There just really isn't anyone except Quinn. Sad, huh?"

"It's life. But I am surprised the CIA hasn't contacted you yet."

She smiled.

"Do you want your listener to render an opinion?"

She'd prefer a shoulder to cry on. "Sure."

He studied her face for a long moment, as if wondering whether or not to believe she wanted to hear his opinion. "Conventional wisdom says not to make a major change within the first year after a traumatic incident."

Tears stung. "But," she whispered, "I need a home and job security like yesterday."

He nodded. "Throws a monkey wrench into the mix, doesn't it? There's always the advice to take two aspirin and drink plenty of liquids."

She frowned.

"What? You wanted real answers?"

"Maybe."

"Sleep on it, Jasmyn. Things will look better tomorrow."

"It's not even noon."

"Another monkey wrench." He smiled.

He smiled a full-on smile.

That smile wrapped around Jasmyn like strong arms lifting her up off of a rock-strewn road and setting her on a horse. A white horse. A steed. She leaned back against a solid wall of armor.

Uh-oh.

Uh-oh indeed.

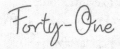

Forty-One

Late Friday afternoon, Keagan knocked on the door of Cottage Eleven, a deep violet-blue windbreaker over his arm, a youth size. They didn't carry women's petite sizes at the gym. They did carry the blue that matched her eyes.

He was thinking way too much about Jasmyn Albright's size and eye color. And poking his nose into her business way too much. A significant other? Had he honestly said those words?

Life had been less complicated when he only noticed her bubbly personality and how much she helped Liv.

The door opened and there she was, the color of her eyes intensified by tears. She was having a rough day.

He steeled himself. That was how one survived the bad guys as well as good women who might exit the scene with his heart in their back pocket.

He cleared his throat. "Need a listener?"

She smiled and shook her head as she wiped her nose with a tissue. "I just talked with Quinn. We're both a mess over Danno retiring."

He nodded. "I come bearing gifts." He held out the jacket.

"Déjà vu. We've done this jacket thing before. There was a motorcycle involved."

The day at the airport, the day of Liv's heart attack. A long time ago, it seemed. An eternity. Before he had noticed Jasmyn Albright.

Her dimples went deep. Her face glowed as if the indentations somehow flipped a light switch. She said, "Do I get to keep this one?"

"If it fits."

"And if I don't have to ride a motorcycle." She took the coat and slipped her arms into it.

"We get them for the gym. You looked cold earlier today. I thought maybe you could use a warmer jacket."

"Ohhh, nice fleecy lining." She zipped it and flipped up the hood. "It has a hood!"

"And a logo."

She glanced down at the small, white embroidered letters, *Seaside Village Gym*, and tied the hood, hiding most of her face. "It's a perfect fit. I'm as snug as a bug in a rug. Can I pay for it?"

He would give her a dozen if it meant seeing those dimples twelve times over. "No. Just wear it everywhere. Free advertising."

"Okay." She looked at him. "Wow. Thank you, Keagan. I really needed this. Not just the jacket but…I don't know."

"A distraction from the mess?"

"Yeah."

"Did you and Quinn decide what to do?"

"No. We just had a good cry."

"That helps." He noticed her tears were gone.

He was noticing too much. When had his reaction to her changed from *she's a sweet kid*? When had he realized she was older than she appeared, that she was near his own age, attractive, competent, and yet full of an innocent, childlike wonder?

He offered some inane parting words and slipped away.

Near his front door, he muttered to a potted bush, "Ten more days and she's out of here. And now I'm talking to plants."

Forty-Two

Still wrapped in the jacket Keagan had just given her, Jasmyn sat down in the rocker and set it in motion. Back and forth. Back and forth. Back and forth.

It was a nervous reaction, of course. The two weeks of delightful bliss were over. Yes, they were definitely over.

Every day she crossed off a calendar date and thought of in-her-face tornado memories and cold shoulders and an ugly studio apartment. Most days she could bury those things and get lost in the bliss.

But now, today, Danno had called with his news. Valley Oaks would not be buried easily.

And then she confided in Keagan because—silly goose that she was—she thought of him as another Casa friend, one with a guy point of view. Like Danno or Zeb Swanson's sons or Quinn's little brother, who had often tagged along with them as kids.

But Keagan smiled, and she thought of knights and white steeds.

And then he gave her a jacket.

She stopped rocking, phoned Quinn again, and told her the story.

Quinn said, "Is Keagan the hot one?"

"There is no 'hot one.'"

"Yeah, there is. You told me he could do men's cologne ads."

"That's Chad. He's super good looking and has a kid-brother personality."

"So who's Keagan?"

"The motorcycle guy."

"Who can break boards with his bare hands and makes you feel safe and scared at the same time."

"I didn't exactly say that."

"You didn't have to." Quinn chuckled. "So what's the problem?"

"I don't know."

"If he were the hot one, I'd say you might want to stay put."

"Honestly, Quinn."

"Okay, seriously. You're attracted to the guy. Probably like all the women there are attracted to him. Angel, knight, Kung Fu Dude. And what was that about that snarly old actor—Clint Eastwood. Wow. Your guy has everyone's attention."

"Hey, you're right. Then it's not a huge deal." She tried out her theory. "Maybe it just says I'm over Nick."

"Definitely. Except it is kind of a huge deal if it means your heart is waking up again."

Jasmyn leaned forward until her forehead rested on her knees and groaned.

"Is it mutual?"

"Mutual? No."

"He gave you a jacket."

"He'd give one to anyone who needed a jacket." She sat up. "'Angel' and 'knight' suit him perfectly. He keeps to himself and then *poof*, appears when someone's in trouble. And the whole time he's so even-keeled, you have no idea what's going on inside."

"He's probably hiding a broken heart."

"Quinn, give it up."

"Okay. Sorry. So, I've been thinking about running the Pig."

Quinn distracted her. They spoke of wild changes they would make to the restaurant, beginning with a French-themed decor, which made no sense at all unless they convinced people that the Eiffel Tower and French fries were somehow connected.

Thoughts of Keagan faded away.

Forty-Three

Liv propped her fists on her hips and walked a slow circle around the front room of Cottage Three. The place was a disaster. "This place is a disaster."

Beau knelt in front of the furnace, a narrow unit in the wall. His tool belt clanked as he screwed in a grate. "Nah. It's made to order for a little TLC."

Liv shook her head. Tender loving care included a good scrubbing and a fresh coat of paint, not major repairs like fixing splintered cabinet doors, holes in walls, broken window panes, and a cracked sink. Not cleaning blood out of hardwood floors.

"Miss Liv, if you don't mind my asking, what happened here?"

"A big mistake." She groaned and sank onto the window seat. "Normally I have an accurate sense of who belongs in one of my cottages." Not wanting to sound pretentious to Beau, whom she did not know all that well yet, she held back. No sense scaring off the competent handyman with descriptions of the Holy Spirit tapping her on the shoulder and breathing insight into her heart about a stranger.

"My guess is you are a woman of prayer, Miss Liv. If God says jump, you ask how high."

She laughed. Maybe she couldn't scare him off. "Something like that. I wasn't paying attention this time. And Keagan, who double-checks my decisions, was out of town. An acquaintance from church asked if her grandson could stay for about a month until his dorm room opened up at school. He was moving down from Sacramento. What she didn't know was that he'd been involved with drug dealers. There was unfinished business between them."

"That sounds like one big made-to-order nightmare."

"They found him here after only a week or so. For some reason he opened the gate for them and let them inside. They almost killed him." She gestured. "And they did this."

"Is he all right?"

"He survived. Oh, it was awful, Beau. It was about two o'clock in the morning. Piper's a night owl and right next door, so she heard the commotion. She called the police and then started the phone tree."

"Phone tree?"

"I'll add you. It's our system for calling each other for emergencies or whatnot." Whatnot. Like her heart attack? Had they used the tree for that? "Piper called Noah and me and we each called others. She called Chad, who went outdoors and unlocked the gate for the police. I don't know if that was stupid or brave."

"You all must have been mighty terrified."

"We were. Fortunately, Tasha and Coco slept through it all. I was kind of glad Keagan wasn't around. He would have done something brave and stupid and gotten hurt."

"Miss Liv, you're getting all stressed out just talking about it. You go on home and have some tea. I'll make a list of what needs to be done here."

She waved a hand, dismissing his concern, and realized she was rubbing her chest with the other hand, trying to relieve a tightness which, according to her doctor, resided in her imagination. "Beau, I've avoided this for six months. Keagan and Noah cleared out what little furniture was in here, but then I locked it up and thought seriously about throwing away the key."

The aftermath—reliving over and over the threat to her Casa family—had been too much for her to bear. The night itself had been so full of terror—shouts, mayhem, flashing lights, cops in the courtyard, the perpetrators sprawled facedown and getting handcuffed. By the time the ambulance carried off the poor boy, by the time the police hauled off the others, by the time she entered Cottage Three and surveyed the damage, it was morning and she had felt ripe then for a heart attack or a stroke.

It took a long time for the Casa folks and the neighborhood to regain their sense of safety. Then the busy summer season was upon them. Then Jasmyn arrived. Then came the real heart attack.

Tending to Cottage Three hadn't even made it onto her to-do list until a few days ago.

"It's high time I address this mess," she said.

"You know what it needs? A good cleaning."

She eyed the stained floorboards again. "Obviously."

"No, I mean a deeper kind of cleaning. The kind my Granny Mibs would give it." He paused and met her gaze.

In an instant she knew what he would say. She wondered why she hadn't noticed before the stuff he was made of. It was plain to see in his open face and hear in the gentle cadence of his speech.

She didn't know much about Beau Jenner. He had come highly recommended by her retired handyman and by Keagan, who knew him from the gym. What else had she needed but their counsel? Now she was curious about the choices Beau must have made that led him all the way from Kentucky to her front door and then to this moment.

Liv folded her hands on her lap. Her chest was fine. It didn't need attention. It didn't need nervous kneading. Her head could do with some kneading, though. How could she not have thought of the obvious?

Because that night…

"It was the most awful thing I've ever experienced."

He nodded.

"Your Granny Mibs would pray and sprinkle holy water over every inch of this cottage, right?"

He smiled. "You got it, Miss Liv."

About time she got it.

∼

While Beau went to the hardware store, Liv walked through the wrecked cottage, praying for God's peace to invade it and spraying holy water from a blue plastic bottle.

It was an old custom she had learned growing up in a liturgical church. Syd had thought the water part was silly, but then he'd never been one for mystery. *Tell God what you need, amen, over and done.*

She wasn't concerned with explaining or arguing or figuring it out. To her the act, at the least, was symbolic of God's presence, and that in itself soothed her soul. The woman Jasmyn had recently met out in the desert—what was her name?—Nova. Nova would understand. Well, insofar as there was anything to understand about mystery.

"And amen." Liv tucked the bottle into a pocket of the canvas bag that held an array of items she used around the property, including a small pair of clippers, baggies of all sizes, a crunchable sun hat, garden gloves, cell phone, and screwdriver. Practical stuff. She was a practical woman who acknowledged a very impractical, unseen world.

She stood in the open doorway, facing the L-shaped living room and kitchen, and smiled. "Peace be with you, Cottage Three."

"And also with you."

Liv turned, surprised to see that Samantha was the one speaking biblical language.

She stepped into the alcove. "A step-aunt took me to church once. She came for a visit and died the next day. I was ten."

Liv relaxed the surprise from her face. "Oh."

"Exactly." She gestured over Liv's shoulder. "You're getting started?"

Liv wanted to ask about the step-aunt, but knowing Samantha, she'd already said all she wanted to say on the subject. "Yes, I am. I think it's time."

"If you're ready, then it's time. That night…" She shook her head, her expression more somber than usual. "It will be good to get it behind us. I for one still give this place a wide berth when I walk to the front gate."

"I wish I would have done it sooner."

Samantha touched Liv's arm, a rare act. "You couldn't. Is there anything I can do to help?" Her offer was rare too.

"Thank you, dear, but I think Beau has it all under control. He's probably the main reason I feel ready. He's quite competent, isn't he?"

"Mm-hmm." Samantha shifted her weight and crossed her arms. And blushed. Or maybe that was Liv's imagination ignited by Jasmyn's gossip about Beau flirting.

"Muscular too, hmm? I like a good bicep on a man. And pecs. My Syd had arms and a chest like—"

"Liv! TMI. Are you coming out of there?"

"Oh." She gave the place one last glance. "Yes, I'm done. You don't care to…"

"No."

Liv picked up her bag and shut the door. They walked a few steps, and then Samantha stopped and turned toward the cottage.

"Liv, it needs something on the exterior. Somehow it still looks like that night."

She stood beside Samantha and studied Cottage Three. "It does. Somehow. What is it?"

"I don't know what *it* is, but if the bluish-greenish color goes, maybe it will go too."

Liv stared at the door. It was aquamarine, not bluish-greenish. The color was carried over to a decorative piece of overhang, the two chairs, and the trim around the window.

"Samantha, dear, that's brilliant."

"Really? I figured you'd say it's been this color since Hector was a pup and we don't mess with decor that old."

She chuckled at the echo of her own words. "It has been here for that long, but I'm not that much of a stick-in-the-mud, am I?"

"Not when it comes to plumbing." Samantha smiled.

"Okay. Well, mark this a red-letter day then. We're going to change the color. It will totally change the vibes."

"Way to go, Liv."

"Thank you. Hey, what are you doing home on a Tuesday morning?"

"I have the day off." She met Liv's stare, almost nose to nose.

"My, my. Shall I bake a cake?"

Samantha rolled her eyes. "My boss made me."

Good for him. He should do that more often. The girl works far too much.

"Jasmyn and I are going patio furniture shopping with Chad. He has a friend's pickup truck in case we find something I like."

After four years Samantha was adding furniture to her home? "You plan on staying then?"

"I thought I might."

They stared at each other for a moment. Samantha giggled first and then Liv laughed.

Samantha smiled. "Maybe when you finish Cottage Three, you'll find somebody nice to move into it. See you later."

Liv watched her walk toward Chad's cottage, too stunned to reply. Samantha was making jokes? Samantha was giggling?

Well. Wasn't that something?

Liv could not help herself. She grinned and sashayed around the fountain and hummed a tune of her own creation. Her heart leapt, this time in a good way.

Forty-Four

Jasmyn sat in the small pickup truck, scrunched quietly between Chad and Sam. The two of them were odd friends, sniping at each other for the entire twenty-minute drive from the Casa.

They were parked now in a lot near Brother Benny's Thrift Shop, a warehouse-sized storefront in a strip mall. Neither of them were making a move to open a door.

Chad said for the umpteenth time, "Samantha, I really can't believe you want to shop in a fourthhand store."

She sighed. "Give it a rest, Chadwick. I told you. Sometimes they have good secondhand stuff. Wealthy people donate things all the time. This is where I got my kitchen table which, according to Liv, is a name brand worth ten times what I paid for it."

"Jasmyn and I would much rather go to Furniture Row. Right, Jasmyn? You don't want to hang out with the sordid underside of San Diego."

"Uh…"

"Chad!" Sam said. "Stop it. You are not an elitist even if you did grow up with a nanny and a butler. Brother Benny feeds and shelters a lot of homeless people from what they make at this store."

"Just because I had certain privileges doesn't mean I'm against recycling and helping the less fortunate."

Jasmyn gaped at him. "You really grew up with a nanny and a butler?"

"Not a butler. A cook. And an *au pair*." He shrugged, a gesture that he somehow made appear elegant in a denim jacket. "And a live-in house-keeper. Not my fault."

"Of course not. It's just that I've never met anyone so filthy rich. I mean…" She made a *whoops* face.

He smiled. He had the straightest, whitest teeth; the most gorgeous eyelashes over eyes like beautiful gray-green glass; and a face so handsome Quinn would have fainted dead away at the sight of him. He always smelled nice too.

"Wealth is relative. Our next-door neighbor was obscenely rich. That's more than filthy."

Sam opened her door. "Why don't you just wait here, Chad? We only invited you along for the truck and the muscle anyway."

"I have an excellent eye for decor."

"Ha-ha." She got out of the truck. "Says the guy who can't find the top of his couch."

Chad turned to Jasmyn. "What do you think, love?"

He was charming too.

"To tell the truth, I've never, ever been furniture shopping in my whole entire life, new or fourthhand. I'm happy just to tag along." She smiled. "Even if you two do argue like an old married couple."

They both went silent and exchanged a puzzled look.

Jasmyn slid over to the open door and hopped out. "Come on, Chad. As long as we're here, let's all go inside. You can choose the next stop, okay?"

He blew out an exasperated breath. "Okay, fine."

The three of them headed across the parking lot with Jasmyn still between them.

Sam leaned around her and frowned at Chad. "We're more like siblings because he's an annoying little brat."

"And she's a bossy big sister." He winked. "But now that I think about it, old married couple fits too. I'm going to call you Mildred. You can call me Robert. Those are good names for an old married couple, don't you think?"

"Whatever floats your boat, Robert."

Jasmyn laughed. To think she had imagined these people were part of a weird cult. That would be true only if goofy and down-to-earth equaled bizarre. They were no weirder than Valley Oaks people.

They entered the store and stopped. It was one of those overwhelming places that had no obvious *start here* direction.

Jasmyn let out a low whistle. "It looks like a football field."

"Only bigger," Chad said. "And a whole lot messier. You're really okay with this, Jasmyn?"

She scanned the enormous facility and wondered if she was okay. As far as the eye could see, furniture and household items cluttered row after row after row. People, strollers, and shopping carts filled the aisles. Rock music thumped, sixties era. It overloaded her senses the way Disneyland had at first. That was a happy place, though, and she had soon felt at ease. This place reminded her of the shopping mall Quinn had dragged her to soon after the tornado. She'd had a major meltdown, and they left without buying clothes she needed for work.

Jasmyn took a deep breath. The mall incident happened within a week of the tornado. That was more than six months ago. She imagined the calendar in her kitchen. Today was the sixteenth. Tomorrow was the seventeenth. Tomorrow marked seven months. Seven months.

It was time to move through it, whatever *it* meant.

"It's not as disorderly as it appears," Sam said. "Clothing is on the left. We'll avoid that whole half." She swung her arm in a wide arc. "We'll check out patio tables in the far back corner. Chad, go find something to do. There's a play area for kids over there in the middle." She pointed toward it. "We'll come find you when we're finished."

"Mildred, you're such a tease." He spoke loudly with animation, his voice spilling onto passersby who turned and watched him. "I'll scope out rockers for Jasmyn, so we can take back the one we loaned her. I miss it so much. I mean, the memories surrounding it. Oh!" He held a hand to his chest. "Rocking our little ones in it, night after night. Treasured stuff, Mil, treasured stuff. Okay, text me." He strode off.

Jasmyn called out, "Thanks, Robert," and looked at Sam. "You're going to catch flies if you don't close your mouth."

She snapped shut her jaw, her face the color of late summer tomatoes. "That guy is impossible."

"He's funny, Mildred."

"A regular hoot."

They strolled down a wide aisle lined on both sides with dining tables and hutches. Jasmyn was surprised to see several pieces like the ones that had filled her farmhouse, old things her grandparents traced back to their childhoods. A wave of nostalgia rolled through her.

"Sam, do you mind if I roam around?"

"Go for it. I'll be in lawn furniture." She walked off.

Jasmyn turned a corner, heading deeper into the forest of furniture. Its thick musty scent reminded her of an attic.

She and Quinn had spent countless hours playing in the attics of both of their houses. Their grandmothers and mothers had been of the opinion that women should never get rid of a thing because somebody might need it someday. The contents of trunks and boxes and wardrobes provided enough entertainment for the countless rainy and snowbound days a Midwest childhood offered.

The thought of all that had been lost saddened her. So much of it she had taken for granted. Maybe someday she would have her own home again. Maybe she would shop like Sam did, at secondhand stores, and find replacements. Not for everything. Not for antiques like the hundred-year-old porcelain bowl—

Jasmyn's eyes locked onto a desk.

It was a rolltop. Dark walnut. Brass handles. Not manly huge, not cutesy lady small. As Goldilocks would say, it was just right.

And it was a dead-ringer for her grandmother's desk.

Jasmyn stopped before it and her breath caught. If she peeked inside the cubbyhole in the lower right-hand corner and found a *J* carved in it, she'd honestly believe the tornado had picked up the desk in Illinois, gently plopped it down in California, maybe at a yard sale where it didn't sell, and then it got donated to Brother Benny's Thrift Shop.

Sudden tears burned in her eyes. She moaned out a long sigh. How had she forgotten the desk? In the aftermath of the tornado, while sifting through mounds of wet trash that had been her home and belongings, she repeated what everyone kept saying to her over and over: *They're only* things. *At least you're safe. The* things *don't matter. You can buy* things.

Now, faced with a replica of the desk, she understood that on the contrary, things *did* matter. They really did. If she had died, they wouldn't have mattered. But she hadn't died, and a deep longing welled inside of her to touch the things of her childhood.

Jasmyn touched the desk. She rolled up the front cover. It clattered into place, revealing an unmarred level surface and a backdrop of cubbyholes and tiny drawers. She leaned over and ran her fingers along the bottom of the narrow opening in the lower right-hand corner. No *J* engraved for June Anderson Albright. No marring of any kind, anywhere. It was in excellent condition.

Her grandmother had told of how she had carved her initial at the age of eight or nine when the desk was new. Her mother had whipped her. It seemed an odd memory for Gramma June to smile about, but she always did. Jasmyn noticed because the woman seldom smiled. As a matter of fact, the only time she appeared happy was when she sat at the desk, reading or writing. She read every book under the sun and wrote poetry, two talents that had totally bypassed her daughter and granddaughter.

Gramma June allowed Jasmyn to use the desk for coloring and doing schoolwork. That might explain why Jasmyn loved it, no matter how much she struggled with schoolwork and coloring inside the lines of princess gowns. Seated in the big, creaky wooden chair, with Gramma June's rare encouragement, she felt as if she were on an island, protected from a scary world.

Jasmyn bent and opened several of the drawers that ran down either side of the desk front. They were empty. Her lost ones had been stuffed with notebooks and papers filled with poems and notes in her grandmother's writing.

She straightened and looked for a price tag on the top. The thing was in mint condition and probably cost hundreds of dollars, way more than she would plop down for something she didn't exactly need to replace.

She squeezed between the desk and a bookcase and found the price tag. Someone had thoughtfully taped it on the back panel where it wouldn't leave sticky residue on the front surface. She flipped it over and gasped. One hundred twenty-five dollars? One hundred twenty-five? Were they batty?

No, she was batty. *Something she didn't exactly need to replace?* Replace? Really? Where exactly was she going to place it? In her suitcase next Monday when she flew back to Valley Oaks?

A hollowness filled her. It felt as if a huge chunk of herself had been gouged out from her insides.

It probably had been. Her things were gone. Things she had touched, smelled, sat on, slept on, ate from, polished, and passed every single day of her life. Most of those things had been touched, smelled, sat on, slept on, eaten from, polished, and passed every single day by her mother and grandparents and those ancestors she never knew. Those things were links to her past, to her roots, to who she was.

And they were gone. Totally gone.

She sank to the floor and wept.

Forty-Five

Jasmyn had allowed herself four extra weeks in Seaside Village after Liv's heart attack. Now time was up.

Saturday morning she scrubbed Cottage Eleven and gathered the borrowed linens and kitchenware.

Saturday afternoon she began returning things to their rightful owners, a courtesy she had not bothered with on that fateful day four weeks ago. Liv had said it was because deep down Jasmyn knew she would be returning, which was why Liv had told her not to bother. She was considering keeping the cottage semi-furnished.

Jasmyn now carried Sam's small television through the front door and out to the courtyard, balancing a box of chocolate truffles on top of it. Sam would have a conniption, but it would be a half-hearted one. The woman really did enjoy chocolate. After loading up Chad's truck with patio furniture the other day at Brother Benny's, the three of them had stopped for gelato and Sam's choice was double-fudge chocolate.

The memory felt bittersweet. Chad had found her while she was on the floor beside the rolltop desk, blowing her nose. He sat down and commiserated with her. The treat had been his suggestion. It was, he had said, the least Robert and Mildred could do for their friend who had suffered great loss.

"Hey." Keagan came into view.

Of course Keagan came into view at that particular moment, the weight of leaving as heavy as the television and probably as obvious.

He reached for the TV. "Let me help."

"It's not heavy." As he scooped the television from her arms, she grabbed the box of candy.

"This belongs to Sam, right?" He veered toward her cottage. "I suppose this means you decided to go back."

"People don't uproot themselves to turn a vacation spot into their permanent place of residence."

"Right."

Jasmyn stubbed her toe. Was that a hint of sarcasm in his tone? The voice usually parked in neutral? She glanced down at her neon yellow shoe. The flagstone had left its mark. She wanted to cry.

"Do you have more to deliver?"

"Nothing big." She didn't want his help.

He turned toward her. A brief flash of sunlight bounced off the lenses of his dark glasses. The corners of his mouth curved. He didn't believe her.

"Really. Sam's fold-up rocker and TV trays. Linens and kitchen things to Riley, Liv, and Inez. Shampoo and soap and stuff to Piper. She gave me way more than I could use. Little things. Chad said he'd get the big ones after I leave, like Inez's bed and his table."

"Okay. So how are you doing?"

"Awful." She winced. The vocal fire hydrant was fully engaged. "I'm okay. There's just too much to do. I should have packed earlier this week, but I didn't want to miss out on anything. I took Tasha to get a DVD and Coco to get groceries. Inez and Louis took me to lunch. Piper helped me pick out a gift for Quinn. And…" The flow stopped. "And a lot of other stuff."

He chuckled.

Chuckled?

"You didn't want to miss out on spending time with people. I'm sure it was mutual. We are going to miss you, Ms. All Bright."

"Ditto," she muttered and stepped around him to knock on Sam's door, the goldenrod yellow one.

"By the way, I'll be happy to drive you to the airport on Monday. In Liv's minivan."

"Thanks, but I'll take a shuttle."

Sam opened the door. "Jasmyn! I said you can keep the TV until you leave." She moved aside for them to enter. "Set it on the counter there. Thanks, Keagan."

"I offered to take her to the airport, but she wants to take a shuttle."

Sam frowned at him. They shook their heads in unison and turned to her. Sam said, "No, you don't want to do that. They'll cart you around the county for half the day and then you'll sit in the airport for the other half."

"I don't mind—"

"Keagan will do it. I can't get away from the office, and Liv's not up for driving the freeway yet."

Jasmyn wondered if they had rehearsed the conversation already. "Whatever."

"Keagan, did you get the word yet? Goodbye pizza party, tomorrow night, on my new, old patio table."

"I did, thanks. I'll go get the rocker and trays." He went back outside.

Jasmyn puffed out a breath.

Sam picked up her television and carried it to the far end of the counter, nearer the kitchen table. "I bet he'll come to the party. I mean, the guy let you ride his motorcycle." She plugged in the power cord. "Did I tell you about the time he let me use his T-shirt for a hankie?"

"What?"

Sam chuckled. "The day Liv had her heart attack. I lost it at the hospital, and he was standing right there when it happened. I've changed my mind about him. He's an okay guy." Her smile wavered. "Actually, I've changed my mind about a lot of people and things thanks to you."

Jasmyn blinked to keep the tears from spilling. She changed the subject. "Is that where you usually keep your TV?"

"Yeah." Sam sniffed. "Sometimes I watch the news while I eat."

"I'm sorry I kept it for so long."

"I'm not." She tore off a few paper towels and handed some to Jasmyn. "Here. Unless you want to wait and use Keagan's shirt."

They laughed and cried and buried their faces in paper towels.

It was going to be a long two days.

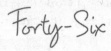

Forty-Six

Early Sunday morning, Liv's courtyard circuit stalled in front of Cottage Three. The aquamarine on its front door all but reached out and smacked her. Samantha had been right. The color had to go. Today.

She whispered, "Lord, have mercy."

It was the easiest prayer in the universe, easier than saying thanks or admitting need or letting someone off the hook. Since the awful incident months and months ago, those words had been the only prayer she could come up with when passing it. Wasn't it time for something different?

Of course she'd already prayed over the work to be done, for creativity and safety for those involved. She had prayed for the boy who had briefly lived in it. She had prayed for the perpetrators. May they all know God's mercy.

But could it be time for the other prayers, the ones that opened her heart to usher someone new into the fold?

She waited, quiet for a moment.

Nothing came to her.

She shook her head. Nope. It was too soon. Or she was too old.

Or Jasmyn's exit was too much to bear.

Oh, dear. She was not herself. Not herself at all.

"Wretched heart attack."

She pulled keys from her pocket, unlocked the door, and entered.

The interior's appearance had changed drastically, thanks to Beau. He had scrubbed down the walls and removed all the kitchen cabinet doors.

There were white spots on the hardwood floors, as if he'd bleached them. He'd probably needed to use extreme measures.

Her heart, with its wretched damage, sank. The work was going to be far more involved than she had imagined. She felt overwhelmed.

"Liv." Jasmyn stepped inside, her eyes wide in alarm. "Are you all right? You're rubbing your chest."

Liv glanced down at her hand and lowered it. "I don't know why I do that. I'm fine. Just fine. Well, except for…" She gestured and sighed. "All this."

Jasmyn grasped Liv's hands between hers and held them tightly. "Liv, if this stresses you out, maybe you shouldn't come in here. Let Beau work. You know he's good. It's wonderful you're feeling up to taking charge again, but you don't have to do it all."

She took a shaky breath. "Growing old is for the birds."

Jasmyn dropped her hands and gave her a quick hug. "Think of it as a vacation."

"A permanent one?"

"You need some cheese and crackers to go with that whine."

"Well, aren't we the feisty one this morning?"

"Somebody has to do it."

"Especially when someone else is having a moment?"

"Exactly." She nudged Liv toward the door and they went outside. "I was wondering if I could go to church with you this morning."

Liv turned to shut and lock the door, hiding what must be a dumbfounded expression. "I hadn't planned on going."

"I know. What's up with that, anyway?"

Liv opened her mouth to speak but didn't have a real reply, except for the standby that was probably becoming overused. She turned and said it anyway. "Heart attack?"

Jasmyn's eyebrows rose, but she didn't voice what she was probably thinking, that Liv's excuse for everything was indeed overused.

"Okay," Jasmyn said. "I thought maybe you'd stopped talking to God."

"Really? Goodness gracious, no. You do realize I think the Holy Presence is everywhere, not just in church."

"I do, but you like your church, right? Don't you feel well enough by now?"

"But I can't drive yet." Actually, the doctor had said she could, but the thought of possibly losing control behind the wheel frightened her to no end.

"Your friends offered to pick you up, Liv. Remember, I was there when you turned them down. Maybe it's the control issue again. Or having a hard time asking for help."

Jasmyn certainly was on a roll.

"The thing is, when I sat in that church on the reservation with Nova, I remembered that I liked going to Sunday school. I usually felt, I don't know, quiet. Deep inside."

Liv had heard the story about the small-town church in Valley Oaks and how Jasmyn's grandmother had gotten her feelings hurt and quit going.

"This is my last day, you know."

Liv shook her head. Several days ago she had announced it was best if she played ostrich and buried her head in the sand. "We are not to talk of that."

"That was your idea. I decided I'd rather not pretend. I'd rather embrace the moment. So, what do you say? Are you up for it?"

"Oh, Jasmyn, dear. I just don't want you to be disappointed. We're all so old at Seaside Village Grace. You might like Noah's church better. It's full of young people and they sing contemporary music. I'm sure he'd be more than happy to…"

Jasmyn's face fell, literally. Liv had no idea such sadness could be expressed in the slight shift of skin.

Fiddlesticks! What on earth was she thinking? This surrogate daughter whom Liv had begged for stood right there before her, graciously putting the kibosh on a silly woman's whining, asking to take that woman to church and not wanting to miss their final hours together.

This is sheer love, Liv. Why can't you accept it?

At the blast of clarity, she nearly plopped down into the aquamarine chair in front of the aquamarine door.

Instead, she straightened her shoulders and cleared her throat. "I have missed church. By the way, I always swing by the donut shop and pick up a couple dozen glazed—"

"Olivia McAlister." Jasmyn smiled. "That is not going to happen. I'm sure everyone will be happy to see you even without donuts."

Forty-Seven

Everyone at Seaside Village Grace Church was indeed happy to see Liv. Jasmyn doubted they missed her donuts one iota. The table—set up for coffee hour on a covered patio between the church and the parking lot—nearly sagged under Danish rolls and whatnot.

Jasmyn stood off to the side, munching the gooiest pumpkin bar she'd ever had. She watched people shower Liv with attention and gave up on separating her friend from the sugar-and-fat-laden goodie someone had handed her and was now making its way toward Liv's mouth.

Jasmyn's hovering stage had to end at some point. Unlike Jasmyn's mother and grandparents, Liv was getting better. Reminding her she had been ill would only reinforce the struggle she'd had earlier that morning about being old.

Whatever old was, it hadn't shown up yet among the mainly white- and silver-haired folks surrounding Liv. Their laughter and energy obviously affected Liv in a good way. The extra crease in her forehead had disappeared.

Jasmyn's phone beeped softly, a text alert. *Oops.* She'd forgotten to turn it off. No one stood nearby, so she reached inside her shoulder bag, expecting to see a note from Quinn. She palmed the phone and angled it so the screen faced up.

Keagan? The text was from Keagan?

His name and number were in her phone because she had entered all the Casa folks' information, a necessity while filling in for Liv. Evidently her number was in his phone as well, maybe from when she had texted him—and everyone—about the potluck.

She rubbed her throat, pulled out the phone, and read the message. *How was church?*

How was church? How did he even know they'd gone to church?

The guy certainly had a knack for knowing, and he seemed to have an angel's way about him when it came to Liv's well-being. Being concerned about her going to church was a little over-the-top. Jasmyn needn't worry that no one would hover after she left. Keagan fit the bill.

She popped the last sweet bite into her mouth, wiped her fingers on a napkin, and typed a reply. *No worries. Liv is happy here.*

Before she could tuck the phone away, another text appeared. *Meant for you.*

For her? How was church for her? Is that what he meant?

Now why would he ask that? Why would the thought even cross his mind to text her when they were neighbors and likely to see each other later that day?

She tapped out *Just fine*, sent it, turned off the phone, and shoved it deep into her bag.

Technology was just plain intrusive. To be able to instantaneously read Keagan's thoughts felt too...well, it made her feel as if they were close friends. Really close friends. Like Quinn.

But not exactly. More like friends who had crushes on each other.

"Are you okay, dear?" Liv came into focus, her face beaming like the sun.

"Uh, yeah. Keagan texted and...um, nothing. He just wondered how church went."

"Hmm. He can be an oddball at times, can't he?"

"A little."

Liv laughed.

Jasmyn suspected that Liv knew that Jasmyn's throat tickled. That she somehow knew Jasmyn felt...what was the word? Discombobulated. As though she were a water balloon that went *splat* because six words zipped through space and time and announced that Keagan was thinking about her.

"Jasmyn, dear, I'm ready to go if you are. Thank you for talking me into coming. What a glorious morning!"

A smile sprang to Jasmyn's lips. Liv was a gem. As Keagan had told her on that very first day when they met, she was the real deal.

And her church was the real deal. It hadn't been just fine for Jasmyn. It had been glorious. The deep quiet she'd longed for had found her there as it had found her out in the desert church. It tiptoed into her heart as she sang and recited and listened to a humble pastor talk simply of God's unconditional love and acceptance.

For Jasmyn, that finished everything. At last she felt really and truly ready to leave Seaside Village. It was time to take this new reality back to her old life.

Forty-Eight

Sam's kitchen table was small and rectangular in shape. An oak border surrounded four rows of white ceramic tiles. She kept two chairs at its long sides, pushed in.

The table occupied the space at the far end of the kitchen in front of the French doors that led out to the patio, as did most of the kitchen tables in Casa cottages.

In the center of the table sat her cell phone. She didn't do centerpieces or place mats. The phone was the only object on the table.

She walked around the table again and again, taking deep breaths, looking at the phone.

Anyone peeking through the window would think her behavior bizarre. But for her it was protocol, her method for preparing herself, each and every time, to make the Phone Call.

Which, given the necessary expended energy, explained why she did not make the Phone Call very often.

Sam glanced around her old-fashioned beach cottage. She liked her home. It was one of four Casa bungalows that had two bedrooms rather than only one. The layouts were basically the same with the living room across the front, the kitchen down one side, a short hallway at the other side that bedrooms and bath opened onto.

Cottage Seven had the yellow door, or, as Liv put it, goldenrod. Bright and glowing, sunrise and sunset and moonlight combined.

Before moving into Seven, Sam had never known such peace. College housing had been a blur of dorms and cheap apartments and, at times, strange roommates. Before that, a small, nondescript house where by age eleven she was sharing her bedroom with three little brothers.

That had not been unbearable. Most days she had the wilderness as her very own space for being alone, for running, for listening to the music of the wind as it whistled through the canyons. Her stepfather provided food, shelter, and a television. Clothes, books, art, and music did not enter into the equation. She once told her high school English teacher that the poverty did not impact her because every student in her school lived in it. The teacher politely disagreed.

Sam wondered if the woman had been right. She was frugal to a fault— no, she was a tightwad. The thought of losing her job caused her to hyperventilate. One reason she continued to live at the Casa was because Liv kept the rent crazy cheap. As long as she had her job, Sam could afford to live in a sleek new condo with ocean views.

From the looks of her cottage, sleek and new were not exactly her style. Except for her bed and some lamps, the sparse, basic furnishings had come from thrift shops, the same ones she had shopped yesterday with Jasmyn and Chad.

Hanging with Jasmyn was bad for Sam's health. There had to be a direct correlation between spending the day with her and this notion to make the Phone Call weeks ahead of schedule.

On second thought, the link wouldn't be all that direct. With Jasmyn Albright there were no straight lines, only labyrinths. Paths led inexplicably to situations Sam had no intention of joining…and yet she did.

Another person tagging along with her for a run? For a ride to the desert when she was working? A shared pizza in her cottage? A dinner at a restaurant with other Casa Detainees to celebrate her achievement? Shopping when she didn't need a thing and buying a useless magnet? Wondering if a pest was, instead, a flirt?

Making the Phone Call before the allotted time had passed?

Why?

Sam liked Jasmyn very much. She had never met a kinder, gentler, more naive woman. The syrupy notes in her voice had all but faded from Sam's hearing, replaced by a genuine sweetness, honey that rendered Sam's gruff bear persona into a version of Winnie the Pooh.

Jasmyn's infatuation yesterday with that old desk touched something inside Sam. Touched? More like it sparked a bolt of lightning, sent it zigzagging through her, head to toe, toe to head, searing open a locked closet of her heart. The subsequent clap of thunder shattered the door, guaranteeing that closing it again would require monumental effort.

More effort than it took to make the Phone Call.

Sam pulled out a chair, sat, picked up the cell, and punched in a number she'd known since childhood. She'd never felt the need to enter it into her contact list.

"Hello?" The familiar squawk resembled that of a pheasant, minus the image of colorful feathers that might soften the sharp edges of such a voice.

"Mom. Hi. It's me."

"Who's 'me'?" Rosie Chee's laugh was an elongation of the squawk. "Hmm. She said 'Mom.' I guess it must be that no-good, long-lost daughter of mine."

Love you too, Mom. "How are you?"

"Peachy. Why are you calling?"

"I'm fine too." She ignored the *why* question, determined to go through the motions. "How are the boys?" She referred to her three half brothers, now in their twenties, still the apples of her mother's eyes, still the *boys*.

"They're right as rain. Guess what? Mike's going to college next year."

"Really?" Sam shouldn't be surprised at anything concerning the boys, but she continually was. They were a goofy mix of loser and not-so-bad.

"Really. You oughta' talk to him about that school you went to."

In your dreams. "Sure." Sam rubbed her forehead. She couldn't remember the last time she'd talked with one of the boys, but being nasty led nowhere fast. "Give him my number. So, anyway, I'm calling because—" A lump closed up her throat.

Good grief.

"Because what?"

Sam coughed away the lump. "I was just wondering about Dad's mom."

"Why on earth— That old windbag?"

As far back as Sam could remember, her grandmother Hannah had been *that old windbag*. She died when Sam was two, at the age of sixty-two, hardly old.

Rosie went on. "I always gave it to you straight. She never accepted me. It was like her son had nothing to do with getting me knocked up. Takes two to tango, honey."

"I know all that." *Get over it already.* "And I know that if you weren't pregnant with me, you never would have married Dad."

"That's true. He sure was good looking, but he was one big pain in the neck. Always acting high and mighty, like he was God's gift to those high school kids he taught, just like her. What do you want to know, anyway?"

"Where was Hannah Carlson born?"

"Up north."

Again, something she already knew. "But where exactly? What state? What city?"

Rosie's exhale could have started up a dust storm. "Why are you asking all of this stuff out of the blue?"

Not out of the blue. Out of a day spent with Jasmyn in the desert, listening to her tales of family and heritage and ties that bless and bind and curse…of a man and a woman who perhaps got together for one reason only: for Samantha Whitehorse, aka Whitley, to be born.

"I just got curious. I vaguely remember your mom, but not Dad's." *Dad's.* When had she stopped referring to him in her mind as *Daddy*? He had been *Daddy* to her when he died. How had she outgrown someone's name while that someone never grew older with her?

"Illinois. The windbag came from Illinois. Like some hippie, way back before there was such a thing. Gonna save the Indians. She was just a wacko poking her nose in where she had no business."

And in the process becoming a beloved teacher whose son became a beloved teacher. "Where in Illinois?"

"How should I know?" She fell silent. Sam imagined the churning of wheels long idle. "It started with 'L' or maybe 'S.' It might've been two words. That's all I remember. She shoulda gone back there. My life woulda been a whole lot easier. I tell you—"

"Did she hold me?"

"What?"

Did my grandmother cuddle me? Did she know I existed? "Did she hold me when I was a baby?"

"Of course she did. All the women did. I was laid up for a long time. You about killed me coming out. I swear, you weighed as much as the boys put together. Besides that, you kicked for nine months, and talk about colicky…"

Sam had heard that stuff her entire life, how she was responsible for her mother's difficult life. But she had never heard about other women holding her.

About her grandmother Hannah holding her.

Hannah had known Sam! Despite her apparent disdain for Rosie, perhaps, just perhaps, she had loved Sam, her only grandchild. As a good teacher and the mother of a good man, perhaps Hannah had even bought toys for her and imagined fun things they would do together in the future.

Sam sighed to herself.

So what? A grandmother's hug from thirty years ago meant nothing in the here and now.

Forty-Nine

Hosting a party was a first for Sam. Of course, never having a BFF before Jasmyn arrived on the scene, there had been no reason on earth for her to throw a party.

From the couch in Sam's living room, Liv raised her teacup. "Kudos, Samantha, dear. The evening was a success."

Seated on the floor, Sam turned sideways as a goofy grin inched its way across her face. She glanced up to see the woman wink. Sam chuckled. "Thanks."

If it weren't for the fact that the occasion was Jasmyn's leaving, Sam might have laughed out loud like a delirious monkey. She had opened her cottage to the entire group of Casa Detainees, tipped the pizza delivery kid thirty percent, spoke civilly to Beau, and honestly enjoyed herself.

The Westminster chimes from her secondhand clock struck ten. The men had left some time ago, but all the Casa females lingered. Except for Coco in her wheelchair, they sat on her secondhand leather couch, her secondhand striped wingback chair, the rocker recently returned by Jasmyn, and on the dark green broadloom rug.

If someone had told Sam a few weeks ago that these women would be chatting inside her cottage, she would have rolled her eyes and said *In your dreams*. But there they all sat...

Liv had her legs tucked under her flowing brown skirt. Her orange cardigan with pockets appeared baggier than usual because of recent weight loss.

Piper as always looked ready for the cover girl shot, even sans makeup.

With her looks and success, she could have been consumed with self, but instead she was always likable and down-to-earth. Sam had noticed how once in a while—and Chad had confirmed—a blankness washed over her face. It was the only hint of sadness she ever exhibited over the death of her fiancé.

Inez rocked in the chair, her hair still thick and black, wearing a red shawl over a white blouse and a bright floral skirt, the ever-present happy expression on her face. She was the epitome of contentment.

Coco slept in her wheelchair, her head upright, her posture still a dancer's. Her blond bob-style wig was a bit askew, her eyelashes prominent as butterfly wings. Sam often zeroed in on her to make sure she was still breathing.

Déja, Noah's fourteen-year-old daughter, lounged on the rug. Her pout had definitely lessened since her arrival, especially after laughing with Piper. Even her dyed black spiked hair, the black jacket, black shirt, black pants, and a dog collar necklace appeared less ominous. Lamplight reflected off her silver nose ring, softening the whole effect.

Riley sat on the couch with Tasha curled up asleep between her and Liv, and she gently stroked her daughter's hair. Her story was another tragedy, and its impact showed. She was an anxious, needy sort. Her wispy, white-blond hair and porcelain skin added to her appearance of vulnerability. Sam always wondered why she didn't move back East to be with family.

Sam's eyes stung. She had never given Riley the benefit of the doubt before. Would Sam have moved back home to be with family if she had a special needs child and the father had left them? Probably not.

Sam blinked and sniffed discreetly.

And Jasmyn. On the floor, leaning against the couch near Liv, she seemed calmer than yesterday when they had cried. Later that afternoon they had gone for a run, but it hadn't—as she put it—cured her of the weepies. She'd spent the evening alone in her cottage, and Sam had not seen her on Sunday until she came over for the party. Evidently she had gotten through the crying period. Or, more likely, she held it all in as she had been doing that first day Sam met her.

Sam had hoped they would get a chance to talk. She wanted to tell her about the phone call with her mother and what she had learned about her grandmother, things too personal to bring up with her neighbors, who seemed in no hurry to leave.

It was odd how the women seemed so comfortable, so at home in her place. Chad, Keagan, Noah, Louis, and Beau had stopped by for pizza and a quick goodbye to Jasmyn. Chad had been his dramatic self, but that was Chad, waxing eloquent about his broken heart over her departure.

The ladies were a different story.

Sam said to no one in particular, "Is it my imagination, or did the dynamics change after the guys left?"

Piper snorted. "You think?"

The giggles started with Riley, setting off a ripple effect that went round the circle.

Coco's eyes opened and she smiled, her small, aged face suddenly animated. "But of course the dynamics changed. Men simply can't engage as we do. Between us girls, you know, we get down to business. We address what life is truly all about."

The giggles erupted into bursts of laughter. Tears streamed down Inez's cheeks. Liv hooted. Jasmyn doubled over on the floor. Sam was surprised that the racket did not wake up Tasha.

Even Déja laughed long and hard. "'What life is truly all about.' Absolutely. I am so happy that I now know, thanks to Piper, the correct way to apply nail polish and that 'burnt sienna' is this fall's to-die-for color."

Inez wiggled her fingers, the reddish-brown polish still drying.

Piper lifted her chin and struck a pose. "Don't forget dusky ocher is good too. And I'm serious. It will match your, ahem, style."

Déja reached over to give her a high five.

Riley said, "But we did talk serious things too, like about Tasha's new class and how hard it is for her."

Liv said, "How we'll all love on her extra and hope that will help ease her adjustments."

Inez added, "And we talk how Louis is so grumpy with his walker."

Sam said, "And we promised to encourage him to use it in the courtyard."

Jasmyn said, "And, Sam, you told us about your project in the desert."

Sam nodded. She had actually described her project, even the new ideas she had offered.

There had been other topics, deep-down, heart-tugging sorts of concerns that flowed between them.

The hardest was Jasmyn's departure and her future plans, of which she had none. All she knew was that she had to go home to figure them out and come visit again as soon as possible.

The clock chimed its ten-thirty piece before they all meandered out to the courtyard to hug Jasmyn goodbye. Tears mixed with soft laughter. The hugs spread from one to another. Even Tasha woke up enough to join in. As usual she hugged everyone, including Sam, to whom she whispered, "Night, Sammi."

There was not an opportunity for Sam to tell Jasmyn about her earlier phone call. Now, as she watched the women drift toward their own cottages, that conversation did not seem to matter much at all anymore.

What seemed to matter— No, not *seemed*. What in fact *did* matter was everything that had happened that evening in her cottage between the girls.

Fifty

Early Monday morning, after an obscenely short night—thanks to post-party hyper mental activity—Sam attempted three times to get out the door. First she forgot to put coffee in her travel mug, then she forgot the mug, then she forgot her briefcase.

The brain fog did not bode well for a productive workday.

"This is why we don't make friends, Sam," she muttered to herself. But the party had been nice.

Except now her final goodbye to Jasmyn would have to be cut short. Which was probably for the best. Getting all emotional was way too exhausting.

She pulled the door shut and stepped into the courtyard shrouded in coastal mist.

Jasmyn waited under the jacaranda tree, her dimples lighting up her face. "Good morning, Sam!"

"You look way too perky for saying goodbye."

"I'm sorry."

"No, I'm sorry. You can be as perky as you want."

"It's not that I want it exactly."

"You just are, naturally. Don't apologize for it."

"I'm going to miss you, Sammi."

She heaved a quiet sigh. They should have skipped this meeting altogether. The paper towel bawling session should have been their final hoo-ha.

"You're running late," Jasmyn said. "Come on, I'll walk you to your car." She led the way toward the back gate. "Seriously, I am sorry for keeping you up so late last night. But I really, I mean really, really appreciated the party. Thank you."

Sam decided not to tell her how many times she had already thanked her. "You're welcome." *Again.*

"I got the sense that you wanted to tell me something in private."

Sam rolled her eyes. Liv's clone was alive and well. "I did. I was just going to mention that I talked to my mom yesterday."

"Whoa. I thought you only did that on Christmas and Easter."

Winter and spring, Sam silently corrected. The holidays had nothing to do with her calls.

Jasmyn pulled open the tall privacy gate and they walked out into the alley. "This sounds significant. Can you give me the short version?"

"There's never a short version when it comes to my mom. Except that I survived the conversation." She stopped beside her Jeep and reached into her jacket pocket for the keys. They weren't there. She shifted mug, handbag, and briefcase to her right arm and dug into the other pocket. She muttered a word that sweet, perky Jasmyn would never say, opened her purse with one hand, and continued the search. "I don't have my keys. I don't have my keys!"

"Well, we'd better go get them."

They walked back to the gate.

"My mind should be in a drainage ditch behind a community center, not focused on getting out the door."

"It was the party on a school night. Throw your next one on a Saturday."

Next party. *Right.*

They stopped in front of the gate. And then looked at each other.

Jasmyn patted the pockets of her sweatshirt and scrunched her nose. "Oops."

Sam groaned and they headed down the alley toward the front gate. Jasmyn trotted to keep up with her long strides.

Sam slowed. "You're all set to go?"

"Yeah. I'm going to finish up some things in the office for Liv and then we plan to walk the pier. She wants to go the whole way, out and back. Keagan said he'd stand by with the guy who drives that little Gator out there for doing odd jobs. I used to have a Gator on the farm. One of those things I did not replace."

In spite of herself, Sam smiled. "I bet Liv's ready to walk the whole way."

"I do too. So why did you call your mom before Christmas?"

They rounded the next corner, their half circle to the front of the Casa almost complete.

Sam shrugged. "It's too complicated for my brain to put into words."

"That's okay. You probably just needed a family touch."

A family touch? Hardly. More like information. "I was wondering why my Swedish grandmother ended up on the rez."

"Hannah Carlson. Did your mom know?"

Sam opened her mouth, but nothing came out. She felt on the verge of tears.

"Good or bad?"

Sam croaked, "Good. Apparently she helped take care of me when I was born."

"Wow. That's beautiful, isn't it? And you never knew this before?"

Sam shook her head at Jasmyn's back as her friend punched in the code. They entered the courtyard and walked toward Sam's cottage. "No. Mom said she came from Illinois. No town name, though."

"Hey, maybe we're related after all."

"Sure. How big is the state?" Sam reached her front door, the yellow one. The goldenrod one. She thought about her keys on the other side of that door. They sat on the little table just inside. They were all on one ring: the Jeep key, the back gate key, the key to her office building, the key to her desk, the key to her locker at the gym, and the cottage door key.

She dropped her things, sank onto the yellow Adirondack chair, leaned over, and buried her face in her hands. *Forget on the verge.*

Jasmyn patted her shoulder. "I'll go in the office and get the extra key. You want to skip work and walk the pier with us?"

Sam burst into tears.

Fifty-One

Jasmyn rested her head on the back of the passenger seat in Liv's minivan, grateful for once for Keagan's dead silence. She shut her eyes to shut out the freeway traffic, shut out Liv's tearful goodbye, and shut out Sam's surprising meltdown.

Liv had made the long pier walk, her arm linked through Jasmyn's for much of the way, more for sweet contact than support. She was a strong woman, physically and otherwise.

"Jasmyn, dear," she had said in her low, confident tone, "I truly believe you will be back here to live someday. I only wish it were today."

Jasmyn listened politely, weary of the question of her future. She had a plane ticket. She would go home because it was her home, she would work because she needed to work, she would pick up where she had left off, perhaps with the in-your-face tornado memory by now a thing of the past.

She would figure out what to do with Danno's offer or with new owners. She would vacation regularly in Seaside Village.

Liv had said, "From almost the very moment we met, I knew the cottage was for you and not just temporarily. It sounds crazy, but God put that thought in my heart. I've heard wrong at times, and I wonder now if I have because why would you be leaving…"

At that point Liv had been unable to hold the blubbering at bay. At least they had reached the Casa and she was able to rest on her own couch instead of on a bench on the pier, waiting for Keagan to come to the rescue with that guy's cart.

Vacationing in Seaside Village was not going to work.

Vacationing in Seaside Village was not going to work.

The thought struck Jasmyn now like a sudden onset of stomach flu. What she had experienced these past eight weeks was a mere blip in her life. So many forces had come together to create it, from tornado to car theft to Casa residents and where they were in their lives at that point in time. How could that be repeated?

Things like Sam's success at work and her slow warming to others and Beau's flirting. Like Tasha starting a new school year and telling Jasmyn about it almost daily. Like Piper's quiet example of moving through each day after a great loss. Like Coco's stories that would soon fade away because the woman was ancient already.

Like meeting Nova in the desert mission church. Like Jasmyn herself taking baby steps in prayer and then in sensing the presence of what Liv called Other, with a capital *O*.

"Jasmyn?" Keagan said. "Are you okay?"

She opened her eyes and sat up straighter. "Probably not."

"Probably not." He threw her his quarter smile. "Nope. Probably not."

She took comfort in his words. In him.

The feather in her throat had begun its tickle a short while ago when he had come to carry her luggage out to the van. It continued through the last goodbyes to Liv and Inez, who had walked with her to the alley. It continued while her eyes were shut.

She reminded herself that, as Quinn had said, it was natural to be attracted to the guy. He made her feel safe. He was single. He had nice eyes. Gorgeous eyes, actually. She'd have to tell Quinn about them.

At the airport, Keagan pulled behind a shuttle van and parked at the curb. "Are you sure you don't want me to come inside?"

She shook her head and they got out. He unloaded her bags, the purple one and the beach bag carry-on, and set them on the sidewalk.

The next moment passed quickly. She had been unable to imagine a goodbye with Keagan.

The night before, she had exchanged hugs with everyone except him. After weeks of living at the Casa, she easily embraced the women, cuddled with Tasha, kissed Coco's downy cheek, stepped into brief hugs with Louis, Noah, and Beau, and laughed in Chad's bear hug. Keagan slipped away when she wasn't looking. But she would be seeing him the next day.

And now, in the blink of an eye, he was waving and climbing back into the van and calling out, "Text us when you get home."

So much for feeling awkward about embracing the guy who made her feel all weird inside.

Jasmyn sighed, disappointed and yet relieved.

It was time she got out of town.

Jasmyn easily found her way this time to the check-in lanes. She was flying straight to Chicago and changing planes there. It would be late by the time Quinn met her at the airport, but Quinn was a night owl. The forty-five-minute drive home would scarcely give them time to begin catching up.

The line was long. No surprise. Lines were always long no matter where she went in California. Jasmyn realized the crowds no longer made her edgy or protective of her space. Interacting with total strangers had become an enjoyable pastime.

She smiled. It wasn't quite the same as knowing everyone she ran into.

Behind a family of four, she parked her suitcase and opened her handbag to get out her e-ticket and driver's license. She spotted her cell phone, its screen lit up with messages.

She took it out, remembering that she had not turned up the ringer's volume. There were texts and missed calls and voice mails, all from Quinn. What on earth? Not bothering to read or listen, she called her friend.

"Jasmyn! Don't get on that plane! You're not on it, are you?"

"What's going on?"

"Are you on it?"

"No. I'm in line at the check-in—oh." She spoke to a woman beside her who was pushing her bag against Jasmyn's. The line had moved forward two steps. "Excuse me. Sorry."

Quinn exhaled loudly. "Well, get out of line, hon. We need to talk."

"Seriously?"

"Yes, seriously!"

"Do you know how long this line—"

"Albright, move this instant!"

Quinn could be bossy. In all the years of their friendship, it had been obvious that she was the leader of their pack of two. Jasmyn never minded. She did not care to be first in anything. And, if not for her friend, she might not have found the courage to try taco pizza, lip gloss, clogs, cross-country, or dinner with Nick Bloome. In all her bossiness, though, Quinn had only screamed at her once before, when the tornado touched down.

"Excuse me," Jasmyn said to the impatient woman behind her and got out of line. "Okay, Quinn, I'm moving."

"Sit down."

"What?"

"Sit down."

"There's no place— How bad is this?"

"It's not bad, it's not— Well, it's just something you need to know right now."

"Are you okay?"

"Yeah."

"Is Danno okay?"

"He is fine. Everyone is fine. Find a place to sit already!"

"I'm finding." Jasmyn eyed an occupied line of chairs and headed outdoors. She strode to a concrete bench under a palm tree. "Okay, I'm sitting."

No sound came from the phone.

"Quinn, are you there?"

Jasmyn heard muffled noises, a hiccup, a soft crying sound.

"This afternoon..." Quinn's voice trembled and then it trailed off.

Jasmyn felt some unknown boogeyman eat up the minutes, precious minutes she needed to stand in line, check her bag, go through security, and get on the plane.

She realized that, once again, she was not going to get on the plane.

Fifty-Two

San Diego Bay across from the airport offered the best and the most immediate respite.

Keagan drove straight to it, parked, and found a bench along the sidewalk. Water lapped at the large rocks that shored up the bayfront. To his left was the downtown skyline. Across the water, a navy helicopter lifted off from North Island. A sailboat drifted by.

He breathed in the salt air and willed his mind to slow, his heart rate to ease up. It took several minutes until he could no longer feel the presence of Jasmyn.

She was nothing like Amy had been. Petite, yes. Fun loving, well, yes, that too. Dimples. Check. Sparkling eyes, yes. Though different colors. But Amy had taken down drug dealers. Jasmyn wouldn't be able to do that in a million years. Wouldn't want to.

When Amy died, when she had been killed...

Keagan blinked the bay into view again.

The point was, he did not want to go down any road that led to entanglements which would, in one way or another, come apart, and that would then rip him apart. It was a good thing for Jasmyn to go home.

He admitted now, without reservation, that she intrigued him. That she touched him deep inside where nothing had touched for years. He assumed the place had closed up shop when Amy left.

Evidently not.

No matter. Life moved on, his life nothing like his parents' lives, nothing like his grandparents'.

He imagined his grandmother, a woman as feisty as Liv, and smiled. She would tell him he missed out on too much because he was stubborn as a mule, and someday he would be sorry for cutting off his nose to spite his face. She liked her clichés.

Sorry, Gram, you got a freak for a grandson. Not your fault.

His phone rang. He considered not answering it.

But he always answered it. Owning a business and being committed to Liv dictated that he always answer it.

He pulled it from his back jeans pocket and saw Jasmyn's name.

"Jasmyn?"

"Hi. Um…"

"What's wrong?"

"It's…well, nothing. Not exactly. Except I'm not getting on the plane. Can you come get me?"

"Of course. Where?"

"Where you dropped me off?"

"Give me three minutes."

"That's all?"

"Yeah. I'm close by."

Her intake was audible. "Okay," she whispered as she exhaled.

Dimples, fun loving, bright blue-violet eyes.

He could almost hear his grandmother laughing.

Jasmyn sat on her large purple roll-along near the curb, her carry-on and handbag on the sidewalk at her feet. She squinted in the late afternoon sun.

Keagan parked and got out of the van.

She twisted her mouth into a semblance of a smile. It was the only movement she made.

Keagan shoved his sunglasses on top of his head and knelt before her, eye level. "What happened?"

"Well." She bit her lip, her brows knitted.

"Are you sick?"

"No. I'm sorry. It's just— We should go."

"Where to?"

Her eyes went wide and she put her hand to her mouth. "Oh, no. Can't I go back to Liv's?"

"I'm sure you can. Is that what you want?"

She nodded and nodded, and then she nodded some more. Her eyes filled.

Tears were a no-brainer. He helped her stand and wrapped his arms around her. She fit neatly, as he knew she would.

She cried against him.

A traffic cop gazed at them, a half dozen cars down the curb. Keagan held up a finger. *Give us a minute.*

Or two or three...

"Jasmyn, what's wrong?"

She looked up at him, nestled in his arms. "Nothing. Not really." She wiped a hand across her face. "I don't know why I'm crying. It's kind of happy stuff. Crazy and weird but— Oh, Keagan. Quinn just told me I have a sister! A half sister, obviously. And she lives in San Diego! And I can meet her on Friday! Do you believe it? My whole entire life, I had no idea."

It was Keagan's turn to be dumbfounded. From what he knew, Jasmyn did not have family, no relatives whatsoever.

"See what I mean?" she said. "Where am I supposed to put that information?"

"Is it true?"

"It seems like it could be." Her bottom lip quivered and her face crumpled.

He pulled her close again. "I guess you just cry till you get used to it."

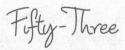

Fifty-Three

Keagan asked Jasmyn if she wanted to adjust to the bombshell of information before going to the Casa.

The Casa. Liv and everyone. What would they think? How could she explain things? Her cottage was clean and tidy, maybe even cleared of the borrowed furniture by now. How could she ask them to start over for her? "Should I go to a motel?"

He lifted her suitcase into the back of the van, shut its door, and turned to her. His chin lowered slightly. He waited, as if the answer were obvious.

She understood. "Mama Liv would have a cow."

"Or at least another heart attack. How about a cup of tea?"

She expected a coffee shop, but he drove them to an out-of-the-way, hole-in-the-wall restaurant not far from the airport. He suggested she bring a sweater as the air was turning cool. She dug the Seaside Village Gym jacket out of her carry-on.

They sat outdoors, the only customers on a tiny white deck, beneath heaters attached to the awning above. Bay water lapped the other side of a low wall with windbreak windows. Their table was one of only a handful. Boats moored to a nearby dock clinked softly. The waiter lit the fat candle inside a clear chimney on their table.

Keagan ordered tea and clam chowder and sourdough rolls for both of them. He winked at her. "No worries. They have to-go cartons."

"Thanks."

He nodded. "What can I do for you?"

"I don't know." She spread her arms. "This."

He smiled and every angle on his face softened.

Jasmyn closed her eyes briefly, blocking the sight Keagan always kept under wraps.

Why had she called him and not Sam or Piper? True, they were at work, but—but Inez's words echoed louder than any coherent thought. *When we women need rescue, he always there for us. He is our knight.* And she had been—she most definitely had been—in need of a rescue.

Her girlfriends, like Quinn on the phone, would have gone on and on, *Oh my gosh* and *What if this… What if that* and *What are you going to do?* They would not have swooped down in under five minutes and hugged her until she quieted inside and whisked her off to just what she needed, a gentle, peaceful place.

But all of that added up to overload. Not only was there the instant-family bombshell to absorb, there was the hug. The Hug. She added the capital *H*.

"I don't have family either," he said. "I was an only child. When I was twelve, my parents and I were in a car accident. They were killed. My mother's parents raised me after that. They've been gone a long time. There was an uncle at some point. I think he died in upstate New York. I can't imagine learning, out of the blue, that I have a half sibling who lives down the street."

Add empathy to the Hug.

"I know. It's like one of those goofy stories you read about online."

"And don't believe."

"Exactly. What's beyond discombobulated?"

He chuckled. "A dozen water balloons going *splat*?"

She smiled. "Right in front of me."

"Want to tell me the whole goofy story?"

She heard Quinn's voice again and her own constantly interrupting the words that made absolutely no sense. She needed to put it in some sort of order. The first thing Quinn had said was that Jasmyn had a sister. Jasmyn said that was impossible. Quinn said she didn't think so. Jasmyn had actually argued with her before she heard anything else.

She looked at Keagan, trying to comprehend how she had gotten from bumping bags in the check-in line to drinking tea and watching the sky turn pink above the hilly peninsula behind Keagan's shoulder.

"They lived there." She pointed.

"Point Loma?"

"Yes. The grandfather was a Portuguese fisherman. He caught tuna. It was big business for decades. I read about it when Liv and I went to the Maritime Museum." She leaned forward. "Now that I think about it, I could have actually seen a photograph of my grandfather there."

"Your grandfather?"

She straightened. She was chasing so many rabbit trails. "This woman's grandfather. This maybe-sister of mine, her grandfather."

"Why don't you start at the beginning?" Keagan spoke gently. "Did Quinn meet her?"

"Yes. She walked into the Flying Pig today for a late lunch. Quinn did a double take. Danno did a double take. Mrs. Benson and Mr. Anderson did double takes. Nancy Standard—she was my sixth grade teacher—said, 'Jasmyn! Holy Moses! When did you get back in town?'"

"Hmm."

"Yeah. Quinn said we could pass for identical twins. No joke. This woman wondered what in the world was going on. Quinn told her about her 'twin' and they got to talking. Manda Smith. That's her name. Manda Smith." Jasmyn repeated the name slowly, feeling the new sounds in her mouth.

"You must not favor your mom or your grandparents then?"

"No, not at all. They were tall and blond. Mom was beautiful. Gramma called her a loser magnet. It's not nice to say, but she was." She scrunched her nose at the memory of the losers her mother dated. It was obvious why Jasmyn had always shied away from men and why she assumed her father was not a man she cared to meet. "I always figured I looked like my dad." The tears stung again. "Manda said he died last year. It shouldn't matter. It's not like I met him or even have a clue if he was my dad."

Keagan reached across the table and touched her hand briefly. "It matters and you do have clues. Quinn told you more, right?"

She nodded. "He grew up out here, on the water. His grandparents came over from Portugal to fish." She stopped again. "Keagan, the first time I saw the ocean, I felt like I was home. Like something inside of me got settled."

He tilted his head, as if he disagreed.

"I know. It's one of those things no one could believe."

"It's not that. I had a friend who went to Scotland once, where her ancestors had come from. She basically said the same thing."

"Really? Then maybe it's not my imagination?"

He shrugged.

"Sorry. Another rabbit trail. I can't focus."

"It's okay. What put Manda's dad in proximity of your mother?"

She took a deep breath. "He was an over-the-road driver. He had his own trucking firm. For a time, he hauled things between here and Chicago. Manda's a driver too. She and her husband run the company now. They cover the West Coast, but she had always wanted to follow her dad's old route someday. He kept a detailed log of every town, restaurant, park, and rest stop he was at. So that's what she was doing in Valley Oaks."

"It's in writing that he was in Valley Oaks?"

She shook her head. "He wrote the name of the truck stop on I-80, twenty miles from Valley Oaks. My mom worked there thirty-six years ago. Manda took the exit, but the place is gone. She got back on the interstate, saw the billboard advertising the Flying Pig, and took that exit. I guess she was hungry."

"And she met Quinn and Danno."

"Right."

"Hmm."

They sat in silence a few moments. Jasmyn picked apart a roll. Keagan dipped his spoon into his bowl of chowder.

"The guy stopped at the place your mother worked. We're not quite into convincing evidence yet."

"You never met my mother."

He eyed her over his spoon.

She was glad not to see judgment. "Mom was eighteen and already had a reputation. It wasn't a nice one. She pretty much kept it going until she died. People weren't always accepting of us."

He lowered his spoon. "I'm sorry."

"The only thing she ever told me about him was that he was handsome and just passing through town. I should get over it."

He winced.

"So I did. Old news. Anyway, Quinn and I agree that this guy stopping by where she worked could easily mean she got pregnant with me."

"Did Quinn tell Manda all of this?"

"No. Goodness, no. She just showed Manda my picture and said she was sure I'd like to meet her. Quinn told her I was in Seaside Village and there was a coffee shop. Manda knew it and agreed to see me there on Friday. She didn't want to exchange any contact information. At first she was all friendly and jabbered with Quinn about why she was there and where she was from. But the more they talked, she became a little standoffish. Although she gushed over Danno's sauce." Jasmyn couldn't help but smile.

"Maybe you could make it for us sometime."

"No way. He's never given the correct recipe to anyone."

"From what you've said, I think you're special to him. I bet when he retires, he'll give it to you. What did he think about all this?"

"Quinn said he ducked out while they were still talking and didn't come back until after Manda had left." She picked at her roll, shredding it to crumbs on a plate. "She could back out. Not show up at Jitters."

"Or you could."

Jasmyn looked at him. "No, I couldn't. She's my sister."

"She's a set of coincidences."

Jasmyn shook her head. "Danno went looking for her semi. They don't exactly fit in our lot. He found it, on a side road, on the edge of town. The road I used to take to the farm." She wondered now if God had directed where the woman had parked. It was a silly thing. Another coincidence, that thing Liv said rarely happened.

Keagan took her hand, turned it over, and brushed crumbs from the palm. "And Danno saw the name of the trucking firm."

"Yes. Anibal Cargo, El Cajon, California. A-N-I-B-A-L. He looked it up online. Nice website, he said. It gave the history, how Carlos Anibal got started by delivering his father's tuna."

"Then Manda's story is true."

"Yeah. The thing is, my mom said she never even knew the guy's name or where he was from. She said she just picked 'Annabelle' out of a name book. She thought it was pretty."

"Annabelle?"

"My middle name. Coincidence?" She shook her head. "I don't think so."

Fifty-Four

After Keagan's heads-up phone call to say he was bringing Jasmyn home, Liv whooped in the privacy of her cottage. The explanation was a tad worrisome—a sister in San Diego?—but the bottom line was that she had been given more time to spend with Jasmyn.

After they arrived, Liv reined in her emotions. To some extent.

Her bear hug was probably a bit overdone. She effused too much about how her casa was still Jasmyn's casa, that the sofa, table, and bed were still in place, that she had stocked the refrigerator with just a *few* items to tide Jasmyn through the night and morning, that they would figure out tomorrow, tomorrow.

At least she had stopped short of tucking the girl into bed. Mama Liv doling out that much smothery effort might send the wrong message. Like she was glad Jasmyn's world had once again been turned upside down.

Jasmyn saw her to the door, clearly exhausted, clearly a jumble of emotions. "How do we pray?"

"Thanks and help." Liv kissed her cheek. "Lots of unknowns, Jasmyn, dear, but they will become known in due time. Get some sleep."

Outside, Liv kept her feet on the flagstones instead of dancing a jig. Jasmyn might be watching from the window. She rounded the corner of her cottage and saw Keagan in the shadows, leaning against the office door, his arms crossed.

She pulled her ring of keys from a pocket. "You kept her out long enough."

"She wasn't ready to come home yet."

"'Home.'"

"Figure of speech."

Liv chuckled and unlocked the door. Keagan entered behind her and shut it against the cool night air while she turned on lamps. Of course he was thinking the same thing she was. "Google?"

He carried one of the overstuffed chairs around the desk, sat down in her leather executive chair, and pulled out the keyboard. "I'll drive."

She smiled and sank onto the more comfy chair beside him. The desk was a big old thing with enough legroom for two. "You can be such a guy sometimes."

"Mm-hmm." He turned on the computer, which she had already shut down for the night. "We went to the Maritime Museum. She wanted to see the displays again about the tuna fishermen in the early days."

"I thought she might have wanted to do some online research."

He shook his head, typing, eyes on the monitor. "I'm not sure she has a technical bone in her body."

"Probably not. She's all heart. She kept saying she doesn't know where to put this information. It's a shock to her system, for sure. How was she when you picked her up at the airport?"

"What you just saw, only ten times worse."

"Weepy and giggly?" Liv tried to imagine ten times worse. Then she tried to imagine Keagan dealing with that. "What did you do?"

For a moment, he did not reply. His hands stilled over the keyboard. "Took her over to the Blue Crab for clam chowder." He typed again.

"Clam chowder? Now that's the way to comfort a woman."

He clicked the mouse, apparently engrossed in where the links were leading him.

Or he might be keeping a private moment between him and Jasmyn private. Had he offered a hug? Any other guy would have, but stoic Keagan? She wasn't sure, but if he had, it had been a significant event.

And she should stop meddling.

"It is the best chowder in the county," she said. "Did you find anything at the museum?"

"No. She studied those faded photos until we were kicked out at eight."

"It's after ten." She winced. *Meddler.*

"Then we drove around Point Loma," he offered, no hint of exasperation. "She seemed to just want to hang out where her distant relatives might have lived."

"Do you think they are her relatives?"

He tilted the monitor to give her a better view. "What do you think?"

Liv adjusted her glasses and looked at a family photo. An elderly couple, a middle-aged couple, a twentysomething couple, and two little tykes stood in front of a fishing boat, its hull and cabin painted an aqua color. The caption read: Carlos Anibal, center, founder of Anibal Cargo, and his family. From Tuna to Total Shipping Services—Transportation You Can Trust.

Except for the young woman, the people faded from Liv's sight. "Oh, my. Do you see the same spitting image of Jasmyn that I see?"

"There's a resemblance in Carlos too."

Liv refocused her eyes. It was true. The hair, the skin tone, the stature, something about the nose. "Oh, my."

There was a rap on the office door and Liv jumped. It opened a crack and Samantha peered inside. "Hey. Private party?"

"Come in, dear. Have you talked to Jasmyn tonight?"

"Jasmyn?"

"She's still here."

Sam, speechless, sat in the chair across the desk. She had just arrived home from work. Liv and Keagan filled her in. They showed her the online photo. Her eyes grew larger and larger.

"This is freaky," she said more than once.

Keagan continued his research. He found the date of Carlos's death— a year ago in September—and Manda Smith's name as his daughter and owner, with her husband Jake Smith, of Anibal Cargo.

He looked up. "What else?"

Samantha stood. "DNA?"

"I'll work on that."

It was hard to tell when Keagan was joking. For all Liv knew, he had a plan to get samples from both Jasmyn and these people. She halfway hoped he did have such a plan. That would be true meddling.

Samantha stood. "I should go see her."

When she had shut the door behind her, Liv turned to Keagan. "Do you think it's too much to hope that Jasmyn finds her biological family and they're wonderful and she decides to move to San Diego? To the Casa?"

His expression deadpan, he shut down the computer. Then he swiveled in the chair, leaned over, and gave her a peck on the cheek. "There's always hope, Livvie," he whispered and left the office.

What an odd evening. Keagan comforting Liv with a son-like kiss. Samantha behaving like a friend to Jasmyn.

She did not think she could have asked for more.

Not counting that little thing about Jasmyn moving into the Casa on a permanent basis.

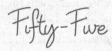

Fifty-Five

Sam had stayed late at work in order to avoid the emptiness waiting for her back at the Casa de Vida. Even before Jasmyn's goodbye that morning, her absence wormed its way inside of Sam, chewing at the joy she felt in her presence.

Evidently Sam had been given a reprieve.

She stood now in the shadows outside Jasmyn's purple door, her hand poised to knock. She hesitated.

Lights glowed behind the drawn bay window curtains, but that didn't necessarily indicate Jasmyn wanted a visitor. Sam wouldn't want a visitor at eleven o'clock at night. Her lights would be on because she was watching the news, not because she was ready to welcome an unannounced guest.

But Jasmyn wasn't like Sam. She was probably the exact opposite in most areas, especially the way she put others first. She was kind. Genuinely kind. Thoughtful.

And she might be in need of a hug. Sam knocked.

Jasmyn opened the door, her eyes wide, her hair half in and half out of a ponytail, her face ashen. "Sam! Did you hear?"

"Yeah. Freaky."

"That's for sure. Um, thanks for stopping by." Her smile didn't hold. "I'm sorry. I just can't talk about it anymore tonight."

"That's okay. I'll catch you tomorrow."

"Okay. Thanks." Jasmyn shut the door.

Sam blinked at the purple door. She blinked a few more times. Her eyes stung.

That hurt. That really hurt. Her stomach felt like a solid knot. Which was the number one reason not to get involved. Not to be friends with anyone. Except it was too late. As far as she could tell, she and Jasmyn were friends. BFFs, actually. Right? And her BFF was not in a good way.

She took several deep breaths, exhaling with each a layer of pride.

Sam knocked again and Jasmyn opened the door. "Jasmyn, you don't have to talk about it. Keagan and Liv told me everything. How about I make some tea? And I'll just sit with you."

Jasmyn started crying, a quiet weeping. Another reason not to get involved. Tears were incredibly messy.

Sam walked inside, shut the door, and hugged Jasmyn. "Oh, good! The couch is still here. Sit. I'll get tea."

Hoping that there was tea, she went into the kitchen and searched the cupboard. Of course she found a box of mixed flavors, no doubt placed there by Liv. She chose chamomile and heated water in the microwave, eyeing Jasmyn as she bundled herself inside an afghan and sat on the couch.

While the tea steeped, she rummaged some more and almost gave up until she opened the freezer. There was the telltale round plastic container. Liv must not have had time to bake a fresh batch of cookies and resorted to her storehouse of frozen goodies. Next she found a small serving tray because the hostess with the mostest figured every kitchen needed one.

A few minutes later she set things on the end table, handed a mug to Jasmyn, and sat beside her.

"Thanks, Sam."

"Shh. We're not talking."

Jasmyn nodded and sipped.

Sam sipped.

Jasmyn smiled. "We could talk about something else."

"Yeah, right, after hearing you have a whole biological family close by. Well, almost whole. A sister and brother-in-law, a niece and a nephew anyway. How can you think about anything else?"

"What? A niece and a nephew?"

Ohhh. Sam groaned softly.

"Sam, what are you talking about?"

"Uh. Um. Oh, nuts. I'm so sorry, Jasmyn. You didn't know."

"Know what?"

"That Manda Smith has a husband and kids."

Jasmyn stared at her. "She didn't mention kids to Quinn. Just that she and her husband owned the business."

Sam wanted to kick herself. "Keagan and Liv got online. They found information about the trucking company. The family trucking company and how—"

"Stop!" Jasmyn held up a hand. "I don't want to hear anything else. I want to meet her first."

"I'm sorry."

"The thing is, what if we're not even related? I don't want to get my hopes all up and then…" She paused. "A niece and a nephew?"

Sam hesitated and then she nodded.

"How old?"

Sam took a breath. "The photo was taken a few years ago. They were little then. One and three maybe?"

Her lips were a straight line.

Sam exhaled. She was not good at the BFF stuff. Not good at all. "Jasmyn, I'm sorry. I am so sorry."

"Sam, you can stop apologizing." She gave her a tiny smile. "Really. It's okay. I think I asked you why you didn't go searching online for your family history. It seems the natural thing to do nowadays."

"If you care to know anything."

Jasmyn's eyes focused elsewhere. She seemed lost in thought for a long moment, and then she whispered, "I'm an aunt?"

"Technically half a one."

Now she groaned. "I couldn't figure out where to put Manda, and now there's a niece and a nephew to fit in."

"What do you mean, 'put'?"

"Put inside of me. In my heart." She touched her chest. "I've been at a total loss about where to put all this new information, these people without names or faces. They're not real, but they are. They need a space in here. I've kept a spare room waiting, but for some reason they don't fit in it now."

"Your heart has rooms?"

"Doesn't yours?"

"I never thought about it. So do you have a whole house in there?"

"Sure. Bedrooms, dens, living rooms, basement, porches. I used to shut the mudroom door on my grandfather when he was being all loud and gruff."

"Mudroom. You're a fruitcake, Jasmyn."

"I am." She nodded. "What do you do with people?"

"Ignore them as much as possible."

"Sammi, you don't mean that."

She actually did, but typical Jasmyn urged her on to higher things. "I probably compartmentalize them in my mind."

"Same thing."

Not quite. Little lockboxes in cubbyholes were not the same thing. She let it go. "Do I have a room in there that you shut the door on?"

"No, silly. Everyone at the Casa is in a big kitchen and family room, an open area, where I spend most of my time. When I go back home, I suppose I'll have to close it all up. Winterize it, like Danno does the patio—Attic! That's where I'll put them for now. They can move into the spare room after I meet Manda in person. I hope, anyway."

"On Friday."

"Yeah." She raised the mug to her mouth, her knuckles white from gripping so tightly. "What do I do until then?"

"Build an attic?"

Once again, her smile went up and slipped right back down.

Sam hoped her own stayed in place and dazzled her BFF with confidence. "Rest assured, Jasmyn, those people in that kitchen and family room of yours will make sure you get through the week in good shape."

Instead of smiling, Jasmyn started crying.

Messy. Messy. Messy.

Fifty-Six

Early Tuesday morning, in the courtyard near the trickling fountain, Liv leaned forward to look straight into Jasmyn's blue-violet eyes. They had begun to resemble those of a woman panicked by the loss of her car and belongings. "Listen, dear. There is nothing to worry about. You are part of the Casa family. Everyone will ask why you're still here."

"Can't we just say my flight was canceled?"

"Oh, applesauce. This news of yours is an exciting development."

"It might be a lot of drama for nothing."

Samantha appeared behind Jasmyn. "And you are such a drama queen."

Liv laughed.

Jasmyn frowned.

Samantha nudged her shoulder against Jasmyn's. "And we are such a nosy bunch."

"I feel like the butterfly I killed when I was in sixth grade. Flutterbee. I never should have named him. I pinned his wings to a two-by-four. It was a science project."

Samantha chuckled. "Liv, what on earth are you going to do with her today?"

"Put her to work scrubbing the walls in Three so Beau can start painting them."

"Good idea. When I get home, Jasmyn, we'll go for a run."

Beau approached from the direction of Cottage Three, wiping his hands on a rag. For a large man, he moved quietly. "I thought I heard voices."

Liv noticed two bright spots erupt on Samantha's cheeks. She smiled to herself. Interesting that she and Jasmyn had been talking for several minutes and Beau had not heard voices until after Samantha joined them.

"Miss Jasmyn!"

Jasmyn rolled her eyes and groaned. "Yes, I'm back."

"Isn't that the cat's meow?"

"Or something. It's a long story. Sam can tell you."

Samantha shook her head. "Gotta go."

"I'll walk you out, Miss Sam. I need to get something from my truck."

At the sight of Samantha hurrying toward the back gate and Beau taking long strides to keep up, Liv couldn't help but laugh out loud. "That was brilliant, Jasmyn."

She smiled. "I didn't mean to put her on the spot. She's just good at giving short explanations."

"Reader's Digest versions." Liv laughed again. "I'm happy to give an uncut version if you'd rather not."

"I'd rather not—oh! Here comes Tasha."

The little girl raced from her front door and around the fountain, squealing, "Jasmyn! Jasmyn!"

Jasmyn caught her up in a hug. "Hey! I'm back."

"Yay!"

Riley appeared as Inez and Louis made their way over from their cottage. Noah emerged from his. She imagined Keagan lurked behind some plant.

Chad called out from his doorway, "What's up? Piper there?" His eyes were at half-mast, his hair a messy tangle. He ducked back inside, probably because he did not see the love of his life and it was only seven a.m.

Liv smiled. Most of the family was up and about, heading to work and school. The shortened account would have to suffice for now. It would be enough for Inez and Louis to invite Jasmyn out to breakfast, for Riley and Tasha to set up a visit to the library after school, and for Noah to offer to bring over a casserole for dinner.

The attention made Jasmyn uncomfortable, but that was life at the Casa. They would get her through the next few days and be there after, when Jasmyn would have to deal with whatever she learned about her biological family.

Fifty-Seven

At a corner table in Jitters Coffee Shop, a third refilled cup in hand—decaf this time—Jasmyn crossed one leg over the other and swung it vigorously.

She glanced at her watch. Twenty minutes to go. She had arrived early. Way early. The crowd had dwindled to a midmorning lull.

She should be having coffee with Quinn at the Flying Pig, figuring out what to do about Danno's offer, moving out of the studio apartment, getting reacquainted with her first-ever brand-new car that was turning old by the hour. It was a nice powder-blue Versa hatchback with tan interior. Driving it off the dealer's lot had been such a kick.

Instead…Her stomach lurched. Excitement. Anticipation. Dread. She took a deep breath.

Instead, she was going to meet her sister. Half sister. Probably half sister.

Maybe half sister.

And learn about her dad. Her *maybe* dad.

A niece and a nephew?

There would have been grandparents. Maybe there were still grandparents.

She checked her watch. Only eighteen minutes to go now.

Lord, help. Help me to be nice to her. Help me not to be stupid. Help me hear the truth about my mom and her dad. And if there's nothing—well, help me deal with that.

She recrossed her legs, stared out the window, and wondered where Keagan was.

Not that he had told her he'd be out there. Nope. He didn't have to. Not that she had asked him to. Nope. She didn't have to do that either.

Keagan. Talk about wondering where to put someone inside her heart. She tried to keep him with the others, in the kitchen/family room. He kept slipping out to the back porch where the sun rose and warmed her and did its *whoosh* and *wham* thing.

She shook her head.

For the past three days, the others had basically taken care of her, much as they had that very first week she had been at the Casa. She didn't have one meal, run, or walk at the beach alone. Keagan asked at least twice a day if she needed anything. Most of the hours she spent working with Liv and Beau on Cottage Three. Scrubbing worked wonders for her frazzled emotions.

She should have let someone join her, in person, to meet Manda Smith. Keagan would have. Sam offered to take the day off from work. Liv and Inez offered, a duo backup team. Chad offered. Even Piper and Riley offered.

Jasmyn checked her watch. Fifteen minutes to go.

She could add up her travel expenses, or rather her going-nowhere expenses. Canceling and rebooking flights were not cheap choices. She hadn't even rebooked the return yet. How could she know what was next? Her future hinged on this meeting.

Sam told her that it shouldn't. Liv had concerns about all the energy she had wrapped up in the event.

Oh, well.

And then, suddenly, there she was. Jasmyn spotted her across the street, on the corner.

Manda Smith. There was no mistaking her.

Jasmyn's heart thumped in triple time, all but closing up her throat.

Except for the facts that the woman was not sitting at a table or wearing a purple V-neck sweater, Jasmyn was looking in a mirror.

The woman stepped off the curb and headed toward the coffee shop. She wore fitted jeans and a collared white shirt under a dark blue vest. Her hair was pulled back and up, ends fanning out on top of her head. Her stride was confident. Dangly silver earrings swung.

Understanding flashed through Jasmyn, a zigzag of light in her mind, a boom of thunder that rattled her from head to toe.

Her life would never, ever be the same again.

Waiting for her destiny to enter the shop and look around for her seemed a stupid plan. Jasmyn bolted from her seat and out the door.

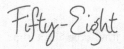

Fifty-Eight

Keagan watched from inside a friend's barbershop, across the street and north of the coffee shop.

He needed a haircut anyway.

Even from half a block's distance he could tell that Jasmyn's friend Quinn had not exaggerated about the resemblance. If no one noticed that Manda Smith was about five foot four and not five two, she could use Jasmyn's ID and board a plane, no questions asked.

The women met on the sidewalk. They seemed to hesitate before speaking, before shaking hands. Then they went into the coffee shop, Manda Smith leading the way. He guessed she was the take-charge type. Assertive. A woman who drove big rigs up and down the coast would require a good dose of moxie.

He ran his hand down his face. Prejudging Manda Smith was uncalled for. He had done further research that indicated she was an upstanding citizen.

He knew the names of her high school and college, that her degree was in business. He knew her political persuasion, the church she married in, her husband's history, their kids' names and birth dates. He knew their address.

He knew the maiden name of Carlos Anibal's widow and that she was sixty-five, lived in a guest house on the Smiths' property, still helped with the business, and belonged to a Portuguese community club. He knew when the parents of Carlos Anibal had died.

He knew Anibal Cargo was a reputable firm. No one involved with it had a criminal record.

So what was his problem?

Jasmyn Albright.

He could have done without the hug at the airport, without the hours spent giving her a safe space to unravel. Being with her, up close, watching her go from discombobulated to calm to resolved had ratcheted up his attraction to her.

He hadn't even wanted to tell her goodbye, but it was obvious he was the one to escort her to the airport. One thing led to another. He responded. Despite what sweet, impassioned Inez insisted, Keagan was not a knight in shining armor, waiting in the wings to rescue damsels in distress.

Later, he and Liv researched Manda Smith. After that, he researched some more. Not to rescue Jasmyn, but simply because he liked to solve puzzles.

He rubbed his forehead. *Yeah, right.*

But it was true. As a kid, he was obsessed with puzzles of all kinds: words, numbers, jigsaw, mechanical, why the neighbor grew strange plants in his basement. Even during his crazy teen years, he did not lose interest. His grandfather finally outfitted a corner in the garage where he could be up at all hours and not disturb his grandmother, a light sleeper.

As an adult, he submitted to officers who ensured he excelled at the whole business of puzzle solving: assess a situation and resolve it. As a DEA agent, his life and others' depended on that ability.

It wasn't something that left one's system like the flu.

He smirked to himself now. The phrase was Amy's, her response to his anger about his inability to slow his brain that ran too often in overdrive.

And what would she tell him in this situation? How would the woman he had loved so deeply—and who surprisingly had loved him so deeply in return—how would she explain his infatuation with Jasmyn?

With a start he realized that was an easy one.

Jasmyn is one of the good ones, caring and giving no matter how crazy her world gets. And you know what, Sean? That's perfectly all right. Six years is long enough to grieve. She would huff and roll her eyes. *Get a life already.*

The past faded from his mind. Through the coffee shop window he saw the indistinct figures of Jasmyn and the twin stranger.

Jasmyn Annabelle Albright.

He'd been unprepared for her. He'd been blindsided. Why her? Why now? What if this newfound family did nothing but propel her back to the Midwest? What if she bought that restaurant and got on with life?

What if... He locked his jaw, willing the questions to stop.

Heart puzzles were the worst.

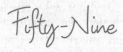

Fifty-Nine

"Unbelievable." Manda Smith shook her head.

"Yeah." Jasmyn shook her head.

They had not said much beyond those two words since meeting out on the sidewalk. The woman—her sister, there was no doubt about it—had chuckled. *Well, we don't need name tags.* Jasmyn had smiled. They shook hands.

Which had felt odd to Jasmyn. Wouldn't sisters— She swallowed the lump in her throat. She was making too much of things.

Now, seated at the table, ignoring their coffee, they stared at each other.

"Wow." Manda chuckled again, a quick humming sound from her throat, her mouth closed. Her voice was lower than Jasmyn's, almost raspy. "I seem to have lost my vocabulary."

"Yeah." Jasmyn smiled. "Me too."

"You have dimples."

"My mom's. You have brown eyes."

Her smile was smaller too, a barely noticeable stretch of lips. "My dad's. Unfortunately, I look like him. I mean, he wasn't pretty. At least I don't have his shoulders. Is your mom still around?"

The lump rolled up again in Jasmyn's throat. Manda didn't have a clue.

Quinn had kept mum with Manda about the possibility that her father might have met Jasmyn's mother at the restaurant where she worked. Still, given the timing of his presence in Illinois, on the interstate that ran past Jasmyn's hometown, hadn't Manda begun to put two and two together?

Jasmyn said, "She died three years ago. I never knew my dad. Not even his name."

"That's a tough one."

"It was okay. Kids teased, though. You know how that goes. I survived. So, you grew up in San Diego?" Jasmyn backpedaled, away from the topic of parents. "It's totally amazing here."

It was Manda's age. If she had appeared years younger than Jasmyn, then she might have introduced the subject. But she guessed they were around the same age, too close. Jasmyn lost her nerve. She simply could not say point-blank that Manda's father must have cheated on Manda's mother thirty-six years ago.

"I've seen a lot of the States, especially west of the Mississippi, but San Diego is still my favorite place. Actually, when I was a teenager, I hung out at Seaside Village beach. My husband and I used to come here before kids. That's why I knew Jitters. Is the ice-cream shop still around?"

"Nonna's Ice Cream Parlor. It's past the library."

"That's it. Quinn said you're on vacation. How did you land in Seaside Village? It's kind of out of the way."

Jasmyn dove into the details of how she had arrived. The verbal fire hydrant switched on. She covered her work, her mother's death, the tornado, car theft, and Casa de Vida. Her throat kept closing up. Her voice warbled, but she pressed on, wanting to avoid what was uppermost in her mind and yet wanting to know more.

Manda listened politely. Her eyes were spaced further apart than Jasmyn's. Her nose was slightly wider. Her teeth were the straight version produced only by braces. She gestured a lot when she talked, tapped her nails on the table and mug when not talking. Her nails were salon manicured, painted the color Piper had put on Inez's nails. What was it? Burnt sienna. The *in* shade for fall.

Overall, Manda seemed more…finished than Jasmyn. It showed in her appearance, but more in airy things like confidence and contentment. She would have handled a tornado better. She wouldn't have chosen a studio apartment. She wouldn't have run away.

Jasmyn asked Manda about her work and family. Manda talked about tuna fishing. About driving a semi. That she was an only child. About how her husband was better with business details and such a great Mr. Mom with their two kids, a boy, six, and a girl, four. They had hired another driver so Mr. Mom could work in the office and be with the kids when Manda was out of town.

Jasmyn could not get enough. She was dying of thirst, and Manda offered only a trickle of water.

Manda checked her watch. "I have to deliver a load of office furniture in Las Vegas by six. I should go." She moved her cup aside and folded her hands on top of the table. "Look, Jasmyn. You seem like a nice person. You're probably thinking my dad could be your dad because we look alike and he stopped in a restaurant twenty miles from your hometown X number of years ago, but I'm not going down that road. Sorry. Too many potholes."

Jasmyn opened her mouth and closed it. She nodded. "I just…" Her voice croaked. Nothing else came out.

"I mean, maybe it's possible. But he's dead and this would kill my mother. How old are you?"

She cleared her throat. "Thirty-five. Thirty-six in January."

"I'll be thirty-six next week. Which would mean— Well, you do the math. If he was cheating on Mom while she was pregnant—" She inhaled sharply. Her jaw set as if she gritted her teeth.

Jasmyn realized that Manda had indeed begun to put two and two together. And she had come up with four.

It was Jasmyn's last chance.

She swallowed the lump. "I'm sorry, Manda, but what he did is not my fault. I don't want to hurt anyone. I just wish I could fill in the blanks of my heritage."

"And what would you do with that information?"

"Nothing except feel like I wasn't such a freak. I don't look like my mom except for the dimples and eye color. She was tall and blond. She worked in that truck stop you tried to find. My middle name is Annabelle."

Manda stared, apparently speechless.

"My boss saw the name on your truck."

She shut her eyes now.

"My mother claimed she did not know his name, but I think that was a lie. It was easier to pretend he was not a real person. She could simply move on. We all could."

"Okay." Her tone revealed nothing.

"What was his name?"

She gawked at her now. "You don't know his *name?*"

"No."

"Any search engine would have taken you there with 'Anibal Cargo.'" She pronounced it *ah-na-ble.* "You didn't look online?"

"No. I didn't want to fill my head with things that might not be true."

Manda's jaw slackened. She exhaled. "Carlos Anibal."

Carlos Anibal. Carlos Anibal. The sound was more exotic than Jasmyn had imagined. She always figured he would be a Joe or Bob or Dan, a Jones or Miller or Wilson. "And did you know his parents?"

"Yeah. They were around until after I got married. Joaquin and Lorena."

Joaquin and Lorena. Her grandparents!

"Joaquin's parents emigrated from Portugal, around 1918 I think. I don't remember exactly. Carlos and Roselo."

Great-grandparents. Jasmyn smiled to herself, deep inside where it wouldn't scare Manda off. "What was your dad like?"

Manda looked out the window, quiet for a moment. "He was confident. A hard worker. He started driving a truck when he was seventeen. He grew the company into a huge success, and not because he was a nice guy. He was fair with clients but a royal pain as a boss. He hated fishing." She turned toward Jasmyn. "He was unfaithful to my mother when I was thirteen. They almost divorced. I doubt that was the only time. I mean, he did long hauls for twenty-five years. Pretty easy to hook up with someone else when you're basically gone four out of every six weeks."

"When did he stop driving?"

"After that incident. She gave him an ultimatum. He hired more drivers and worked in the office."

"He drove to Chicago all those years?"

"No. He built up a territory on the coast and gave up that run."

"When?"

"I don't know exactly. It was before I was born."

"So…" Jasmyn hadn't felt the bubble of hope until now, as it popped. "Then he might not have known that Jerri Albright was pregnant."

"Or he did and he bailed." She sighed. "I loved my father. We were friends. He taught me everything about the business. I'm a good driver because he was a good driver. But given his history, I don't know what he would have done if he had known."

"When you drove to Chicago, you were following a diary of his?"

"It's more of a list. He liked to keep track of places he visited. A quirk of his."

"Are there dates in it? Like exactly when before you were born he was last in Chicago?"

"That would be in the manifest." She paused, lost in thought. "I think we still have them from back then, buried somewhere in the garage. I can't promise when I'll get to them— I'm sorry, but I have to say this. My mom is taking Dad's death badly. I hope you won't contact her?"

Jasmyn sat back, surprised. "I wouldn't do that."

They stared at each other.

"No, I believe you wouldn't. Thank you." Manda scooted her chair from the table. "I really have to go. Maybe someday we can…" She shrugged.

Jasmyn stood with her and smiled. "Maybe."

Manda returned her smile and they shook hands.

"Did you ever want a brother or a sister?" Jasmyn asked.

"Nope. Guess I was having too good a time being the one and only. Take care."

"You too."

As Manda hurried to the door, Jasmyn sank back into her chair. Her legs weren't quite ready to carry her to the door, let alone down the street.

Well, she had wanted a brother or a sister. Not that it mattered now. She had one and did not even know her phone number or email address. They hadn't been offered, and after Manda told her not to contact her mother, Jasmyn wasn't asking. It was clear they were going nowhere.

That last smile of Manda's? The tip of her nose had tilted, her brows rose up just a bit. It was the same smile Jasmyn gave customers who changed their order umpteen times and then asked for the moon.

Sure. No problem. *Maybe someday we can…* Do what? Exchange contact information? Send Christmas cards—

"Hey." Manda stood beside her. "I just wanted to tell you something about my dad. For all his macho posturing, he liked gardening. He spent a lot of time taking care of our yard." She paused, as if deciding whether to go on or not, and then she took a breath. "The whole back fence was lined with jasmine." With a quick nod, she scurried off again.

Jasmyn's chest felt as if a whole rack of barbecued ribs had gone down the wrong pipe.

Sixty

After Manda left the coffee shop a second time, Jasmyn sat for several minutes, waiting for the pain in her chest to clear.

Carlos Anibal apparently liked the jasmine plant.

Jasmyn Annabelle's mother had chosen her name well. Purposefully. Which meant…

Honestly? It probably meant very little except Jerri knew a lot more about Jasmyn's father than she had admitted.

A loud banging on the window caught her attention.

On the other side, Chad grinned at her. He made senseless sweeping gestures. She shrugged. He put his palm against the pane, mouthed *Wait*, and walked toward the door.

Like she was going somewhere? Breathing was still an issue.

Chad plunked a large shopping bag on the table and disappeared behind it as he sat down. "How'd it go?"

"How'd what go?"

He peeked around the corner of the bag. "Oh, dear. That bad?"

Jasmyn's forehead hurt, as if the skin were all knitted into furrows. "I'll be fine."

"PDA alert!" he called out. "PDA!"

"What?"

Before the word was out of her mouth, he was at her side and pulling her up into his arms. "Public Demonstration of Affection."

The hug felt awkward. Her head was buried in his shoulder, but she knew people must be watching after his announcement. He held on to her tightly, until it began to feel like exactly what she needed.

"But," he murmured, "I don't do public display of tears."

"Me neither." She disengaged herself and wiped her eyes with her sweater sleeves. "I did once, in front of my smashed-up house. Got my picture in the newspaper in five counties. It was awesome."

"Oh, Jazzie." He pointed to the bag. "This will cheer you up."

She looked inside and saw rubbery material, black with a wide streak of pink. "A wetsuit?" She lifted the thick, bulky suit out partway.

"My sister's. I recalled this morning that she had left one at home. She's taller than you, so it might be a bit long, but it should suffice for today. We never did get to our surfing lesson. I don't know where the time went. You'll probably be winging your way back to Illinois soon, so we better hop to it. As in right now. Seriously, the surf's up, dude."

"Chad, the tag is still on this suit."

"What can I say? My sister bought it and never used it. She takes wastefulness to new heights. I suppose all we Rutherfords have that habit. I hope you won't hold it against me." He exaggerated a sad face. "Mildred does."

Jasmyn giggled.

"That's better." He smiled and looked somber at the same time, as only handsome Chadwick could. "You know, Jasmyn, the biological family is not all it's cracked up to be. Which explains my presence at the Casa. We're family without being family."

She nodded and folded the wetsuit back into the bag. "Which explains your presence here too?"

He grinned. "I suppose so! Okay, let's go hang ten and all that business."

As they headed toward the door, she noticed a coffee mug in his hand. "I forgot to put my cup in the bin. Here, I'll take that one too."

He yanked his hand away. "I'm stealing this one."

"Not really."

"Yeah, really. They don't sell these and you can't find them anywhere. The heft is perfect. I could offer to pay an inordinate amount of money for it. Or tell them we need it for a criminal investigation and I left my badge at home."

She touched his arm and stopped walking. "Chad, what are you doing?"

He rolled his eyes. "Now everyone is looking." He leaned forward and whispered in her ear, "It's for the DNA. Keagan can do something with it."

Jasmyn took the mug from him, walked back to the table, picked up her mug, and deposited both of them in the collection bin. At the door, she smiled at Chad. "Thanks but no thanks."

"You're sure?"

"I'm sure. She's my sister."

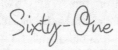

Sixty-One

Friday evening Liv opened her front door and saw, of all people, Samantha. She couldn't remember the last time Samantha had knocked on her cottage door without a specific invitation. Typically, she sought Liv out in the office. This might be a first.

Liv was all but certain that the expression of concern on the girl's face was a first. "Samantha—"

"She's not at home. Is she here?"

There was no need to ask who. "Yes, she's here."

"Mmm. Do I smell mac and cheese?"

Liv smiled. "There's plenty."

"Thanks."

Liv followed her across the living room. Samantha still wore her work outfit—black slacks, black blazer, plain off-white silk shell, small gold stud earrings. According to her clothing, her company did not have casual days. Liv figured that suited their prestigious reputation.

They entered the kitchen, where Jasmyn sat at the table. Samantha sighed loudly, a sound of relief. "Jasmyn."

"Hi." She smiled. "Just in time for mac and cheese."

Samantha slid onto a chair beside her. "You're smiling. That's a good sign."

"Chad taught me to surf."

"Okay. Nice." She leaned forward. "And the meeting went how?"

Jasmyn held out a hand and rocked it back and forth. "Did you ever try surfing?"

"Yes. I bruised a rib and nearly broke my arm. You're changing the subject."

"There's not much to tell, really."

Liv got another plate from the cupboard and set it in front of Samantha. "Why don't we eat?"

Samantha said to Jasmyn, "Just tell me one thing. Is she or isn't she?"

"She is."

"Wow." She blinked. "Wow. Manda Smith is your sister?"

"Half."

"Half. That's exciting. Isn't it?"

"Yeah. It is. Really. But it's also sort of…I don't know. That's that?"

Liv pulled her casserole from the oven.

Earlier in the day, Jasmyn had poked her head in the office, relayed the same noninformation about her meeting with Manda Smith, and held up a wetsuit. Liv invited her to dinner later. No matter how at ease the girl appeared, Liv figured comfort food would be in order. She prepared her famous three-cheese macaroni, chicken, and truffle oil dish.

Samantha chatted about her day. Samantha, chatting and making small talk! Who would have imagined she could do that? Jasmyn had worked wonders in her short time at the Casa.

What were they going to do without her?

Liv busied herself setting the table with a bowl of spinach salad and adding lemon slices to glasses of mineral water. She put the eleven-by-fourteen-inch casserole dish near her plate.

"Liv, where's the army?" Samantha asked.

"I never could cook for just a few." She pulled out her chair, and there was another knock on the door. "Syd asked every night where the guests were."

"There they are."

Liv went to the door.

Keagan was less a surprise than Samantha.

He stated with certainty, "She's here."

"She's fine."

He cocked his head, waiting, not moving along as he usually would.

Mr. Antisocial wanted to come in? Liv wondered if there was a virus going around.

She shut the door behind him. "Mac and cheese?"

"No, thanks."

They went to the kitchen and she got out another plate and fork.

"Ladies." Keagan pulled out a chair and sat.

Jasmyn's brows rose and Samantha squinted a question behind his back at Liv.

Liv shrugged.

There was another knock.

"Really, Liv?" Samantha's tone accused.

The girl probably thought Liv had called a meeting. "I didn't. I swear."

Keagan said, "She always makes enough to feed a platoon."

Samantha asked, "Is that smaller than an army?"

Liv opened the door.

Beau stood on her doorstep. "Evening, Miss Olivia. I was just on my way out and smelled something burning."

"It's cheese. It overflowed out of the casserole."

He grinned.

She smiled. "Hungry?"

In the kitchen he said, "Well, hey, everybody," and sat.

Samantha crossed her arms. Keagan nodded. Jasmyn waved.

Liv added a place setting in front of Beau, slid out a chair at the oval table, and noticed the vacant sixth chair. "Why don't I just stand until Chadwick knocks. He usually has a nose for my mac and cheese."

Jasmyn said, "He told me he was having dinner with his sister tonight."

Liv sat.

She was at a loss how to melt the ice. It was an odd combination gathered round her table. Keagan avoided socializing, so he was no help. Samantha's small talk had gone silent after Beau arrived. Jasmyn was off, closed in on herself. Beau could normally talk to a wall, but tonight he seemed tongue-tied. Perhaps because he sat next to Samantha?

Liv asked him to say grace.

He shut his eyes. "We thank You, Lord, for this food we are about to receive, and bless the little hands that prepared it. Amen."

Samantha said, "'*Little* hands?'"

"Something my granddaddy always prayed."

"I take it Granny Mibs had *little* hands."

"Why yes, as a matter of fact, she did."

"Liv doesn't. And she prepared this platoon-size feast with a whole lot more than just her hands."

"That's mighty true, Miss Sam. I appreciate you calling that to my attention. Miss Olivia, I apologize for any offense I might have committed. I realize you put your whole self into this feast, a lot of time and energy, and heart and soul."

"No offense taken, Beau." Liv spooned a scoop of the casserole onto Jasmyn's plate. "Samantha, hold up your plate, dear. So you think I have particularly large hands?" she teased.

"No!" Samantha's cheeks reddened. "They're regular women-sized hands. 'Little hands' sounded derogatory, that's all. Like…like you're insignificant and incapable unless you're in the kitchen cooking. If you feed the men, then you'll get noticed."

Oh, my.

Beau said, "I meant no disrespect, Sam."

Her cheeks were two beet-red circles now and she lowered her eyes. "I know," she mumbled.

Liv touched Samantha's shoulder lightly and said a silent prayer for healing whatever triggered her unease around Beau. It was obvious the man adored her.

Keagan helped himself to the casserole. "Say, how about those Padres?"

Liv said, "I thought you didn't want to eat."

"Changed my mind. It seems a night to indulge in comfort food. You baked brownies too, right?" He winked at her. "Cream-cheese filled with milk chocolate icing?"

Liv stared. She had never seen sugar pass the man's lips. There had to be a virus in the air.

Jasmyn said, "Who are the Padres?"

Keagan chuckled.

Beau laughed.

Samantha snickered.

The virus was most definitely contagious.

⁂

Liv shut the door on her guests and walked through the cottage, turning off lights.

The kitchen was immaculate, compliments of Jasmyn and Beau. They insisted she relax and that the other two stay out of the way. Samantha and Keagan were all thumbs when it came to simply clearing the table.

Her guests. It seemed too detached of a description for those four young people. Was "family" going overboard?

Jasmyn had finally shared details of her meeting with Manda Smith. Naturally, the big letdown was that there seemed to be no future relationship in store.

Beau had offered, "It's like with adoption. Sometimes the kids or the biological parents don't want to meet the other."

Samantha said, "Exactly. If there's the slightest possibility that a meeting would throw a major wrench into their status quo, they'd just as soon not."

Beau said, "Upsetting the applecart isn't on anyone's agenda."

"Exactly."

Liv said, "But who knows? Manda might get in touch with you again now that she's met you and sees what a sweetheart you are. She might want her husband and kids to meet you."

Jasmyn said, "But she might not because then her kids would wonder why we look alike and tell their grandmother and then Manda would have to explain who I was."

"Still," Samantha had said, her eyes watering, "you met her. You got to fill up that spare room in your heart."

Keagan had rested his arms on the table, leaning enough toward Jasmyn to force eye contact. "Who needs genetics? You have us."

Liv's head spun. What had happened? Samantha and Beau agreed on something. Samantha talked about the heart. Keagan suggested they were all family.

Her surrogate daughter announced she was leaving as soon as she got a ticket.

But Liv sensed that certain things had been cemented tonight. She and Jasmyn and everyone at the Casa would always be surrogate family.

And for that, Liv sang hallelujahs. She hitched up her shoulders and swayed her hips in rhythm to her spur-of-the-moment tune. She shuffled around her living room in little circles, her version of a jig.

If she kept looking for wonders, they never ceased and they continued to amaze her.

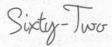

Sixty-Two

Beau, Jasmyn, Keagan, and Sam said their good nights outside Liv's door and veered off in four directions through the courtyard shadows.

And then Sam veered off to follow Beau down the path to the back gate.

"Beau," she called out softly, not wanting to disturb Inez and Louis, whose open window she scooted past. "Beau!"

He turned and she caught up with him.

His size always struck her. In the dim glow of solar lamps along the walkway he appeared even larger, as big as the polar bear she'd seen at the San Diego Zoo the one time she went for a work-related event.

And as cuddlesome as the midsized brown teddy bear her dad had given her.

She jerked her head as if that would shake loose the sappy images glomming onto her mind's eye. It didn't work.

Bearkins was his name. She slept with him for years, clung to him during her dad's funeral, whispered secrets to him, and screamed at age nine when her stepdad pitched him in the trash because Sam had head lice.

"Miss Sam?" Beau stood before her and lowered his chin to his chest.

The movement was a habit of his. She figured it helped him see faces rather than tops of heads.

She lowered her own chin, not wanting to see his face. The way his green eyes always sparkled was too…kind.

"Everything all right?" he said.

"Yeah." *No.* "I just, um…" Wanted a hug.

A hug? *Good grief.* Where had that come from? From the stupid teddy bear link because Beau happened to be a big guy?

Or from Liv-induced thoughts? The woman had hugged them all goodbye, explaining that their emotional health needed twelve touches a day. Hugs were the best bet and, by golly, she was going to do her part to add to their tally.

Sam never got twelve touches a day. Nowhere near.

"Sam?"

Sam. Just Sam. No *Miss* attached. Exactly what she had asked him to do a while ago, at the potluck for Liv. Why had he waited until tonight to comply?

When he had done it earlier, at the dinner table, she hadn't only heard it. She'd felt it, like a tug on a thread which, if pulled anymore, would unravel her.

And now he was tugging on it again.

"I, um, I…" She took a breath and risked a glance upward. "I just wanted to say I'm sorry for snapping at you earlier. That's all. Good night." She spun on her heel and took off.

Beau's chuckle followed her down the walkway. "Hey," he called out softly. "Don't you want to hear me accept the apology? Or not?"

She shook her head, zipped around the corner lickety-split to her door, unlocked it, and slipped inside.

His quiet laughter echoed long after she'd put on her pajamas and brushed her teeth and watched the news. Oddly enough, the sound didn't set her off. He had not laughed *at* her. It was more like a friend letting her get away with being a hothead.

With being herself. Curious. Too curious to welcome sleep.

Thoughts poured in, the kind she always preferred to ignore. They were the heavy ones that took her down dark alleyways, asking ridiculous questions.

What did she mean, *being herself*? Who was she? Was she still Samantha Yahzi Whitehorse, acting out of fear as she had since her father died? A hothead spouting caustic remarks that kept the likes of Beau Jenner at arm's length?

Couldn't she be Sam Whitley, respected professional with a tiny dose of Jasmyn's sweet naïveté to soften the edges?

That might be a bit much, though. It would be like a leopard changing her spots.

But still. Sweet, naive Jasmyn had changed into a more confident woman during her stay at the Casa. The passage of time since the tornado partially explained it. Managing the place for Liv had boosted her tremendously. Facing that stranger today and coming to terms with her heritage certainly made an impact.

There had been an obvious peace about her tonight. It was not exactly spot changing and her voice still dripped with maple syrup. Yet Jasmyn was in a new space. She had filled up that spare room of hers in her heart.

Spare room.

Nah. There wasn't a spare room in Sam's heart. It felt more like a hole.

Holes in hearts were not healthy. They just weren't.

Sam got out of bed, grabbed a sweatshirt, and shuffled into her second bedroom, aka her second office. In one continuous motion she flipped on the desk lamp, slid onto the chair, and turned on her laptop.

Avoiding familial research no longer seemed an option.

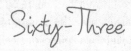

Sixty-Three

Jasmyn added cream to her first mug of coffee and noticed that the container was almost empty.

Which begged the question: Should she buy more or go home to Valley Oaks?

Of course Quinn had already given her opinion on the phone yesterday. After Jasmyn told her about the meeting with Manda, Quinn said with relatives like that in California, why would she stay another minute out there with the weirdos?

Jasmyn walked over to the bay window. Shadows still enveloped the courtyard, but patches of sky between the treetops were clear, a promise of early sunshine. Except for two rainy days, it seemed to be an autumn thing like the slanted sun rays. She saw a figure moving slowly. It was Liv, making her morning rounds.

How would Liv decide what to do?

Jasmyn smiled. The point no longer was what Liv would do. It was what Jasmyn would do.

Praying might be too strong of a word to describe what had woven itself into her everyday life. Morning and evening she consciously said simple things like *Thank You* and *Help me do such-and-such* and *Bless so-and-so*. Between the two, though, something else had developed. It was a quiet assurance that she was not alone.

Even yesterday at the coffee shop, before Chad appeared, while she reeled from how things had turned out with Manda, she knew at some level that she lived and moved within the confines of God. Loneliness was not a constant companion.

Jasmyn saw Liv now pausing at the other side of the fountain, in the proximity of Cottage Three. How lovely that she prayed for all the tenants, even the ones not yet at the Casa.

She set down her mug, went into her bedroom, and knelt before the bed on the nice, thick throw rug Inez had loaned her along with the bed.

"Thank You for the rug. Maybe when I'm Nova's age I can manage with a hardwood floor or even flagstones." She smiled. "Thank You for all of my new friends here."

She rested her forehead against the mattress, her arms outstretched, her hands folded, and she began to imagine each of them, one by one, round the ring of cottages.

"Take care of Coco today. Ease her arthritis pain. Bless her nephew and niece and the visiting nurse who take care of her.

"Use Keagan to take care of others. And let him know through others that he is cared for too.

"Help Chad with his struggles to find where he belongs in this world. Give his parents wisdom. Give him a path to a more independent, satisfying life.

"Give Piper a good, productive day at work in the store. Comfort her when she misses her fiancé.

"Take care of Noah. He always looks a little lost except when Déja is here.

"Keep Riley's head above water. Being a single mom of a special needs child and working as a dental hygienist is a lot. Take care of Tasha as she plays with friends today. And tell her dad, who has never been here since I arrived, to pay some attention to them.

"Help Sam to know how to relax. Heal the rift between her and her family.

"Bless sweet, funny Inez and Louis. Take care of all those kids and grandkids and great-grandkids."

In her mind's eye she arrived at the laundry room and thought of Beau.

"Bless Beau and his big hands that he uses to fix and maintain things. Give him the right words to say to Sam so she will hear them and realize how much he cares.

"And Liv. Continue to make her strong and healthy. Comfort her when I leave."

When I leave.

She raised her head.

Yes. It was time to leave. To end her vacation, to end her time of hanging in between worlds. To return to Valley Oaks and her life there. To create a new home.

"Thank You and amen."

She stood.

And wiped a sleeve across her eyes.

"I guess I could use some comfort too."

＊

Jasmyn worked at Liv's computer in the office, trying to rebook her flight home but making little progress. She wasn't that great with technology, but she didn't think it was her fault when the airline website kept giving her the message that they had no record of her.

Liv would say the difficulty was a sign that she should not leave, not just yet. Last night, after the mac-and-cheese dinner, she had said, *Would another week or two matter?*

How could she tell Liv, Sam, and Keagan that yes, spending another week or two with them would matter?

Sam had become the younger sister she'd always wanted, the one who needed looking after and to have life lessons taught to and to eat pizza with. Liv had filled in countless mothering gaps. And Keagan...

Keagan.

The honest truth was she wouldn't mind another hug from him or even riding on the back of that motorcycle if it meant holding on to him. She wouldn't mind watching his smile come and go, a subtle movement of lips that were just so. She wouldn't mind listening to his low voice for another whole week and bask in that all-is-well sensation that flowed around him like dirt around Pig Pen. She wouldn't mind—

Well, there were a lot of things about everyone she wouldn't mind experiencing for at least another week. She loved all the Casa residents. They were definitely the family that Manda Smith could not offer.

But the longer she stayed, the more she'd have to cry saying goodbye.

"Sorry, Liv, but the website is not giving me a sign." Jasmyn picked up the telephone.

The airline put her on hold. She gazed through the windows and the open door. It was a gorgeous late October morning, the air cool with hints of sun-kissed warmth. The sight of blooming bougainvillea and bird-of-paradise and begonias still amazed her. Autumn was as full of flowers as summertime had been. She wondered what changes winter would bring.

She spotted Sam crossing the courtyard, angling toward Jasmyn's cottage, and called out, "Sam!"

Her friend circled the jacaranda tree—full of green leaves—and entered the office. "There you are. What are you doing?"

"Booking." She disconnected the call. "Attempting to book anyway."

"So you decided for sure to go."

Jasmyn laughed. "Like I told you last night, yes."

"Yeah, yeah, yeah. I know exactly what you said. You went surfing and got all the biological family baloney thrashed out of your system. You realized home is not here. But none of us wanted to believe it."

She had seen the sad expressions on their faces. Even Keagan had frowned briefly. "I never said 'baloney.'"

"Sorry for the paraphrase. It wasn't baloney. It was just such a letdown for you, I felt bad."

"I was putting too much weight on it. I can't believe I didn't rebook right away and save hundreds of dollars. It was totally stupid to wait until I met Manda, like that would keep me here longer."

"But at least the spare room in your heart got filled up, right?"

Jasmyn wrinkled her nose. "I think I have to keep the Anibal family in the attic. But that's okay. The attic is in my heart too."

"I feel like I have a hole in my heart." Sam's eyes went wide and her mouth formed an *O*.

Jasmyn stared at her. "That sounds painful."

Sam closed her mouth and cleared her throat. "Yeah. It might be like your spare room, though. It just needs some attention. Then it'll get closed up and I can get on with life."

"I think Liv would say it'll get healed before you get on with life." She waited for Sam to roll her eyes, but she didn't. "That's what happened after I met Manda. I mean, it still hurts about never knowing my dad and now about being a nonperson to the only family I have. But we met and now the whole thing feels finished somehow."

Sam nodded, her lips pressed together.

Jasmyn leaned across the desk. "Sammi, who do you need to meet?"

"Hannah." She shrugged. "I found her."

"Really?"

"Mm-hmm. Last night I joined all those online heritage groups. I paid to join them." Now she rolled her eyes. "I could have gone downtown to the library and done it for free. Hannah Susanne Carlson grew up in Lynn Center, Illinois."

"No."

"Yes." Sam smiled. "A hop, skip, and a jump from Valley Oaks."

Jasmyn giggled.

Sam said, "So." She inhaled deeply and then she exhaled loudly. "Can I come home with you? There's a courthouse and a cemetery I want to visit."

"That's wonderful!"

"It's something. Why is it I want to do this in person?" Sam swiveled the monitor toward herself and pulled over the keyboard. "You're a bad influence on me, Jasmyn Albright. In a good way. When shall we go?"

"Tomorrow."

Sam stopped typing and looked at her. "Good grief. How much money did you make on the sale of your land?"

"Enough to splurge, I guess. The thing is, I'm just so tired of saying goodbye."

"Oookay." Sam turned back to the monitor. "I'm still paying off school loans. I'll check the cheap flight sites. You don't mind making sixteen stops between here and Chicago, do you? Or taking a red-eye? Sleeping in LAX?" She rambled on, typing and clicking.

And, knowing Sam's abilities, she would make it all work out.

Sixty-Four

Early Sunday morning, before the sky had rolled every shade of blue into one and taken on its pearly glaze, Jasmyn and Sam stood outside the airport, looked at each other, and laughed.

The shuttle bus from the long-term parking lot had just deposited them and their luggage at the curb. Despite Beau's offer to drive them, Sam had insisted on driving her car and parking in the long-term lot. Jasmyn figured the two-way crush was still in effect but not making much progress.

Sam said, "Whew. We made it."

"So far, so good."

"Come on. We agreed that the third time's a charm. You'll get on board this time."

They wheeled their bags toward an entrance.

Jasmyn said, "I hope so, after all you went through to get us here. Half a day online and how many phone calls?"

"I lost count, but it was worth it. We ended up with only two layovers and twelve hours travel time."

"And we still have money in the bank."

"Yes. The biggest hurdle, though, was getting you and Liv through another set of goodbyes."

Jasmyn smiled sadly. It had been bittersweet hugging Liv in the predawn shadows, not knowing when or if they would ever see each other again.

Sam nudged her with an elbow. "But don't answer your phone, and if you see Keagan, duck."

"Good idea." As they walked, she pulled her phone from a jacket pocket. "I'm going to turn it off— Oh, no." She stopped, read the screen, and set down her carry-on. "Three missed calls. A text. All from Keagan."

Sam groaned.

"The text says, 'Where are you?'"

"Tell him we're on the plane. We got an earlier flight. *Hasta la vista,* bud."

She felt light headed. Her stomach clenched. "But what if it's—"

"It's nothing, Jasmyn." She took the phone. "I'm calling him. There is absolutely nothing that can keep you from leaving today." She put the phone to her ear. "No matter who got sick or who needs—Keagan!" She spoke sternly into the phone. "You know where we are!"

"Now I do." His voice was loud.

Too loud to be coming from the phone.

He was at Jasmyn's side.

Sam lowered the phone. "You have got to be kidding me."

"Liv forgot to give this to you." He held out a small cloth bag. "Cookies for the trip. You know her. She was distraught because she'd baked them especially—What's wrong?" He looked back and forth between the two of them.

Sam grabbed the bag from him without a word, her scowl saying more than enough.

Jasmyn could only shake her head and hope her breakfast toast stayed down. She tried to inconspicuously press her stomach and breathe normally.

Light seemed to dawn on his face. "Ohhh. You thought something had happened."

Sam said, "Given your history at the airport with Jasmyn, uh, yeah."

"I'm sorry. I am so sorry." He smiled and spread his arms. "Everything is fine." His eye caught Jasmyn's.

And there was a shift in him. In the air. In Jasmyn herself.

She wondered if it was the sunlit peacock blue or the intriguing shape his jaw took on as the smile faded or the expression that contradicted what he said. Everything was not fine.

She agreed. Everything was not fine.

She stepped nearer to him, stood on tiptoes, and kissed his jaw where the leather jacket collar touched it. "Thanks, Keagan," she whispered.

His arms came around her.

And then everything was fine.

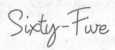

Sixty-Five

"What was that all about?" Sam handed Jasmyn a coffee and sat down next to her with her own cup. They were at the gate, half an hour early, time enough for coffee, a cookie, and an explanation.

"What was what all about?" Jasmyn eyed her over the cup, a distinct expression of mischief on her face.

"You're having short-term memory issues."

Jasmyn grinned and lowered the cup. "It was about *whooshing* and *whamming*."

"I wasn't asking about getting our things through security."

"You're so funny."

"I'm funny? You kissed him and he kissed you, and the two of you hugged for a really long time and I had no idea anything was going on between you."

"I didn't think there was. Really. Actually, nothing's going on. We're just friends. He only kissed my forehead."

That hardly mattered. To see Mr. Kung Fu Dude kiss in any way was almost disconcerting. For never expressing emotion, he sure could put a lot into one peck on the forehead. It probably had to do with the way his hand cradled the back of her head and how it was not a simple brush of his lips on her forehead.

Sam said, "Whatever. It's none of my business. I was just surprised."

"That's okay. I was too. I admit that I have felt an attraction of sorts. He kept showing up and doing things, like delivering my lost luggage and just appearing at the beach when I was sitting there and needing to talk."

"Being drawn to that behavior is a hormonal reaction, Jasmyn. That's all it is. He was there at opportune moments."

"He has that knight and angel reputation. Don't roll your eyes."

Sam blinked and refocused. "That's for the old ladies."

"But he is kind and attentive. He was even sort of funny last night."

Sam chuckled. "Okay, I'll give you that. He was. And he ate junk food. Very un-Keagan-ish. It seems, then, that this crush is mutual."

"There isn't one. I mean, it was really nice to hug him, but I'm going home."

"'Nice?' That's what *whooshing* and *whamming* is? Nice?"

Jasmyn blushed.

Sam smiled. "I guess it was more than nice."

Jasmyn shrugged. Then she shrugged again. She swallowed. "All right, yes. It was more than nice." She stopped talking.

Sam stared at her. "You're in love with him?"

"No! No. We hardly know each other. Honestly, this is Keagan we're talking about. Antisocial, odd, no first name. I mean, he has a first name. It's Sean. But nobody uses it. And I'm going home. I shouldn't have said anything."

"But you did. Jasmyn, you're morphing into a lovesick teenager, and I signed up to spend the next five days with you. If it's not a crush and you're not in love with him, what is it?"

"I don't have a word for it." She paused and bit her lip, looking more uncomfortable than even the day Sam had met her.

"You have two words for it, *whooshing* and *whamming*. What is that?"

Jasmyn sighed. "It's sunrise and sunset and the ocean. It's the desert. Remember where you took me? Where we stood on the overlook and could see absolutely forever?" She stopped again. "That's the feeling."

Sam started to shrug and then, suddenly, she understood. Her shoulders went down.

In her mind's eye she saw again the desert floor, its massive display of valleys and mountains and rocks and vegetation. She saw the sky above it all. She felt the enormity of creation, the mystery of life, the promise of terrifying goodness.

And she saw herself with Beau, being snarky or stammering because in his presence she felt exactly the same way.

Sixty-Six

Liv heard Keagan's motorcycle roar to a halt in the alley all the way from her living room with the door shut.

Although it was out of character for him to be obnoxious with his bike, she assumed it was him. Typically, no other motorcyclists used the alley. He could be parking in Samantha's vacant spot for some reason.

He gunned the engine again.

"Good heavens." She put down her book and went outside to the courtyard, half expecting to hear Louis yelling. His patio backed up to the alley fence.

The motorcycle was turned off. Liv waited, curious. She heard the gate open and shut. A moment later Keagan appeared on the walkway.

He was in his all-black mode, wearing jacket, pants, boots, and sunglasses with even a stocking cap and gloves. It was a cool morning, no doubt cold while going seventy on the freeway.

He veered her way, removing his hat and gloves. There was no little bag in his hand.

"Thank you," she said, referring to the cookies he had insisted on rushing down to the airport. Earlier that morning, he had happened to pass her the exact moment she realized she'd forgotten to give them to the girls. She had said to herself, apparently aloud and with much feeling, *Oh, applesauce.*

His overboard reaction had been to insist on delivering them.

Now she wondered if his engine revving and totally unnecessary trip were related. "You found them."

He nodded and stood before her. "Okay if I park in Sam's spot for a while?"

"Of course. I am sorry for making you drive all the way to the airport, park way over in the lot, and track down the girls, and then come all the way back home. My goodness."

His chuckle was more a puff of expelled air. "Liv, it wasn't a problem."

"Oh?"

He stuffed his hat and gloves into his jacket pockets and kept his hands in them as well. "How are you doing?"

"I'm fine. How are you?"

"Fine."

She pulled her cardigan more closely about herself, crossed her arms, and gazed at his sunglasses. "Sean Michael Keagan, I have never known you to speak an untruth. You are no more fine than the moon is made of ricotta."

His mouth twitched. "Or provolone."

"Or Muenster."

"Or Jarlsberg."

"What happened?"

He turned aside for a moment. He slid the glasses on top of his head and looked at her. "I told her goodbye."

When Jasmyn and Samantha had left for the airport before dawn, no one was up and about, excluding herself, naturally. But she had expected at least Keagan to appear. "You missed her earlier."

"I was at the gym. Issues came up about three a.m."

She understood. During the winter and on extra-cold or wet fall nights, he and his co-owner offered the gym as a sleeping shelter to a handful of homeless men. They had been doing it for a few years now. Once in a while there were problems and Keagan was needed.

No wonder he had insisted on rushing down to the airport. He had wanted to tell Jasmyn goodbye.

And their parting must have jarred something inside of him. Well, wasn't that curious?

She hated to pry, but— "So, you told Jasmyn goodbye."

"Mm-hmm." His eyes were focused behind her, in the direction of Jasmyn's cottage. "Big mistake."

She touched his arm. "Sean, it's never a mistake to show you care."

"No, it's not. The other part is. When it's given back to you."

Liv's spirit sank and jumped at the same time. Keagan and Jasmyn? Yesss. He was admitting it. But...

But Keagan's heart had been broken. Liv had seen that the very first day he showed up. He was not a cold man, simply a cautious one.

"Why are you afraid?"

He looked at her again, his face softening. "It's too trite and maudlin, Livvie. Let it rest. I am fine."

She straightened her shoulders and held up her chin. "I'm fine too because she is coming back. I know this for a fact. Just don't ask me how I know."

"It really doesn't matter. We're here. She's not. Life goes on. See you later." With that, he walked off.

She stared at his retreating back, watched him cross the courtyard toward his cottage, and disappear around the large bird-of-paradise.

Oh, Lord, don't let him shut down. Please don't let him shut down.

Sixty-Seven

Driving through Illinois at midnight was a trip. The word *trip* had nothing to do with travel.

Sam chalked up her catty response to the long day: three plane changes, a late arrival in Chicago, a line at the rental agency, and a drive on an endless stretch of interstate that offered less exits than Arizona highways and was twice as dark.

She exaggerated. How could anything be twice as dark as dark?

Jasmyn directed her to an exit in the middle of nowhere. They followed a narrow highway that felt more like a path through a forest of cornstalks. Sam's eyelids itched.

Jasmyn flicked her hand toward the left. "That was part of our land."

"It's too dark to see much…" Much? She couldn't see anything but a ribbon of road and weird-looking figures reflected in the headlamps alongside.

"I don't want to see much yet. Construction started already. It's not my idea of a welcome back."

They drove on for several more minutes. Sam imagined that if a strip mall went in where Jasmyn had indicated, travelers would easily stop there rather than continue on.

"Here we are," Jasmyn announced.

"Where?"

She giggled. "Sammi, you crack me up. Where do you think? See the lights up ahead?"

"That distant glow?"

"Gas stations. We have two now. Talk about controversy. I guess they all lived through it. No dead bodies have turned up, anyway."

The headlamps flashed on two signs. *Reduce speed ahead*, and *Welcome to Valley Oaks, Established 1867, Population 1100.*

"You'll want to slow down here."

Sam eased up on the pedal. "It's after midnight."

"They roll up the sidewalks at eight, but old Deputy Kropp can't sleep so he sits out here. The man is ancient, but he'll catch you three feet past the thirty-five speed limit sign if you're going thirty-six. Yup, there it is and there he is. Hey, Rudy!" she called out as if the man could hear her and waved. "Sheriff Cal won't let him carry a gun. Turn left here, between the stations."

Sam would have blown right on past the turn. There was no obvious indication of a street or a town beyond it. Maybe the dark hid everything. It was so dark.

Jasmyn chattered. She had grown more excited the closer they got to town and now seemed almost ecstatic. She lowered the window a crack and cold air flowed in. "Mmm. Smell that? Sycamore. There's a grove in that yard. That's the Westin Mansion, built in 1914. Remind me to take you out to see Wharton Castle. It's a real castle. Oh, look. That's the Pig."

They passed a nondescript building with a parking lot to one side. Sam could not read the low sign in front. In spite of streetlights, it was too dark.

"My home away from home. At least before I landed at the Casa. Here's our downtown. Post office, library, Lia's pharmacy, Ron's barber shop, Dottie's beauty shop. Dottie's been gone for twenty years but the name stuck. Keep going straight here. See the water tower over there? That's really old. There's a little park down that way." She pointed right and left and behind them. "Oh my gosh, it all looks so small."

"Compared to San Diego, it is small."

"Teeny-tiny. I haven't been gone that long, have I— Oh! Listen!" She paused and whispered, "It's so quiet."

There was absolutely no sound, no movement, no traffic.

"See the big building on the left?"

Surprisingly, it was big, perhaps three stories and made of brick.

"You can turn in here. This used to be Wilmington School. My great-grandparents and my grandparents went here. Do you believe it? I hope you're not allergic to chalk dust."

Sam pulled into a lot where about a dozen cars were parked and found a spot. Before she had turned off the engine, a squeal erupted and a shape streaked past the windshield.

Jasmyn added her own squeals and jumped out of the car. The blur must have been Quinn.

Sam unhooked her seat belt and pocketed the key, giving the friends a moment. From the intensity of their hug and the shrieks of laughter, she understood they were true BFFs, a dozen levels beyond what she and Jasmyn teased about sharing.

Sam's resolve wavered. What had ever possessed her to make this spontaneous trek to the Midwest? She had enjoyed Jasmyn's company back in Seaside Village and more so during their day of travel. Jasmyn possessed an ability to make her laugh and think and feel comfortable. She coaxed a better version of Sam out into the open. She made Sam believe that tracing down Hannah Carlson was a Big Deal.

But Jasmyn needed to get on with her life back here. Sam was going to be an intrusion. Not to mention a fish out of water. What was she going to do for five days in the middle of nowhere?

Ew. It was beginning to feel like her hometown. Small and cramped with a tight-knit circle of people that never slipped a stitch to allow space for her to enter in.

A knocking on the side window startled her.

Quinn motioned for her to get out.

Sam did so. "You must be—"

"I am." Quinn was short, like Jasmyn, but she threw her arms around Sam's shoulders and drew her into a fierce hug. "And you are you." She rocked her back and forth. "Any BFF of Jasmyn's is a BFF of mine. Welcome to Valley Oaks."

Sam almost melted into tears.

It had been a long day.

♒

Quinn was a flightier version of Jasmyn with short blond curls and, thank goodness, a lower voice. She seemed in perpetual motion, carrying more than her share up to the second floor to Jasmyn's studio apartment.

Jasmyn had not overstated the dreariness of her temporary home. The ceiling light cast shadows on drab walls and thin carpet, both nondescript.

They stood in the middle. Without much of a stretch, each woman would be able to touch the bed, the love seat, and the table.

"Sammi, I'm sorry it's not the Ritz."

"Did you ever take me for a Ritz person?"

"Well, no, but—"

"I'll be fine if you're sure you want to give it to me. I'm happy to check into a motel."

The other two burst into laughter.

Quinn said, "Forty-five minutes down the road."

Jasmyn said, "Don't worry about it, Sam. I'm fine on Quinn's couch for the week. I thought you'd prefer having your own space here."

"Thank you." Sam smiled. Jasmyn understood she would want that.

They showed her light switches, the coffeepot—tucked into a corner because there was no other space on the counter for it—and the trick to flushing the toilet. The shower appeared to be a closet.

Quinn had gotten things ready for her, clean linens and a few food staples. "Including our all-time favorite ice cream. Call if you need anything. We're half a block away. Yellow house, third on the right, one oak tree and a bunch of dead mums in pots. Missed your green thumb, Jazz."

They left and within a few minutes, an exhausted Sam crawled into the small bed. Her feet hung off the end. It made her think of Abraham Lincoln. She was in the land of Lincoln. She was also in the land of her ancestors.

She wondered how tall Hannah Carlson had been.

As she drifted to sleep, she felt content, glad that she had come.

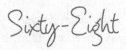

Sixty-Eight

Quinn handed Jasmyn a bowl of Melly's Mississippi Mud ice cream and plopped down on the other armchair in her living room. "I like Sam."

"I do too." She spoke around a mouthful of chocolate fudge, Oreo cookie chunks, and Kona coffee ice cream. "She's the one I told you was uptight."

"Nah. No way."

"Yes."

"Then I guess our Miss Sunshine has been busy."

Jasmyn crinkled her nose and changed the subject. "Mmm, Melly could make a fortune if he sold this ice cream on the West Coast. I have missed it."

Quinn laughed. "Did you miss anything else?"

"You." She scooped another spoonful. "You and Mississippi Mud. That about covers it."

"Girl, you are a puzzle. You bring home a stranger. All you talk about is Liv and Coco and Inez and Tasha and Piper—what kind of a name is Piper? I don't know, hon. Somehow you're just different."

"Is that good or bad?"

"You tell me."

She smiled. "It's good, Quinn. It's very good. I'm ready to tackle the world. Or at least Valley Oaks. I seriously think I want to take over the Pig when Danno retires. With you as co-owner."

"Jazz, I love the idea of running it together, but I can't co-own anything. You know I don't have the money—"

"Shh. Think outside the box." She smiled at hearing Keagan's words come out of her mouth. "There might be a way to do it. What do you think? Would you want to?"

Quinn stared at her, clearly taken aback.

Jasmyn waited for the idea to take hold.

"Wow. It actually sounds fun. Better than a beauty shop. But come on. You just told me you didn't miss anything about Valley Oaks. Why would you go into business here?"

"For a new start." She shrugged. "What I didn't miss was the old me in Valley Oaks. It was good for me to get away and meet people. Gain new perspectives. Reinvent myself." She swirled the ice cream with her spoon. "Okay, this is going to sound totally like a cliché because it is one, but I don't have another way to say it." She looked at Quinn. "God did something in me. He let me know that He's in every breath I take."

Quinn stared at her.

"Weird, yeah. I lose my family. I lose my house and belongings. I can't work. I lose the rental car. I'm glad I didn't lose you too, but the point is—even before any of that happened—I felt lonely and pointless."

"You did? You never acted like it."

"Like I said, I *felt* it. I functioned okay. Except for work and you, though, did I have a life?"

"You had Nick."

"Evidently, not for real."

"True. I thought you liked being alone out on the farm."

Jasmyn pondered her words. "Being alone isn't the same as lonely. Lonely happens when you're with other people and yet know you're not with them."

"Because your family were outcasts and you always got chosen last for a team?" Quinn made her dried apple face, scrunching her nose, lips, and eyes. "Sorry. I'm just trying to understand."

Jasmyn sighed. Quinn's delivery had always been right between the eyes. "Yes, that sums it up."

"And now you don't feel lonely and pointless?"

"I do sometimes, but deep down I know I'm not."

"How does knowing deep down make a difference?"

"It feels like there's solid ground under my feet. Quinn, it's what you've heard all your life in church about God."

Quinn's eyes unfocused, a sign that her thoughts were chasing down an answer. She shook her head. "But you're tweaking things. You're saying God is not Santa Claus."

"That's what you hear in church?"

"Basically. He has the list going, checking it twice."

Jasmyn chuckled. "He loves us, silly."

"Oh, that." Quinn winked. "But it's more personal to you now."

"Yeah. I wasn't in very good shape when I left here."

"Understatement of the century."

"I was that bad?"

"More than that."

"Oh. Anyway. I met Liv at one of the really bad moments. She showed me God. She's the closest thing to Jesus I can imagine. And so I started paying attention. I started listening. Then I got on my knees. When I got up, life wasn't the same."

"Hmm."

"Hmm."

"Hmm. Well, Jazz, however it happened, here's what I think changed. The sunshine got a little brighter."

Jasmyn frowned.

"Sorry, you're not losing the nickname. Sunshine just happens when you're in the room."

It just happens?

Did that mean she wasn't responsible for making sure it glowed?

Of course it did.

That was Someone else's job.

Talk about not feeling lonely and pointless.

*

"Nice car," Sam said from the passenger seat.

Jasmyn flashed her a smile. "It still smells new, doesn't it?" She turned her attention back to the highway, the morning sights almost too much for her eyes to take in at once. The rolling hills. The knots of oaks and pines. The fields of corn and beans ready for harvest. The white puffy clouds skittering.

"It's the color of Keagan's eyes."

Jasmyn whipped around. "Sam!"

"I'm just saying…" She grinned. "Hey, you want to watch the road?"

Jasmyn watched the road. Sam grinned? That might be worth putting up with her teasing about Keagan. Sam had even told Quinn about him at breakfast.

They had been talking about the Casa Detainees, as Sam referred to them. The mention of Keagan's name drew Quinn's attention because it reminded her of Sheriff Cal and Jasmyn's comparison of the two guys. One thing led to another and— And, well, there really wasn't anything to tell. Somehow, though, Quinn found things to ask and Sam found things to tell.

Sam pointed at the windshield. "What is that huge green machine up there with the line of traffic behind it?"

"A combine. They own the highways this time of year, going between fields. Be sure to watch out for them when you drive. And the grain trucks too."

"Grain trucks?"

"You'll know them by their overflowing corn kernels." She slowed, flipped on the turn signal, and turned onto a side road. "They're not powder blue like my car."

"They're not?"

"Peacock blue," she muttered.

"I'll take your word for it. All blues are not created equal. I knew that. I guess I never looked at his very closely." She laughed as if she'd said the funniest thing ever.

Now she was laughing?

Maybe getting away from home and work had given Sam a new perspective, similar to what had happened to Jasmyn in San Diego. She vowed to take regular vacations from now on.

Jasmyn's stomach churned. Given her plan for the morning, she should have skipped breakfast.

They had eaten at the Valley Café downtown. To her surprise, a few people stopped at their table and welcomed her home.

Welcomed her home.

Two of them—Jonah Thurm and Hayley Banks—mentioned how smart she had been to sell her land. Jonah's son, a project manager, and

Hayley's nephew, an electrician, were in on the windfall of the mall's construction jobs.

Windfall of jobs. Imagine that.

After Quinn had kicked Jasmyn's leg under the table, she realized her jaw hung open.

Despite the encouraging words, though, she wasn't exactly eager to see the construction work in progress.

She turned again, at a tight clutch of tall, fat pine trees onto a lane of cracked blacktop. It was short, maybe half a football field long. It felt like a driveway, although it led nowhere. Two willows drooped along one side. A soaring walnut tree stood alone, round walnut shells dangling from its leafless branches.

Sam said, "Is this it?"

"Yeah." Jasmyn braked at the widened end, switched off the car, and crossed her arms over her stomach. "This is it."

Sam touched her shoulder. "You okay?"

"Sure. But I should have skipped the pancakes."

"Seven months isn't all that long. You must still feel sick about it."

Jasmyn gave her a wan smile, grateful for Sam's presence. "It's so empty here. That just doesn't compute. My whole entire life there were willow trees on both sides of the drive. There were a dozen apple trees off to the right. There were six walnut trees and four oaks around the…" She gazed at the emptiest of empty spaces. "Around the house."

"Show me?"

Jasmyn nodded and they got out of the car. They walked across flat, graded dirt. "It's unrecognizable. Where was the front door?" She zigzagged over the ground.

She had been to the area once after all the broken wood and glass, the roof tiles, and concrete blocks had been hauled away and the basement filled in. There had still been vague outlines in the dirt of the house and barns, remnants of the grass yard. Now even those references were gone.

"Nuts. I can't see it."

Sam turned sideways. "I'm facing the sun. It's midmorning, late October, so the sun is lying to the south and east." She looked over her shoulder at Jasmyn. "Did you see it from the kitchen window when your grandmother cut up the apples for pie?"

Instantly Jasmyn tasted a thin slice of apple coated with cinnamon and sugar. She shut her eyes and saw the kitchen…its east-facing window over the sink…the corner table where her grandmother sat, cutting board and a large bowl of apples before her, windows behind.

Jasmyn looked at the sun and walked to a spot. "Here. This was the corner in the kitchen where the autumn sun hit, where Grammy June cut the apples for pie." She turned in a slow circle, and then she moved slowly, this way and that, describing what she saw in her imagination.

Kitchen, mudroom, back porch, doorways to dining room and back staircase, living room, entry, front stairs, front porch. She pointed a finger upward. Grandparents' bedroom, mother's bedroom, spare rooms, bathroom, attic stairs. She raised her arm high. "And there, in the northeast corner of the attic, was my room."

Sam smiled.

Jasmyn smiled. "Come on. Let's go do the barns and then we'll take a run."

Sixty-Nine

Sam's phone rang as she jogged alongside Jasmyn on a wide path. To the left was a stream bank lined with trees, their leaves a liquid gold color. To the right were cornstalks, thick and tall.

They ran on Albright property—or rather former Albright property. The crop belonged to someone named Zeb. It would be his last ever planting in that field.

Sam unzipped her hip bag and pulled out the phone. "It's Randy," she panted. "I gotta…"

Jasmyn nodded and pointed down the field. "Meet you there."

She waved and answered the call. "Hey, Randy." She slowed to a walk, tilting the phone upward so she wouldn't huff and puff in her boss's ear.

"Sam, how's it going?"

Inhale. Exhale. Lower the phone. "Good." Lift the phone.

"Great. Sorry to interrupt the first day of your first real getaway, but Creighton's breathing down my neck about the Chula Vista project. There's a board meeting tonight, and he wants his ducks in a row…"

Sam stood still to answer Randy's questions and direct him to her files. Nothing had been pressing on the docket that week, which had made it ideal for her to leave. But the big boss lining up ducks redefined pressing. It was why she carried the phone.

"Thanks, Sammi. I promise not to call again."

"It's okay. I was getting bored."

"Really?"

She chuckled. "No."

"Did you find your grandmother yet?"

She had told him a little bit about her quest. It was her only plausible explanation for flying last minute to Illinois. "You mean in the ten hours since I arrived?"

"Probably not?"

After their goodbyes, Sam looked around. The air was crisp, the sky clear and almost as blue as Jasmyn's definition of Keagan's eyes. Wind rustled the cornstalks, a whispery, soothing sound. Now and then she heard a gurgle from the stream.

And then she felt them: the low, silent hum of the earth itself, the gentle touch of air itself. They were different from and yet the same as what she had always known in the desert. The seen expressed the unseen. Creation and Creator became one.

Her father had tried to explain it to her little girl mind when they hiked.

Perhaps she had, after all, found her grandmother. Hannah Carlson moved far from her homeland, but she took with her that understanding of the Creator and she fell in love with a kindred spirit, Sam's grandfather. In their son, the understanding lived on.

Now at last, Samantha Yahzi Whitehorse began to grasp the deeper truth. Nature spoke to her as it had to her father and his parents before him. It announced a living God.

*

Sam found Jasmyn where the corn gave way to—of all things—a construction site.

It was incongruent and just plain ugly.

Jasmyn sat on the ground, her knees bent up, her chin on them.

Sam joined her. She had nothing to say. Apparently neither did her friend.

About a hundred yards away, like a kid's erector play set, there were vertical and horizontal beams, crossing each other. People in hard hats scurried about. Noisy trucks churned around. A short distance beyond, tiny vehicles zipped along the interstate.

"What used to be here?"

"Soybeans or corn. Zeb planned for beans this year. I had to buy him out."

"At least he had the other fields, right?"

Jasmyn nudged her with her elbow. "We'll make a farmer of you yet."

"This will be the strip mall?"

"Yes. Fast food, gas, and a midsized discount store."

"For Valley Oaks, that could mean…"

"A big ouch. Or not. Townies, generally speaking, will probably still mainly shop in town. This will serve other outlying areas." She frowned. "The people who now drive into Valley Oaks. This is Phase One. Phase Two, if the farmer across the road sells out, will be an outlet mall."

"Those are popular. That could bring business to the specialty shops." She had noted gift and antique shops in town.

"I hope so. Phase Three will be condos where the house and barns were. That, actually, could be positive."

"Definitely. New people, larger tax base, more customers close to town. Wow, I had no idea how huge farms could be."

"The landscape is shot to pieces."

"True, but there are still some wide open spaces. It is beautiful here."

"It's nothing like it was, and after this is built up…" She shook her head. "I can't quite get over the fact that I have money in the bank because of this mess."

"Oh, Jasmyn. You have money in the bank because of a tornado. That's not your fault."

"But if I hadn't sold—"

"Zeb would have soybeans, and you would have a studio apartment and an empty lot. From what I hear, you're giving back to the community, even if it doesn't seem like it."

"I guess I know that."

"You don't sound convinced. Maybe we should call Liv and the girls. Get some more pep talk."

Jasmyn smiled. "You did a good job, Sam."

"Anytime. What's for lunch?"

"If we sit here long enough, we could try that fast-food joint."

"Not going to happen." She stood. "Come on. Race you to the car."

Instead of racing, they walked. Jasmyn told stories about growing up

on the farm, about silly cows and mean goats, playing in the creek with
Quinn, ice skating on it in the winter, driving the tractor as a kid, snow
sparkling in moonshine. Sam laughed. But inside she felt a little bit sad.
Neither she nor Jasmyn could ever go back to those snippets in time when
home had seemed good.

☙

They ate lunch in another diner, this one in the county seat of Oxford.
It was a little bit like going to Liv's for dinner. Sam's dietary pickiness went
by the wayside. Organic and fresh vegetables and whole grains seemed,
oddly, to be missing from the heartland of agriculture.

But instead of whining about it, she dug into a luscious chicken pot-
pie with the flakiest crust she'd ever tasted and smiled at Jasmyn across
the booth table.

Jasmyn giggled. "You can run off the calories later."

"Right after the nap."

"This must be a major culture shock to you."

"It's nothing compared to my first day at UCLA after leaving Arizona.
The hordes of people. The strange food. The crazy traffic. Sheesh."

"It's funny how none of that affected me when I was in San Diego."

"I suppose you stayed there long enough for the culture shock to go
away."

"No, it was instantaneous. I never felt any culture shock. The minute
I stepped outside the airport, I was at home. I wonder if it was the Portuguese fisherman's DNA in me. The smell of the ocean triggered something
that made everything absolutely okay."

"That's—well, I was going to say off-the-chart wacko. But this morning
in the cornfield I sensed that my grandmother loved this land."

Jasmyn's smile creased her eyes into slits. "You get it."

"Yeah. Don't tell anyone." Sam smiled. "Back to the culture shock.
What's it like now, going backward? Being here at home?"

"It's amazing! I feel like the world is my lobster."

"Oyster."

"That too. I am so ready to start a new life. I want a new place to live,
maybe a condo. I want to buy the Pig next year and make a go of it."

As Jasmyn talked excitedly about her plans, Sam thought about their first conversation, the day they ran at the beach. At the time, the topic had been a bit heavy-duty for her, but Jasmyn being Jasmyn drew her out. Sam ended up confessing hurts she never spoke of. How that as a child, like Jasmyn, she had not felt safe unless she was alone. Family did not offer safety and nurturing. Neither did townspeople.

Although Jasmyn was at her sunniest and most confident—more so than Sam had ever seen her—something felt off. Maybe it was Jasmyn's reaction at the farm site earlier. For whatever reason, Sam couldn't buy into the rosy picture she painted.

It reminded her of how she had encouraged Jasmyn to reinvent herself. This wasn't exactly what she had in mind. But who was she to tell Jasmyn how to start over?

In Seaside Village, Jasmyn had fit into life at the Casa de Vida in the same way she had described her arrival in San Diego. Her sense of being at home hit her almost instantaneously with Liv and Cottage Eleven and many of the Detainees.

While Sam always pooh-poohed the Casa camaraderie, Jasmyn had fallen into it as slickly as a seal skimming through the ocean. She called Sam her BFF, but in reality they were all her BFFs: Liv, Inez, Coco, and the others. BFFs or, more precisely, family.

And now it seemed that Jasmyn's Valley Oaks home offered just one big fat challenge: starting over by herself. Where was her cheering section? Aside from one lone BFF in Quinn, where was her safety net?

Sam should tell Liv. She would want to know.

Seventy

Liv cuddled Tobi on her lap in an armchair in the office, and listened to Samantha on the phone.

"Did I mention the courthouse was built in 1880?"

Yes, Samantha had mentioned it already, but Liv let her ramble on. It was such a wondrous thing to hear Samantha Whitley ramble.

"The workmanship is incredible. Why don't we build like this anymore? I mean, besides the obvious—cost. The stone and marble, the colors, the artistic way it's all put together—well, it's too…it's just too *too*." She sighed.

"Use your words, Samantha."

She chuckled. "Anyway, the records people were also incredible. They helped me find my great-grandparents' marriage license and my grandmother's birth certificate. My great-grandfather sold insurance, and his business was listed. They told me about local history books at the library that should have more information. I'll check those out tomorrow."

Liv heard the satisfaction in her voice, a deep contentment even. "You might want to talk to the old people. Your grandmother would only be in her eighties, right? Someone could remember her."

"Great idea. How's Beau? And, um, Chad and Coco and everyone?"

Liv almost laughed out loud. How was Beau and *um*? "We're all about the same as we were forty-eight hours ago." There was a light rap on the door and Beau opened it. "Speaking of Beau, he just came in. Beau, Samantha wants to know how you are."

Samantha protested in her ear and Beau's cheeks glowed.

"Tell her fit as a fiddle." He backed out of the doorway. "I'll catch you later, Miss Olivia." And then he was gone.

Liv wondered what was up with him. He had not been himself that day. Either he was fighting an infection or he was perturbed about something. About Samantha's absence?

"Liv, the main reason I called is Jasmyn."

Liv listened as Samantha shared her concerns. Although awash in emotion regarding her grandmother and perhaps Beau as well, she was a pragmatic girl and Jasmyn's plans did not set well with her. They were airy ideals that included, of all things, to remake who she was in Valley Oaks.

Lord, have mercy.

She promised Samantha she would pray that Jasmyn would have wisdom to make the best choices. Now was not the time to explain that sometimes not-so-good choices ended up being the best for growth as well as for blessings. That life was never perfect and that stumbling allowed one to seek grace like nothing else could.

Liv did not want to hear that stuff herself. She preferred to hear that God answered the prayers of a woman of faith, even if those prayers were purely selfish demands. *Just bring her home to the Casa, Lord. Just bring her on back.*

She stroked Tobi's furry neck and listened to her sweet purr. "What are we going to do, Tobi? Prayer is a work in progress. Faith has no handles. We can only keep on keeping on."

She sat in silence and listened to the whispers in her heart.

And she understood that keeping on keeping on was not a solo affair.

And that faith did have handles. They came in the form of friends, three women in particular.

Liv referred to them as her top people. Although separated through the years by situations or distance, they remained her touchstones when it came to the spiritual.

But what she loved most about them was that they prayed at the drop of a hat.

She set Tobi on the floor, went to her desk, and composed a quick email to her friends and sent it off. Technology and backup were also wondrous things.

Liv found Beau in Cottage Three, sitting on a tarp in the living room, staring at three opened cans of paint.

"Beau?"

He turned, his cheeks still tinged with pink. "Sorry to have bothered you while you were on the phone, Miss Olivia." He gestured to the cans. "I can't remember which color you wanted where."

The man never forgot the slightest detail about what she asked him to do. They had discussed the colors on Friday for a long time. She had even gone with one of his suggestions. And by now in her presence, he would have politely risen to his feet.

She said, "I liked your suggestion about the pale yellow in the living room and the lemon yellow in the kitchen."

His eyes glazed over.

"Beau, are you all right?"

"Hmm?"

"You seem to be somewhere else today."

"Well now, Miss Olivia, I am sorry to say that your observation is true. I apologize for my subpar performance."

"Can I help you?"

He looked somewhere over her shoulder and exhaled a big-man sort of exhausted breath. He got to his feet and removed his cap. "I'm afraid I need some time off. A week." He shook his head. "Or so. I'll get someone to cover for me. I have a trustworthy friend who can work here between his other jobs. You don't need to worry about a thing."

Liv felt her hand moving toward her chest and lowered it. Her mind was already drafting a postscript to the email she had just sent. "I do worry. About you, though, not about the work."

His shy smile flashed. "Miss Olivia, you could pass for my Granny Mibs."

"Except for the small hands."

A crimson red flushed his cheeks now.

She had hoped for a full-on grin. What was going on with Beau, the steady, unflappable guy?

He cleared his throat. "I do thank you for your concern, but there is no need for you to worry. We know rain is going to fall now and then in every life. I seem to be in the middle of a flood. I'll just run up to Hollywood to see if I can't rebuild the riverbanks before any more damage is done."

River banks? Hollywood? She had no clue what he was talking about.

He reached into a back pocket and pulled out his wallet. "If you don't mind, I'll close up these paint cans and give my friend a call. Here's his card." He handed it to her. "Nice guy. Knowledgeable. Excellent."

Liv touched his hand. "Beau, will you save the cottage for whenever you get back? Please."

"Of course, Miss Olivia, if you're sure that's what you want."

"It is. This is our project. I don't want to move ahead without you."

He held her gaze for a long moment. Then he nodded, as if he understood there was no practical reason for her request. She was asking him to come back because she simply could not lose another member of her home.

Seventy-One

Tuesday morning at the Pig, wrapped in Danno's bear-sized arms, Jasmyn shut her eyes. She felt the soft flannel against her cheek, smelled the familiar barbecue scent, and wished more fiercely than ever that he was her dad and not that fly-by-night stranger who just happened to meet Jerri Albright on his way through the state.

"Welcome home, Jazzie." Danno moved her to arm's length, his eyes soft and his forehead creased. "That girl was honest-to-goodness for real?"

There was no need for him to explain which girl. "She was honest-to-goodness for real."

"Well, I'll be switched. You got family in California."

"Sort of."

He gave her shoulders a quick squeeze and let go. "I bet the guy never knew you existed. Have a seat."

She smiled to herself. Quinn had filled him in on the details of her meeting with Manda Smith. He was sweet to try to make the situation okay.

He yelled toward the kitchen, "Hey, Biscuit!" He winked at Jasmyn and said in a low tone, "I found a new way to annoy Quinn."

As if on cue, there was a loud smack against the swinging door, and Quinn burst through it, frowning. "Seriously, Danno? You're going to keep that up?"

Jasmyn laughed. "He will as long as you keep reacting like a wet hen."

Danno led them through the dining room, vacant at this time of day. "Step into my office, ladies."

They sat near the French doors that led to the screened-in porch at a large round table, where Danno typically conducted business. If vendors came during business hours, he'd offer them a stool in the kitchen beside the stainless steel counter. His official office was a messy, closet-sized nook, where the only clear spot was the computer. Jasmyn did not know for sure if there was a desk underneath it.

Danno eyed them one at a time. "Ready?"

Jasmyn nodded and saw Quinn do the same.

The evening before, he had called to ask if they could meet before she returned to work on Wednesday. He wanted to discuss the possibility of her buying the restaurant, if she was still interested. She was, but she hadn't imagined he would bring it up on her second day back in town. But then, she had absolutely no clue how to take over an established business. She had told him her idea about partnering with Quinn. He invited her to join them.

"Let me start by saying that you two are the best." Danno's expression seemed more sad than businesslike. "In my thirty years here, you two have been the absolute best. Separately and as a team. I know if anyone can keep the Pig flying, it'll be you ladies."

Jasmyn exchanged a glance with Quinn. Her brows inched upward too. The praise was overboard for Danno.

"You know I'm not full of hot air, so just accept what I said as true." He pulled a sheaf of papers from a file folder and laid them out. "I want to show you exactly what you'd be signing up for."

Jasmyn listened as he explained some of the financials. The numbers were not unfamiliar. He had brought her into the loop years ago, needing her to fill in for him now and then to order supplies or help with the pay-roll. She knew he made a decent living, but it was hard work.

"It's more a labor of love than anything. I think you both get that. You gotta love people and make them feel special. You gotta make top-notch food and make the place comfortable. We're getting a little dated, but that's an easy fix. Fresh paint, new lights. Just takes time and creativity. You'll want to put your own stamp on it. Maybe even change the name."

They protested that idea.

He smiled. "Remember, it was the Factory when I bought it. I called it the Rib House for years before adding the Flying Pig because the wife thought it needed some pizzazz." His expression turned somber again, and he muttered something to himself. "I need to quit beating around the bush." He took a deep breath. "The thing is, Ellie has breast cancer."

Jasmyn imagined his wife, several years younger than Danno, a vivacious redhead who was involved in theater, mostly in Rockville where they lived. When it came to the Valley Oaks community and barbecue ribs, she was usually absent. She and Danno seemed mismatched. Somehow, though, they had made their marriage work. They never had children. The restaurant and Ellie were his life.

As Jasmyn and Quinn began to sympathize and ask questions, he held up his hands. "They got it early, but this is it. She means more to me than the Pig. It's time to retire. She's already moved down to Florida where her sister lives. She'll have surgery and treatment there. So, ladies, I am leaving."

Jasmyn stared at him.

He nodded. "In two weeks."

"Two weeks?"

"Yeah. I'm sorry. That messes with the timetable."

Timetable? What timetable?

Suddenly Jasmyn realized that her eager-beaver return was all about some fuzzy future. It was not about two weeks from now.

She looked over at Quinn, who mouthed, *Red flag.*

Seventy-Two

The Valley Oaks Library resembled absolutely nothing Sam had ever seen before. Which was, surprisingly, a positive.

It fell somewhere between her childhood library—three shelves in a doorless closet off the community meeting room—and the bibliophile's dream-come-true at UCLA. Valley Oaks was a happy medium with an old-fashioned card catalog, a few computers, and, most importantly, books on local history.

Sam sat at a table alongside tall, sun-filled windows, lost in the thickest book titled simply *Patrick County*. It contained the county's history including photographs, a few from the 1860s. She flipped pages in search of a Hannah Susanne Carlson born in 1924.

Sam muttered, "How can there be so many Carlsons in one place? I should start with her parents' names. Or the grandparents."

"What you need is the genealogy collection."

Sam jumped at the squeaky voice behind her and turned to see a very small bird of a woman in a wheelchair. "Excuse me?"

"The genealogy collection. It's in the basement." She scowled, jerked on the wheel, spinning it toward the front desk, and called out, "Gloria! Gloria! Go get her the genealogy collection."

The librarian, a fortyish blonde who had helped Sam find the local history books, stepped from behind the counter and came over to the table. "Hattie, what do you need?"

"*I* don't need a thing. *She* needs the genealogy collection."

The librarian smiled at Sam. "Which township?"

"I don't know. Whichever one Lynn Center is in."

Hattie shouted, "Denkmann Township! The red-bound ones on the east wall. Do I have to get them myself?"

"Would you like to? I'll take you on the elevator."

"No, I would not like to! You know they made me retire. I don't work here anymore, missy." In a huff she wheeled herself away.

The woman chuckled. "When I was a kid she was the librarian, always shushing me and my friends because we whispered too loudly. How can I help you? I'm Ann, by the way, not Gloria."

"I'm Sam, and I guess I want the genealogy collection for Denkmann Township, red-bound, on the east wall." She smiled.

"Actually, Hattie helped collect and organize the information on local families ages ago. I'm sure we have more details than you can find online. I'd ask Hattie for help, but she doesn't seem to be in the mood today. Do you have an idea of the years you want? Some of the families are in several books, depending on when they settled here and how long the descendants stayed around."

"My great-grandparents were married in 1920 in Andover. Does that help?"

"It's a good start. Who were they, by the way?"

"Hilma Sofia Bengtson and Charles John Carlson. My grandmother was Hannah."

"Hmm. Doesn't ring a bell, but I'm from a town west of here. Let's see." She scanned the large room. "Ah, perfect. Do you see that gentleman over there, reading the newspaper?"

A white-haired man sat in a corner, in a grouping of armchairs around a coffee table.

"That's Otto Green. Come on, I'll introduce you." She smiled at Sam. "He's eighty years old but still one of the sharper knives in the drawer."

Ann introduced Sam to the white-haired man and left them to fetch the red-bound volumes.

"Have a seat, young lady." Mr. Green folded the newspaper and removed his glasses. "Now tell me, who was your family?"

Sam slid onto a chair next to his and told him names and dates.

A playful smile grew on his face. "Of course I remember Hannah Carlson."

Sam slumped against the chair, stunned at the idea that this man had known her grandmother. "Really?"

"Yes, but I'm afraid only from afar. She was older and our paths never crossed. She lived over in Lynn Center and came into town here for high school. That building has been torn down, by the way. Let's see, I must have been in the eighth grade when she was a senior. I noticed her because she was one of the stars, you know. Won all the smart awards, so her picture was in the newspaper a lot. She was a vision, let me tell you, with golden curls and a grin that would melt the meanest heart. And tall, like you." He shrugged. "She went off to college and I started paying attention to girls my own age."

"You don't know where she went to college?"

He shook his head. "Sorry. Girls didn't go that often. We were still coming out of the Depression. But, like I said, she was smart. She wasn't going to stay around here for long. I bet you're a smart one."

Sam smiled. "I do all right."

He laughed. "Where did Hannah eventually end up?"

"She moved to Arizona and taught school."

Hattie wheeled up to the low coffee table before them. "We got newspapers!" she snarled. "If you're talking Depression era, they're still in microfiche. Town can't come up with enough money for us to finish our work around here. It all ought to be online by now. Tell Gloria to take you downstairs." With that, she spun around and rolled away.

Mr. Green sighed. "Some days I want to park my golf cart in the middle of that ramp outside so she can't get her chair up to the front door." He grinned. "But then I'd probably carry her inside because I'd feel bad. I took her out once or twice before the war. At least I think I did."

They chatted a few minutes about his time in the navy and the bride he brought home from Virginia who loved his hometown. Sam could have listened to his stories for a long time, but Ann appeared with a stack of red-bound volumes. She and Mr. Green went to the table, where the librarian explained their contents.

The pages were photocopies, obviously from a variety of sources, some of them even handwritten. Ann and Mr. Green helped her find the book that contained the lineage of her grandmother's father. They left her to peruse lists of names and dates. It seemed a silly thing to wonder at, but her imagination took hold.

She had grown up learning about her Navajo heritage, how scholars disagreed on the people's origin, how they were hunters and gatherers and migrated in the 1500s to the Southwest. She learned the legends of the Diné and the four sacred mountains. She learned about the wars with Spaniards, Apaches, and Americans. She learned of the Long Walk in 1864 to New Mexico and back to the homeland in 1868 when the reservation was established. A great-great-great-grandfather had been a part of it.

Those facts had never been enough. Half of her had always been a blank slate, a blank canvas. But now...an artist stood before it, dipping his brush into his palette and, with great sweeping motions, painted the colors of sunrise and sunset on it as she read *Charles John Carlson, born in Sweden, 1864.*

As one ancestor was being forced to march across Arizona and New Mexico another was a baby in Sweden.

Somehow the paths of the descendants of these two men crossed, and Samantha Whitehorse was alive today.

Good grief. Jasmyn would have a heyday with this one.

ote

Jasmyn indeed had a heyday with Sam's information as they ate dinner at the Flying Pig, a cozy den of tasty comfort food with a Beau-like owner making the rounds. Danno was a bit gruffer around the edges but obviously a gentle guy who knew how to make customers feel welcome.

Jasmyn clapped her hands. "See, Sam? What did I tell you? Your grandma went to Arizona to meet your grandpa so your dad could be born so—"

"I get it!" Sam chuckled. "I just can't wrap my head around it."

"Why would you want to? Liv would say accept it as a love note from God."

"Liv would, huh?"

"Okay, I would too." Jasmyn picked up a rib dripping with sauce. "Even if it does break down when I try to factor in a half sister who doesn't want anything to do with me, I still accept that. Is this too much?"

"No. It's amazing. Not overly spicy or sweet."

"Not the sauce. I meant talking about God, and how I think He loves all of us and that reassures me that everything is going to be okay, no matter what it looks like."

Sam knew what Jasmyn had meant. The only aspect that seemed too much was that it was not too much. "It's not too much."

None of it was too much. God talk, Jasmyn's maple syrup voice, the too-short bed, Quinn's constant interruptions as she alternately served them and joined them, the library that closed at noon and kept its red-bound volumes behind locked doors, thoughts of Beau every time Danno passed by... She bit into a French fry.

Jasmyn eyed her over the rib in her hands, a spot of sauce on her cheek, surprise written in the raised brows.

She wasn't the only one surprised. Sam smiled and pointed to her own cheek.

Jasmyn laughed and grabbed a napkin from the pile on the table. "There is only one way to eat these, and it's messy."

"But worth it." Sam picked up another fry. "Did you know the library closes at noon on Tuesdays?"

"And it's closed all day on Wednesdays. You have to wait to look at the newspapers. Will you go back to Rockville?"

Sam had found her way to the so-called big city about forty minutes away and spent the afternoon in that library, mostly online. Ann, the librarian, had been right. Valley Oaks was leaps ahead when it came to local history. "I have something better to do."

"You're having lunch with Otto Green and Hattie."

"Not quite. They gave me an idea, though. They think the house Hannah grew up in might still be standing. Neither of them know the exact street, but they figure that Ruthie Moore will know it. She's lived in Lynn Center for eighty-eight years. Ann gave me her number and address, and Otto promised to call her to say I'd be dropping by."

"That town hasn't changed at all. You'll be walking exactly where Hannah walked."

Sam nodded and felt again the thrill she had earlier while reading about her ancestors.

"Maybe you'll even see her house. Whoa! Maybe you'll even go inside it."

Sam stared at her. "I hadn't thought of that. I could just knock on the door and explain— Maybe not. I'm beginning to feel like that baby bird in the kids' book who asks every animal 'Are you my mother?'"

She smiled. "Since you have an introduction to Ruthie Moore, start there and win her confidence. She can put in a good word for you at the house. If there is a house."

"With someone in it. Want to come with me?"

"I'd be as much a stranger as you are. You'll be fine. I have some things to take care of and then I have to work. Why do you keep looking at Danno?"

"I don't." She glanced at him. Again. "He reminds me of Beau."

"Danno?"

"Size-wise. Maybe."

Jasmyn looked over at her boss. "I guess I can see that."

"He seems, uh, nice."

"He is, but with Beau you get that right away. Danno hides it. You're thinking about Beau?" Jasmyn gazed at her a little too intensely.

Sam shook her head a little too vigorously and changed the subject. She pretended that all was well, that she did not miss Beau Jenner. She pretended her life had not turned downright messy.

Seventy-Three

Jasmyn and Sam lingered at the Pig after hours, drinking decaf coffee and tea. It had been a slow night. Cleanup did not take long. Danno told them to lock up whenever. He and the rest of the crew said good night and left.

Coffee mug in hand, Quinn slid onto the bench seat next to Jasmyn. "What's up?"

Sam said, "She was just telling me about—"

"Beau Jenner." Jasmyn winked. "At least I tried to."

Sam seemed flustered again but clamped her mouth shut. Maybe she decided to finally give up dodging the subject Jasmyn had been attempting to discuss for a while.

Quinn said, "Beau, the handyman." She glanced back and forth at Jasmyn and Sam. "Ah. He's something more, huh?"

"We're not absolutely sure," Jasmyn said.

Sam raised her hands in surrender. "I'm absolutely sure. I have a crush on the guy. Okay? I do. Nutty as that sounds. And I can't believe I said it. I hadn't even admitted it to myself. Good grief! What was in that barbecue sauce?"

"Truth serum." Quinn smiled.

"Well, it worked."

Jasmyn figured a combination of things was at work in Sam that had breathed life into her. She was clearly excited about the whole family history thing. Taking a vacation had to have helped. Jasmyn hoped her information would not pop the whole bubble. "Sammi, it's obvious he likes you too, but something has come up." She paused. "I talked to Liv today." She stopped again.

"Okay. And?"

"And she said that Beau left. He went to Hollywood for a week. Or two." Popping bubbles was such a painful process. But Sam needed to know. Didn't she?

"So?"

"It might be nothing. But you should know. I think."

Quinn blew out an exasperated breath. "Albright, say it already. Why did he go to Hollywood?"

"I don't know why. All I know is that his ex-fiancée lives there."

Sam sank against the back of the bench seat. Her face sort of went blank, as if a shade had been pulled over it, darkening the light. She resembled the chic, aloof woman Jasmyn had met that first day at the Casa.

Quinn said, "Uh-oh."

Jasmyn said, "Maybe it's not related."

Quinn added, "Yeah, he probably went to take one of those movie star home tours."

"Or maybe Liv heard wrong. He went somewhere in Los Angeles to get some tools he couldn't buy in…" Her voice trailed off.

Sam straightened. "Or else he went to see her. It really doesn't matter."

Jasmyn said, "I'm sorry. When you brought him up earlier, I thought, oh no. Absence has made your heart grow fonder. I thought I'd better tell you what I know."

Sam rolled her eyes. "Don't worry about it. Did Liv tell you this?"

"No. She doesn't know anything except that he went to Hollywood, which seems to have upset her. When I first met Beau, I asked him how he got from Kentucky to Seaside Village, and he said he came with his fiancée, his hometown honey. She's an actress and she made it big. Because he lives in San Diego and she doesn't, my guess is they split."

Quinn said, "Curious that he told you."

"I caught him at the right moment. Her latest movie had just been released, and I think it bothered him."

"Jazz, who is she?"

Jasmyn hesitated. Hollywood was a big deal to Quinn. She would make the fuss Beau wanted to avoid.

Quinn sighed. "Like I don't live three thousand miles away."

Jasmyn looked at Sam.

"You know I can keep my mouth shut. And honestly, I'm fine. We weren't exactly seeing each other. If he's hung up on someone else, I don't want us seeing each other."

"Yeah," Quinn said. "What good is a crush if you can't dream about taking it to the next level?"

Sam frowned. "I was nowhere near dreaming that. I never asked him how he got from Kentucky to Seaside Village because he annoys me to pieces."

Jasmyn wasn't sure she bought into Sam's words. There was still a hint of emotional shutdown in her face.

Quinn said, "So? Who is she?"

"Tallie Shay."

"Oh. My. Gosh." Quinn almost squealed.

Sam said, "Who's Tallie Shay?"

Quinn said, "One of the hot new ones. There's talk of her being nominated for best supporting actress in her latest movie. Even before that, her face was plastered everywhere. Some of it was tabloid stuff."

"Hmm." Sam's shoulders relaxed. "That's Beau's style?"

Jasmyn smiled gently. "I can't really see it."

"Well, he had me fooled."

Quinn huffed. "Men."

"Speaking of which. Of whom? Anyway." Jasmyn hesitated. "While we're on the subject…" Her voice faded out. Her thoughts tumbled like clothes in a dryer. What was there to say?

The other two stared at her, waiting.

At last Quinn said, "The subject is men." She gestured for Jasmyn to get on with it. "Come on. You can do it. Does he have a name?"

Sam's eyes widened. "Mr. Kung Fu Dude."

Quinn grinned. "The guy with the last name for a first name. The angel, knight, kung fu dude who doesn't talk much. The one who gave you that jacket lying there next to you."

Jasmyn glanced down at the purple folds on the bench seat and vowed to stop wearing the jacket. "He's weird. He lives far away. I'll stop thinking about him eventually. A week or two. Three, tops."

"It was the kiss at the airport," Sam said. "That wasn't fair."

Quinn said, "Whoa! A kiss at the airport?"

Jasmyn shook her head. "A peck on the forehead. Like between friends. Like it's been fun getting to know you, have a good life."

"It sure didn't look that way to me. Quinn, in the three years I've known him, I have never seen the guy show even a hint of emotion."

Jasmyn squirmed. "This is a pointless conversation. I only brought him up because I ate the barbecue sauce too."

The other two laughed.

Jasmyn realized the talk wasn't totally pointless. Her confession released some tension inside. She really did like Keagan in that way.

Quinn finally caught her breath. "Seriously, Jasmyn, love knows no distance. But if he shows up here, I will ask him the tough questions. Like, is he standoffish because he has a broken heart or because he's a serial killer?"

"Well." Sam cleared her throat. "It's the first."

"What did I tell you, Jazz? That's exactly what I said. He's hiding behind a broken heart."

"Sam!"

"I can't say for sure. This came from Chad, who was drunk when he heard it and not quite sober when he told me."

Quinn said, "Chad's the hottie who could pose for cologne ads?"

"Yeah, that's the one. He's been known to go off the deep end now and then. Keagan has helped him through some bad times. He dumped his alcohol more than once and intervened for him with Liv."

Jasmyn said, "I didn't know that."

"Keagan and Liv don't talk about it. And Chad's been doing well the past six months or so. One time Keagan brought him home from a bar. You know how crazy Chad is about Piper."

"Piper," Quinn interrupted. "The drop-dead gorgeous shopping expert."

"You have been paying attention." Sam grinned. "Anyway, Chad was whining about her complete lack of interest in him and what a snob she could be. Keagan pushed him up against a wall and said that until he saw his fiancée gunned down, he had no right to talk like that."

Jasmyn turned to Quinn. "Piper's fiancé was killed in Afghanistan."

"How awful."

Sam nodded. "The thing is, Piper didn't see it happen, and it was an IED, not a gun that killed him. Chad might have the words all confused, but Keagan's extreme reaction was real enough. It struck him that Keagan was referring to himself."

Quinn said, "Which would explain why he's brokenhearted and standoffish."

"Totally unapproachable."

Jasmyn disagreed, but kept her thoughts to herself.

Quinn said, "That's a sad story too."

"Mm-hmm. Even if Chad imagined three-fourths of it. Do you have a sad guy story?"

"I do."

Jasmyn said, "Quinn, you and Andrew are crazy about each other and he's a keeper."

"Except he's in Chicago most of the time now, for work. Even on weekends."

"You didn't say anything."

Quinn shrugged. "It's too sad to talk about."

They sat in silence for a long moment.

Quinn said, "What's really sad is that those three men are going through life without us."

Jasmyn snickered first. Sam snorted. Quinn giggled. Soon each of them were doubled over in laughter.

It felt like a balm seeping into wounds long scarred over, softening them, pouring new life into them. It felt like a promise that no matter what, Quinn and Sam would always be there for her.

Seventy-Four

Liv's office door opened and Keagan walked in. "Liv, are you okay?"

Seated behind the desk with Tobi on her lap, she wondered how he knew. They hadn't seen each other since Sunday. He didn't have firsthand knowledge of her phone calls with the girls, her witness of Beau's odd behavior, or of her own rattled demeanor. How did Keagan do it?

He sat across from her. "The gate. You left it unlocked and it's eleven p.m."

"Well." She glanced at the computer screen with her favorite gardening website in view, at her hands stroking Tobi's fur, at the monitor again as it winked off, and finally at him. "I'm okay."

He grunted.

"I talked to the girls. They're fine. Except Sam voiced concern yesterday about Jasmyn, who seems a little too over-the-top idealistic about her plans to buy the restaurant. Jasmyn called today and confided that her boss's wife has cancer, which means the sale needs to happen immediately. Beau took off for Hollywood. I have no idea for how long. Louis's gone into the hospital for tests, Tasha has strep throat, and the new van driver, who brought Coco back from her senior activities center, couldn't find the Casa, so it took forever to get her home. She was frazzled."

"You've had a day."

"Yes, I have." She waited, giving Keagan time to ponder. "What do you think? Besides the life-is-difficult stuff."

A muscle in his jaw twitched. "It's too soon for Jasmyn to make a major commitment like that." His voice was brusque. "She needs to give herself a whole year to recover."

Liv had not expected such a harsh response from him. "Maybe I could offer that bit of wise advice to her."

"I already did."

"She's a stubborn little fighter. She could make it work." Liv's shoulders sagged. How she hoped Jasmyn would not make a mistake. No. How she hoped Jasmyn would just change her mind and leave Valley Oaks altogether.

Keagan stood, muttering something about stubbornness, and went to the door.

"Keagan, why is Beau in Hollywood?"

He stopped and turned. "It's complicated."

"You brought him into my world and now I'm hooked. I like him in it. Is he coming back?"

"I don't know." He sat down again. "When I met him a few years ago, he'd work out every day at the gym like a man possessed. Eventually he calmed down. He told me that he and Tallie Shay had been engaged."

"The actress?"

"Yep. I don't know why he lives here and she lives there, but he goes up every so often."

Liv sighed. "And here Jasmyn and I thought he had a crush on Sam. I guess I can cross that romantic scenario off my list."

He gave her a funny look.

She smiled and refrained, as she had so often refrained, from asking why he did not have a significant other, other than herself, in his life.

He soon left and she burst out laughing. "Oh, Tobi. Evidently, I am his only significant other. Dear Lord, I do appreciate how he watches over me, but let's get real. He needs someone else, and I am willing to share."

❧

The next morning, Liv's unease still festered.

"Lord, I don't want to meddle. You know I don't want to meddle, but..."

She found the phone number for the Flying Pig in Valley Oaks and hoped Jasmyn was not there.

Danno Johnson answered the phone. His voice sounded exactly how Jasmyn had described him, gruff and yet gentle, distant and yet approachable.

Expressing her motherly love for the young woman he had watched over for years was like having a chat with an old friend.

They were on the same page.

Seventy-Five

Two characteristics were fairly easy for Jasmyn to admit about herself to herself without thinking she was obnoxiously tooting her own horn.

One, her memory was good.

Two, her heart was good. She felt compassion for most of the people she knew, including the townspeople who were not so nice to her after she sold the land.

Her memory and heart combined made her a good waitress. She hoped they would make her at least an average business owner who gave to the community and paid her own bills.

The only drawback now sat across the wide conference table from her and Quinn in a downtown Rockville office building. His name was Nick Bloome. He did not have a room in her good heart, not even a corner in a closet. And in his presence, her good memory was turning to oatmeal.

He smiled his phony smile. The straight, white teeth she used to admire seemed yellow. The uniquely shaped nose—broken twice when he was a wrestler—that had intrigued her now, almost, nauseated her. The thatch of unruly black hair looked plain messy on a guy in a black suit and gold tie.

He said, "Jazzie, you with us?"

She blinked, long and slow. Why had she agreed to this? True, he was the best local business consultant. True, Danno was his client and highly recommended him. True, she and Quinn needed his input and expertise. But still...

"Sure."

Quinn stood abruptly. "Will you excuse me, please? I'm going to the ladies' room." She sent a glare in Jasmyn's direction and scooted out the door, closing it firmly behind herself.

A clock ticked. A distant train whistle blared.

At last Jasmyn looked at him. "I don't think this is going to work. I'm sorry."

"Don't be sorry. I'm sorry." His brown eyes—the ones that used to seem so romantic—reminded her of a doe's. Not a buck's. A doe's.

He was soft. Nothing at all like Keagan.

"I'm sorry for everything."

By that, she supposed he meant for dumping her when he got Becka Piehl pregnant. Surely he wasn't sorry for his marriage and his one and one-on-the-way children or for his successful business.

She sighed. "Nick, I'm not angry or hurt anymore. It was for the best for both of us. But there's this…" She waved her hand between them.

"Baggage. I understand."

"I think I'll leave now." She stood.

"Wait. Please." He gathered papers and folders together. "I need to tell you something. You'll hear it soon, but maybe not soon enough. You did not hear this from me, okay?"

"Okay."

"Two gung-ho type guys wanted to buy the Pig."

"Danno told me that."

"Well, when he told them that you had dibs, they made other plans. You know the empty lots on the other side of the bank?"

She nodded.

"These guys are building two restaurants. Somehow they've managed to keep things hush-hush. In a couple of weeks, the town council will most likely approve their plans. They're set to go after that. And no, they're not working with me."

"Two restaurants?"

"First a sports bar, big screens, the works. They plan to open in time for the Super Bowl. By summer they plan to open a second one, a family-friendly, hamburgers, pizza, indoor playground, rah-rah-siss-boom-bah place."

Jasmyn sat back down. "Wow. In Valley Oaks."

"Yeah."

"Worth a drive from the interstate."

"It won't have the history or the small-town ambience the Pig is known and loved for."

"Or the sauce."

He shook his head. "Nope. No sauce."

"So you're saying we shouldn't buy?"

"I'm not saying that."

"Do we have to pay you to say that?"

He smiled. "No, Jazzie. Speaking in generalities, if you paid me, I would show you numbers and they would show that you had a fighting chance. And it would be a fight. It would be a long shot, but a shot nonetheless. There's nothing like Danno's place."

"Maybe for good reason." She shrugged and stood again. "Thanks, Nick."

"You're welcome." He moved around the table, opened the door for her, and shook her hand, holding it and the eye contact a tad longer than necessary. "Good luck."

She hurried down the hall, grabbed Quinn as she emerged from the ladies' room, and steered her through the well-appointed office.

"Jazz, what happened?"

She didn't answer until they had gone through the glass doors and were almost to the car. "The short version is that Nick just made up for every mean thing he ever did to me."

ᨦ

Jasmyn and Quinn treated themselves to the Chinese buffet across from the Rockville mall.

"What are we going to do?"

They took turns asking the question.

Quinn said, "Get jobs at the new place."

"Which one? Screaming kids or screaming sports fans?"

She wrinkled her nose.

Jasmyn said, "Or let's just go for it. We'll stop at the bank this afternoon. Sign some loan papers." With the amount she had tucked away there, she assumed asking for a loan would not be a problem. "We can just slide on in and keep things as is. Nobody will even notice Danno's gone. We don't shut down for redecorating. We can do that some other time."

"At least, supposedly, business would continue as it is."

"It should."

"Do we tell Danno?"

"Do you think he knows?"

They stared at each other a moment, and then they shook their heads in unison.

"Nah." He would have told them.

Jasmyn said, "This is all starting to feel complicated."

"I wish I could blame it on the crazy year you have going, but it feels the same to me. It's another red flag. A huge one."

"I want to take a long nap."

"Don't check out on me yet, hon. We'll talk to Danno. He'll know best. He might even be able to keep the place open long-distance, and we could just run it for him while he's gone."

"Maybe."

"There's always the beauty shop idea. Or Andrew's dad's auto shop."

They had joked about combining the two shops. One-stop car and hair repair.

Andrew had graduated a few years ahead of them. He went off to college and landed a big-time job in Chicago, something to do with software. When his mother died and his father got sick, he returned to Valley Oaks to care for him and his auto shop.

That was when he and Quinn got together. When his father passed away some months back, Andrew had begun to work more from home for his old company and less at the shop. Lately, he'd worked from the office...in Chicago.

Jasmyn said, "What's really going on with Andrew?"

"Who knows? Let me count the days since he's been in town. Or since we've talked on the phone long enough to get past the weather report and how busy he is."

"I'm sorry." Jasmyn thought of how the two had hit it off, how perfect Andrew was for Quinn.

"His dad's partner is finally ready to buy him out, and Andrew's back in love with Chicago."

"Does he talk about moving there permanently?"

"No, but there's nothing to keep him here anymore."

"Quinn, stop. You're here. He loves you."

"It's a tough competition. Me versus Chicago. What would you choose?"

Their eyes met and they each set down their chopsticks.

Quinn said it first, "Me versus California?"

"It's not exactly the same."

"Close enough. With Danno, your job, and your house gone, there's only me here for you."

They sat in silence, old, close friends whose minds—Jasmyn figured—were running the same circuit.

At last Quinn said it only because Jasmyn would not voice it first. "I could go with you."

"You have your mom and dad and brothers and sisters and your grandma's house, and you're halfway to getting a beautician's license."

"Three-fourths." She bit her lip. Quinn never cried but she clearly was on the verge. "Jazz, you know you're more family to me than they are." Her hushed voice quivered.

Jasmyn wasn't sure if she wanted to laugh or cry or take that long nap.

Seventy-Six

Sam stood on the large front porch of a rambling, two-story, neatly kept old house in Lynn Center. Painted white, it had dark green shutters on every one of its countless windows. Through the tall ones that ran along the porch, she saw lace curtains.

A corner of the curtain moved and then the door opened. A man stepped onto the porch, his hand extended.

"Hi. I'm Ruthie's grandson, Jack Moore." The guy was tall and narrow with wavy dark blond hair and a friendly smile. He wore blue jeans and a long-sleeved shirt the shade of green that she had noticed on farm equipment and caps. "Otto called."

She shook his hand. "Sam Whitley."

"Nice to meet you. I hope you don't mind me butting in. Gran sort of comes and goes. I might be able to help keep her coherent."

"I'm sorry. Maybe this is too much to ask?"

"Not at all. She will love talking to you. Come on inside." He opened the door for her.

Sam walked through it, noticing the logo on his shirt. "Did you have to take off work?"

"No problem. My dad and I run the dealership in town here." He followed her inside. "To the right. Gran! That lady I told you about is here."

Sam turned from the entryway with its staircase and stepped through a wide arched opening into what could only be described as a parlor, something out of another era. There were overstuffed sofas and chairs with high backs and spindly legs, end tables with old-fashioned globed lamps, and lace everywhere. A sweet fragrance greeted her, and she spotted a huge bouquet of white roses.

Ruthie Moore, white-haired and frail looking, smiled from the chair beside the white brick fireplace. She wore a floral dress and a lacy white cardigan. "What lady was that?"

Jack winked at Sam. "This one. Her name is Sam."

The woman frowned as if confused.

Sam reached her chair and leaned down to greet her. "Samantha."

"Oh." Ruthie smiled and grasped Sam's hand between hers. "Hannah's girl."

Neither Sam nor Jack corrected her. If she remembered there was a connection between Sam and Hannah, that was enough.

Ruthie studied her closely, her blue eyes sweeping Sam's face and hair, right to left, left to right, up and down, down and up. "The coloring's all wrong. But." She smiled again and squeezed Sam's hand. "The spirit is there. See this, Jack?"

He stepped closer. "See what?"

"This." Ruthie touched Sam's right cheek, near the corner of her mouth.

Sam met Jack's gaze. His brown eyes were clearly apologizing.

Ruthie tapped Sam's cheek. "That little crease. Hannah had it. It folded up whenever she talked. My mother said it gave her face character and it showed she was full of goodness. Have a seat."

Sam sank onto the nearest chair, at a loss for words.

"Gran." Jack sat on a loveseat. "How do you remember a little thing like that?"

"Little?" She laughed. "Mother compared me to Hannah Carlson almost every single day of my life, and I always came up with the short end of the stick. I hated the girl."

"Gran, you didn't hate her."

"I most certainly did. We didn't play all that much together. She was—what? Probably two years older. Smart as a whip. Another bone of contention." She chuckled. "Let me tell you, I was glad the day she went off to college. Got her out of my hair. Not that Mother stopped talking about her."

Sam said, "Where did she go to college?"

"Where all the girls went back in the day. That teachers' school down in Normal."

"What did she look like?"

"Don't you know?"

"She died when I was two."

"Two! How can that be? She wasn't here when you were two, was she?"

"No. She was in Arizona, where I grew up."

"My goodness." The light seemed to fade from Ruthie's eyes.

Sam's heart sank. *Don't go away.*

Jack stood. "How about some tea? I'll be right back." He left the room.

Ruthie said, "I hope the weather holds. Jack needs to get in the fields soon. If he would have kept the insurance business going without Father or Charles, we wouldn't have to depend so much on weather." She shook her head. "But Jack doesn't like book work. I don't mean to complain. He's a good husband."

Jack was her husband. That was probably young Jack's grandfather. But Charles? And insurance? It rang a bell from her research at the courthouse. Charles Carlson was Hannah's father and he owned an insurance business. "Charles Carlson?"

"Did you know him?"

"No."

"He and Father got along famously. Everyone said that's why they were successful businessmen. Even during the Depression they did all right."

"He was Hannah's father, right?"

"That's the one. Nice man. He'd bring me and my brother candy from Rockville. They were good people, Charles and Hilma. Such a tragedy."

"What happened?"

"Haven't you heard?" She tsked. "Influenza. Took both of them practically overnight. Poor Hannah had to come home from college and bury them. She was their only child, you know. Her grandparents were already gone. The two who lived here. She might have had other family in Sweden."

Sam sat back in the chair, speechless. Her great-grandparents had died at the same time? And so young? At the courthouse, their death certificates hadn't been found. The staff apologized, blaming clerical error and promising to keep hunting. Yes, poor Hannah!

"What did Hannah do?"

"Buried them, I told you. In the Lutheran Cemetery out on County Road NN."

Jack reentered the room, carrying a tray. "Everything all right?"

Sam tried to give him a reassuring smile.

He handed her a mug. "Green okay?"

She nodded and sipped while he served his grandmother.

"So," he said, "the Lutheran Cemetery. Samantha, have you been there yet?"

"No."

He rattled off easy directions. Two turns. The Carlsons were near the Moores, far northwest corner. Couldn't miss it.

Sam said, "Hannah didn't move back here?"

Ruthie's cup rattled against its saucer. "Heavens to Betsy, no. She sold the house to the first buyer—dirt cheap, Father said—and skedaddled. She never even collected her entire share from the business. He sent checks that she never cashed. Oh, we heard such crazy things. Some said she went to Chicago and worked in a nightclub. There was a rumor that she married a hotshot *Eye*-talian from New York. Mafia. Mm-hmm. That was before she went to Africa and died while climbing Kilimanjaro. Somebody said she went out West to teach school to Indians. You know she had to have gone a little off her rocker after such a tragedy."

Jack said, "I never heard all that."

"You have so. You just forgot. And what about the photographs?"

"The photo—right." The guy was infinitely patient with his grandmother. "Samantha, we didn't have a chance to get photos from the attic. If you leave your address, we'll send some to you."

"Of Hannah?"

"Yes, from when she and Gran were young girls."

"Oh my gosh." She hadn't imagined actual photos.

"Jack, take her over to the house."

"I will."

Sam said, "What house?"

He looked surprised. "Your grandmother's. Didn't Otto tell you? It's right across the street. The owner said we're welcome to see it."

Her grandmother's house?

Sam clutched her mug tightly. She didn't want the tea to spill while she tried not to burst into tears.

A short time later, Sam stood inside a house very similar to the one across the street.

Jack shut the door, which had been left unlocked. It was generally left unlocked. That was what people did in the small town.

He smiled. "Welcome to the house your great-grandfather built. If Gran is to be believed, Charles built after her father finished his house and shamelessly copied it. Of course it could very well have happened the other way around."

She turned slowly, taking in the current owner's lifestyle. Children's toys and books lay about. Clothes and shoes of all sizes were strewn. The chairs and couch were worn and sprawling with pillows and afghans. Vertical blinds covered the windows, not lace curtains. Scents of old coffee and burnt toast permeated. The room was not Ruthie Moore's quaint parlor.

But the hardwood floor shone at the edges of an area rug and the wide woodwork was oak, unpainted. The place had been cared for.

Jack picked up a paper from the entryway table. "Here, before I forget. The owner asked me to give this to you. It has her contact information in case you have questions."

Sam read the note, a kind offer from Matt and Heather Williamson. "She says to snoop and take pictures."

"That's the Williamsons. They're both at work. The kids are at school and the sitter's."

"Am I related to them?"

He laughed. "I don't think so."

"To you?"

"No. I take it Hannah did not die in Africa?"

Sam shook her head. "She went to the Navajo reservation, taught school, and married my grandfather. My dad was their son. I lost them all early."

"I'm sorry. It's a little bit like Hannah's story."

"Hmm. I hadn't thought of it that way."

"It sounds like she lived an extraordinary life. She must have been a special woman. From what I've always heard, Gran really did grow up in her shadow."

"Funny. My mother felt the same about Hannah."

"It must have been the crease." He touched his own cheek. "And you have it."

She laughed. "Yes, I do."

"You wear it well. Okay, I'll leave you to your snooping and picture taking."

"You're sure the owners won't mind?"

"I'm sure. Heather was sorry she couldn't be here. By the way, Gran says that Hannah's bedroom was in the southwest corner." He spun around and pointed to the ceiling. "That one, facing the backyard." He turned again to her and shook her hand. "It has been a pleasure, Samantha. Oh, here." He pulled a business card from his back pocket and gave it to her with another full-on, small-town, friendly-as-all-get-out smile. "If you need anything else, give me a call. I'm just around the corner."

She gave him one of her own business cards, writing the Casa's address on the back for any photos he could send.

After he left, Sam listened to the silence.

And then she imagined a smart, energetic little girl growing up in such comfort and—what must have been—wealth.

And then she imagined the young woman who buried her parents and chose to move far away and live in dire poverty.

If she believed Ruthie Moore's report and the words the old women had told Sam long ago about Hannah Carlson Whitehorse, her grandmother had been a remarkable woman.

Sam walked through the house, in Hannah's footsteps, in the footsteps of her great-grandparents, Charles and Hilma. She felt grateful for the sliver of heritage.

It hinted that she was neither an accident nor insignificant.

Some indescribable, unnameable knot at the core of her being was released.

Seventy-Seven

Her first evening back to work, Jasmyn walked through the restaurant's noisy dining room, an empty tray under her arm, and straightened the Cat in the Hat stocking cap on her head. The place was a zoo, speaking animal-costume-wise.

It was Halloween and Danno's advertisements for trick-or-treat bags of coupons and candy had done their own trick. Half the adults wore some sort of token getup for Halloween. Kids were totally hidden behind masks and costumes.

Danno would have enjoyed the hoopla, but he was home, presumably packing up his house. Jasmyn and Quinn had not had a chance to talk to him about business matters. He had been too distraught after talking with his wife in Florida and left work early, an unheard-of event.

Jasmyn only hoped he hadn't left the state.

Sam caught her eye from the hostess stand and gave her a thumbs-up.

Jasmyn bypassed the kitchen door and went over to her. "Are you doing okay?"

"You tell me." She grinned. The silver Minnie Mouse ears on the sequined headband bobbed.

"I'd say you've done this before."

Sam laughed. "Hosted in a restaurant. Yeah, right."

"You're a natural."

"You're a good liar."

Jasmyn smiled and wondered to herself again at the change in Sam Whitley. It wasn't just the mouse ears.

Most evenings Danno hosted, bused tables, poured water, delivered food, and sometimes cooked. He'd gone home at four thirty. The kitchen was covered but not the dining room. The staff Jasmyn phoned could not fill in. Sam showed up, assessed their shorthanded situation, and immediately offered to help.

"Hello." Sam smiled over Jasmyn's shoulder, picked up a stack of menus, and stepped around her. "Welcome to the Pig."

Jasmyn watched her friend for a moment as she seated a family of four. There was a distinct change in the way she carried herself, with an air of confidence. True confidence, not the phony aloof kind. She smiled, and her face seemed relaxed enough to do it often.

By ten o'clock the last customers were gone. The kitchen staff headed out soon after. Jasmyn locked the front door and turned off the outside lights. Quinn took off her pig nose and ears and closed the window blinds. Sam blew out the votives on each table. They met in the middle and sank onto chairs at the long rectangle table.

Sam propped her feet on another chair. "I have never, ever been this tired."

Quinn laughed. "Come in on Friday after the football game."

Jasmyn added, "Or the Friday after Thanksgiving."

"You two love it," Sam said. "Are you going to buy it?"

Jasmyn and Quinn groaned. They filled Sam in on the latest red flag, the big unknown in their future. "I guess it depends on what Danno has to say. Tell us about your day."

Sam pooched her lips together as if she might cry. "I went inside my grandmother's house."

"Whoa!" Quinn whooped.

"Sammi! Really?"

She beamed at them, and then she began to tell an amazing story. "After I left the house, I found my great-grandparents' graves. I saw that they had lost two babies before Hannah was born. There were small headstones. One baby lived two days, the other not even a day. It's so strange, how significant this old history seems to be for me."

"I understand." Jasmyn shrugged.

Sam reached over and touched her arm. "Of course you understand. At first I didn't get why Manda and the Portuguese fishermen and the trucking firm mattered to you. But that past is a part of you, isn't it?"

"Exactly. It's not a practical thing you can explain. Learning about that part—I don't know. It sort of finishes you."

Quinn said, "You're both a little weird."

Jasmyn said, "What would you know? You grew up surrounded by every living relative on both sides. Your parents knew their parents and their grandparents and greats. You've always known the grave sites and houses, your whole line of Olafssons and Bensons since 1850. You didn't have any holes to fill."

Quinn grimaced. "Holes? As in graves?"

"You know what I mean."

Sam said, "Back up. Benson?"

"Yes. My mom's maiden name. Originally it was Bengtson, with a *g* and a *t* but they Americanized it. Why do you ask?"

"That was my great-grandmother's maiden name. Bengtson. Hilma Bengtson."

"My great-grandmother had a *ton* of siblings."

"Hmm."

"Hmm."

Jasmyn laughed and clapped her hands. "You two are probably related."

Quinn smiled. "There's a genealogy book at my house."

Sam grinned. "Are you too tired?"

"Nah. Come on, ladies. Let's go fill some holes."

As she and her friends gathered their things in the kitchen and flipped off lights, Jasmyn felt a wave of homesickness. Its suddenness and intensity scared her to pieces.

She turned her back to Quinn and Sam so they could not see it on her face and ask what was wrong.

She knew what was wrong, and it didn't have anything to do with genealogy or the new challenges surrounding taking over the restaurant.

No. It was something far more intangible.

In San Diego the feeling of homecoming overwhelmed her. Now, in spite of her excitement to return to Valley Oaks and start over, she felt homesick.

It seemed totally backward.

Seventy-Eight

Early Saturday morning, Jasmyn, Quinn, and Sam stood beside Sam's rental. The mild weather had turned chilly, and Jasmyn worried about Sam's driving to O'Hare Airport without a heavier jacket.

"I'll be fine." Sam tightened a black scarf at her neck. "It's not snowing."

Jasmyn's worry ran deeper than weather issues. "Saying goodbye stinks."

Sam's eyes filled. Quinn grabbed her newest BFF in a bear hug. "It's been awesome, cuz."

They all laughed. Quinn and Sam had found a possible distant family link in the genealogy book. One branch of the Bengtsons in Sweden eons ago led to a name that might have been connected, a name which Sam had seen on her own family tree. Even if it were true, it was beyond shirt-tail, but enough to make Quinn a believer in heart holes and their closings. She was giddy about having a maybe, sort-of cousin in California.

Jasmyn and Sam hugged and sniffed through goodbyes. There were no more words to exchange. They had already told each other to visit again. Sam had already echoed Liv's sentiment, that Cottage Eleven belonged to Jasmyn.

As Sam drove down the street waving in the rearview mirror, Jasmyn thought about another kind of heart hole, the one ripped open when sadness took hold.

Quinn threw an arm around her shoulders. "Come on, Sunshine. Let's move you back into your apartment."

"Are you kicking me out?"

"I am."

Jasmyn smiled at her friend, doing her best to wear the sunshine face.

They carried Jasmyn's few things from Quinn's house to the studio, put away her clothes, and changed out the linens. They worked side by side, old friends comfortable with silence, in tune with what they left unspoken.

Housekeeping finished and the first hour or so of Sam's absence gotten through, they sat on the floor. Because only one chair fit at the tiny kitchen table, the floor was the best place for eating cereal and drinking coffee. And catching up on the unspoken.

"I really, really don't like this apartment."

"In this case, you're allowed to say 'hate,' Jazz."

"I hate that word."

Quinn smiled sadly. "I made a list of possibilities. Two condos for rent, a two-bedroom house near the high school, a one-bedroom really, really close—like right next to—the railroad tracks. Unless you want a farmhouse or something in Rockville, that's it for Valley Oaks. Well, unless you want to buy. There are a few nice— From the look on your face, that's a no."

"Thanks, though."

"Mom's offer stands too. My old room. Dirt cheap. She'll knock more off if you cook twice a week."

They laughed.

Quinn then proceeded to sob. "I loved him. I *love* him. Really and truly. What'd I do wrong?"

"Aw, Quinn, Andrew hasn't said it's over, has he?"

"Actions speak louder than words. It's quite obvious he's moved on. Which is what I have to do." She jumped up, took her bowl to the sink in the corner that was the kitchen, tore off a paper towel, and blew her nose. "Come on. Let's go buy a restaurant."

Jasmyn hesitated. She adored Quinn. She ached for her over the Andrew development. She could not imagine anything more fun than running the Pig with her.

But the homesickness still sat like one of those enormous boulders in the desert, smack-dab right in the middle of her chest.

Danno's first reaction to the news about the gung-ho guys building new restaurants in town was to let loose a rare, thundering expletive.

Before he shouted another one, he hurried away from the big round table, aka his office, and disappeared through the kitchen door. Subsequent cussing was muffled.

Jasmyn and Quinn stared at each other.

"I don't think he knew," Quinn said.

"Nope."

They busied themselves preparing the dining room for lunch. Danno eventually reappeared and motioned them to rejoin him at the table.

He paced a little before he sat down again. "They said they would buy me out if my potential buyer—you, Jasmyn—did not say yes by January. I thought I had a gentlemen's agreement with them. Young whippersnappers wouldn't know one of those if it whacked them on the nose. My bad." He folded his hands. "All right. Let's plow through this and see where we end up."

They ended up with a temporary arrangement. He would keep things going financially until the first of the year.

"I promised Ellie I'd be done mid-December, before Christmas, but we can manage this. Our house buyers want me out yesterday, so that gives us some leeway. I just do not want to be involved here except on paper. I'm outta here a week from tomorrow. I am not coming back. I do not—I repeat, do *not*—want daily phone calls. Got it?"

They nodded for the umpteenth time.

"You two use the next eight weeks as a trial run. You manage, I take a percentage. If you don't love it, we'll shut it down. Get a feel for what the new guys' impact might be. Play with the numbers. I realize it's long before they open for business, but once the word gets out about that, you'll get a sense of the future. If it's not a good one, we'll shut it down and I'll put the property up for sale."

Jasmyn said, "Sounds fair."

Quinn added, "Reasonable."

He smiled. "You two don't have a clue."

They agreed with him.

"We'll put it in writing on Monday." He shook their hands. "I have your backs, ladies. You do not have to go through with this."

His words, as always, comforted Jasmyn. It was the underlying tone of temporary that struck her, though, and not in a good way.

She was eight months into the world of temporary and growing weary of it.

Danno leaned sideways and looked over Jasmyn's shoulder. "What in the name of Sam Hill is that?"

She turned.

Through the windows she saw a huge white horse gallop across the parking lot and come to an abrupt halt. His rider pulled the reins and turned him. They approached the windows. The rider leaned down to peer through the blinds.

Jasmyn grinned. It was Andrew, Quinn's long-absent boyfriend, recognizable by his black, horn-rimmed glasses. His black hair stuck out beneath an odd gray helmet that was topped with a patch of fake hair. The rest of him was very shiny, covered in—

"Foil?" Quinn nearly shouted. "He's wearing foil? Are those tin pie pans on his shoulders?"

Danno chuckled. "It's tough to find a good set of armor these days. Stores just don't carry them anymore."

Tears pooled in her big blue eyes. "Is he…"

"Oh, yes." Jasmyn laughed. "He most definitely is."

Quinn raced across the dining room, grabbing her coat as she passed the rack, and hurried outdoors.

Jasmyn wiped at her own tears. "Is it rude to watch?"

"Are you kidding? The guy rode through town on a white horse. Who does that belong to, anyway?"

Andrew grinned widely and offered Quinn an arm. She appeared, for once in her life, to be speechless. He pulled her up onto the horse behind him, and they trotted away, out onto the street.

Jasmyn sighed. "I guess she was wrong about him losing interest in her."

"What was your first clue?"

She smiled and met Danno's gaze.

He said, "So, what do you think?"

"If she says yes, then I've lost my business partner. Andrew has all but moved back to Chicago. His work is there. They won't stay here."

Danno reached across the table and squeezed her hand. "Happy and sad, huh?"

She shrugged and nodded and cried. "It's…" She unrolled a napkin, dumping the silverware from it, and buried her face in the thick paper. "It's just too much to take in since the tornado."

"I know."

She blew her nose. "I'm sorry, Danno. You've had a horrific year. Mine is nothing—"

"Let's not compare. Life can be a real pain in the neck. We deal with it one day at a time."

"I could still take over the Pig—"

"Hush. We'll save that talk for later."

Silverware clanked as she took apart another place setting. She cried into the fresh napkin.

Danno rubbed his bristly chin. "I suppose she'll want the day off."

In spite of herself, she laughed. "I suppose."

"I suppose you'll want your own knight-in-foil—I mean, shining armor."

The thought of Keagan flashed and fizzled. He was the Casa's knight and a good friend to her, but the ache of homesickness quickly pushed aside romance. Her Valley Oaks family was disintegrating on the spot.

"I'd rather have a home and a family."

They sat for a long time. Jasmyn's imagination raced down one rabbit trail after another. There were no cozy bunny homes along the way, only black holes.

Could she manage the Pig without Quinn? There was the staff to consider. They were good workers: two cooks, two other waitresses, some part-timers. Everyone was on edge, wondering what was going to happen when Danno left. Could she take care of everyone without Quinn's help?

Then there were the customers. The food. The state inspectors. The maintenance of everything, including the coming winter snow in the parking lot and—

And where would she live?

"Jasmyn." Danno's voice broke through her crazy thoughts. "You have a home and a family out West."

"Seaside Village? Valley Oaks is my home. I don't fit in out there."

"Good golly, Jasmyn Albright!" He scowled. "You said the same thing about Valley Oaks. Get over yourself, already."

"I never said…" She never? Of course she had. As far back as she could remember—as far back as to four years old when she got the distinct impression that she was the reason her grandfather glared and snarled— she had believed she did not fit in. She had been saying it aloud for a long time.

"Honey." Danno's voice became soft. "Once you make yourself fit in with yourself, then you're okay anywhere. Get my drift?"

"I guess so."

"My hope was that you would go away and learn how to be comfortable in your own skin. I think you got that. You came back all jazzed, ready to plug in here in a new way."

She nodded. It was true. Except for feeling homesick in her hometown, she had been all set to reinvent herself.

"But I agree that you don't quite fit in with this community, up to a point. Sure, people are getting over the sale of your land and seeing the benefits of it. And sure, your customers love you and will remain loyal as much as they can. And sure, the staff here supports you one hundred percent. But unless you have some close local friend hidden in the wings, I'm afraid that once Quinn and I leave, on some level you'll be alone."

A friend in the wings? Nope. None that she knew of. Her stomach knotted.

He went on. "The way I see it, you could move to Florida or Chicago or to Seaside Village to be near people who care for you."

Tears seeped out and she could not speak.

"I like Sam a lot." He paused. "I like Liv a lot."

"Liv?"

"We talked. She called the other night." He shook his head as if in disbelief. "She almost had me convinced to pull our potential deal right off the table then and there. But I don't think that was her point."

"What was her point?"

"To make sure I know that she loves you like a daughter. That if things did not work out here, there's a whole bunch of people out there who hope you come back to stay."

Jasmyn yanked another napkin away from silverware and wiped her eyes.

"I wasn't convinced, though. A little bit of ego got in the way. I mean, I liked the idea of you stepping in here, keeping my legacy going. I believed you were ready. Partnered with Quinn, it was a winning plan.

The dynamite duo would be unstoppable." He chuckled. "Then Andrew and that horse show up."

She stared at him. "Are we having that talk you were saving for later?"

"Yeah, I guess we are. You don't have to decide this moment. Give it ten minutes or so."

"You really think I can move to Seaside Village?"

"Of course you can, Jasmyn. You've come a long, long way these past few months. You're coming into your own. It won't be an easy transition. Nothing worthwhile is ever easy. The question is, do you *want* to move to Seaside Village?"

Move to Seaside Village and away from owning a business that would consume her time and money? Away from living alone in some unfamiliar condo or whatever with no one around who cared if she came or went? Away from memories that lay around every corner, memories that were, for the most part, unpleasant?

He spread his hands, as if offering her a gift, and smiled. "Why not?"

She had no answer for that.

Seventy-Nine

Late Saturday night, Sam rolled her suitcase into her cottage, flipped on a lamp, stepped back outside, and shut the door. The first thing she wanted—even before doing email, even before stretching out full-length on her own bed—was to see Liv.

Ew. That was a purely emotional response.

But why should it surprise her? She should be getting used to purely emotional responses. Unearthing ancestral ties and seeing—basically—the hand of God bringing together two far-flung histories that resulted in Sam's existence had seriously messed with her core being. And before all that—

She shook her head. Before all that, she had been primed for it. Meeting bighearted, honey-voiced Jasmyn had been the beginning of the end of Samantha Whitley. Jasmyn was an industrial-strength version of Liv but didn't know it.

Jasmyn had taught Sam that she could be social and that people would actually accept that side of her. Such an image of herself made Sam squirm inside, and yet it also made her want to go for it, to find a life outside of work.

That thought led directly to Beau.

Which led to facing the fact that he already had a life, one that ruled out their paths crossing in a social way.

Which led to the idea of moving from the Casa to someplace where their paths would never cross in any way.

Which led to craving a hug from Liv.

She paused now in the deserted courtyard and took a deep breath of salt air. *Good grief.* What did people do with such a clutter of emotions?

Her phone rang and she pulled it from a pocket. Jasmyn's name showed on the screen and a wave of calm flowed through Sam.

"Hi."

"Quinn got engaged."

"You're kidding. To the guy who dumped her?"

"Evidently that was all in her head. He showed up on a white horse, and he was wrapped in foil. He took her to the baseball fields at the high school. They love baseball. He proposed on the pitcher's mound and said he had to live in Chicago and he would buy them season passes to the Cubs if she said yes. She said yes. She'll text you a picture of the diamond ring."

Sam laughed until the words sank in. "Wait. Chicago? She's moving? Jasmyn! What does this mean for you and the Pig?"

"Well." Jasmyn sniffled and giggled at the same time. "Well. You know." The sniffles won and she stopped talking.

"I know?" What did she know? She knew that buying the restaurant was Jasmyn and Quinn's future together, not separately. She knew that Jasmyn did not have a real home, nor did she even feel at home in her hometown. Now she didn't have a job. Or a BFF. Or a surrogate dad in Danno.

Sam's breath caught. "Really? For real, Jasmyn? You're coming here? You're *moving* here?"

"Is that crazy?" she whispered.

"Crazy wonderful." And then Sam started crying. She was a goner for sure now.

Eighty

Eavesdropping was like a reflex. Keagan did not intentionally engage in it. It just happened. In his past life, when information was everything, it had served him well.

He had spotted Sam near her cottage and began to go over to greet her when her phone rang. He stopped beside a large bird-of-paradise, in its shadow. Reflex.

Her voice carried—the fountain was off—and it became apparent she was talking to Jasmyn.

"Really? For real, Jasmyn? You're coming here? You're *moving* here?"

He heard the words, those precise words. Still, he would have questioned his understanding of the one-sided conversation if not for the fact that Liv had said Jasmyn would return to stay.

Why did he ever doubt Liv's intuition?

He felt, for the first time in a very long time, hopeful.

And maybe even a little bit happy.

Eighty-One

Every once in a while, like now, Liv sat in her recliner, completely incapacitated, overcome with...

"With You, Lord. Just with You."

It was not always a significant, happy event that triggered the moment. Sometimes it was the sight of a dolphin swimming past the pier. Sometimes it was a memory of Syd. Sometimes it was deep sadness.

But tonight it was most definitely a significant, happy event.

Samantha had stopped in, thoroughly flustered. She smiled as tears poured from her eyes, turned down the small casserole Liv had prepared for her homecoming, and promised to tell her all about her trip tomorrow.

Liv wondered who the stranger was and what she had done with Samantha.

At the moment, Samantha said, it didn't matter. Jasmyn was going to call any minute with news.

Any minute proved to be unbearably long for Samantha. She spilled the beans. By the time Liv answered Jasmyn's call, she too was in a tizzy. Many happy tears were shed.

It was too soon for plans. Jasmyn had much to do before she could leave Valley Oaks.

Liv smiled now, simply overcome...

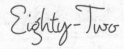

Eighty-Two

Two weeks and four days after Jasmyn realized that her life in Valley Oaks was over, she arrived in San Diego in time for Thanksgiving dinner.

Was she home?

She stood on the curb at the busy pickup area outside the airport and shut her eyes. The familiar ocean air and the bone-warming sunshine engulfed her. *Welcome home, Jasmyn Albright. Welcome home.*

It felt right, but butterflies still whipped around inside of her. The questions still bombarded.

Was she making the right choice? Would she find a job? How would she find a job? Would she truly fit in at the Casa? In a big city?

The past two weeks and four days had been a nonstop string of cleaning, packing, gatherings, and goodbyes.

She and Quinn observed the eighth-month anniversary of the tornado with lattes in Rockville. They agreed that was enough commemorating and spent the rest of the day at bridal shops and choosing Quinn's gown.

She and Quinn threw a going-away party for Danno. It seemed that half the town stopped by to wish him and—surprisingly—Jasmyn good luck. He officially shut down the Pig and she hugged him goodbye beside his pickup truck the day he left for Florida.

She helped Quinn pack, hugged her and Andrew goodbye beside a small U-Haul, and took comfort that she would see them in the spring for their wedding.

She packed her own few things, stuck them in her car, and made arrangements for it to be shipped to California. It was expensive, but unlike her half sister Manda, she had no desire to drive cross-country by herself.

There was no one left to hug goodbye except Quinn's younger brother, who kindly drove her to the airport in Rockville.

None of it had been easy. It had all been downright awful. She desperately needed a hello hug from Sam to remind her that the past was past. That today was a brand-new beginning full of unimagined possibilities.

Amen.

She blew out another anxious breath and opened her eyes.

Keagan stood in front of her, smiling, his sunglasses on top of his head. The full-on impact of his peacock-blue gaze set off another batch of butterflies.

"Hi."

"H-hi. Uh, Sam's picking me up."

"Change of plans. I told her you and I have this airport thing going." He paused. "And maybe something else."

Her breath caught. Sean Keagan cared for her? But— "You didn't text or call."

He shook his head. "I didn't want to confuse the process. I didn't want you to come back here for me."

She thought of Danno's comment about her having a knight. She remembered her response, that a family and a home were what she needed. "I truly did not."

His mouth twitched. "Not even a little?"

She shrugged and tried not to smile.

They stared at each other for a long moment, smiles fading as something else began to blossom.

His hands were propped on his hips. He wore a dark gold T-shirt, one with the small logo on the front, and blue jeans. As always, the air shimmered around him. She felt safer than she had in her entire life.

She took the first step toward him, into the strong arms she knew would enfold her.

"Welcome home, Jasmyn," he whispered in her ear. "You have been greatly missed."

Unlike Labor Day back in September, Jasmyn entered the Casa de Vida via the back gate with Keagan carrying her luggage. The courtyard, however, was once again decked out in festive mode, this time for Thanksgiving.

She spotted long, cloth-covered tables with autumn floral centerpieces. Orange Japanese lanterns were draped here and there. Stacks of real plates, cloth napkins, and silverware—no plastic or paper in sight—waited on the serving table. Liv and others were setting things in order.

During the ride from the airport, Keagan had filled her in on the Casa's Thanksgiving tradition. Or, rather, Liv's tradition. It was her day to welcome the street people to dinner.

Liv saw them first and she shrieked. "Keagan! You were supposed to call!"

Jasmyn hurried over to greet her with a hug.

From that point on, things became almost chaotic. Jasmyn received a full quota of hugs and then some. The smiles and welcomes went on and on. Liv, Coco, Inez, Louis, Noah, Déja, Piper, Riley, Tasha, Chad, and Sam.

Sam waited until last, pulled her aside, and spoke in a low voice. "Sorry about the airport surprise."

"You owe me for that one. Not even a text warning?"

"He can be really persuasive."

"Tell me about it."

Sam's eyes narrowed. "Maybe you want to tell me about it?"

Jasmyn smiled.

"You have the Cheshire cat bit down good. We'll talk later. So, welcome to Liv's annual madhouse. I'm not staying, by the way."

"Why not?"

"Randy and his family invited me for dinner." She tilted her head, right and left. "The homeless crowd makes me nervous. And Beau will be here."

Sam had not spoken to Beau since she returned. He was back from Hollywood, but she had so far managed to avoid him.

"Sam, you have to talk to him at some point."

"I will."

"What are you waiting for?"

Her mouth set in a straight line. The hurt in her eyes was unmistakable. She still had a crush on him.

"Oh, Sammi. I'm sorry."

"I feel like such an idiot. But…" She smiled. "Other than that, I'm all about being social. Come on. Number Eleven awaits."

They walked toward the cottage. Liv had texted almost daily about its condition. Many borrowed items were still in place. The hand-me-down couch from Inez. The hand-me-down end tables, lamps, and kitchen table from Chad's parents' garage. Inez insisted the rollaway bed stay. Liv insisted her kitchen items stay. Sam donated her television and rocker again for however long Jasmyn might need them.

Jasmyn eyed the grape-purple door with its matching Adirondack chairs and breathed a *thanks*. She thought of the jasmine plant in the back and offered another *thanks*. She thought of the furnishings inside, the cream that was probably in the fridge, the calendar she had left on the wall, the Casa friends—those who were the family of her heart—and gave *thanks*.

She stepped on a thick mat in front of the door.

A thick mat? What happened to the thin rug—

Her name was on it. Small, purple lettering in the upper left-hand corner. The center image was a large bouquet of colorful flowers.

It was the same mat that all the women had in front of their doors. The men's mats had trees instead of flowers.

"Ohh."

Sam said, "You're official now."

She grinned and pushed open the door, already ajar because Liv had gone ahead with Keagan and the luggage. Jasmyn and Sam walked inside. The sign caught her attention first and she stopped dead in her tracks.

It hung across the arched doorway that separated the living room and kitchen. *Welcome Home, Jasmyn!* The letters were big and fat and solid purple, surrounded by rainbows and flowers. It looked like Tasha's handiwork.

The trio caught her eye next. Keagan, Liv, and Chad stood shoulder to shoulder, along the side living room wall, a vacant space that was not vacant now.

As if on cue, they parted and then she saw it. The desk? The desk! The rolltop with all the cubby holes just like her grandmother's. The one she had cried over in the secondhand shop.

She gasped and started crying again.

Chad said, "Do you like it?"

Sam explained that the day they saw it, Chad had bought it and had it delivered to his parents' home, where he stored it with their other castoffs. Yesterday he, Keagan, and Beau had moved it into the cottage.

"It was such a steal," Chad said. "And we all hoped that you would use it someday."

Jasmyn thought she just might melt into a puddle on the floor.

Eighty-Three

Although Liv told Jasmyn she should rest and not help with the Thanksgiving dinner, Jasmyn jumped in with both feet and both hands.

True, she was exhausted, and yet she was home, in Seaside Village, at the Casa, surrounded by people who cared for her. She even had her first piece of furniture, a desk. How could she rest? She wanted to dance and serve dinner and clean up and hug everyone.

Except maybe for Burt. He stood across from her at the serving table in the courtyard, a small, weathered man who could have been anywhere between thirty and fifty years old. He wore a black stocking cap, grimy blue jeans, and a stained gray sweatshirt several sizes too large, and he loved to tell jokes.

"What time is it when you have to go to the dentist?" He leaned over until she was forced to meet his wide, clear blue eyes. "Think about it. What *time* is it when you have to go to the dentist?"

She pressed a plate, laden with turkey and all the traditional fixings, into his hand, but he didn't budge. Apparently he'd rather tell her jokes than eat because this was his fourth one. "I don't know," she said and turned her attention to the table.

Large foil pans and four slow-cookers covered the pretty white lace tablecloth. The food was dwindling, but Liv was out on the sidewalk, eager to pull in anyone, homeless or not, who had nowhere else to eat Thanksgiving dinner. Despite overcast skies and a thick mist, Liv's courtyard dining room remained open with plenty of hot cider, coffee, and pie.

Some of the street people lived regularly in the area, sometimes on park benches, sometimes in a shabby motel. Liv knew them by name because she talked to them often. She knew they would rather stay close than trek out to the centers serving Thanksgiving dinner.

Ignoring Burt didn't work.

He chuckled. "You're sure you don't know? You don't know what time it is when you have to go to the dentist?"

She gave him her best fake waitress smile, the one she had to pull out now and then for the offbeat customer who got the better of her. Not that she'd ever run across one quite as offbeat as Burt.

Keagan appeared beside the man and put an arm around his shoulders, looking at her. "Really, Jasmyn? You don't have a clue?"

"No."

He exchanged a glance with Burt, their jaws dropped in disbelief. Keagan said, "We'd better tell her, Burt."

They looked at her and in unison said, "Tooth hurty. Get it? Two thirty."

They laughed and laughed as Keagan steered the man away from the table. "Burt, what do you call it when a martial arts guy gets sick?"

"That's an easy one, dude. Kung flu!"

They laughed some more and walked across the courtyard to one of the long tables where others sat, obviously enjoying the meal and the company.

Jasmyn organized the remaining food, still amazed at Liv's ability to put on such an event. She used several of the ovens in the complex to cook dinner for up to forty. Jasmyn had counted thirty-one, not including herself and the few Casa folks.

Many of the residents had helped set up, but, like Sam, had gone to eat dinner elsewhere, except for Piper, who went to work because the mall was open. After seeing Chad in an elegant suit and silver tie—the holiday was a formal affair at his parents'—Jasmyn wondered how Piper could have turned down his invitation to join him.

Beau, Riley, and little Tasha were serving pie now. Coco was eating it along with the other guests.

"Knock, knock."

Jasmyn jumped at Keagan's voice from across the table.

"Sorry." He took a piece of foil out of her hand and wrapped it neatly around the pan of yams. "Work with me here. Knock, knock."

She rolled her eyes. "Who's there?"

"Apple."

"Apple who?"

"Knock, knock."

She stopped tucking foil around the sliced turkey. "Keagan."

"Just say, who's there."

"No."

He said, "Okay, I'll fill in for you. Who's there? Now I say, apple."

She ignored him.

"Trust me. It's a good one. Now you say, apple who?"

"Apple who?"

"Knock, knock."

"Seriously?"

"Come on. What's next? You can do it."

"Will you go away if I answer?"

He winked. "You don't really want me to, do you?"

"I thought you were the strong, silent type."

"I have my chatty moments."

She dipped her head to hide a smile. Flirting with Sean Keagan was going to add to the Casa's attraction. As if she needed anything more.

"I repeat," he said. "Knock, knock."

"Who's there?"

"Orange."

"Not apple?"

"No, orange. And you're changing the script."

"Okay, okay. Orange who?"

He smiled. "Orange you glad I didn't say apple?" He took a clean plate from the stack. "Have you eaten yet?"

"No."

He handed her the plate and took another. "Me neither." He lifted the foil off the yams.

"We just covered everything."

"Life is difficult."

They filled their plates, recovering the food as they went, and sat at an unoccupied patio table nearest the serving table.

"Since the day I met Liv, I thought she was amazing. But this is something else."

"Reaching out to the needy is her passion, for sure. She grew up wealthy and married a rich man. Somehow, though, she connects to everyone who crosses her path. Burt doesn't stress her out." He smiled. "He was pulling your leg, you know."

"Was he? I've waited tables for twenty years, and thought I knew how to handle anyone's leg-pulling."

"You probably never served a crowd like this. Did you even have people living on the streets?"

"No. There is poverty and mental illness in Valley Oaks, but nothing like this. The local chapter of the Veterans of Foreign Wars serves holiday meals for people who live alone or can't afford a turkey." She picked apart a roll. "It's a little unnerving to think about this group sleeping outdoors tonight."

"A few of the men I know actually prefer that."

"How can they?"

"Unimaginable baggage." He glanced around. "But our group here...see those two women?" He tilted his head toward a far table. "Liv will ask me to drive them to a shelter. The other two with them are living at the motel until probably next week when their money runs out. They have jobs but don't make enough to make ends meet. Most of the men, like Burt, sleep at the gym."

"Your gym?"

"We don't make a big deal of it. There's only space for ten and only during inclement weather. It costs us. Upkeep, third-shift employees. Enforcing rules like sobriety is a hassle sometimes. Overall, though, it's working."

"That's wonderful."

"We do what we can with what we have. Jasmyn, you don't need to worry about our group here. They'll be looked after."

"All right. I guess."

"Trust me?"

"Probably too much." The words popped out and she saw his brows go up. "Oops."

He grinned. "You're running on fumes and Central Time."

"I'm discombobulated too."

He leaned across the table and spoke softly. "And fragile and vulnerable. But you're in a safe place. You can stop serving everyone else for a while."

Said the angel-slash-knight.

Despite the unanswerable questions of what was next, despite her exhaustion and discombobulated state, Jasmyn sank into the safety net known as Sean Keagan. He wouldn't press. Their friendship would grow. She would get through her first post-tornado year before taking on any more major changes.

Falling in love would be easy, but she would take the scenic route this time.

Eighty-Four

Late Thanksgiving night, Sam entered the Casa's back gate and smelled roast turkey. The heavy air must have trapped the aroma, a leftover from Liv's afternoon gala in the courtyard.

Guilt tweaked her conscience. Selfless Liv would have set aside leftovers for Sam, despite Sam's annual avoidance of the annual courtyard turkey dinner. Joining in Liv's *love me, love my homeless friends* attitude had never quite taken hold of her.

Sam wondered how Jasmyn had fared with it all. No doubt, just fine. She was cut from the same cloth.

For the first time, Sam had accepted her boss's invitation to his home for a holiday gathering. The image of him, his wife, their kids, and a host of relatives around the Halls' Thanksgiving table came to mind. They were all certifiable, in a positive way. Open, honest, giving, teasing, opinionated chatterboxes, real and refreshing.

Sam had—surprise, surprise—enjoyed herself tremendously and even forgave Randy's wife for the obvious attempt to match her up with a cousin. She might be feeling freer in a lot of ways, but Sam was not about to let herself be attracted romantically. She still smarted from the emotional ambush Beau had created when she wasn't paying attention.

Nope. No more of that.

She turned the corner at her cottage.

"Psst!"

The sound came from behind her.

"Mildred! Are you there?" Chad called out too loudly. It was not the recommended nighttime courtyard voice, nor was it without a slur or two.

Sam followed the sound of his chuckle and the faint odor of cigar smoke. She found him at the trickling fountain, his feet propped on its side, his body poured into a patio chair.

Beside him, in another patio chair, sat Beau. "I'm sorry, Sam. I told him to hush and let you be."

She took in the scene. Chad was obviously zoned out. Family holiday gatherings were triggers for him. She saw no telltale glass or glowing cigar stub, though. Beau must have already cleared away the evidence.

"Ah, Mildred. How are you, darling?"

"Better than you, Robert." She pulled a chair next to his and sat. "Our landlady would not be happy with you right now."

"Oh, tsk, tsk yourself." He loosened his tie. "You know, if you weren't such a nag, I'd love you instead of Piper."

And if you weren't so pathetic, she might love you back. Sam bit her lip.

Beau said, "If y'all don't mind, I'll go make my granny's soup. It's a surefire cure. That is, if either of you have some beef broth and noodles?"

She stared at him. "I don't cook. Chad cooks even less. Coffee will be fine because that's probably all we have. Will you help me get him inside?"

Before she could move, Beau had Chad on his feet, his arm around his waist. Chad walked steadily enough. Perhaps he was not as far gone as she feared. She followed them through the shadows, hoping Liv could not hear them.

"Sammi, he called me an embarrassment."

From Chad's past confidences, Sam figured he now referred to his father.

"Not merely a 'disappointment.'" He shook his head vigorously. "Not merely a 'loser.' You know, those make complete sense. I am *obviously* a loser and a disappointment. No argument from me. But an embarrassment? He said it with force, Mildred. With force in front of aunts, uncles, and cousins. That's low, don't you think?"

Sam ignored the question. Chad could talk the paint off a wall when he was sober. He was worse inebriated and performed monologues with no need of a responsive audience. The good news was he never turned into an ogre.

"Right," he said. "Don't talk to the drunk guy. Sammi, I'm not that far gone. I'm just so tired of being the only idiot in the room."

"I'm an engineer, Chad, not a counselor. Get professional help." *Get a job. Get a life.* Maybe she should speak her mind to him. Again.

Beau opened Chad's cottage door. "She is a wise woman, your Mildred."

"That she is." Chad dropped onto the couch. "You ought to hang out with her more."

Sam hurried into the kitchen to make coffee.

Beau soon joined her. "Does this happen often?"

"He's been good the past six months or so. He hunkered down, got serious about school, surfed more with some new friends. He even went to summer school." She filled the carafe with water. "Family dinners. I don't know why he goes."

"Family is family."

"I beg to disagree." She poured the water into the coffeemaker and turned it on.

"Separating yourself from them doesn't heal the wound."

She faced him, leaned against the counter, and crossed her arms. Facing him was not a good idea. How could she be crazy about the guy and never have noticed how she felt? She looked at the floor. "So what does heal it?"

"Granny Mibs would say prayer."

"Can you put some feet on that?" She risked a peek and saw him smile crookedly. His face was the kindest she had ever seen. It could be a stand-in for all the old Jesus paintings. Jesus with green eyes and reddish hair.

"Miss Samantha, you are a tough cookie."

"Yes, I am. But it's an honest question."

"Agreed. No, I can't put feet on prayer or faith or the unseen world. They just are. The key to hitching a ride even on their coattails is to forgive. Forgive ourselves and others. Let it go. Nobody's perfect." He shrugged his broad shoulders. His down-filled brown vest rustled. "But if my daddy called me an embarrassment, I'd avoid family dinners."

Her mother came to mind. "My mom basically does the same thing. I avoid even calling her."

"What do you think about forgiving her?"

Sam began to say *not in this lifetime*, but stopped. Her smart come-back tasted sour. What had she discovered in the Midwest? That ances-tors' choices and the situations imposed on them by governments were the warp and woof of her life. She didn't have a say in the past. Only in what lay before her.

"I'm working on it."

He grinned and creases all but hid his twinkly eyes. "How was your trip?"

"Great. How was yours?"

"Great." Now he looked down at the floor.

The coffeemaker chugged along.

Sam gave up. It was too late after a long day to figure out how to for-give Beau for just being himself. He was strong, talented, loveable, a gen-tleman to everyone, and he paid attention to her. News of his girlfriend aside, what was not to like about him?

She redirected the conversation. "What did you do with his stash?"

Beau looked at her. Clearly, his mind was elsewhere.

She pointed her thumb toward the other room, where Chad had prob-ably fallen asleep. "His booze and cigar."

"There wasn't any stash."

"He showed up like that? He drove himself home?" Sam felt a surge of anger. Criticizing a son was one thing, but allowing him to drive while intoxicated—

"Mildred." Chad strode into the kitchen. "No worries." He spread his arms, all innocence. "This was simply a little ruse."

"You're sober."

"You sound disappointed." He smiled his rakish smile and steered her away from the counter. "Excuse me. The coffee smells good." He took a mug from the cupboard and filled it.

Sam exhaled. "I can't tell you how *not* disappointed I am. Did your dad—"

"Oh, you know he did."

"I'm so proud of you."

He gave her a thumbs-up. "I did enjoy a few puffs, just to get the aroma going for you."

Beau said, "Am I missing something?"

"Well." Chad took a sip of coffee. "Yes, old boy, I'd say you are missing something huge. Her name is Sam Whitley. And Sam, your stubbornness has become rather tedious."

She and Beau stared at him.

"Enough with the clueless expressions. You both know what I'm talking about. You've been dancing around each other for months now." He set down his cup and made shooing gestures. "Go now. Go make up somewhere else."

Sam gaped. "You faked this whole thing?"

"You can thank me later. The timing was tricky. Not letting Beau go home, sitting outside in the cold until you eventually decided to come home way past your curfew. What was up with that anyway? Never mind. Shoo." He took hold of their arms until they moved toward the door.

A moment later Sam stood in the courtyard with Beau as Chad firmly shut his door.

"Sam, I'd invite you down to the coffee shop where it's warm, but it's closed for the night. We really do need to talk. Now."

She gaped again, this time at Beau, at a loss for words.

"Please, Sam."

She invited him to her place, probably because of the way he said her name, a gentle singsong that stretched it out into two syllables. As though it was worth the emphasis.

Sam offered coffee and tea. Beau declined and asked if they could sit.

Her armchair all but disappeared behind and beneath him. She curled up on the couch and pulled the throw from its back to wrap herself in. Her teeth chattered.

Beau wrung his hands briefly. "Chad's right. We—I've been dancing around for months. I want to tell you why."

"Dancing around what exactly?" Sam knew what she had been dancing around.

"You're a tough cookie and a straight shooter." He stilled his hands and looked at her. "Which I like. A lot. To tell the truth, Miss Samantha, I'm head over heels in love with you."

Love? *Oookay.* That pushed things up a notch. Her dance was because she liked him and, since her return, because he had a girlfriend. Avoidance was a necessity, not an option.

"I don't want to scare you away. It's just the truth. I'd rather deal in the truth and not dance anymore."

She nodded, her throat too tight to speak.

"Back home I grew up with a girl named Tallie. We'd always loved each other. We were best friends. Our families were best friends. I proposed when we were ten years old, and then again when we were nineteen. She said yes both times. I considered it like an old-fashioned betrothal. Things were sealed. I figured we'd keep our word to each other, no matter what, no matter how long it took."

Sam wanted to tell him to shut up and leave, but he'd only return at her another time. He was the type who had to set things right. Steeling herself to hear the inevitable was beyond her abilities. She shivered and pulled the blanket closer.

"Tallie always wanted to go to Hollywood and become an actress. So we went. She worked hard and she made it. Then she made it big." His eyes seemed to lose focus, as if he went inside a dark place. After a moment, he blinked. "And I didn't belong with her. I stayed for a while, though. She needed help. You probably don't read the tabloids, but they pretty much got her stories right. She'd want me to remind her of her roots, get her straightened out. Jump, Beau. How high, I would ask."

Sam listened for bitterness in his voice, but did not hear any. He was so...so *Beau.*

"Anyway, this has been going on for years now. She still wears the engagement ring when it suits her. Wore. Not wears." He focused on Sam's face now, totally present to her. "I went up to see her while you were gone. It was my last trip. I took the ring back."

Sam cleared her throat. "What if she needs you?"

"Oh, she will. No doubt about that. She's one confused woman. But she's a movie star first. She'll find someone else to cater to her. I'm over feeling responsible for her because of a childhood promise."

The tension slid from Sam like the syrup down the stack of pancakes she ate in Valley Oaks. Slow and meandering.

"I was foolish, no two ways about it. I guess I never had a reason not to be until I met you. Do you have anything to say?"

She shook her head and smiled.

"Okay." He looked at her in a way he'd never looked at her before.

Something had slid away from him too.

They were, Sam figured, at the beginning of something that could not yet be put into words.

Eighty-Five

The day after Thanksgiving, Liv stood outside her cottage and observed the courtyard. It was all back in order, thanks to her Casa family, who indulged her whims. They had pitched in without complaint, moving tables and chairs, washing dishes. Samantha and Jasmyn laughed now as they took down the orange Japanese lanterns.

So much joy flowed through Liv that she wasn't quite sure what to do with herself. Having Jasmyn back made her absolutely giddy. Samantha's blossoming made her want to dance a jig. Was it possible to spontaneously combust?

Movement at the front gate caught her attention. A stranger entered. If Liv were not looking at Jasmyn near the fountain, she would swear the woman was Jasmyn Albright.

Liv went over to witness the reunion she knew was coming.

Yes, she was a busybody with a hint of a mama bear now on alert. If Manda Smith upset Jasmyn, Liv wanted to be close enough to put the kibosh on it.

Manda had phoned the Casa's main line earlier, asking for Jasmyn's number. Liv had grilled her, naturally. The woman explained that she had called the Flying Pig, but that number led nowhere. She remembered Jasmyn had mentioned the Casa de Vida.

Liv held back, not mentioning that she could have gotten Jasmyn's cell number weeks ago when they had met. But no. Manda had wanted nothing to do with her half sister. What had changed?

Liv had asked politely.

Manda explained.

And then Liv explained that Jasmyn was in town.

Now, Jasmyn spotted her half sister and stared in disbelief. "Manda!"

"Hi." She shrugged a shoulder, hesitant as all get out. Not the confident girl Jasmyn had described.

"Hi. Uh, this is Liv and Sam."

Hellos were exchanged.

Samantha seemed to tense. Maybe she had some mama bear in her too.

Manda was still at a loss for words.

Jasmyn, the vocal fire hydrant, filled in. "How did you know I was here?"

"I didn't. Liv told me when I called to ask for your number. I asked her not to tell you. I-I didn't want to scare you away before we talked, face-to-face." She hesitated, eyeing each of them. "Do you mind if I talk in front of your friends?"

"They're family."

Liv truly thought her heart would burst.

"Okay." Manda took a deep breath and released it. "I told my mom yesterday. It was Thanksgiving and I-I couldn't help it. I can't keep secrets from her, and the thing is…I'm so thankful for you, for my sister."

Earlier, when Manda had said those words to Liv, Liv's heart ached for the girl's mother. How devastating for a widow to hear such a thing. But Manda said that hurtful as the news was, it only confirmed her mom's suspicions. She had learned to forgive her husband years before and would continue to do so. She was, Manda said, a generous woman who refused to be bitter.

As Manda spoke now, Jasmyn's eyes grew wider, but evidently the fire hydrant had shut down.

"Jasmyn, I'm sorry. I lied to you about not wanting a sister. I've *always* wanted a sister. I hope I can be yours."

Jasmyn grinned. Tears spilled down her cheeks.

"And," Manda said, wiping at her own tears, "you have a niece and a nephew and a brother-in-law who can't wait to meet you. They're down at the beach."

Jasmyn grabbed Manda in a hug, long and tight, as if to make up for a lifetime of missed ones. Their laughter filled the courtyard.

Liv exchanged a look with Samantha. One of them was going to have to fetch some tissues.

Instead Samantha wrapped her arms around Liv. "Mama Liv, why are families so messy?"

Oh, dear. Liv would need an entire box of tissues.

Discussion Questions

1. The loss of her home sends Jasmyn down an unpredictable path. Besides the tangibles, what else does she lose?

2. In the long run, Jasmyn's losses lead to much gain. What are some examples?

3. How do others help Jasmyn? What gifts do Quinn, Danno, Liv, Sam, and Keagan give to her?

4. What gifts have others given to you to help you along life's journey?

5. Jasmyn learns that physical things can be important. What things speak to her? How? Do you have examples from your own life?

6. How does Sam change from the beginning of the story to the end? How do Liv and Jasmyn eventually win her over?

7. Liv is older and wiser than Jasmyn and Sam, but she is still learning and growing. What are her weaknesses? What are her strengths?

8. What makes the Casa de Vida a safe harbor? Do you have a similar place to live in or to visit? What makes it safe?

9. How does Liv define a "thin place"? Have you experienced a moment such as Jasmyn does in the old church? What was it like for you? How did it impact you?

10. Both Jasmyn and Sam learn about their ancestors. What did that mean to them? If you know about your own, what does that mean to you?

Don't miss the continuing story
at the Casa de Vida in

Take My Hand

**Book 2 in the Family of the Heart series
coming soon**

Author **Sally John**'s passion is writing stories about relationships. Her 20 novels explore marriage, family, and friendship in today's world.

Initially inspired to write after penning a computer software manual, Sally has also published nonfiction articles in a variety of magazines and speaks at workshops and conferences about writing and family issues.

A winner of an American Christian Fiction Writers' Carol Award and a three-time finalist for the Christy Award, Sally has two married children, two granddaughters, and one grandson. Illinois natives, she and her husband, Tim, live in Southern California.

www.sally-john.com
email: sallyjohn.readers@yahoo.com
Facebook: Sally John Books